THE BOSS
SHE CAN'T RESIST

BY
LUCY CLARK

HEART SURGEON,
HERO...HUSBAND?

BY
SUSAN CARLISLE

MILLS &
BOON

THE BOSS
SHE CAN'T RESIST

BY
LUCY CLARK

MILLS
BOON

First published in Great Britain 2012
by Mills & Boon, an imprint of Harlequin (UK) Limited.
Harlequin (UK) Limited, Eton House, 18-24 Paradise Road,
Richmond, Surrey TW9 1SR

© Anne Clark & Peter Clark 2012

ISBN: 978 0 263 89146 1

Harlequin (UK) policy is to use papers that are natural, renewable and recyclable products and made from wood grown in sustainable forests. The logging and manufacturing process conform to the legal environmental regulations of the country of origin.

Printed and bound in Spain
by Blackprint CPI, Barcelona

'You know you're beautiful, Honey, and that makes you dangerous to be around.'

She itched to lean forward, to close the distance between them, to throw her arms about his neck, to urge his head down so their lips could make contact. But she'd already sensed Edward was an old-fashioned type of man. She could nudge him a little, but if she went too far, too soon, she'd scare him off for good—and that was the last thing she wanted.

Slow and steady. She stayed where she was but angled her head slightly, her hair sliding off her shoulder to reveal her neck. She watched as Edward's gaze dipped momentarily to the smooth skin, his pupils dilating for a fraction of a second, indicating that he liked what he saw. It made her feel all warm and fuzzy inside.

'Dangerous for whom?'

Lucy Clark is actually a husband-and-wife writing team. They enjoy taking holidays with their children, during which they discuss and develop new ideas for their books using the fantastic Australian scenery. They use their daily walks to talk over characterisation and fine details of the wonderful stories they produce, and are avid movie buffs. They live on the edge of a popular wine district in South Australia with their two children, and enjoy spending family time together at weekends.

THE BOSS SHE CAN'T RESIST
is Lucy Clark's 50th book
for Mills & Boon® Medical™ Romance!

CHAPTER ONE

HONEY changed gear, slowing the hot-pink car as she neared the outskirts of Oodnaminaby, the sub-alpine town where she would be spending the next twelve months of her life. It was through her friends Peter and Annabelle that she'd been fortunate enough to gain employment in the Oodnaminaby GP practice while Dr Lorelai Rainbow went on maternity leave.

Honey had a good feeling about this town. She'd worked in several towns over the years, searching, yearning for the place where she might feel at home. 'Oodnaminaby.' She spoke the name of the town out loud. 'Hello, I'm Dr Huntington-Smythe and I live in Oodnaminaby.' She smiled and shook her head at her own folly. 'One day, Honey. You'll find the place where you fit and the place that fits you.'

Here, in Oodnaminaby, she would be working with Peter's brother, a man she'd never met before but one she knew Peter held in high esteem. Her job interview had been conducted over several phone calls with Lorelai, the two women immediately bonding and becoming firm friends.

'I told Edward not to worry,' Lorelai had said two days ago, just before Honey had set out to drive from

Queensland to New South Wales. 'I told him I'd found the best replacement ever.'

'Is it me?' Honey had joked, and Lorelai had laughed down the line.

'I can't wait to meet you face to face— Oh, and thanks for the herbal tea you sent me. It's really helped my indigestion.'

'It makes my heart sing to hear that. I'll be there soon enough to take over so you, sweet Lorelai, can really rest because I've heard that growing a baby can be quite exhausting.'

Lorelai had laughed once more and soon their conversation had ended. Honey smiled at the memory and her hope that Oodnaminaby would be *the* place for her increased. She picked up the piece of paper that was on the seat next to her and glanced at the name of Peter's brother. '"Edward",' she read out loud. She was looking forward to meeting him, too. Peter had often spoken of his family. He had five brothers and Edward was the eldest—Honey had often found herself completely muddled as to who was who in the Goldmark family.

'"Edward Goldmark. Oodnaminaby Family Medical Practice, Lampe Street, Oodnaminaby,"' she read, before looking out the front windscreen searching for street names. She couldn't see any surgery and the houses she was passing had no numbers. When she saw an old weather-beaten sign that said Shops, she pulled into the parking lot. There were steps leading up to a brick colonnade sheltering a row of shops and right in front of her at the top of the steps was a clean glass window with the words Doctors' Surgery. She switched off the engine.

'I'm here.' She couldn't resist smiling as she unclipped her seat belt and opened the car door, stepping out into the crisp March morning. 'I'm here!' The words were louder, her tone filled with renewed energy and excitement as she quickly stretched her arms overhead before heading up the steps. The last two towns she'd worked in had felt promising to begin with but over time she'd found too many obstacles, both literally and figuratively, to stop her from settling down.

For most of her life, she'd been searching for the place where she belonged in this world. Being raised in what many people would call a 'hippy commune', she'd often found herself dissatisfied with life. At eighteen she'd left the commune, changed her name and continued looking for her mental, spiritual and emotional home. She'd been looking ever since.

Breathing in, her senses were tantalised by the fresh scent of sweet blossoms from native trees and surrounding shrubs. 'Glorious,' she pronounced. There didn't seem to be any sign of life this early and as she turned and looked at the scenic view of mountains, trees and a crystal-clear lake, she couldn't contain her joy. It was picture perfect.

Stretching both her arms out wide, her face tilted towards the sun, she spun in circles, her long purple skirt fanning out wide as she twirled.

'This. Place. Is. Gorgeous!' Honey punctuated each word as she continued to whirl around, breathing in the freedom of the morning.

'Can I help you?' A deep male voice spoke from behind her and Honey stopped spinning so suddenly, one of her multicoloured hair braids flicked her in the face. Wrinkling her nose, and a little disoriented from spinning, she realised she was still facing the wrong way. Turning quickly, she found a stern man standing with his feet planted firmly just outside the door to the surgery. He was dressed in navy trousers and a navy polo shirt, the top button undone.

'Oh. Hi.' Honey felt a tad self-conscious at being caught twirling but quickly swallowed it.

'What are you doing?' the man asked.

Honey's smile increased as she momentarily considered explaining the way majestic views, such as the one spread before them, made her feel. However, she'd discovered over the years that a lot of people didn't understand her connection to nature so she'd stopped trying to explain it.

'Twirling,' she offered, and smiled brightly, lifting her sunglasses to rest on the top of her head. The man before her was tall, dark, handsome and scowling, his arms crossed defensively over his firm chest, his dark brown eyes shuttered. 'This place is amazing.' Her smile was still bright as she spread her arms once more to encompass the view surrounding them. 'The mountain air just infuses your body and zaps it to life, doesn't it? Fantastic!'

'Is there something I can help you with?' Impatience had crept into his tone.

'Yes.' She faced him again, taking her sunglasses off her head and running her free hand through her long multicoloured hair. 'You can tell me how on earth anyone gets any work done when you're faced with such stunning views each morning?' She held out her hand. 'I'm Honey.'

The man gave one long blink as though he couldn't quite believe what he was hearing. '*You're* Honey?'

'Last time I checked,' she replied cheerfully. 'And you must be Eddie.'

'Edward,' he instantly corrected.

'Sorry. Edward,' she repeated, then looked closer at him. 'The family resemblance is certainly very strong. You and Peter could be the twins rather than Peter and Bart.'

Edward nodded. It wasn't the first time he'd heard that. Being the eldest of five boys, though, they were all bound to resemble each other in some small way. He stepped forward and placed his hand in hers, accepting her polite greeting, even though he wanted to tell her to turn right around and head back to whatever carnival she'd sprung from. She looked so different from any doctor he'd ever met that he had to wonder whether his brother was playing a practical joke.

With her slim hand enclosed in his, Edward couldn't help but be aware of the oddest tingling sensation. So soft, so delicate, and his frown deepened before he quickly released his hold and folded his arms back across his chest. He stared at her again, as though not quite sure exactly what he was seeing. His new locum was dressed in a sleeveless orange top that buttoned down the front, a long, flowing purple skirt that swirled down to her ankles and her feet were strapped into a sort of flat leather sandal. Her hair was long and honey blonde in colour, except for the parts that were streaked purple, blue, red, green and pink. Her eyes… He squinted in the sun and almost leaned forward, trying to figure out exactly what colour they were before finally deciding that they were indeed a rich, deep blue, although sometimes in the light they looked almost violet.

When his business partner for the last six years, Lorelai Rainbow, had told him she would be taking twelve months off for maternity leave, he'd been more than happy for her. Although Lorelai had agreed to fill in for the odd clinic here and there, Edward had realised he'd need to find a locum. However, Lorelai had beaten him to the punch.

'Your brother Peter knows a doctor who's free to fill in for the year,' Lorelai had told him. 'I've read her résumé and I have to say it's highly impressive. I've also spoken to her on the phone several times and she sounds great. We hit it off right away. Her name is Honey and she's just perfect for this position. I've completed all the paperwork, Ginny's filed it. It's a done deal. No need for you to worry.' Lorelai had patted him on the shoulder. 'I'd never leave you in the lurch so relax, Edward. It's all taken care of. Trust me.'

And he did. He trusted Lorelai implicitly both in business and personal matters but he'd known Lorelai for most of his life and considered her part of his family. Edward also trusted Peter's judgement, knowing his brother would never do anything to upset the family medical practice, which was their parents' legacy. Staring in stunned disbelief at the woman before him, he couldn't help but think that both Lorelai and Peter had had rocks in their heads at such a ludicrous recommendation.

This Honey woman was completely unsuitable for the traditional family general practice his parents had started over thirty years ago. The majority of people living in Oodnaminaby and surrounding districts, who had lived in the area for most of their lives, were very set in their ways and didn't take well to change.

'So...Edward. Would you like to give me a tour of the place?' Honey glanced around at the shops, rubbing her hands together, desperate to ignore the way her fingers had tingled as soon as they'd touched his. She may be searching for a home, a place where she felt she truly belonged, but she was most definitely not searching for any type of romantic entanglement.

'Or is this it?' She pointed to the general store, which, from the display in the windows, seemed to cover everything from groceries to clothes to pharmaceuticals. Next to it was a hot-food take-away shop, then a post office and a ski-hire/fishing-tackle shop.

'Uh…this is basically it.' He was still frowning, still highly unsure of this strange but vibrant woman who stood before him. He watched as she walked—no, not walked, *glided*—a few steps away from where he stood, momentarily mesmerised by the gentle swish of her hips, the swirl of her skirt around her ankles, the way she rubbed her brown bare arms as the crispness of the morning started to raise goose-bumps on her skin.

'Not that there's anything wrong with all of this being "it",' she clarified, her voice as smooth as…well…honey. 'I like small towns. They form a tight-knit community where you can always rely on having a good ol' chinwag with your neighbour over the back fence. Ooh, look.' She took a step closer to the door of the medical clinic. 'You have brass plaques.' She quickly read them, reaching out to run her fingers over the engraved etching of Edward's name and the plaque below bearing Lorelai's name and credentials. 'I love these things. I've always wanted one but I've never been in one place long enough.' She touched Edward's plaque again, that deep need to truly belong filling her through and through. 'One day,' she murmured softly.

'Why is that?'

'Hmm?'

'Why have you never been in one place long enough?' And should he be worried about hiring a nomadic locum? Surely her wandering feet would stay grounded for the duration of her twelve-month contract. He'd make sure of it.

Honey shrugged. 'I guess I haven't found the place where I belong.' She turned to look at the scenery, sighing once more. 'It is extremely beautiful here.'

Edward watched her with interest, noting her effort to change the subject.

'It would be a fantastic place to raise a family. So peaceful with lots of open spaces and fresh air and...' She nodded. 'I could definitely raise my children here.'

'You have children?' Edward was stunned. What *had* Lorelai been thinking?

'Hmm? Uh...no. I meant in the future. Future children.' She waved a dismissive hand at him. 'Don't mind me. I'm just...' Another sigh. 'Dreaming.' She gazed at the scenery once more before turning back to him. 'You were raised here, weren't you?'

Surprised by the question, Edward found himself answering immediately. 'My parents moved here from Canberra when I was three, just before Mum had the twins.'

'Oh, it must have been wonderful.' She laughed, a sweet tinkling sound that seemed to blend in perfect harmony with the early-morning calls of the native birds. Edward felt a tightening in his gut at the sound and quickly turned away from her. With his gaze straight ahead, looking at the scenery that was usually quite calming to his senses, he couldn't believe what he saw. He blinked one slow blink as though to clear the picture before him but it didn't work.

'Your car's a little...bright, don't you think?' he asked, shielding his eyes against the glare shining off the paint-work from the early morning sunlight.

Honey smiled. 'It is. It has sentimental value but runs like a dream. Hubert gave it a complete tune before I left.'

'Hubert? Who's Hubert? Your...mechanic?'

She smiled. 'My grandfather. He likes to tinker with classic cars.' Honey looked lovingly at the small vehicle.

'It was a birthday present, which he enthusiastically restored for me.'

'So he chose the paint scheme?' Edward starting wondering whether Honey's entire family had rocks in their heads. He turned to look at her and found himself mesmerised by the smile touching her lips.

'No. I chose the colours and he knows my favourite flowers are daisies. He said I should try to stop fitting into this world because I was born to stand out.' Honey sighed and clutched her hands to her chest. As she stood there, the early-morning sun surrounding her, multicoloured hair loose and flowing over her shoulders, Edward sucked in a breath. There was a twinkle of happiness about her sparkling eyes, the tug of a smile evident on her perfectly sculpted mouth. Her face was completely devoid of make-up and he couldn't help but admit she was an extremely beautiful young woman.

'How old are you?' he blurted. 'You look about the same age as my youngest brother.'

'Oh? And how old is he?' she queried, seemingly not at all put out that he was questioning her in such a personal way.

'Er…he turned seventeen last month.'

'Ah. Right. Well, I'm *much* younger than him.' She pointed to the surgery behind where they stood. 'So…shall we go in? You can show me around and I can ask you three trillion questions so that by the time the patients start to arrive, I'm all hunky-dory with the set-up.' She raised her eyebrows. 'Yes?'

He didn't seem to be moving, still rooted to almost the same spot as when she'd first laid eyes on him. He was tall, about six feet four inches, she guessed. She liked tall men. 'Or I don't mind winging it if that's what you'd like.

I'm very versatile and completely adaptable.' She raised her eyebrows in a teasing gesture and Edward was astonished to find his body reacting with increased heat and awareness.

'Adaptab—' Edward closed his eyes for a brief moment, and pinched the bridge of his nose, needing to block the woman from his vision. He felt as though he'd just been sucked into some alternate dimension and that the last five minutes of his life had been one of total confusion and disbelief.

'Problem?' she queried.

He squared his shoulders and glared at her, trying not to be affected by her nearness or the hypnotic scent she brought with her. What was that perfume? It seemed to be a mixture of cinnamon and an earth-bound naturalness with just a hint of something sweet and seductive. It was confusing his usually ordered mind. 'Yes, there's a problem. What do you mean, you're younger than my brother? Are you sure you're a qualified doctor?'

He'd obviously pigeonholed her. The clothes, the car, the colours in her hair, and he'd shoved her into a stereotypical box and labelled it 'fruitcake'. If that was the case, who was she to deny herself a bit of fun? 'Don't I *look* qualified?' Honey couldn't resist twirling slowly in a circle, swishing her hips, teasing him.

Edward swallowed the lump that instantly formed in his throat at her provocative movements. There was no doubt whatsoever that she was an incredibly attractive young woman and there was no doubt that she would create havoc amongst the single men in Oodnaminaby, including the elderly widowers. He instantly knew she was completely wrong for this town no matter how sensually appealing he might find her.

'In a word, no. You look as though you've just come from some bohemian fancy-dress fair, driving here in a car that looks as though you borrowed it from the circus.'

Honey pretended to frown. 'Shh. He'll hear you.'

Edward rolled his eyes. 'No wonder you and my brother get along. You both share that same warped sense of humour.' He dragged in a breath, trying to keep his calm so he could control this situation. 'What are you doing arriving so early in town? You weren't expected for at least another two hours. It's only just after six and every other town in the district is well over half a hour's drive away. Where did you start off from this morning?'

'Oh, I only came from Canberra. I stayed with friends last night and left just after four o'clock because I simply *adore* watching the sunrise. The way the colour starts to seep into the surroundings...' She stretched out her arms and wiggled her fingers, her movements adding a flourish to her words. She wore a few rings on her fingers, the jewellery sparkling in the morning light. 'Turning things from shades of grey to shades of green and blue and pink and orange, and it's just breath-taking.' She sighed and dropped her arms back to her sides. 'The show this morning certainly didn't disappoint.'

Edward blinked again, still unsure what to make of her. What on earth had Lorelai and Peter been thinking? This woman most certainly didn't fit the profile of a studious general practitioner. 'And your age?'

'Yes, yes. Of course. Sorry.' She smiled at him. 'In this stunning scenery, it's easy to get sidetracked. I'm seven and a quarter and quite proud of it. My birthday was only last week. Not a huge celebration like my last real birthday but still a spiffy one.'

'Seven and a…?' Edward's frown intensified but then it cleared. 'You were born on February twenty-ninth?'

Honey's answer was a wide and beaming smile. 'See. I knew there was a reason I liked you, Edward. You're quick. It usually takes people a good few minutes to figure it out.'

'You like me?' Her words stunned him a little. 'You don't even know me.'

'Ahh…that's where you're wrong. I've known Peter and Annabelle for years and I've met Peter's twin brother Bartholomew and both of them talk about you with such reverence and awe. Lorelai also thinks the world of you and it definitely takes a special man to do what you've done, Edward.' There was none of her earlier humour in her words and Edward realised she was completely serious with every word she spoke. It made him stop and take notice, intrigued by this different side of her.

'To be thrust into the role of father figure from the age of twenty-four,' Honey continued. 'To keep your family together, to put Bart and now Benedict through medical school, to keep your parents' dream of the family medical practice alive, and to do all of that while grieving for their loss…' Admiration lit her eyes and heartfelt emotion flowed through her words. 'That makes you quite a man, Edward Goldmark.'

'I had help,' he felt compelled to point out, lest she think he was a modern-day saint, which he wasn't. It was odd the way her words, her praise, the light in her violet eyes, shining with respect, made him feel as though he was someone important.

'I've no doubt about that. Lorelai told me how her father was always there for you, guiding you, offering advice, but when it came down to the bottom line, you made sacrifices for everyone around you, Edward, and that proves to me that you're a man of honour and great principle.'

Edward recrossed his arms over his chest, desperate to put up barriers between himself and this woman. He *had* made sacrifices for the sake of his family but he'd done it quietly, never once speaking out about the injustice he'd often felt. He'd put his brothers, the medical practice and the people of this community before himself and, while he didn't necessarily want any fuss to be made of his actions, it startled him that Honey was astute enough to see it.

'You're an old-fashioned gentleman whose word is his bond and I have to say it's not only a delight to find someone like you in this day and age but also that I am so honoured to be working alongside you for the next twelve months.' Honey's smile was bright, lighting her pretty features, and Edward felt mesmerised by her once more.

He'd just been about to tell her that he didn't think she was at all right for this practice. That even though Lorelai had made all the arrangements, he didn't think it was going to work out. That he appreciated her time but he could do without her help. It would be difficult, he would be burning the candle at both ends, but he'd survived worse. He could run the busy practice on his own for a few months until arrangements could be made for a more suitable locum.

Then she'd mentioned honour.

Honour *was* important to him and Lorelai had been acting on behalf of the practice, offering Honey a contract. Family *was* important to him and he wasn't sure he could bring himself to tell Peter that he thought Honey unsuitable for the position. Honesty *was* important to him and if he was completely honest with himself, he would accept that he *did* need Honey's help.

He realised there was obviously more to Honey than met the eye and that he'd be foolish to act impulsively. Besides, it wasn't his style. He was the type of man who thought everything through, who didn't make snap decisions.

'There are quite a few rules and regulations you'll be required to follow whilst working at the practice.' He spoke briskly.

'I wouldn't have expected anything less. Small communities are often very set in their ways and that's not always a bad thing.' Honey leaned forward and looked intently into Edward's brown eyes, a twinkle in her own. 'However, sometimes giving things a little bit of a shake-up is good for the soul. Right?'

Why did he get the distinct impression that she was talking directly about him and not the town? 'No.' He shook his index finger at her. '*No*. There will be *no* shaking-up... of *anything*.' Especially not him. He knew his brothers thought he was too set in his ways but Edward was a creature of habit. No beautiful, eccentric woman, barging her way into his world, was going to change that.

'This practice has run just fine since long before either of us was born. My parents built this practice up from the ground with the dream that it would be run as a family business, providing care and support to the people in these often isolated parts. The people who attend our clinic demand a certain level of care and I intend to see that standards are upheld so there will be no shaking up. Understood?'

'Absolutely. I agree with you one hundred per cent,' she said with a nod, her coloured hair shimmering in the morning sunlight as she inched towards him, allowing his preconceptions about her to work to her advantage. She'd seen the moment of hesitation in Edward's eyes as he'd looked at her and she'd had the feeling he'd been about to give her her marching orders. She couldn't let that happen. Oodnaminaby was calling to her, speaking to her in a way a place never had before. She needed to stay here, to discover whether this was the place she would finally find not only peace of mind but peace of heart.

'You won't know that peace until you feel it,' her grandfather had always said. 'But once you find it, oh, Honeysuckle, darling, you hang onto it with all you've got.' She couldn't leave Oodnaminaby. Not yet.

'Well…uh…' Edward wanted to step back, to put some distance between himself and this woman who was slowly advancing towards him. 'Good.'

Honey took another step closer and whatever scent she was wearing teased at his senses. She angled her body inwards and said in a quiet, low but somehow sensual tone, 'It's nice to know we're on the same page, Edward, even if we're coming at it from different angles. Caring for people is a high priority on my list of lifetime goals. Good to know it's on yours, too.' Her gaze held his while she spoke, her words winding their way around him. Edward swallowed, his Adam's apple sliding up and down his throat. How was it she could make him feel so uncomfortable and so aware of her so easily?

When her gaze dipped to travel quickly over the length of his body, he couldn't help the tightening in his gut. She was attractive, she had sex appeal and it was clear she knew how to use it to disarm a man.

'I like a man of principle,' she said, her gaze meeting his again.

Edward couldn't contain his discomfort any more and, clearing his throat, he edged back, needing to put some distance between them. He uncrossed his arms, wanting to show her she didn't affect him at all. She was his locum for the next twelve months and, despite how wrong he might feel she was for the practice, he knew asking Honey to leave would bring questions not only from Peter but from Lorelai as well, and the last thing Lorelai needed in her heavily pregnant state was to think he'd doubted her judgement.

No, it appeared Honey was here to stay and he would have to do his level best to keep a safe distance between them. Their relationship would remain strictly professional. He took another step back and let his hands hang by his sides.

'Let me show you the clinic.' He was proud his words came out calm and controlled, brisk and professional.

'Edward…' she winked at him and took his hand in hers, tugging him towards the door of the clinic '…I thought you'd never ask.'

Momentarily stunned, allowing himself to be led into his own medical practice, Edward once again felt as though she'd knocked him off balance. It was an odd and dizzying sensation and for the first time since he'd learned of his parents' death he felt as though he really had no idea which way was up.

CHAPTER TWO

'No, IT's perfectly all right,' Honey said as she escorted Mrs Etherington towards Reception. 'Of course you can take it with you. I make it up myself and it's never difficult to find empty jars.'

'And you're sure it will work wonders for my arthritis? Because I've tried everything else and nothing seems to give me relief.' Mrs Etherington held a small jar of white cream in her hands, hope in her eyes as she waited for Honey's reply.

'I'm sure it will but if after three days of applying the cream as I've shown you, you're not satisfied, come and see me. We could always try acupuncture.'

'Oh!' Mrs Etherington's eyes widened at this news but there was an excitement in her wise brown eyes.

'The most important thing is to find what's going to work for *you*.'

'Yes.' Mrs Etherington nodded. 'Thank you, Honey.'

'You are most welcome.' Honey smiled warmly. 'You have a lovely rest of the day.'

'Why, thank you, dear. Of course you need to be getting on with your patients. Don't let an old girl like me hold you up.' Smiling brightly, as she hadn't done in years, Mrs Etherington stopped to chat with some of her friends who were in the waiting room, no doubt telling them all about the new doctor.

Edward caught this exchange as he waited for Mr Winton to manoeuvre his walking frame into the consulting room. In all the years he'd known Mrs Etherington, he'd never seen her look so happy. He glanced at the waiting room, noting the curious delight on the faces of the people. They were all looking at Honey as though she were a new and exciting present they simply couldn't wait to unwrap.

Honey, however, seemed oblivious to the wide-eyed stares she was receiving and after spending a moment with Ginny, saying something to make the sixty-three-year-old receptionist smile, she picked up her next set of case notes and called in her next patient. Mr de Mingo, an elderly man who never seemed to move faster than a snail, went eagerly with her, stepping sprightly.

Edward frowned, not happy she was handing out personal remedies to his patients. There could be anything in that cream! What if things went wrong? *He* would be the one to pick up the pieces, to pacify patients like Mrs Etherington, who could be quite temperamental. No. This wouldn't do at all. As soon as morning clinic was finished, he'd have a quiet word with Honey and lay down the law. He heard laughter coming from her consulting room, her sweet tinkling sounds mixing with the deeper ones of Mr de Mingo. Edward tried not to grit his teeth.

When Mr Winton cleared his throat and murmured a husky 'Aren't you coming, Dr Goldmark?' Edward snapped his thoughts back to the present, pushing his new locum from his mind. He'd deal with her later.

As the morning progressed, Honey couldn't believe how welcoming her patients were. There were one or two who were naturally a little cautious, especially if she recommended an alternate course of treatment, but for the most part she thought things were moving along swimmingly.

From the moment she and Edward had entered the clinic that morning, Honey had been aware of the distance he maintained between them. She'd listened to his deep, modulated tones as he'd outlined the intricacies of the practice and what was expected of her.

He'd told her that in the summer months the town was often infiltrated with campers, hikers and fishermen, whilst in the winter months skiers, snowboarders and families wanting a winter break made up the visiting population. Although Lorelai had covered things in quite a bit of detail during their phone conversations, this was, to all intents and purposes, Edward's practice and as such Honey gave him her full attention.

She noted he was highly methodical, not wanting to leave anything to chance. He'd taken extra copies of her documents, saying they were for his own records, and she'd watched as he'd stapled everything together. Neat and tidy. Straight and organised.

Once the paperwork had been completed, he'd taken her on a tour of the clinic facilities, pointing out the location of the bathroom and kitchenette. He'd indicated where the receptionist—Ginny—sat, and the system for calling in patients.

'Ginny put the system in place and as she's been working here for as long as I can remember, we don't change it.'

'Warning me again not to rock the boat?' Honey had smiled brightly and Edward had shoved his hands into navy trousers as though her smile had been tempting him to touch her.

'Well…we wouldn't want to upset Ginny. Trying to get her to use a computer a few years ago was bad enough,' he'd muttered, shaking his head. 'Still, she mastered it but wasn't happy for quite some time.'

'Contrary to what you might believe, I'm not here to upset anyone, Edward. I'm here to *help*.' Helping people was what she did. When she'd been a child, she'd helped animals, nursing them back to health with dedication and care. Her parents had been more than happy to encourage her to become a vet…until the day when she'd changed her mind, realising that human medicine was for her. They hadn't been so supportive then.

When Lorelai had arrived at about seven-thirty, the two women had embraced warmly, as though they were life-long friends, excited to see each other again.

'You're far more beautiful in person than in photographs,' Lorelai said.

'You've seen pictures of me?' Honey had been surprised.

'Peter and Annabelle have some, from the time they visited you up in Queensland.'

'Oh, yes.' Honey had nodded. 'That was when I was in Port Douglas. My hair was shorter then and I think it was black.'

'Yes.' Lorelai had touched the multicoloured strands. 'But this style definitely suits you. You're so pretty.' Then Lorelai had turned and looked at Edward. 'Don't you think so?'

Put on the spot on a topic he'd rather not contemplate, Edward had quickly nodded and muttered something highly intellectual like 'Er…yes,' before excusing himself. He'd stayed in his clinic room until his first patient had arrived.

By the time lunchtime rolled around, Edward was eager to find out just how well his new colleague had coped with the clinic. He'd managed to find some time to peruse Honey's résumé and had to admit that she was almost over-qualified for a position as general practice locum. Aside from her medical qualifications, she held a degree in psychology and graduate diplomas in midwifery, naturopathy and acupuncture. It also stated that she was presently studying for her PhD.

It made him wonder, given she was only twenty-nine years of age, where she'd found the time to have a normal life. Part of him was streaked with jealousy that she'd been able to accomplish so much. He'd always intended to be a surgeon and, in fact, two days before his parents' deaths he'd been agonising over which university to apply to.

He'd had a rough plan for his life and had been in the midst of discussing his options with his parents when tragedy had struck. Not only had he then been responsible for his siblings but he'd had to give up the life he'd built for himself as a medical professional in Canberra.

And then there had been Amelia.

He breathed in deeply at the thought of the woman he'd been planning on marrying and still felt the slightest twinge of pain. It had been seven and a half years since he'd proposed to Amelia and seven and a half years since she'd rejected him. Even now he could hear her hurtful words.

'Edward. I love you. I really do but I'm not cut out to go and live in a little town and become an instant mother to grieving children. I've spent the past six years at medical school, I'm exhausted from my internship and marriage is so not on my agenda. And besides…' her eyes had lit with delight '…I was going to tell you later but I can't hide my excitement any longer. I've been accepted into the surgical training programme in Melbourne for next year. They don't usually accept interns so early but I made the cut. Isn't that fantastic?'

Edward closed his eyes and remembered how he'd murmured polite responses to her news. Amelia had continued to talk about herself for a while longer, brushing aside his proposal, and had had the audacity to ask him why he wasn't more excited for her.

Over the years he'd realised he'd had a lucky escape, not having been able to see before then how self-centred she was, but he knew he couldn't really blame Amelia. He'd been selfish in wanting her to give up her dreams, her goals, just for him. *He'd* had to make that sacrifice and he hadn't had a choice so it had been wrong of him to expect it of her… But if she'd really loved him, she would have been willing.

It wasn't that he didn't love his brothers, he did, even though Hamilton was driving him insane right now. Having his parents die just after he'd turned twenty-four, being legally responsible for his two younger brothers, had meant Edward had had to make certain sacrifices. Benedict had been only thirteen and Hamilton only nine. The twins, Peter and Bartholomew, had been twenty. Bart had been off attending medical school in Sydney and Peter had been getting ready to move out of home. Somehow they'd struggled through, managing to keep the family together, but all of his aspirations, dreams and hopes had died along with his parents.

Edward was pleased with what he'd managed to achieve, knowing it was what his parents had wanted. He'd held true to their legacy for their sons and he was grateful for the help he'd received both in and around the town of Oodnaminaby. But what of *his* dreams? Looking at Honey's résumé, seeing the scope of her experience and qualifications, he couldn't help but feel a little jealous.

No one had ever asked him what he'd really wanted in life. Everyone had always presumed he was quite content running the family practice and caring for his brothers, and in a way he was. He'd done what needed to be done but at the end of this year Hamilton would be finished at school and would probably move out.

Then what? He would have done his duty but what was he supposed to do next? He'd wanted to accomplish so much back then but now...things were different, *he* was different. What *did* he want to do next? His new locum seemed to have a direction for her life even if it was to find somewhere to one day raise her family. He could almost picture her with a gaggle of children around her, all of them with their arms out, twirling in the sunshine.

A slow smile touched his lips at the thought, then he shook his head to clear the image. He looked at Honey's résumé once more, noting her full name was Honeysuckle. Her surname was listed as Huntington-Smythe. Such a weird mix of a name.

He paused for a moment, then frowned, remembering he'd heard the name Huntington-Smythe before. It took only a second to recall, his eyes widening as his early-morning conversation with Honey replayed in his mind. 'Hubert Huntington-Smythe is her *grandfather*?' Before Professor Huntington-Smythe had retired, he had been one of Australia's leading pioneering neurosurgeons... and Honey was his granddaughter?

Edward put the document back into his in-tray and stood. Picking up his coffee cup, he headed out of his clinic room. When he walked into the kitchenette, he was surprised to find Lorelai sitting in a chair with her feet up on Honey's lap, his new colleague massaging Lorelai's feet. Neither woman seemed to notice his presence so he kept quiet, listening to Honey's smooth and modulated tones.

'Reflexology is more about pressure points. Acupuncture works on the same principle. Applying pressure to the base of your big toe helps to relieve abdominal and back pain, as well as releasing endorphins to help you relax.'

'Ooh, that feels so good,' Lorelai murmured, her head tilted back in the chair, her eyes closed. 'I feel so calm and the pain in my lower back has disappeared.' She sighed and sank down further into the chair.

'I can teach your husband exactly where he needs to be pressing so that during the birth he'll be able to help you.'

Lorelai opened her eyes slightly but didn't move. 'John won't do this. He hates it that I'm pregnant and refuses to be there for the birth.'

'Then *I'll* do this for you at the birth and if the pain gets bad at night, give me a call.' Honey's tone was still soothing and calm.

Edward clenched his jaw, unimpressed with Lorelai's husband. John wasn't his favourite person in the world but Lorelai had married him and therefore Edward and his brothers had done their best to get along with the man— for Lorelai's sake. They considered Lorelai and her father BJ as part of their extended family.

'What if I get a pain at three in the morning?' Lorelai asked.

'Then call me.' Honey's words were insistent. 'Enduring lower back pain when you don't have to will only lead to further discomfort. Besides, when I'm not working here at the clinic, I'm presuming I'll have quite a bit of free time. I'm not being polite, Lorelai. I'm quite serious.'

Lorelai sighed again and closed her eyes, her breathing once more nice and relaxed. 'I wish I'd known about these acupuncture pressure points before now,' she murmured.

Edward gritted his teeth, annoyed with another reference to acupuncture. 'If you melt into that chair any further, Lore, you're going to end up on the floor,' he murmured as he took his cup to the sink to rinse it.

'I don't care,' Lorelai replied, not bothering to open her eyes. 'Honey has managed to take away the pain I've been living with for the past few months.'

'You've been in pain?' Edward's tone was filled with instant concern.

'No more than any other pregnant woman who has only four weeks left to go.' Lorelai chuckled as she opened her eyes and smiled at her friend. 'Didn't I tell you I'd found the perfect doctor to replace me?' Lorelai looked from Edward back to Honey. 'Thank you, Honey.'

He watched as Honey continued to massage, kneading deeply. 'You're welcome. Helping people is why I became a doctor,' she replied, as a happy smile spread across her features.

Edward felt a tightening in his gut at the sight of those gorgeous lips of hers curving upwards and quickly turned back to the sink and washed out his cup. The more he looked at her, the more he couldn't believe how extraordinarily beautiful she was. There wasn't a scrap of make-up on her face, her multicoloured hair was tied back into a ponytail at the base of her neck with a red ribbon, and her Bohemian clothes were hardly what he would call stylish. In short, she was not the type of woman he was usually attracted to. In fact, she was quite the opposite and yet he was definitely attracted.

Edward glanced at the two women as he slowly dried his cup, watching Honey as she spoke in that calm tone of hers, relaxing Lorelai even further. Honey's neck was long and smooth and when he breathed in, that same scent he'd detected earlier that morning once more surrounded him. He became mesmerised by the way her arms and hands moved, the fluidity of her body, the way she seemed completely focused on her task, as though nothing else in the world mattered.

Exotic. Quixotic. Hypnotic.

'Lorelai?' Ginny walked into the kitchenette, bursting the bubble. Edward quickly turned and began filling the kettle, needing to do anything other than being caught staring at his new colleague. 'So this is where you all are.' The receptionist stopped and looked at the three of them. 'I'll have a tea, thanks, Edward,' Ginny said, after seeing him at the sink. 'Lorelai, your husband's on the phone...' There was a briskness to Ginny's words as though she really didn't like Lorelai's husband but her voice gentled as she continued. 'Honey, your first patient for the afternoon called to cancel so I've shifted some of Lorelai's patients onto your list.'

'Sounds great,' Honey replied, smiling at the receptionist before helping Lorelai out of the chair. 'In fact, give Edward and I all of Lorelai's patient's because she needs to be off her feet and at home, resting.'

'No. It's all right. I can...' Lorelai tried to protest but was cut off by a yawn. 'Oh. I think you've relaxed me too much.'

'Honey makes a valid point,' Edward interjected as he began making a cup of tea for Ginny. He turned and looked at the three women in the room. Two of them were like family—a surrogate mother and sister. The other one, well, she was just a new colleague. Nothing more. At least, that's what he seemed to need to tell himself over and over.

'And we don't want to argue with Edward,' Honey continued. 'Time to rest, Lorelai. Edward and I can hold down the fort.'

'Good idea,' Ginny agreed, as Lorelai tried again to protest but only succeeded in yawning once more. 'I'll see to it,' she said, ushering Lorelai out. 'You two need to get ready for afternoon clinic…but only after you've brought me a cup of tea,' she said with a twinkling smile.

Honey chuckled and the warm sound washed over him. He turned back to the task at hand, trying not to be conscious of the fact that they were both alone in the small kitchenette. He felt rather than saw her draw closer and hated himself for the heightened awareness he was feeling.

'I might have another cup of tea as well,' she said, coming to stand beside him. He shifted over, ensuring that not one part of his body touched hers. It didn't work, especially when she leaned across him to extract a cup from the cupboard, her bare upper arm brushing lightly across his chest.

She gasped at the touch, then turned to look up at him. 'Sorry.' Honey shook her head as though to clear her thoughts. 'I didn't mean to…nudge you.' Honey's mouth started to turn up at the corners. 'We *haven't* met before, have we, Edward?'

Edward swallowed, his Adam's apple sliding up and down his throat. His gut tightened as he realised she was watching his every action. If there was one thing he'd noticed so far today, it was that Honey gave her full attention to whoever she was with and right now all that attention was focused on him. He swallowed again. 'I think I'd remember.' Now why had his voice come out so deep, so husky, so mesmerised by the woman in front of him?

'So would I but I have the strangest sensation that we have definitely met.' She leaned in a little, her gaze dipping momentarily to encompass his mouth. 'Maybe we met in our dreams because there's a strange sort of…connection between us, don't you think?'

'Uh…'

Honey paused a moment before shifting back and reaching for his hand, holding his palm up in her own. 'You have nice hands. Hard-working hands. I think you can tell a lot about a person simply from looking at their hands.' She tenderly brushed her fingers across his palm, somehow igniting every nerve ending in his entire body. She swapped hands, caressing the other. 'Caring hands.' She turned his hand over and caressed the back, her fingers stopping at a small scar at the base of his thumb.

Edward swallowed again and found he was powerless to move, allowing the fresh scent she wore to once more hypnotise him.

'How did you get this scar?'

'Uh…' He cleared his throat, willing his vocal cords— and his mind—to work. 'I broke my thumb when I was seven.' He gave a little shrug. 'Fell off my bike.'

Honey looked up into his eyes. 'Did you cry?'

'I tried not to.' He looked away from her penetrating gaze, unable to believe how she could make him feel so… special. It had been a very long time since *anyone* had made him feel special.

'Brave. Even back then.' Honey bent and pressed her lips to the scar and then released his hand.

'Wh-why did you do that?' he queried as he rubbed his thumb, trying to dispel the wildfire of heat that was burning through him.

'What? Ask you questions or kiss your hand?'

'Both.'

Because I'm interested in getting to know you, not only as a colleague but as a person. This is a small community where people tend to look beyond the occupation, the qualification or the title.'

'Ah…actually, speaking of titles,' he said, and edged back from her, desperate to put some much-needed distance between them. 'I noticed on your paperwork that your surname is Huntington-Smythe.'

'That's correct.'

'And that means your grandfather—Hubert Huntington-Smythe—was the world-renowned Australian neurosurgeon.'

'That's right. Until he retired a few years ago.'

'And started restoring cars?'

'Yes. He says the insides of the car are not that dissimilar to a human brain. His eyesight isn't what it used to be so he jokes that if he makes a mistake, it doesn't really matter. Jessica, my grandmother, is more than happy to have him home rather than working all hours at the hospital. The house was quiet when he wasn't there and I was always so worried we'd get a call and be told that he'd had a heart attack due to the stress but thankfully that didn't happen.'

'You lived with them?'

Honey nodded and finished making her tea. 'Since I was eighteen.'

This surprised him. From the way she dressed and her outlandishly coloured hair, she didn't appear to be the sort of woman who had been raised in a well-to-do household. She was such a contradiction he couldn't quite figure her out. He decided to try and dig a little deeper. 'And what about your parents? Did they live with them as well?'

'No. No, my mother ran away from home just after she turned seventeen, changed her name, married my father. They travelled from place to place, living the alternative lifestyle in communes and squats, always protesting against any injustice no matter how big or small. She hasn't been in contact with her parents since.'

Edward listened closely, again realising there was more depth to Honey than first met the eye. 'Is that what you did? Ran away from home?' Edward asked, thinking of Hamilton at the back of his mind. His brother had just turned seventeen and was wanting to leave school now, not bothering to finish his final year. He kept threatening to go live in Canberra with Bart, saying that he would leave home because Edward was a controlling tyrant.

Honey shook her head. 'I was eighteen. I *left* home as a legal adult. Big difference.'

'And went to live with your grandparents?'

'Yes. Jessica was lonely, especially with Hubert working so much. They put me through medical school and gave me the stability I'd always craved.'

'Stability? Your parents are unstable?'

She laughed without humour and shook her head. 'I guess it depends which way you look at it. They've been called hippies or gypsies or the more politically correct term of alternative lifestylers. By the time I turned eighteen, I'd realised that way of living wasn't for me, so I did something about it. I left.'

Edward continued to process what she was saying. 'Wait

a second.' He held up his hand. 'If your mother is Hubert's daughter, how come your surname is Huntington-Smythe?'

'I changed it. In essence, I guess you could say I took on the life my mother rejected. She felt suffocated by the rules and regulations my grandparents had stipulated but I seemed to thrive in that environment. Children, even young adults, need boundaries.' Honey frowned for a moment.

'Your parents didn't give you boundaries?'

'Raised my brother and I free and natural, as they used to term it.' She shook her head. 'I left, I went to live with my grandparents and to honour them, I took their surname.'

'So...what *was* your surname?'

She shrugged one bare, elegant shoulder. 'Moon-Pie.'

He blinked one slow blink. 'Moon-Pie?'

'Go ahead. Make all the jokes you want. I've heard them all. My brother and I were teased at every different school we went to. Honeysuckle Lilly-Pilly Moon-Pie.'

'That's...quite a name.'

'Tell me about it. I'm going to call my daughter something easy, like Clara or Elizabeth. Something...normal that you can easily find on a door plaque for their bedroom door.'

'So now your name is Honeysuckle Lilly-Pilly Huntington-Smythe?'

'It is.' She angled her head to the side, her hair still secured by the shiny red ribbon, and Edward found himself momentarily distracted by her soft, smooth skin.

It had been one thing to ogle her neck from across the room but it was quite a different matter altogether to ogle it when she was right in front of him. He worked hard to control his breathing, to keep his desire under wraps. He

cleared his throat and edged back a bit more, far too aware
of her body so close to his.

'Did changing it make you happy?'

'In some ways, yes. In other ways…I'm still searching.'

He nodded as though he completely understood. 'Aren't
we all. I've always had to be what everyone else needed
me to be. A father, a brother, a breadwinner, a discipli-
narian.' He wasn't quite sure why he was telling her this.
No doubt Peter had told her the story but it wasn't something Edward often talked openly about, mainly because
everyone in town already knew his past. 'Even now with
Hamilton, when I'm not sure how to deal with his utter
stubbornness, I still have to stand firm, to be the one in
charge. Some days, I just want to give it all a big miss.'

He frowned, momentarily lost in his own thoughts, but
when he looked at Honey he could see empathy in her eyes.
He instantly straightened, wishing he hadn't revealed so
much to a woman he barely knew. She was his locum. He
was her boss. He couldn't allow himself to be drawn in
by her natural charm, even though it felt like she had the
ability to see right through his barriers. That was just another reason why he needed to keep her at arm's length.

'We're governed by the rules that bind us,' she stated
with a knowing nod.

'And speaking of rules, I have something I need to say,'
Edward continued, collecting his teacup and Ginny's, his
tone becoming more sharp. 'I'd appreciate it if you didn't
hand out your own personal remedies to the patients. If
something were to go wrong, the malpractice insurance
might not cover it.' He started to walk out of the room,
pleased at the distance he'd managed to find, both literally and figuratively. Being so close to Honey, having her
kiss his hand, had temporarily blinded him to his initial

purpose, but now he was back and he needed to be sure she understood her position in this clinic.

'The use of acupuncture needles is also out of the question and I'd appreciate it if, starting from tomorrow, you would wear something more befitting a qualified general practitioner.'

With one firm nod Edward turned and walked from the kitchenette, no doubt leaving a bemused and bewildered Honeysuckle Huntington-Smythe in his wake.

CHAPTER THREE

THE rest of the clinic proceeded without a hitch and by the time Ginny announced they were done for the day, Honey was starting to feel the fatiguing results of her early-morning start.

'Do you know where I'm supposed to be living for the next year?' Honey asked the receptionist as she handed up the last of the completed case notes.

'Oh, dear, Honey. I'm so sorry.' Ginny hunted around on her desk for a set of keys. 'Lorelai was going to take you over after clinic and show you around because Edward was supposed to have a house call in Adaminaby but that's been cancelled. She left the keys with me… Ah…here they are.' Ginny handed them over, then switched off her computer and picked up her bag.

'Where is—?'

'I'd take you there myself but I have to go and pick my husband up from Tumut and I'm already late. He's part of the amateur theatre group there and it does him good to get out of the house but as he doesn't drive any more after his stroke, it's up to me to get him there and back.'

'Well if you could just let me know where the—'

Ginny wasn't paying attention as she bustled around to the door. 'Sorry. Don't like dashing off on your first night here but I'm sure you'll be fine. Edward will look after you. Have a good night, Honey.'

Honey held out the bunch of keys Ginny had handed her. 'Well, if you tell me where the—' She stopped as the clinic door tinkled closed and Ginny disappeared. Honey sighed and looked down at the keys in her hand. She wasn't sure she wanted to ask Edward anything after the way he'd laid down the law. She knew he had every right to dictate the way she treated the patients but she felt he was out of line regarding the way she dressed. It wasn't as though she was filthy or indecent. She simply dressed differently. Still, it wasn't the first time she'd encountered such a close-minded attitude and she'd survived through worse. Tomorrow she'd dress the way he wanted because she really wanted to give Oodnaminaby a chance. First, though, she had to find out where she was staying and that meant asking her new fuddy-duddy colleague for his help.

'Problem?' Edward's deep voice came from behind her and she turned to see him leaning against the reception counter, a stack of case notes next to him. She was glad he couldn't read her thoughts.

Honey indicated the keys in her hand. 'Apparently I have a place to live in and I have the keys to the castle but unfortunately I have no idea where my palace is situated.' She shrugged. 'I guess Ginny was in a bit of a rush.'

Edward nodded. 'She has to pick up Harry from Tumut.'

'So she mentioned. I don't suppose you know where I'm living?'

'As a matter of fact, I do.' He jerked a thumb over his shoulder. 'Let me show you how we lock up and then I'll take you over.'

'Or you could just give me the address and once we've locked up, I'll get out of your hair.'

Edward shrugged. 'It won't take long.'

As Edward went through the lock-up procedures, she listened attentively, knowing there would be times when this would be a part of her duties. Once they were done, she collected her bag and car keys, heading out the front door. Edward put the alarm on and followed her, dead-bolting the surgery door.

'How's the rate of crime in Oodnaminaby?' she asked as she walked down to her car.

'Basically non-existent but with the equipment and drugs in the surgery—'

'Oh, I wasn't criticising,' she interjected. 'I was simply curious.'

'We have two full-time police officers but they cover a wide territory and work closely with the Kosciuszko National Park rangers.'

'Good to know.' She opened her car door and waited for Edward to give her directions. 'So…where am I headed? Left or right? Up or down?'

'It's not far.' He walked to the passenger seat. 'Better if I show you rather than tell you,' he remarked, feeling highly self-conscious as he climbed into the brightly coloured, daisy-covered car. 'It really is…pink.'

Honey was about to protest, but his attitude was a little more relaxed than before and perhaps she'd been too quick to judge him. She smiled and nodded. 'I guess here it does seem a little over the top but I do love it and given I only really have a birthday every four years, the presents become all the more special.'

'Fair enough.' He tried to ignore the way her fresh scent wound its way around him in the small confines of the vehicle. How was it that after travelling since four o'clock in the morning as well as doing a very full clinic, she could still smell so incredibly sweet? He cleared his throat, returning his thoughts to the task at hand. 'Er...turn left at the end of the car park, then up the hill and then turn into the third street on the right.'

Honey nodded, easily remembering his instructions. 'Where to after that?' she asked.

'Nowhere. You will have arrived at your destination. Oodnaminaby isn't that big.'

'So where exactly am I staying?' Honey turned into the third street on the right and slowed down.

'The coach house. Many years ago, it housed the horses and carriages of the early Australian pioneers but today it's been renovated with all the comforts of home. It's at the rear of my house.'

'*Your* house?'

'Problem?'

'Uh...no. None at all.' Honey wasn't sure how well she'd manage working and living so close to Edward. 'Actually, didn't Peter and Annabelle live in the coach house at some time? I thought I remembered her saying—'

'Yes, they did,' he confirmed. 'For the first year after they were married.' Edward nodded and pointed to the large family home built on stilts and with a sloping A-frame roof. 'It's this one here.'

'Wow.' She pulled the car into the driveway and came to a complete stop. 'Unbelievable!'

'What is?' He was a little confused.

'This place. It's just how I imagined it would be.'

'You imagined what my house looked like?'

'Not specifically your place. You know, the type of place that dreams are made of. It's a complete picture, what with the house, the trees, the garden, the scent of possibility in the air. Everything is beautiful and just...perfect.'

She pointed to the different things as she unclipped her seat belt and climbed from the car. 'Lovely, lovely, lovely.' She clapped her hands in delight, her face alive with happiness. 'I've never lived in a house with a sloping roof before. Excitement plus.'

'It's just a roof, Honey, and, besides, you'll be staying in the coach house, around the back,' Edward remarked as he unfolded himself from her small car, unable to stop watching the way Honey seemed to be drinking in the sights before her, eyes wide in wonderment. He stopped and looked at his property, trying to see it the way she did, but he shook his head. It was simply a house. Nothing more.

'It may be just a roof to you but to me it's a new and exciting experience. Everything in life can be seen as a new and exciting experience if you look at it the right way.'

'You're a real nature girl, aren't you,' he stated rhetorically, trying not to drink in every aspect of her inner beauty, which seemed to be shining out, illuminating her. She came and stood beside him.

'Do you get much snow here in winter?'

'Quite a bit.'

'Ooh. I can't wait.' Excitement burst forth as once again she was struck with the feeling that Oodnaminaby was special.

'You've never seen snow?' Edward raised his eyebrows at the question.

'Oh, sure I have. I've had holidays at the Australian snowfields over the years, I've skied in Switzerland, France and Austria. All beautiful, all fantastic, but I've never *lived* in a sub-alpine town before, hence the happy Honey you see before you.' Then with utter glee shining from her gorgeous face, she all but skipped up the driveway.

'Come on,' she called, beckoning to him. 'You have to show me *everything.*'

Edward knew she wasn't going to take no for an answer so went with her, quickly catching her up.

'Beautiful!' She waved her free hand at the colours, the floral scents from the row of flowers that lined the drive, the birds chirping in the air, the present blue sky with only a few fluffy clouds, the reds and oranges of sunset starting to filter their way through.

They came around the coach house and to her immense delight, opposite the door, Honey found the most incredible little garden with a rockery around the edge and stone steps leading down to a perfectly manicured patch of grass.

'Oh, my!' she breathed, stopping still so suddenly that Edward almost bumped into her.

'This is…' She stopped, as pleasure, awe and fascination at the beautiful garden engulfed her. It was clear that it had been lovingly cared for as there didn't seem to be any weeds anywhere. There were neatly trimmed hedges, tidy shrubs, native flowering plants and trees, and a birdbath with a feeder in the centre. As they stood there, Honey drinking in the sights, two bright red and green rosellas flew down and started pecking at the seed and fluffing their feathers in the water.

'Don't move,' she whispered.

'Wouldn't dream of it,' he answered, and Honey was secretly delighted to find that Edward didn't think stopping and watching two birds was a silly thing to do. Kennedy had, but, then, Kennedy's idea of slowing down was to actually stop walking before drinking his coffee. Still, being in this stress-releasing garden was not the time to ponder her past relationship with Kennedy. They hadn't been able to agree on what they really wanted out of life, so Honey had ended it. That had been over five years ago and now she was standing looking out over one of the prettiest gardens she'd ever seen, watching two little birds having fun in the water. A moment later they shook themselves then flew off, chirping to each other.

'The garden is...breath-taking, Edward.' As she kept looking, she noticed new and different things. 'Oh, look. There's a seat.' As she headed over, she realised it was engraved.

'FOR HANNAH AND CAMERON. YOUR LOVE ENDURES FOREVER.'

She turned to face Edward, her hands clutched to her heart, her eyes filled with a mixture of sadness and happiness. 'Aw...that's a lovely dedication.'

He nodded, astonished to find his throat thickening with emotion and in that one split second, with Honey by his side, looking down at the bench, the pain and loss of his parents' deaths settled over Edward again. He hadn't felt this way since he and his family had scattered their parents' ashes into the wind and he'd said goodbye.

'My...uh...' He stopped and cleared his throat. 'My mother planted this garden. So many years ago. It was *her* garden. Always has been, always will be.'

'Hannah's garden.' Honey spoke the name out loud and then nodded. 'It *does* suit it and you've kept it tended in her memory.' She looked up at him and Edward was surprised to see tears glistening in her eyes. 'That's perfect, Edward.'

'It's not meant to upset people.' He shifted away, feeling if he stood there for too much longer, looking down into her shining face, he'd end up giving in to the urge to hold her hand, to touch her, to pull her close and wrap his arms around her. It was an odd sensation to be so attracted to a woman he'd only just met. Still, deep down he appreciated that whilst this was *his* mother they were talking about, Honey was the one overcome with emotion.

Honey sniffed and laughed. 'Sorry. I'm a highly emotional being, especially when I discover something extraordinary. Peter's shown me pictures of your mother and I can quite easily imagine her here, wide straw hat on her head, kneeling on a rug as she pulls weeds or trims the bushes.'

'Yes.' Edward exhaled slowly, a sense of calm settling over him. 'You know it's odd, I come out here and look after the garden, so does Peter and BJ, Lorelai's father, and even Hamilton mows the grass and pulls the odd weed or two. Sometimes Lorelai comes, more often than not lately, and we all do our little bit to keep it neat and tidy, but I think this is the first time in a long while that I've just stood and appreciated it.' He put his hands on his hips and nodded, slowly turning as though drinking in what the combined efforts of his family had produced. 'My mother planted this.' He spoke the words as though they were really only now penetrating his mind and Honey could hear that his voice was thick with emotion.

'She left you all a sanctuary and one that was designed and made from her heart, a heart filled with love. She must have been quite a mother, so loving, so caring, so thoughtful.'

'Yes.' He looked at Honey for another moment then turned his back but not before Honey had seen his eyes become glazed with repressed sorrow. She wondered how much he'd actually been able to grieve for his parents before the heavy burden of responsibility had settled on his broad shoulders.

Honey moved further into the centre of the garden and looked around her, wanting to give Edward some space.

She sniffed a flower or two, watched the bees and admired the view of the rolling hills beyond, the colours of the sky beginning to intensify even more. Her heart filled with pleasure as the small daffodils danced nearby.

'It's so incredibly perfect,' she whispered, then, unable to contain her joy any longer, she put her arms out and her head back and twirled around. Edward watched, captivated by the freeness of her heart. Honey seemed to see the world he thought mundane and restricting as wild and free. The first time he'd seen her twirl like this, he'd thought she was quietly insane, but now it seemed right that she would appreciate such beauty in such a way.

'Don't you think it's lovely?' she said, but the instant the words were out of her mouth, she overbalanced and came tumbling down onto the grass.

'Honey!' With two long strides he was at her side, only to find her giggling with glee. He looked away, to the view beyond the garden, the sunset meeting the tops of the mountains. It was a view he'd seen for most of his life and of course he knew it was pretty, but actually stopping to look at the garden, at the view and really appreciating them was something he rarely did. However, the view was far safer than the enchanting woman at his feet.

Honey sat up, the smile still on her face. 'Why don't you sit down? Join me on my magic green carpet.' She stroked the grass. 'We can go *anywhere*!' She beckoned him down and he had the feeling that she wasn't going to let up so did as she asked.

'You're acting like a child,' he said, but there was no censure in his tone. It was more of a statement and one that held just the slightest hint of jealousy.

'Well, I am only seven and a quarter,' she pointed out matter-of-factly.

'A ready-made excuse. Lucky you.'

'You don't need an excuse to let go, Eddie. Everyone's entitled to reactivate the child within and just have a tantrum. Lie on the grass and kick your arms and legs, scream, yell, let it all out. Let your frustrations, your anger, your pain be expelled from your body. Come on. Try it.' She nodded enthusiastically. 'You'll feel great afterwards.'

'I am not going to lie down and yell.' His words were calm and well modulated and he shook his head for emphasis. Honey could see she was losing the battle...for now, but right then and there she accepted the mission to loosen Edward up and to help him deal with the repressed grief she could see behind his eyes. 'Is that what you used to do as a child? Lie down yelling, kicking and screaming out your frustrations?'

Edward had merely meant the question as a form of deflection and was astonished when he saw a slight flicker in the smile on her lips. An apology was already forming in his mind when she gave a tiny shrug and shook her head.

'No. There was never anyone around to pay attention. If you're going to have a full-on tantrum, you want witnesses. Anyway...' she patted the grass again '...why don't you tell me about your childhood? I love that you've lived in the one place for most of your life. How grounding that must have been.' Honey's eyes twinkled with anticipatory excitement and Edward had to admit she looked very becoming. 'What are some of the best memories you can think of about this garden and this house?'

'Why? So you can assess my psyche? I know you hold a degree in psychology. I'm not some broken toy you need to fix while you're working here.'

'I never said you were. Besides, if you stop to think about it, we're all broken in one way or another. We've all had our share of hurts and disappointments and they scurry around in our minds, finding places to hide like a Jack-in-the-box and then they *jump* out at us and go *blah*, unleashing those carefully boxed-up emotions all over the place. It's usually when we least expect it.'

'Really? So *you* have some…' He stopped, unable to say the words she'd used because they sounded silly.

'Jack-in-the boxes…' she encouraged.

'Hiding in your mind?' He finished.

'Of course.'

'What are they?'

Honey smiled as she ran her hand over the grass, liking the way it tickled her palm. 'Oh, where to start. Shall I lie down?'

Edward couldn't help the smile that spread across his lips. 'Sitting is fine, Dr Huntington-Smythe,' he remarked in his best doctor voice. Honey closed her eyes, took a deep cleansing breath and then slowly released it.

'I'm ready.' She opened her eyes. 'Ask what you will.'

'Just like that? You'll open up to me?'

'I'm hardly an espionage agent, Edward,' she responded with a smile.

'Uh…OK.' He thought of a question that was really burning in his mind. 'What brings the granddaughter of a classic, iconic surgeon all the way to Oodnaminaby for twelve months?'

'The opportunity to help people,' was her reply.

Edward watched her carefully. 'There's more to it than that,' he murmured.

'Possibly.'

Edward waited, keeping silent, knowing it would prompt her to expand on her answer.

Honey raised her eyebrows. 'You're really getting into the part of the psychologist,' she said after they'd sat in silence for a minute. 'All right, if you really want to know, I'm looking for a place where I can...truly belong.'

'And you think that might be Oodnaminaby?' His eyebrows were raised. Was she looking for a permanent job? Wanting to *live* here in town? A thousand different scenarios flooded through Edward's mind at the thought of this gorgeous woman living here, seeing her every day, around the town, infecting his clinic with her alternate remedies. Or worse...what if she started up her own medical practice, where if people weren't satisfied with the response at his clinic, they'd go to hers? What would that mean for his parents' legacy?

'I don't know.' Her words were honest.

Edward let out a deep breath, unaware he'd been holding it while waiting for her answer.

'I feel as though I've been looking far too long. Probably since I was about six years old.'

'Six years old? Or are you referring to when you were *really* one and a half?' He smiled and was pleased when she reciprocated.

'Yes. Only one and a half when I first remember my parents leaving me.'

His eyebrows raised. 'They left you?' Edward shook his head. 'I don't understand.'

'They went off to protest something or other, they were—still are—always protesting something. The bigger, the better as far as they're concerned. Clean water. Fresh air. Greenhouse emissions. Don't dam the river. Bring home the troops. Anything and everything. My brother calls them professional protesters and in a way he's right.'

'So...they went off to protest something and left you alone?' he prompted, eager to hear her story.

'Hardly alone. I was six years old and they left me "in charge" of my three-year-old brother, four-year-old twins

and a ten-month-old baby. The baby and the twins belonged to two other families we were living with. Three
sets of parents left the commune and didn't come home
until three days later. In their defence, they thought they'd
only be gone for a matter of hours but the peaceful protest
turned not so peaceful and they were all arrested, spending two nights in gaol.'

Edward was stunned. 'And no one came to find you?
Social services? Anyone?'

Honey shook her head. 'Nope. If they told social services about their children, they risked having us taken
from them. When they returned, they were astonished
I'd coped. I knew how to change nappies and I fed us all
mashed potatoes because that's all I knew how to cook.
Everyone went to bed on time and washed in the morning
before they dressed. I was a right little mother.'

Honey folded her knees beneath her skirt then hugged
them to her chest. 'As I coped so well at such a young age,
they would often leave me in charge of several children.
Animal healing and childminding. Those were my primary duties wherever we lived for the next decade.'

'And I'm sure you learned to cook more than mashed
potato.'

Honey smiled, pleased he hadn't offered any empty
platitudes. 'Yes, I did and my brother was forever grateful.'

'What do you mean by animal healing? Do you have
magical powers?'

'Don't I wish.' She smiled. 'I would have magicked myself and Woody out of that life a lot earlier. No, the animal healing is what my father called it. When I was about
five, I found an injured ring-tailed possum and I nursed it
back to health. Splinted its little tail, fed it milk through an

eyedropper, kept it warm, that sort of thing. After that, if anyone found an injured animal, it was brought my way.'

Edward shook his head, completely bemused. 'It sounds like a life that was never dull.'

'It sounds like a life that was never happy,' she counteracted, her voice barely above a whisper.

'You're looking for happiness, then?'

'Isn't everyone? I *did* find a level of happiness, though. When I left and went to live with my grandparents, I had people who cared about me, who were interested in *me*, not simply in what I could do for them. I was happy but I can't live with my grandparents for ever, now, can I,' she stated with a small smile.

'According to your résumé, you've certainly travelled a lot, working in different places for six- or twelve-month contracts.'

'The place that fits me has been rather elusive,' she agreed with a small nod. 'But I am determined to find my home. I can't give up because I simply know it's out there somewhere.'

'You don't see your parents at all?'

Honey looked away from him, into the stunning sunset that surrounded them. 'My parents and I have never seen eye to eye. You think I'm bad, offering patients an alternative to traditional medicine, but my parents are way off the charts as far as that goes.' Honey tried not to scowl as she remembered the way her mother had refused to have her pregnancy checked, even though she'd been in her mid-forties. The result had been disastrous. 'If there isn't a natural cure, they don't want to know. I'm not that closed minded, Edward. I was raised to use honey on bee-stings, to place aloe vera on rashes, to chew root ginger to relieve intense pain. It's true that we can learn a lot from nature but I also agree to prescribing antibiotics when warranted, that terminally ill patients should make use of the synthetic barbiturates as pain relief and that X-rays and ultrasounds are the inventions of complete geniuses.'

Honey put one hand over her eyes, willing her breathing to settle, willing for the peace she'd spent years learning to find to wash over her. With one deep breath she removed her hand and gave Edward a lopsided smile. 'Next question?'

Edward returned her smile, seeing that she was mentally exhausted. It was then he remembered she'd had a very long day. They were both silent for a moment, watching the changing colours of the sky. 'Do you think we'll see a star soon?'

Honey glanced at him, grateful he hadn't asked her another probing question. 'I hope so. I'd like to make a wish.'

'Wishing to find your home?'

Honey hugged her knees closer, her head back as she looked at the sky once more. 'Wishing for a happier future. For my children to have a life of stability and understanding. You had that. You had parents who loved you, who provided for you, who left you their legacy.' She ran her hand over the grass once more. 'Such a beautiful garden.'

'Thank you,' Edward said a minute or two later. 'I appreciate your openness, Honey. It's something I…struggle with…opening up to people,' he clarified.

'Well, you live in a town where everyone knows your story so it's not as though you'd have to repeat it all that often.'

'True.'

'But they don't know the *real* you, the man deep inside, do they?'

Edward slowly shook his head, still looking into her eyes. 'Sometimes I'm not even sure if *I* know me.'

'You've been wearing too many hats.'

He nodded, amazed at how well she seemed to understand him. 'Exactly.'

They both sat there on the grass, neither of them moving, their gazes locked. He was captivated, watching her as they'd watched the rosellas, not daring to move a muscle as he appreciated the incredible beauty that was Honey. His heart started to pound beneath his chest and his palms began to sweat as he realised he was powerless to look away from her gorgeous eyes.

'What colour are your eyes?' he murmured softly. 'Sometimes they look blue, other times they're more like a violet colour.'

'They're bluey-greeny-grey but I'm wearing coloured contacts.' Her tone was as soft, and as intimate as his own. 'They sometimes appear to alter the colour of my irises. I have green contacts, too.'

It was odd. Sitting there. So close. Looking at her. Giving in to the urges he'd been fighting ever since they'd met. It was as though they were having two very different conversations. One was quiet and restrained, the other—the non-verbal one—was a rage of riotous emotions.

How was any man to ignore such a woman?

'Why do you colour your hair?' His hands were itching to reach out and touch it, to feel if it really was as silky as it looked.

Honey smiled and then without another word she removed the red ribbon and let her hair fall loosely around her shoulders, enticing him further. Then she reached up, fiddling with a clip or something at the top of her scalp. A second later he heard a faint 'click' and she removed an artificial plaited blue braid, holding it out to him.

'It's fake?'

'Well…that one is. So is the green one, but the others are real.'

'But why?' Unable to contain the need, he reached out and scooped a handful of her long hair from her shoulder, allowing it to sift through his fingers. It was as soft and as silky as it looked and it left his hand tingling with delight.

Honey tried not to gasp at his brief touch, swallowing lightly over the instant dryness of her throat. 'Why not?' she countered, not at all surprised that her words came out more huskily than she'd thought. 'It's just colour. Don't you think it suits me?'

Edward couldn't help but nod, even though he knew she was fishing. 'You know it does. You know you're beautiful, Honey, and that makes you dangerous to be around.'

She itched to lean forward, to close the distance between them, to throw her arms about his neck, to urge his head down so their lips could make contact, but she'd already sensed Edward was an old-fashioned type of man. She could nudge him a little but if she went too far, too soon, she'd scare him off for good and that was the last thing she wanted.

Slow and steady. She stayed where she was but angled her head slightly, her hair sliding off her shoulder to reveal her neck. She watched as Edward's gaze dipped momentarily to the smooth skin, his pupils dilating for a fraction of a second, indicating he liked what he saw. It made her feel all warm and fuzzy inside.

'Dangerous for whom?'

'For both of us. We don't fit, Honey. We come from two very different worlds and our lives appear to be heading in two very different directions.' He shook his head again before getting to his feet, brushing the grass from his navy trousers. 'Hamilton will be home from sport practice now so I'd better get inside and start dinner.' He took a few steps away from her, then turned. 'Welcome to Ood.'

CHAPTER FOUR

THE next morning, Honey woke up feeling highly optimistic about the day ahead. She'd slept incredibly well and with the sunlight streaming in through the open curtains of the coach house she couldn't resist getting up and facing the dawn.

Looking out the kitchen window at Hannah's garden, she smiled as she pictured Hannah Goldmark working hard to make her garden sanctuary. As a mother with five boys, no doubt she would have needed it. Honey's thoughts turned to Edward and his impeccable manners...although she wasn't quite sure what he'd meant when he'd said they were a wrong fit.

There was no fooling herself about her attraction to him but that didn't necessarily mean she was ready to jump into a relationship. First, she wanted to get to know the town and the people, to see if Oodnaminaby really did possess the magic she was looking for, but she had to admit that Edward's comments had piqued her interest. If she was going to do a psychological evaluation on her new colleague, she'd say he'd been caught so tightly in a web of duty he wasn't sure how to get out. Had he denied himself any sort of private life during the past eight years since his parents' deaths? Had he ever really had the time to come to terms with their loss before he'd stepped up to the plate and taken over the reins?

'You raised a good, strong man, Hannah.' She aimed her words towards the garden. Even yesterday evening, after he'd turned and walked away, she'd found him later, with his youngest brother, out at her car, unloading her belongings.

'G'day,' Hamilton had said when he'd spotted her. 'Nice wheels.'

'Thanks,' Honey remarked, after introducing herself.

'Do you think I'd be able to score a drive some time?'

'Hamilton,' Edward warned, but Honey laughed and held up her hands to show she hadn't taken offence at Hamilton's enthusiasm.

'It takes a secure man to drive around in a hot-pink, daisy-covered car,' she pointed out, but nodded. 'If you'd like to go for a drive, we can.'

'Now?' Hamilton pushed.

'Homework,' Edward growled as he lifted two canvas bags from the back seat and thrust them both at his brother. 'Take these to the coach house.'

'I'm sitting my driver's licence test next week,' Hamilton continued brightly as he headed up the driveway.

'Heaven help us,' Edward murmured, and Honey couldn't help but smile.

'He's not that wild, is he?' she asked as she opened the boot to reveal two boxes.

'Pete's been teaching him to drive because I simply wouldn't have the patience.' Edward pointed to the boxes. 'Is this it?'

'Yep.'

'You travel light.'

'For a woman,' she added.

'I didn't say that,' he countered, taking out one of the boxes.

'Ah, but you were thinking it.' Honey had removed the other one, shut the boot, then headed up the driveway.

Within another five minutes she'd been officially installed at the coach house. Edward had outlined the facilities, with Hamilton shifting back and forth around the place, pointing out different white goods as Edward rattled them off. 'You have a fully equipped kitchen, washer and drier, bathroom and sitting room downstairs with the bedroom upstairs.'

Hamilton's teenage comedic antics had made Honey laugh as he'd ended up pointing upstairs as though he were directing an aeroplane, both hands pointed forward towards the stairs. Edward had rolled his eyes but Honey was positive she'd seen his mouth twitch.

'You'll also find bread, milk, sugar, tea and coffee in the cupboards and fridge.'

Hamilton had skidded around the floor, opening the cupboards and then the fridge, swiping his hand through the air as though he'd been a model on a game show. Honey hadn't been able to resist laughing again.

'Clown,' Edward had murmured, which had only made Honey giggle even more. 'Go have a shower before you slide and crash into something,' he'd instructed his brother, his tone not as brisk as it had been before. Hamilton bowed, a wide grin on his face, before waving to Honey as he'd left the coach house, leaving Honey and Edward alone again.

'Thank you, Edward,' Honey murmured, stepping over one of the boxes she'd carried in, coming closer to his side. 'The coach house is perfect.' She looked around the room, admiring the décor. 'You've been more than helpful—with everything.' Before he could leave, she quickly leaned up and pressed a kiss to his cheek.

'What was that for?'

She shrugged. 'For making me feel welcome.'

Edward had held her gaze for a moment longer before he nodded once, then turned and headed out the door.

Honey sighed and closed her eyes, wishing she'd been able to read his mind. The kiss to his cheek had been prompted by an overwhelming sense of thankfulness. In some of the towns she'd worked at over the past five years since her break-up with Kennedy, she'd either spent the entire time in a rented room in a rundown hotel or in an apartment with the barest furnishings. Compared to most of the places, the coach house was pure luxury and Edward's thoughtfulness in providing her with the basics had been the cherry on top.

She hadn't expected him to understand how she'd felt but even though he'd asked her to tone down her outfits and to refrain from giving patients alternate treatments, he'd still taken the time to ensure she was settled.

'Yes, Hannah, you raised a good man,' she said again, and looking out at the perfect morning spread before her. Unable to contain the happiness that bubbled through her, Honey flung open the door and skipped out into the garden, breathing in the freshness of the day, and lifted her voice in song.

When he first opened his eyes, Edward could have sworn he heard singing. He checked the clock. It was just after six and for a moment he thought he'd set his radio alarm to the wrong station. No. His alarm wasn't supposed to click in for another half an hour. So where was that singing coming from?

No doubt Hamilton had turned on a radio somewhere but after a moment of lying in his bed and listening to the sounds of the house he realised it wasn't a radio. He rubbed his eyes as he climbed from the bed and stretched. Pulling on a pair of jeans, he padded barefoot down to the kitchen and turned on the coffee machine. While he was waiting, he headed to the window and opened the blind, squinting as he peered out into the morning sunshine. The house was quiet, the world outside was still, but he could definitely hear the faint strains of a beautiful voice.

He gazed towards the coach house and then nodded, realisation dawning on him. *That* was where the singing was coming from. Honeysuckle. One of the most mind-blowing, off-the-wall, disruptive women he'd ever encountered. It was now twenty-four hours since they'd met and yet he felt as though he'd known her for much longer.

Grabbing a cup of coffee, he opened the back door and stepped out, breathing in the brisk air before sipping his hot drink, which warmed him through. He probably should have stopped to pull on a T-shirt and some shoes but he was intrigued. The singing was louder outside and he realised that Honey wasn't in the coach house, as he'd originally thought, but somewhere in the garden.

Walking gingerly in his bare feet on the cold ground, Edward went in search of the early morning songbird and around to the side of the coach house. He found her—in the small garden his mother had loved. Honey was standing barefoot in the grass. She had flowers, shrubs and trees around her and her arms were out to the sides, her eyes closed, her face tipped towards the sky. His gaze travelled over her, taking in the singlet top and the love-heart cotton pyjama bottoms she wore, her long, multicoloured hair scrunched messily into a hair band, tendrils escaping here and there as though refusing to be bound.

As the last note of her song died upon her lips, she breathed in deeply then sighed. Birds in the nearby tree seemed to chirp in appreciation, almost as though they were cheering her. A smile spread across her lips and Edward was suddenly pierced with an overwhelming sense of jealousy and longing. To be so free, so happy, as Honey looked right now… He shook his head, clearing the emotion as quickly as it had come.

'That was beautiful,' he remarked, knowing he should announce his presence sooner rather than later, lest she turn and think he was spying on her. Her feet remained stable as she looked at him over her shoulder.

'Oh. I'm sorry if I woke you. I didn't…mean…' Her words faltered as she took in his state of undress. Swallowing over the sudden dryness in her throat, Honey couldn't help the way her gaze lingered on his lightly tanned bare chest. He wasn't hairy like her father or even pale skinned like her brother and whilst she was a trained medical professional and had seen many a naked chest before, this was entirely different. This was *Edward*, the man she hadn't been able to stop thinking about.

Her heart did a little flip-flop as her tongue slipped out to moisten her lips. Her eyelids fluttered closed for a split second as she tried to reboot her brain so she didn't end up a babbling twit in front of such a handsome man.

'It…er…was such a beautiful morning and the song just burst out.' She gave a slight shrug of her shoulders.

Edward sipped his coffee, his male pride secretly pleased with the way she'd given him more than just a cursory glance. His skin was not only being warmed by the rising sun but also by her appreciative gaze.

When he didn't say anything else, Honey turned her attention back to the flora nearby and bent to breathe in the scent of the beautiful flowers. Anything to stop herself from ogling Edward again, even though she desperately wanted to sneak another long look. She walked to the stone bench and brushed her fingers across the engraved words. 'Do you miss them?'

'Every day.'

She turned to look at him then, glad he hadn't moved and that there was still a good distance between them. 'I can't imagine what it must have been like for you, to lose both of them at the same time. No wonder you're searching for some peace.'

'Who said I'm searching for peace? Was it Peter? Or Lorelai?'

Honey raised her eyebrows. 'It was neither of them.'

'Then what makes you say I want peace?'

'Uh…how about the way you're flipping out right now?' She smiled at him, as though she was indulging him.

'I am not flipping…' He stopped and raked his free hand through his hair.

'You haven't had time to grieve properly for your parents.' Honey's voice gentled. 'You had a lot on your mind back then, and have had for the last eight years. Have you at least had a holiday? Gone away for a good long break?'

'Of course,' he said. 'I used to take Ben and Hamilton away for a few nights every holidays. Sometimes we'd go canoeing or hiking. In winter, we'd go skiing or snowboarding. Lots of camping, lots of outdoorsy stuff.'

'Great. It's good for stress release.'

'Exactly.'

'But did you ever go away…on your own…just you?'

'I don't have time for those types of vacations, Honey.

Between the clinic and home and conferences and eating and sleeping and—'

She held up her hands and he stopped. 'I get the picture.' She paused for a moment and Edward had the strangest sensation she was trying to choose her words carefully. 'Would you consider going away now? Just you? By yourself for...' she shrugged '...a few nights?'

'I can't. Lorelai's just taken maternity leave and, besides, Hamilton needs stability, someone to stand over him so he gets his homework done.' There it was again, just a slight hint that something was going on between the two brothers. Honey filed the knowledge away for now. It was clear Edward was stalling, putting obstacles in his own way to avoid the pain and hurt that had been buried deep within him for the past eight years. She also realised there was no point in pushing him, not just yet.

He sipped his coffee and stuck his other hand into the pocket of his old denim jeans. Seeing him standing there, Honey couldn't help but contrast this picture with the man she'd met yesterday morning at a similar time. The man yesterday had been dressed, defensive and determined. This man was raw, impatient and demanding. Honey also realised she was equally attracted to both aspects of the man but, then, what female wouldn't be? Edward Goldmark was definitely quite a catch and while she hadn't come to town looking for a relationship, she was starting to realise she couldn't completely rule it out.

'Life has a funny way of sneaking up on you,' her grandfather had often said. 'One day, Honeysuckle, you're going to find the man that fits perfectly with you. Your heart nestled comfortably with his. That's the way it was with me and your grandmother and although we've had our ups and downs over the years, we've never let go of each other's heart.' Hubert had nodded. 'It'll happen. One day. Just you wait. You won't be expecting it, girl, but it'll happen.'

Honey tried not to stare at Edward's firm, sculpted chest but it was difficult when the man was so incredibly gorgeous. 'What about—?' she began, but stopped then closed her eyes, trying to catch the train of thought she'd just lost.

'What about...what?' he asked a moment later.

'Uh...' Honey opened her eyes, forcing herself to look directly into his. 'I've, uh...forgotten what I was, uh... Hey, would you mind putting on a T-shirt or a jumper or something? Please?'

'Oh?' Edward looked down at his naked torso, an unbidden slow smile spreading across his lips as he realised why Honey had been a little jumpy. 'Sorry. I guess I'm not used to having a woman around the place.'

'Fair enough, but this is your one warning. Dress all bare and sexy like that again and I don't know if I'll be able to control myself.' She winked at him, adding punch to her words.

He blinked twice, utterly shocked at the way her open and honest words burned through him, igniting the flame of deep, primal need. He'd never felt anything so intense or powerful before. 'Uh...yeah.' He eventually nodded. 'Point taken.' He turned and took a few steps away before she called his name.

'I remembered what I was going to say.'

'What's that?' he asked, mildly embarrassed when his words came out a little huskily. It wasn't every day that a beautiful woman told him she found him sexy. Clearly, she'd affected him.

'Are you free on Saturday?'

'Saturday?' he frowned. 'Why?'

'So you can meet me after morning clinic.'

'And why would I do that?' He took a sip of his coffee, needing to do something other than stare at her in those tight little pyjamas she was wearing, which did absolutely nothing to hide the luscious curves of her body. 'What do you want to do?'

Honey's smile slowly widened, her eyes twinkling with delight. 'What will we do?' She asked, her tone deep and sultry and sexy, and he wasn't at all sure whether or not she was teasing but right now all he could do was swallow and watch as she came to stand before him. 'That's for me to know and for you to find out, mister.'

When Edward turned up at the clinic later that morning, dressed appropriately in his usual trousers and polo shirt, his tongue nearly rolled out of his mouth and hit the floor when he saw a sleek, professionally dressed Honey in the kitchenette, making herself a cup of herbal tea.

'Hi, again.' She smiled and held up an empty mug. 'Tea?'

'Uh…ah…' Edward stopped trying to speak and simply blinked a few times to clear his vision. Honey was dressed in a grey pinstriped pencil skirt, which came to just above her knees, her legs were bare and her feet were enclosed in a pair of sensible court shoes. She wore a matching jacket and a cream blouse. Her hair was pulled up into a chignon and he could only see one or two glimpses of the different coloured strands blending with her honey-blonde locks. She wore a touch of mascara and lip gloss, her jewellery kept to a minimum.

In essence, she was the consummate medical professional, the general practitioner he had initially expected to appear on his doorstep yesterday morning—Dr Honey

Huntington-Smythe. Yesterday he'd found her attractive, even though she wasn't his type. Today made him realise that it honestly didn't matter what she was wearing—loose swirly skirts and tops, tight-fitting pyjamas or a pinstripe suit—the woman was absolutely stunning and he was having the most difficult time *thinking* around her.

That had never happened before. Not with any of his other colleagues, not with any of the girls he'd dated during medical school and his internship, and it most certainly hadn't happened with Amelia. He'd always managed to appreciate their looks, to acknowledge their beauty and to keep his brain functioning with no ill effects whatsoever, yet Honey turned him into a blithering idiot with one simple smile.

'I'll take that as a yes,' she replied and placed a teabag into the empty mug. 'Did Hamilton catch the school bus all right this morning?'

'What? Huh?'

Her smile increased. She hadn't expected her clothes to have such a paralysing effect on Edward but she was extremely pleased they had. She'd learned years ago that in order to fit in more smoothly with people, she needed to dress a certain way. Power dressing was what her grandmother had called it and together they'd gone shopping for just the right outfits.

'Remember, Honeysuckle,' Jessica had said. 'They're just clothes. Clothes do not make the woman—the woman makes the clothes. It doesn't matter whether you're wearing three-piece suits or lacy-frilly things, you be yourself. Always.'

And she had. During her internship, she'd wear her suits to work, blending in like everyone else, but as soon as she arrived home she'd change into her 'hippy', freer-flowing clothes, feeling as though her soul could breathe once more. Today, though, it had been well worth the effort to see Edward's reaction. Besides, she was only doing what he'd asked.

For the rest of the week Honey wore the suits, with Ginny remarking that she looked very fancy, very swish, and that perhaps Edward should start wearing a shirt and tie in order to bring himself up to Honey's standard.

He came out of his consulting room one afternoon to find her standing by Ginny's desk, cradling a young month-old baby in her arms.

'Little Imogen is simply gorgeous,' Honey told Carrie, Imogen's mother, before cooing at the baby, 'And now that we're sorting out your colicky problems, you'll be even more irresistible.' She pressed her lips to the baby's bald head, kissing her lightly. 'Yes, you will, sweetheart. So precious. So special. I'll bet your Mummy and Daddy can't stop kissing you.'

'You're right,' Carrie remarked. 'Even though she hasn't been well, she's still our angel.'

Honey smiled and sighed as she handed Imogen back to her mother and Edward could see a secret yearning in Honey's eyes. He knew she yearned that one day her wishes would come true and she'd find a place where she felt at home, where she could stay for ever and raise her family. Children. Honey had made no secret that she wanted children.

Edward shook his head and disappeared back into his consulting room, closing the door behind him, blocking his attractive colleague from view. He was determined to maintain a controlled distance with her given they both wanted different things from life. Even though he was incredibly drawn to her, like a moth to the flame, Honey was looking to settle down and have children, and whilst he may not know exactly what he wanted to do once Hamilton finally left the nest, he knew for certain he didn't want children. He'd done his time. That part of his life was over.

Still, that hadn't stopped him from wanting to spend time with her, to chat with her, and when Hamilton had suggested one night that they ask Honey to join them for dinner, Edward had jumped at the chance.

'Small-town manners,' he'd told himself as he'd walked to the coach house and knocked on the door. 'It's polite to ask her to join us for a meal,' he'd muttered, waiting for her to answer. He'd knocked again, wondering if she was in the shower, but after a few more minutes of waiting he'd walked around to where her car was usually parked and found it gone. She wasn't home. The deflation of his spirits couldn't have been faster than that of a balloon losing air.

The following morning when he bumped into her in the kitchenette, he casually enquired as to her whereabouts the previous evening and she'd laughingly told him that, apart from her first night there, she'd been invited out every night to someone's place for dinner.

'It's so lovely,' she told him. 'Everyone is making me feel so welcomed. I'm quite overcome.'

He had to admit she had been warmly welcomed by the community and he was pleased people weren't giving the new locum a difficult time. In fact, Honey seemed eager to fit in. She'd definitely adhered to his wishes of offering only traditional medicine to his patients and he'd seen no more of her hippy clothes around the clinic rooms.

Edward leaned against his desk, now wondering if he hadn't made an error in judgement, especially when she looked so dynamic and stunning in the feminine business suits she wore every day. Perhaps he should let her dress however she wanted, for either way she seemed to be driving him crazy.

Honey let herself into the coach house, pleased that for tonight at least she hadn't been invited out to dinner. The community at large had been incredibly welcoming but even she needed a break, a bit of time for herself.

She'd done well to follow Edward's stipulations for working at the clinic, dressing sensibly and only offering 'normal' medical treatment to the patients, but this afternoon when Mrs Etherington had popped in to report a vast improvement in her arthritic pain, Honey had been pleased and handed over the recipe so Mrs Etherington could make the special cream at home.

'It's just a recipe, after all,' she told herself as she slipped out of her suit and into a cotton T-shirt and loose, flowing skirt. She was about to settle down to some beans on toast and some research reading for her PhD. when she heard deep male voices, locked in battle, coming from the main house.

The anger in their tones made her wince inside and never being a person who could put up with loud confrontations, without another moment's hesitation she quickly reached for an empty cup and headed over. Eavesdropping had never been her style. Honey preferred to tackle whatever was happening head on, if she could, but as she came closer to the house, she couldn't help but overhear what was being said.

'I don't understand why I need to finish school. It's almost positive I'll get picked to play sport. The talent scouts have been at school all week,' Hamilton yelled.

'You are not throwing away your education *just* to play sport,' Edward yelled back.

Honey knocked loudly on the door, waited a second then opened it, surprised to find the door opening straight into the kitchen, a large wooden table off to the side, eight chairs around it. 'Hi. It's only me.' She held out the empty cup. 'I've run out of sugar and forgot to pick some up at the store after clinic ended.'

Both Goldmark men looked at her, Hamilton's face all red and hot with a belligerent gleam in his eyes. Edward looked a little embarrassed, arms crossed defensively over his chest, reminding her of the first morning they'd met. The atmosphere in the room was so thick she could have sliced through it with a blunt scalpel.

'I can get it if you just tell me which cupboard contains the sugar and then the two of you can go back to fighting. I have headphones. I promise I won't hear a thing.' She walked towards the cupboards as she spoke and it wasn't until she'd opened the first one that Hamilton broke the silence.

'Honey, you can be our impartial judge,' he said, determined to plead his case to her.

'Don't go bringing Honey into this,' Edward retorted. 'Go to your room and finish your homework.'

'You never listen to me. I'm not a child any more,' Hamilton yelled, before stomping from the room.

'Then stop acting like one,' Edward called back. He shook his head and sat down at the table, burying his head in his hands. Honey put the cup down on the bench and walked towards him.

'Here.' She placed her hands on his shoulders, pleased when he didn't shy away. 'Just try to relax for a moment.'

'Ha!' The word was wrenched from him without humour but he dropped his hands and sat up straighter in the chair. 'Impossible to do with him around. Honestly, he's the stubbornest of the lot. So determined, so pig-headed—and if you say he reminds you of me, I'll have to ask you to leave.'

Honey bit her tongue.

'We *are* the same,' he continued as Honey's fingers carefully started to work at the knots that had turned into boulders, buried in his trapezius. 'I know that but that's also why I need to push him. He's capable of so much more than running around an oval, kicking a ball.'

'Then again…' Honey spoke softly, calmly, the way she had when she'd been massaging Lorelai's feet on her first day at work. Edward closed his eyes, allowing her ministrations and her soothing words to wash over him. 'How often do talent scouts come to schools to look for players? Come to schools that aren't in the major capital cities? You're not wrong, though,' she continued. 'Education is vitally important and will most certainly give him a greater range of options.'

'Yes. Exactly. See? You get it.' Edward could feel the tension starting to seep from his muscles, unable to believe just how tight his shoulders felt. Honey kneaded on in silence, Edward's thoughts started to drift and a few minutes later he felt her clever fingers coming up his neck to the base of his skull, where she applied small strokes. His head was lighter, his anger and frustration at Hamilton starting to float away.

'Just listen to my voice and know that everything is going to be all right. Everything will work out just fine and there will be no more yelling, no more confrontation. Things will be smooth and calm with Hamilton. Just listen to my voice. You're doing a great job, Edward. Just relax.'

Edward felt his lungs fill completely with air before he slowly exhaled, allowing all his tension to float away, just as Honey had suggested.

'That's it. Focus on your breathing. In and out. Nice and slow and steady.'

'What are you doing?' Hamilton asked from the doorway behind her, and Honey smiled as she looked at him.

'Just helping Eddie to release his tension. Why don't you come and join us?' She inclined her head towards the table, her smile welcoming. Hamilton did as she asked but sat almost at the opposite end of the table from his brother.

'Would you like a massage?' she asked Hamilton, but he quickly shook his head. 'You're like my brother. He hates them, too. Says they give him goose-bumps.'

Edward chuckled at that and Honey removed her hands and sat down, bridging the distance between the two brothers. 'So? Shall we talk? Hamilton, you go first.'

Edward opened his mouth to protest but Honey simply reached over and placed her hand on top of his. 'Edward will listen.'

He closed his mouth.

For the next hour the two brothers talked, with Honey mediating the discussion, her tone calm and controlled, which helped the conversation to stay civilised. By the end it was decided that should Hamilton be offered a position by the sport scout, then a family meeting would be held with their other brothers to discuss the pros and cons. In the meantime, Hamilton wouldn't continually argue about going to school and would apply himself to his homework.

'You're good at mediating,' Edward said after Hamilton had headed off to bed. 'Do you do it often?'

Honey smiled. 'No. Quite the opposite, really. I was usually the one who required the mediation. My poor brother would more often than not be the one sitting between myself and my parents, making sure both sides were heard.'

'You? A troublemaker?' Edward smiled at her but shook his head, as though he didn't believe it. 'Never.'

Honey laughed as she collected her empty cup from the bench. 'And now, Dr Goldmark, if you'll excuse me, I have some reading to do and an outing to plan.'

'Do you mean *our* outing on Saturday?'

'Yes.'

'Can you give me a hint?'

'Nope.' She grinned at him. 'Goodnight.'

She was at the door before he called her name. 'What about the sugar?'

Honey chuckled. 'What sugar? I don't need any sugar.' With that, she waved goodbye and headed out the door, leaving a smiling Edward in her wake, concerned about Saturday, highly appreciative for what she'd done and completely confused about his feelings for her.

CHAPTER FIVE

By the time Saturday rolled around, Edward felt completely on edge. Honey had flatly refused to allow Lorelai to come into the clinic for the rest of the week, saying she was a quick study, had things completely under control and that Lorelai needed to rest. He had to admit she was true to her word and he had received comments from many patients about the wonderful Dr Honeysuckle.

'She gave me this special cream, one that she made up *herself*,' Mrs Etherington had said when she'd bumped into Edward at the general store. 'And it has been the only thing that's given me any relief from my arthritis *for years*. She says it's all natural and she gave me the recipe so I can make it up myself.'

The glee on Mrs Etherington's face had stunned Edward and he'd been hard pressed to recall a time when the woman had looked so happy. 'It's nice that she's not locked into doing things in just the traditional way,' the woman had continued, and for a split second Edward had wondered whether she was having a dig at him, but in the next instant Mrs Etherington had nodded. 'I'm happy to keep coming back and seeing Dr Honeysuckle for as long as she's here.' Then she'd patted his hand and said more softly, 'I think your mother would have liked her.'

Edward had been too stunned to say anything. When

he'd been a young boy growing up, he'd been afraid of brisk Mrs Etherington and never had he heard her speak so gently or so intently. He'd nodded and smiled and that had appeared to be enough for Mrs Etherington who'd finished paying for her purchases and headed out the door.

'She's right, you know,' Connie, the owner of the general store, had agreed. 'Greg and I went to see Dr Honeysuckle on Thursday because, you know, we're having trouble conceiving and stuff, and she not only recommended some herbal treatments but she was so...' Connie stopped and shrugged. 'I don't know. She just listened to me as though I were the only patient she had. It was as though I really mattered to her. She made me feel...'

'Special?' Edward had supplied, when Connie had seemed to be searching for a word.

'Exactly. It's not that I don't like you or Lorelai but I grew up with you guys and even now it sometimes feels a little weird...you know, talking to you about such personal things, but that Honey, well, she's a *real* honey.'

At the petrol station, in the pub, even down at the fishing wharf, the whole town seemed to be buzzing with praise for Dr Honeysuckle. No smirks, no sniggers, just down-to-earth respect for the new locum.

Edward knew he should be happy, should be relieved that everything was working out perfectly, but he was still on edge. He knew it had little to do with the way Honey was settling into the practice and more to do with where she was planning on taking him today.

Initially she'd arranged to meet him at midday, after morning clinic had finished, but given there were only two patients booked in and that Lorelai had insisted on seeing them, he was now due to meet her at eight o'clock—in fifteen minutes' time.

He sat at the old wooden kitchen table in his big family home, the table where he'd eaten so many meals, drunk so many cups of coffee, made many difficult decisions. The familiarity brought him little comfort. It was all *her* fault. Being around Honey unnerved him. That much was obvious. The whole town seemed to have taken to her, his brother Peter had called him a few times to check to see that everything was going all right, and Lorelai was certainly singing Honey's praises, too. Wherever he turned, someone, somewhere was telling him how much they liked the new locum.

It was rare for the practice to have a locum. If they'd needed one before, it had usually only been for a few days—a week at most—whilst he and Lorelai had attended conferences. Honey was the first big, long-term change the practice had undertaken and she was certainly proving to be a success. He knew it was more than her simply being a great doctor, it was also her bright, easygoing manner, her personality. He should be jumping for joy, knowing his patients were happy with the change, especially as Oodnaminaby wasn't a town to easily accept change. He should be incredibly happy that things had worked out.

So why was it that ever since Honey Huntington-Smythe had arrived in his home town he'd had a constant headache? Why was it that he hadn't been sleeping properly? Why was it that just thinking about Honey—the way her hair fell about her shoulders, how her clothes, whether suits or the more bohemian look, which suited her infinitely better, seemed to highlight her incredible body, how her fresh, cinnamony-earthbound scent seemed to linger around him after she'd left his presence—made him feel so shaken up?

Edward closed his eyes and pinched the bridge of his

nose. She seemed determined to encourage him to talk about his parents, although she hadn't said anything more about the idea since their chat early on Tuesday morning… when she'd caressed his body with her eyes and called him sexy. Was it any wonder he was having trouble sleeping?

Amelia had never made him feel so raw, so exposed, so primal and he'd been considering marrying her. What did it mean when he couldn't stop thinking about a woman who was obviously so wrong for him? Then there was the way she'd helped him with Hamilton, the way she'd released the tension in his shoulders, making him feel renewed and refreshed. He'd realised afterwards that she'd used the acupuncture pressure points and wondered if he hadn't been a little harsh when he'd told her he wanted none of that 'alternative' stuff practised at his clinic. To that end, she should also be allowed to dress however she felt comfortable because he'd noticed that as soon as she arrived home from the clinic, she changed her clothes.

Oodnaminaby Family Medical Practice wasn't about rules and regulations, that wasn't what his parents had intended. They'd intended it to be a practice where the doctors worked with the patients to find the best outcomes, the best treatment, and he knew without a doubt that if Honey's alternative remedies worked, why shouldn't the patients try them? Mrs Etherington had certainly been impressed and willing to give it a go.

Either way, it didn't change the fact that Honey had come into his life and rocked his previously even-keeled existence.

'Hello?' She knocked twice on the back door before opening it and coming in. Edward quickly stood, almost knocking the chair over, and shoved his hands into his jeans pockets. 'Hey. There you are. All ready to go?'

He took in her attire of jeans, hiking boots and long-sleeved top, a thick Aran jumper tied around her waist. Apart from when he'd seen her in her colourful pyjamas the other morning, it was the first time he'd seen her in anything but dresses or skirts and he had to admit she looked fantastic. Then again he was sure she could wear a garbage bag and still look amazing.

'I take it I'll be needing a thick jumper?'

Honey shrugged. 'Depends if you're partial to the cold. As I've spent the better part of my life either living on the beach or in the tropics, the cold and I are not the best of friends.'

'A beach baby?' Now, why did the image of Honey in a bikini suddenly pop into his mind?

Her tinkling laughter surrounded him. 'Give me a summer's day over a winter one any time.'

'We get some cold weather here,' he added, collecting a jumper from the closet by the back door where he kept his thick coats, gumboots and wet-weather gear.

'I know.' Excitement lit her eyes. 'A new experience for me. I can't wait.'

Edward wasn't too far away from her and when he looked down into her face he was astonished to discover her eyes were now a vivid shade of green. Just like the sea on a stormy day.

'Wow.' The word escaped his lips before he could stop it as he stared into her eyes. 'You look…different.'

'Good different or bad different?'

Edward swallowed, then licked his lips, completely hypnotised. 'Er…your eyes are so…green.'

Honey laughed and nodded at his reaction. 'Good different.' She took a step closer, pleased that he hadn't looked away. She liked it when he looked at her as he was now, as though she was the most beautiful woman he'd ever seen. She wanted so desperately to put her arms around his neck and urge his head downwards until his lips met hers but she knew there was no rushing a man like Edward. From the discussions they'd had, it was clear he needed some time to himself, some space to sort things out, some room to get his head together, and she was more than happy to give him whatever he needed.

'Green is supposed to be a soothing colour,' she added, forcing herself to look away. Self-control. This day wasn't about her and what she wanted, it was about Edward, and although he may be looking at her right now as though he really did want her, she also knew that moment would pass.

'So…' She stepped forward and just as she'd done on her first day in Oodnaminaby, Honey took his hand in hers. 'Ready?'

'For?'

'A bit of fun. We're taking my car and you're driving.'

'To where?'

'That's for me to know and for you to find out!'

An hour and a half later, Honey and Edward stood at the bottom of a chairlift. It had been enjoyable watching him drive her pink car along roads he knew so well.

'Why are we taking your car?' he'd asked when she'd handed him the keys.

'Because I need to see how it handles on the mountain roads and as you drive them regularly, it seemed logical for you to be the one to drive.'

Honey had held her breath as she'd waited for his decision. He could have overruled her and demanded they take *his* car, to do things *his* way, that her plans for the day be brushed aside in favour of whatever *he* wanted to do. That was the way Kennedy had been.

'Fine.' Edward had accepted her keys and folded his six-feet-four-inch frame behind the wheel, loosening up as they drove along and in the end being quite impressed with the handling of her little car.

Now, as they looked up towards the top of the chairlift, Edward raised his eyebrows. 'This is your spontaneous idea? Walking up Mt Kosciuszko?'

Honey nodded, a large smile on her face as she took off the backpack she'd brought and handed their lift tickets to the attendant. 'It's a nice day, it's not too far from where you live and I confess I've always wanted to walk to the highest point of Australia.'

'So this is more about you than me?' Edward wanted to know, but Honey's only answer was a squeal of delight as she sat down next to him on the chairlift.

'Why should you get to have all the fun?' She waved brightly at the attendant. 'Thank you,' she called as Edward pulled the safety bar down across them, the weather gradually becoming cooler as they rose. 'It's exciting.'

'You're like a child at Christmas,' he remarked, unable to resist smiling back. Her excitement was infectious.

'How many times have you been up here?' she asked.

'On the chairlift to ski down, too many times to count. Walking from Ramshead Range to Mt Kosciuszko, only twice.'

Honey raised her eyebrows. 'And here I thought you'd be an experienced guide.'

Edward shrugged. 'My dad and I came up a week after my twelfth birthday. We walked up to the summit, took pictures and then headed to one of the camping areas where we pitched a tent for the night. Just the two of us, in the crazy Snowy Mountains weather. It was early December, which is of course summer here, and it was pretty cold overnight in that tent, but in the morning we woke to find ourselves surrounded by snow. It was incredible. It sparked a tradition and after that, every time one of my brothers turned twelve, dad would organise a camping trip when the weather was fairly safe, then he and the birthday boy would walk to the summit and tent it overnight.'

'What happened when the twins turned twelve? Did he take them together?'

'No. Each boy had their own special adventure.'

'He sounds like quite a man, your dad.' A pang of jealousy ripped through her. She wished her father had spent time with her. 'All I received when I turned twelve was a card stating I'd donated a chicken to a village in Africa. Not that that's a bad thing,' she quickly added. 'They needed the chicken more than I needed a gift, but it was still a little…'

'Disheartening for a twelve-year-old?' Edward ventured.

'Exactly. Anyway, tell me more about these camping trips. They sound fantastic.'

Their chair bounced up and down as they went through the first tower's sheaves, the calmness of the mountains surrounding them. Honey listened intently to everything Edward said, hearing the love and respect he carried for his father in his tone.

'Benedict was the last one to go on the birthday hike.' Edward paused, as though trying to control his emotions whilst relating the story. 'The next winter season was the year of the avalanche. The year my world changed. The year my parents died.'

Honey wanted to hold him, to touch him, to reassure

him, to do anything she could to take away the pain and regret she could hear in his voice. The world about them was still, the sounds of the chairlift engines working in the distance, the coolness continuing to surround them.

'They were in Charlotte's Pass, doing house calls.' He shook his head, sadness and regret filling him. 'The avalanche came without warning and forty-three more people died that day. BJ was leader of the rescue team and Peter, who was only twenty years old, was a junior member, out on his first major job.'

Unable to contain her need to let him know that she was here to support him, Honey reached out and covered his hand with hers, giving it a little squeeze. She didn't want him to stop talking because she had a sense that he didn't discuss his parents' deaths all that often. She was also humbled he was doing it with her.

Edward turned to look at her, his voice shallow, his eyes filled with pain, regret and deep sadness. 'Poor Pete. So young to see such a sight.'

Honey nodded, trying to control her own emotions, blinking back the tears. One look at Edward's face and empathy had flowed through her. She squeezed his hand again, trying to be strong and supportive for him. 'Peter once told me that he grew up that day. It helped him to focus on what he really wanted to do with his life and now look at him, a national park ranger.'

Edward dragged in a deep, cleansing breath, unable to believe how incredible he felt saying this to Honey. Amelia had been in his life when the tragedy had struck. She'd offered her condolences, she'd stood beside him at the funeral, and once his parents had been buried she'd expected his life to carry on as planned. What she hadn't expected was all the 'baggage', as she'd termed his younger brothers, that had come with his parents' deaths.

Honey, however, hadn't gushed with emotion, she hadn't offered bland apologies for the tragedy that had struck his life. Instead she was supportive and uplifting. He'd seen her blink back the tears, he'd seen that she'd been affected by what he'd related and, even though she'd heard the story from Peter, her reaction to *his* words was just what he needed.

'That's Pete,' Edward agreed with a nod. 'Always seeing the glass as half-full rather than half-empty. So do you, Honey. No wonder you and Peter became friends.'

'You're like that, too, Edward.'

'No.' He instantly dismissed her words with a shake of his head. 'I'm far too pessimistic. I'm old and set in my ways.'

'You're thirty-two!' She chuckled. 'That's far from old and if you're so set in your ways, why are you riding up a chairlift and getting ready to walk to the highest point in the country?'

'Because you're making me?' he asked, a slight smile touching his lips, but she rolled her eyes and shook her head.

'No. It's because you're daring.'

He laughed at that. 'I am not daring, Honey.'

'I disagree. Don't you realise that in accepting full custody of your brothers, being the Rock of Gibraltar for your family and friends, supporting a community in a time of need, you've been more bold and daring than anyone I've ever met? You've shared experiences with your brothers that are unique and precious and I'll wager that on the whole the good times far outstrip the bad.' She squeezed his hand again, desperately wanting to show him that he *was* an incredible man. 'And I'll bet that three years after your parents' deaths it was you who brought twelve-year-old Hamilton up this very route so that he wouldn't miss out on his birthday camping trip. Am I right?'

'Pete told you, didn't he?'

Honey shook her head and blinked back the tears that were threatening to dash onto her lashes. 'No.' Little puffs of air came from her mouth as she spoke and she gave him a watery smile. 'You're a quiet achiever, Edward. A man who perhaps gives too much of himself to other people. How often do you stop to consider what *you* want from life? What are those deep thoughts you've pushed to the furthest reaches of your mind? You work and you work and you work. You get stuck in the day-to-day rut and it's easy to leave those deep thoughts out of sight, not stopping to think about them, but you have to. At some point, you just have to or those deep thoughts can turn poisonous and start to infect your life.'

'You sound as though you're speaking from experience,' he murmured, unable to believe how close to the truth she'd come.

'I am. It was the reason I studied psychology. I wanted to try and understand where my parents were coming from, to understand their rationale. When my mother was in her late forties, she became pregnant. She'd always struggled with pregnancies, saying that Woody and I were her little miracles. Yet she refused to have scans, to see a GP or even a midwife to check that everything was all right. She kept saying she could do it the natural way, that everything was fine.' Honey paused and shook her head. 'Everything wasn't fine. If she'd had her scans, if she'd had an amniocentesis, then she would have discovered the baby had a congenital heart defect. They could have delivered the baby at thirty-seven weeks and performed surgery to fix the problem but instead my mother wanted to do it naturally. As a result, my little sister lived for an hour before she died.'

'How old were you?'

'Almost eighteen. I couldn't believe their blinkered view of the world. Things are not black and white, right or wrong, traditional or alternative. There needs to be a balance. I knew if I stayed with my parents, the poison in my mind would eat away at me. So, when I turned eighteen, I left. I went to live with my grandparents and over the years I was able to rationalise what happened. I started focusing on the simple things in life that make it so grand, such as helping my grandfather restore his old cars. Or going shopping with my grandmother, or hanging out with my brother and going to the movies. Or sitting on the beach at sunset.'

'Putting your arms out to the side and twirling around, absorbing the delights of the world?' he asked, recalling far too easily how beautiful she'd looked the first moment he'd laid eyes on her.

'Yes. Exactly. Those awesome, fun-filled, simple things that make life so worthwhile. That's what counts and I'm sure you have a plethora of memories, things you've shared with your brothers over the years.'

Edward nodded, remembering times when he and his brothers would roll around on the floor rough-housing, or when he'd come home late from an emergency to find eleven-year-old Hamilton had prepared baked beans on toast for dinner. If that was what was important in life then, yes, he'd had a terrific amount of those 'simple things' Honey was talking about. 'I have.'

She smiled at his words and let go of his hand as they

were coming to the end of their chairlift ride. The attendant at the top helped them to disembark safely, Honey carrying the backpack as they walked passed the tall building that housed Australia's highest restaurant to the sign that indicated the different mountain walks.

'It's brisker up here.' She opened her backpack, pulling on a beanie and a pair of gloves. 'Here.' She handed over gloves and a beanie to Edward. 'I found these in the coach-house cupboard. I didn't want to give too much away about our destination so I packed them for you.'

Edward put them on. 'Worried that I'd refuse to come?'

She shrugged before putting the pack on, flatly refusing his offer to carry it for her. 'It doesn't matter now. You're here.' She smiled brightly, her earlier enthusiasm bubbling over once more. 'Come on. Let's get started. I can't wait to get to the top of Australia.'

'OK.' He peered out at the clouds. 'March is supposed to be the best month for walking up here but the weather can be very unpredictable. Here's hoping it won't give us any trouble today.'

They headed down the paved path before crossing a metal bridge, the small stream babbling along nicely, patches of ice visible here and there. In some areas around them were beautiful wild flowers, just starting to bloom. In other little valleys, where the sun didn't often reach, were patches of snow.

Honey oohed and ahhed at it all, pulling a camera from her pack and snapping photographs all around her. 'It's glorious,' she breathed as they reached the lookout. They'd passed a few other people along the way, most of them on their way down, others stopping to take photographs. There was an elderly retired couple, a family with three teenagers and a young couple, dressed warmly, the father carrying a toddler strapped firmly to his chest.

'Here. Let me take your photo,' Edward insisted, and Honey immediately struck a pose, laughing and changing position as he kept snapping.

'Now let's get one of both of us,' she said. 'To mark this auspicious occasion.' She drew closer to him, putting her arms about his waist, startling Edward so much he almost dropped the camera.

'No. I'll just take pictures of you.'

'Don't be silly. Quick. Hold your arm out straight and watch the birdie.' She smiled and held the pose. There was nothing more for him to do but to take the picture. 'There,' she remarked. 'That wasn't so bad, was it?'

They continued on, walking carefully on the raised metal-grate path that had been installed in order to protect the surrounding flora from being trampled. Edward had to admit things looked different from the time he'd walked up here with his younger brother. It had been a difficult trip for him, reliving memories of the time he'd walked the same path with his father. Hamilton had been oblivious, running on pure excitement which, in the end, had made the trip worthwhile.

When they finally reached the summit, they both stood there and breathed out at the rolling hills before them. 'We did it!' Honey stood on top and twirled around, her arms out wide. Edward quickly raised the camera and took several pictures. Although she was dressed in jeans, boots and Aran jumper, the beanie, gloves and scarf she wore were bright and colourful, making her stand-out against the backdrop of granite rocks with tufts of grass here and there, blue sky above.

She laughed and stopped spinning, turning to smile up

at him. They were at the highest point in the country and they were all alone. When she looked at him like that, his gut tightened with desire. Good heavens, she was beautiful. Her cheeks were brisk and rosy from the walk, her red lips enticing as she smiled, and her eyes glowed bright with excited delight.

'Let's have our picnic,' she said, pulling off her gloves, stuffing them into her jeans pocket and opening her backpack. Within five minutes Edward was sitting on a rug, sipping a hot mug of coffee and eating a sandwich.

'If someone had asked me earlier this morning where I'd be eating lunch, I wouldn't have had any idea it would be at the top of Australia.' Edward bit into his sandwich and chewed, seemingly completely satisfied.

'That was the general idea.' Honey swallowed her mouthful. 'Do you know, you can shout anything up here.'

'Shout?'

'Sure. You can go really bizzonkers.'

'Bizzonkers?' He raised an eyebrow as she stood and turned her face into the breeze. The weather was starting to change again, to become cooler, but she loved the briskness.

'Yep. You can shout anything into the wind. It doesn't even have to make sense. Watch.' Honey took a deep breath and cupped her hands around her mouth. 'Hey, everybody, it's time to walk your fish and milk your moose. Woo-hoo.'

Edward laughed at what she was saying, admiring her lack of inhibition. It was *that* quality which was drawing him in.

She took another deep breath and yelled again. 'Standing here, I feel complitified.'

'Com-what?' Edward finished his sandwich and headed to stand next to her.

'Complitified,' she said in her normal tone, brushing
a stray strand of hair out of her mouth and tucking it beneath her beanie. 'It means you're completely verified.'

'You just made that up.'

'That's the point. You try it.'

'*You're* bizzonkers,' he muttered with a laugh, her silly
word tingling on his tongue.

'Sure am. Now it's your turn. Take a deep breath and
yell anything you want.'

'No.'

'Go on, Edward. You'll feel complitified afterwards. I
promise.'

'I'll be fine,' he remarked, and bent to start packing the
food away.

'Edward.' Honey reached for his arm and tugged him
up, hoping he wouldn't fob her off. She could tell he was
resisting because it was a big step outside his comfort zone
but deep down inside she knew if he gave her a firm and
resounding 'no', she'd stop. Kennedy had said no whenever she'd suggested something that little bit different or
daring and in the end he'd tried to repress who she really
was. It was one of the reasons why she was determined
to try and be exactly who she was right now, and she desperately wanted Edward to free himself too.

'Come on. Just yell something. It's all part of doing
something crazy, something different, something no one
expects you to do. Let go. Be free. Achieve emancipation!'

Edward looked down at her, knowing she wasn't going
to let this go. If there was one thing he'd learned about
Honeysuckle Huntington-Smythe this week, it was that
she was a highly determined woman.

'Fine.' He turned his face to the wind, feeling the first
sprinkling of mist pass over. It felt fresh, it felt new.

'Hold your arms out,' she encouraged, a thrill passing through her at his acceptance.

He did as she suggested and tried to think of something to say. He frowned.

'Don't think too hard, Edward. Just yell the first thing that comes to mind.'

He nodded, then closed his eyes as though he couldn't believe what he was about to do. He took a deep breath, then yelled, 'Coffee tables can't sing karaoke.'

Honey was delighted, laughter bubbling up within her. 'Brilliant. Do another one,' she urged.

Edward's smile tugged at his lips as he thrust his arms even wider to the side. 'Coconuts look good in red nail polish!'

Edward couldn't believe how free he felt. It was as though yelling ridiculous things into the wind, as though not caring about what anyone else thought had lifted an enormous burden from his shoulders. He looked at Honey and felt incredibly grateful she'd brought him here today. If she'd told him where they were going, he might have baulked about coming to Mt Kosciuszko given the memories he'd shared with his father. Right now, though, he knew that had his father been alive, had his father come with them on this trek, he would be turning his face into the wind and yelling things no doubt more ridiculous than Edward could imagine. It made him feel closer to the memory of his father.

'That's it,' she encouraged.

He did another. 'Yelling into the wind at this altitude is making me light-headed.'

'Hey, that one made sense,' she protested. 'But I'll let it slide because it's also very true.' The wind was starting to increase, swirling around them, and not too far off they could see mist heading their way. She put her arms out wide and yelled, 'This place is awesome. I love being in the clouds.' Then turned to look at Edward. 'And I've enjoyed sharing it with you,' she finished in her normal tone. 'Thanks for trusting me, Eddie.'

He nodded, just looking at her, drinking her in, liking very much what he saw. Standing there in her bright scarf and beanie, stray strands of hair sneaking out to tickle the side of her face, she looked glorious. 'You keep calling me, Eddie.' His tone was deep, thick with repressed desire, and Honey found it completely addictive.

She took a small step closer. 'Tell me to stop and I'll never do it again.'

He didn't utter a word. Instead, he reached out and picked up the ends of her scarf and tugged her closer. He didn't know if it was because they were alone on the highest peak in the country or whether his light-headedness was affecting his otherwise rational judgement, but right now he wanted to know what it felt like to have that hypnotic mouth of hers pressed against his.

He had thought about her perfect lips throughout the week. Every moment he spent with her made him feel knocked off balance. He couldn't deny that there was a definite attraction pulsating between them, intensifying the more he tried to fight it.

'Why are you…?' he started to ask but stopped, his breath mingling with hers as he continued to look into her upturned face. 'You're so beautiful, Honeysuckle. I don't understand how you can still be single.'

Honey hesitated and, for a brief moment he saw sadness and pain reflected in her bright eyes. So there had been someone and something had gone wrong, causing her pain. A surge of protective energy shot through him at the thought of anyone hurting this incredible woman and he had to stop himself from gathering her close to his chest and never letting her go. The emotion felt right yet he knew it shouldn't.

She cleared her throat and gently shrugged one shoulder. 'Never found the right man. How about you? Why are you still single?'

'Never found the right woman,' he returned, and her lips tilted upwards at the edges.

'An amazing man like you?'

'An amazing man who upon the death of his parents gained custody of his younger siblings,' he returned pointedly, edging her even closer, his hands sliding up her scarf as though ensuring she wouldn't turn and walk away at his words.

'Ahh.' Honey nodded, pleased he wanted her near. 'Were you engaged?'

'We had discussed marriage.'

'She couldn't handle the thought of instant motherhood?'

'No. Her career was far too important.'

'She was a fool to let you go.' She slipped her arms around his waist and leaned into him even further.

He bent his head, now almost desperate to have his lips pressed firmly to hers, to taste and to experience the perfect flavours he knew her perfect mouth would provide.

This was it. Edward was going to kiss her. Honey could tell. She could see it reflected in his eyes as he looked from her mouth to her eyes and then back again. Her tongue slid out to wet her lips in an involuntary action of nervous anticipation. She rested her hands on his hips and rose up on tiptoe, angling her head back in order to close as much distance between them as possible.

His lips were almost there…almost…almost… And at the split second that she felt the slightest, most tantalising pressure of his lips against hers, the heavens above them opened up and the rain poured down.

'Quick!' Edward called, and both of them turned to pack up the remains of their picnic, the rug almost being blown away. Honey pulled two lightweight waterproof ponchos from the pack and they quickly helped each other to put them on. Edward insisted on taking the backpack and Honey was in no mood to argue.

'Let's head back. Chances are it won't be so bad fifty metres down the track,' Edward called near her ear, before taking her gloved hand in his. Honey more than willing for him to play the role of big strong hero. Besides, he knew the erratic weather in this part of the country far better than she did so it seemed only right that he be in charge.

They made slow but steady progress, visibility often reduced to about five metres in some of the small valleys. The entire time, though, Edward kept a firm hold of Honey's hand. 'Slow and steady is definitely going to win this race today,' he remarked as they continued.

'You know, Eddie, you don't have to make conversation with me to keep me calm or to slow me down. I love walking in the rain and being up this high. We're literally in the clouds. I have no objection to slow and steady,' she continued, her tone holding a hint that she wasn't only talking about the weather surrounding them. Edward cleared his throat but tightened his grip on her hand, deciding to ignore the double entendre.

'Even though you're practically soaked through?'

Honey's laughter mixed with the clouds swirling around them. 'Absolutely.'

'You are so different from the women I know.'

'Yeah?' She certainly hoped that was a good thing.

'Yeah,' he replied. They kept walking, hand in hand,

treading carefully on the wet and slippery metal-grate path. They were heading downhill now and one slight error could cause them both to tumble.

The visibility started to increase so they could see a little further ahead.

'It's so quiet and still and peaceful and scary and ex-hilarating and I'm having so much fun.' Honey continued to step carefully but Edward could almost feel the excite-ment of their situation zinging through her gloved hand. 'I'm walking in a cloud. Another thing to cross off my bucket-list.'

'Bucket-list?'

'You know, the things you want to do before you "kick the bucket", before you die.'

'I know what a bucket-list is, Honey. I guess I just hadn't expected someone like you to have one.'

Honey glanced up at him very briefly but returned her gaze to the path beneath their feet. 'Someone like me?'

Edward was surprised he could detect the teasing note in her tone. 'I just meant you seem to live every moment to the fullest.'

'I *try* to. Sometimes I don't succeed,' she called, the wind starting to pick up around them, the visibility de-creasing again. They were already talking fairly loud but as there was no one around, it didn't matter.

They came to a small valley where Mt Kosciuszko and Rams Head met. Edward squeezed on her hand, urging her to stop walking. Honey wasn't sure why they'd stopped and was about to ask him what was going on when he tugged her close, ignored the rustling of their wet ponchos and quickly dipped his head to capture her cold lips with his. Not a brief brush kiss this time. His lips lingered tantalis-ingly on hers, with the promise of so much more.

CHAPTER SIX

KISSING Honey was like receiving manna from heaven and he drew her body closer to his, annoyed both of them were dressed in weatherproof ponchos, gloves and beanies. He wanted to run his fingers through her long and silky hair; he wanted to nibble at that delectable neck he'd caught glimpses of during the week. He wanted to have her arms wrapped around him as he took his sweet time exploring the wonders of this extraordinary woman.

Kissing her now had been a spur-of-the-moment thing, completely spontaneous, and while he was the type of man who for years, had meticulously planned everything, standing here with his mouth pressed firmly against Honey's he couldn't deny the appeal of following through on a thought.

He'd wanted to kiss her—so he had.

'Nice,' she said against his mouth, drawing the word out slowly, savouring it. 'Who knew the simple touch of your mouth to mine would be so incredibly...dynamic?'

Edward murmured his agreement, then closed his eyes and kissed her again, wanting to commit every shared sensation to memory. He'd locked his own wants and needs away for so long but now he'd broken the drought, so to speak, he wanted to continue sampling her sweet, flavoursome lips.

It felt right holding her in his arms, even though they

were encumbered by wind, rain and plastic ponchos. Something deep within him felt as though it were breaking open, a crack in the armour he'd surrounded himself with for so long while he did what had to be done. It was as though freedom was close at hand, that his reward was near, that his life would soon start to make sense. He'd be able to walk his own path, rather than following the footsteps of others.

And Honey? Did she fit into that new world of freedom he'd been searching for? Was she merely the gatekeeper to show him the way? To put him on the right path? Was there room for her to walk along beside him? The thoughts jolted Edward back to the present, his mind zinging with possibilities, probabilities and a ton of questions.

He savoured Honey's addictive lips one last time, before pulling back, the wind having changed direction, the rain urging them to keep moving.

'I'm happy to continue exploring every contour of your lovely face…' He exhaled slowly, then glanced around at their present surroundings. 'But I fear now is not the time.'

'Or the place,' she added as he took her hand in his once more.

'Let's get to somewhere drier,' he suggested, and together they headed back onto the track. The rain had eased, the atmospheric disturbance having calmed down somewhat, and visibility was better.

Honey was elated because Edward had just kissed her. There had been no build-up, no shuffling dance towards each other. Edward had simply pulled her close and kissed her. Right out of the blue! She'd hoped that by bringing him here today, he'd have the opportunity to relax, to take some time out for himself, to do what *he* wanted to do. She smiled to herself. Edward had wanted to kiss her—so he had. The knowledge warmed her heart faster than any heater.

'One more kilometre to go and we'll be back at the restaurant.' He stopped and looked over his shoulder, the path they'd walked along obscured by cloud. 'Do you want to take any more photographs now the weather is clearing up?'

'That's all right,' Honey replied, knowing the camera was stowed safely in the backpack. 'I've been taking plenty of mental snapshots and my memories are more reliable than any mere photograph. Plus, I can remember far more with my senses. I can remember the feel of the wind and the rain; the excited apprehension of being up so high; the sight of those clouds whirling around before covering us like a big white blanket and...I can remember the glorious taste of your lips against mine.'

She stood on tiptoe and brushed an extremely brief but highly tantalising kiss across his lips. 'Thank you for sharing this with me.'

Edward's mouth was still tingling from her touch and he swallowed. 'You knock me off balance, Honey. It's new and exciting and believe me when I say that I like it but it's all mov—'

A loud, blood-curdling scream filled the air and both Honey and Edward turned their heads, looking in the direction of the noise.

'What on earth was that?' she asked as they both stepped off the metal-grate path, being careful as they walked across the cushion plants and herbfield. The area around them was nowhere near as steep as it had been before but on both sides of their path were granite boulders and rocks, jutting out here and there. The ground was uneven but as they continued to walk in the direction of the scream, they heard more cries.

'Help. Help. Somebody—*help*!' It was a woman's voice and, judging from the direction, they couldn't be too far away.

'Just behind that stand of rocks.' Edward pointed with his free hand, his other one firmly holding onto one of Honey's.

'We're coming,' Honey called back. 'Where are you?'

'Over here,' the voice said from behind the rocks, just as Edward had indicated. 'Help me. Please. It's my son. He needs help.'

'We're on our way. Just keep talking,' Honey encouraged.

'What sort of supplies do you have in the backpack, Honey?' Edward asked as they drew closer to the woman's voice.

'Just a small, very basic first-aid kit. Sticking plasters, crepe bandages, disinfectant, triangular bandage and two small gauze pads. Oh, and some paracetamol. That's it.'

'Is there still some water left in the water bottle?'

'About half.'

'Over here,' the woman kept calling. 'Help me, please. My son's hurt.'

'Is he conscious?' Honey asked, as she allowed Edward to help her scramble over the rocks before them.

'No. Well, I don't know. I can't tell. Leonard? Leonard? Talk to me. Talk to me, please!' The woman's voice was starting to become hysterical just as Edward and Honey rounded the rocks. It was only then that Edward let go of Honey's hand, both of them quickly rushing to where a boy of about fifteen lay in an unconscious tangled position on the gravel at the base of the rocks. Honey recognised him as part of the family they'd passed when they'd been heading up to the summit.

'I'm Honey. This is Edward. We're both doctors.'

'Doctors.' The woman clutched her hands to her chest. 'Oh, thank you for stopping.'

'What's your name?' Honey asked the mother as Edward performed a quick assessment on the unconscious Leonard.

'Penny. Is he going to be OK? He was taking photographs and he...well, he just slipped. He was on his way down. I'd already told him to get down,' Penny commented, her words running over each other in her haste to get them out. 'He likes taking photos. Even saved up all his birthday and Christmas money to buy the camera.' Penny looked down at the smashed camera nearby. 'Now it's broken.' The woman choked on her words, clearly distressed by the situation and probably wondering whether her son was as badly broken as the camera.

Honey stood, crossed to where Penny was standing and put her hands on the woman's shoulders. 'It's all right. We're going to help Leonard and you can help him too by staying nice and calm.'

'Honey, I need you,' Edward called, and Honey crossed back to his side. He'd already retrieved the small first-aid kit from the backpack and had pulled off his gloves. The rain was starting to disappear now, heading off to swirl around on the other side of the ranges, but Honey had a feeling it would be back. If there was one thing she'd learned during her week in Oodnaminaby, it was that if you didn't like the weather, you only had to wait about fifteen minutes and it would change.

'What can I do?' She knelt down on the other side of Leonard. In essence, it was the first time she and Edward had worked together but both of them knew what needed to be done and had the skills to see it through. Edward was calling to Leonard, trying to see if the boy would respond, but to no avail.

Edward looked at their patient. 'Carotid pulse is strong, which is a good sign and indicative of no internal bleeding, respirations are conducive to head trauma.' As he pointed to Leonard's head, Honey noticed some blood on Edward's fingers. 'Head wound to the right side of the cranium just above the temporal pulse, possibly two centimetres in length. I don't want to move him any more at this point in order to confirm. Right leg is at an odd angle, possibly fractured at either the acetabulum or femur or both; right radial pulse is intermittent indicative of a possible radial or ulna fracture.' Edward extended his hand as he spoke. 'No doubt he put his hand out to help stop his fall.'

'Good heavens,' Penny mumbled, her trembling fingers covering her mouth as she stood by and listened to Edward's report. 'Is he in any pain? Oh, my poor boy.'

Edward looked up at the mother. 'He's unconscious, Penny, but he's breathing well. His airways aren't blocked and from what I could see when I lifted his eyelids, his pupils were the same size and reacted to the light.'

'Is that good?'

'It means the possibility Leonard has suffered any brain damage is minimal.'

'Brain damage?' Penny looked down at her supine son, fresh tears gathering in her eyes. Honey stood and put her hands on Penny's shoulders again.

'Penny. Look at me.' Honey's voice was soft but direct. When Penny finally lifted her eyes from her injured son, Honey smiled reassuringly. 'Where is the rest of your family? Does anyone else know about this accident? Have they gone to raise the alarm?'

Honey was fairly sure she knew the answer, given she and Edward had been the only two people walking on the path and hadn't seen anyone else after they'd heard Leonard's scream.

'N-no. Oh, no! Howard will be so cross. He didn't want Leonard to come over this way, to leave the path, but Leonard wanted to take some photos. He does a class at school. He's very good but Howard doesn't understand and all they do most of the time is fight,' she explained as she wrung her trembling hands. 'I told him to take the younger two children back to the chairlift and that I would get Leonard and follow them down. I couldn't find him at first but, just before we were engulfed in the misty rain, I found him. He was on the rocks, taking photographs of the clouds rolling in. I begged him to get down, to hurry up...and...' she hiccuped '...that's when he...he jumped.' New sobs peppered her words. 'Oh, Howard's going to be so cross when he finds out.'

'Do you have a phone on you?'

'Yes.' Penny looked hopeful. 'I forgot about my phone. How silly is that?'

'Not silly at all,' Honey reassured her. 'You were focused on Leonard.'

'There should be fairly strong phone reception,' Edward interjected. 'There's a cellphone base station at the restaurant and as we're not that far away, the signal should be strong enough to call for help.'

'Oh, good. Yes. I'll call Howard,' Penny said as she dug through the layers she was wearing in search of her phone, her tone much calmer now.

'Call emergency services first.' Honey told Penny the number to dial. 'Ask for the paramedics, tell them we're approximately one kilometre from the restaurant.' Honey knelt down to help Edward with getting Leonard as stable as they could. Edward had applied some sticking plasters to the minor areas where Leonard had sustained a few cuts and was presently bandaging the right arm.

'Radial pulse has improved. Vital signs still good. I've just placed one of the padded bandages beneath his head where I could see the cut in order to provide some pressure to stem the bleeding. As far as his leg goes, I don't have a clue what to use as a splint.'

Honey looked around them. 'We're above the tree line. There are only rocks, no branches.' She thought quickly, mentally working through what was in her backpack. 'I have a couple of books in there—just small ones but enough to supply a bit of stability until the paramedics arrive.'

'You brought books with you on our date?'

'Hey, this isn't a date, Eddie. When we go on a date, you'll know about it.'

Edward glanced at her and couldn't help smiling at the way she was all fire and determination. The more he discovered about Honey, the more he liked what he found. She was a clear thinker, resourceful and able to think outside the box. It was true that since his break-up with Amelia he hadn't even bothered to try dating again. Raising Benedict and Hamilton and stabilising the family practice had been his main concerns, and paying for Bart to go to medical school. He'd been left with little time for dating.

Now, though, things were different. Things had changed. Benedict was now at medical school and Hamilton was in his final year at school. Edward had the time to date and, lo and behold, along came Honey, the most flamboyant, humorous and sensual woman he'd ever met. She was so incredibly different from Amelia, from the sort of woman he'd always thought he would end up marrying, that it was no wonder she'd made such an impact.

She was by no means traditional in her approach to life; she most certainly didn't have a boring sense of style and her personality…well, he couldn't shake the feeling that in helping him to step out of his very comfortable comfort zone, she was showing him how vibrant life could be. Plus, he had to admit, seeing the world through Honey's eyes—standing on the highest mountain, with his arms back, yelling ridiculous things into the wind—had been incredibly liberating as well as a lot of fun.

Kissing her had been equally so.

He looked at the woman kneeling beside him as they worked together to get Leonard as comfortable as they possibly could. Penny had managed to phone through to the emergency services and, with their help had relayed information about their current position and what injuries Leonard had sustained. Once that was done, Penny took a deep breath and called her husband, Howard, letting him know the situation.

Edward and Honey splinted Leonard's leg with the books, which Edward discovered were two paperback books about the history of the Snowy Mountains area. Honey pressed her fingers to the boy's tibial pulse.

'Blood is flowing much better now that it's splinted,' she reported.

'Good.' Edward took Leonard's vital signs again, pleased with the outcome. 'He's as stable as we can get him. Now we just need to wait for the paramedics.'

'How long should that take?'

'About an hour,' he replied as they covered Leonard with the rug they'd used for their picnic. 'Given his clothes are wet, we need to ensure he stays as warm as possible.'

'Agreed. Let's wrap my scarf carefully around his neck to act as a soft cervical collar. If only I'd packed a magazine or something.'

'First books, now magazines. Did you think you were going to get bored, coming out with me?' Edward asked, and Honey gave him a quizzical look, detecting a veiled hurt beneath his words.

'Has that happened to you before? Have you been out on a date only to have a woman prefer the company of her book to you?'

Edward's eyes widened at her words. 'How did you...?' He stopped, looked down at Leonard as they carefully secured the scarf in place to protect the spine, then back at Honey again. 'Yes, but in my defence, I was only nineteen at the time.'

Honey shook her head disgusted with the unknown woman. 'It doesn't matter. No one should be treated that way and that woman was a fool. When we go out on *our* first date, I promise you my *full* attention.'

'You usually give everyone your full attention, no matter what you're doing. Whether it's your patients, or Ginny, or Brad at the service station, or Connie at the grocery store.'

'Have you been watching me?'

'I've been *told* about you, by so many people. You've really made an impression on the whole town, Honey.'

'I usually *do* make an impression on people,' she countered, but he could tell she was pleased. 'Whether or not it's a positive one is the debatable point.'

'Well, I can tell you it's all extremely positive.' He studied her for a brief moment. 'And I have to say I was wrong in asking you to dress more formally. You should feel comfortable when you're consulting and you always look nice in everything you wear.'

She raised her eyebrows. 'No more suits?'

'That's up to you. Also…' He paused, meeting her gaze. 'If you feel a patient will benefit from alternative means of treatment, then I have no objection. The massage you gave me the other night really helped to reduce my tension and I know you were using pressure points.'

Honey gave him a sheepish grin. 'Yeah. I was. I wasn't sure you'd notice but you…well, I thought you needed it. You were pretty stressed at the time.'

He nodded. 'I was but you diagnosed the situation quite accurately and applied the necessary remedy. It's clear you honestly care for the well-being of the patients and at the end of the day that's what matters most. You provide your expertise and you listen to them. That's special.'

'You're right,' she agreed. 'That's all every single person wants in life—for someone to listen to them. Not just half-heartedly but to really listen, to take what they say seriously, to understand what they might be going through or feeling.' She looked down at their patient as they once more performed observations, Honey helping Edward to change the pad beneath Leonard's head, both of them pleased the bleeding seemed to have stopped.

'Take poor Leonard here. It doesn't sound as though he gets on all that well with his father.' She inclined her head towards Penny, who was still talking on the phone, having put a bit of distance between them. 'And the expression on Penny's face tells me she's a little scared of her husband. No doubt Howard has his own set of problems, just as we all do, but if everyone simply stopped and really listened to the people who are the most important to them, chances are the world would be a lot nicer to live in.'

'Who do you talk to, then?' Edward asked.

'My brother. My grandparents.'

'Not your parents?'

She shook her head. 'I haven't spoken to them in years.'

'You can't forgive them? Leave the past in the past?'

Honey shrugged. 'It's complicated.'

Edward shook his head. 'No, it's not, Honey. It's as simple as picking up the phone and saying "Hello". Do you have any idea just how much I'd love to be able to do just that. To speak to my parents one last time? Life's too short, Honey.'

She held his gaze for a moment before looking down at their patient, her mind whirring with his words. She picked up Leonard's left wrist to check his pulse. 'Pulse is strong. Leonard? Leonard?' She called to their patient. 'Can you hear me?'

This time, for the first time since one of them had called to Leonard during the course of treating him, they got a response.

'Mum?' It was only a slight murmur but it was such a good sound.

'Penny?' Honey called, and beckoned the mother over. 'He's starting to stir.'

'Oh. Oh.' Penny disconnected the call from her husband, even though he was no doubt in mid-bluster, and crossed to their side.

'He's still very groggy and you need to keep very calm when you talk to him. He needs to remain as still as possible and not to panic.' Honey glanced at her watch. It hadn't been all that long since the call had gone out and the only pain medication she'd brought was paracetamol. Still, it was better than nothing.

'The emergency call will be relayed to the first-aid team

in Thredbo village and they're situated at the bottom of the chairlift,' Edward said to Penny. 'They'll come up first with the stretcher so hopefully by the time the ambulance arrives we'll have Leonard at the bottom of the mountain.'

'Leonard?' Penny called, bending down next to Honey. 'It's Mummy.'

'Mum?' The word was stronger now and Honey could hear the rising panic in the teenager's voice.

'Stay calm,' she said.

'You've had an accident,' Edward confirmed in his deep, authoritarian tone. 'I'm Edward and this is Honey. We're both doctors and we're looking after you,' he informed the teenager. 'We need you to lie very still until the stretcher arrives.'

Leonard went to nod his head but immediately cried out in pain.

'Keep very still, including your head,' Edward instructed again, placing his hands on either side of Leonard's head to steady him.

'Just look at your mum, sweetie. She's here for you. So are we. Everything's going to be just fine.' Honey's voice was soothing and calm. 'Just keep looking at your mum and know that everything will be all right.' She reached beneath the blanket for Leonard's left arm, quickly checked the pulse, pleased it was stronger than before, then stroked his arm a few times before applying pressure with her thumb to the inside of his wrist. 'Close your eyes. Know that you are loved, that you are cared for,' she continued, her tone almost hypnotic. 'Breathe easy. All will be well with your world.'

Leonard did as she said and the stress lines that had moments ago been evident on his face relaxed.

'That's it. Keep relaxing. Let your body heal. Everyone

is looking after you and there is nothing for you to worry about. Your mum is here and she loves you very much. You're safe. You're wrapped in a cocoon of happiness, light and love.'

Leonard's breathing eased and his chest rose and fell as though he was relaxed and ready for a nice long sleep.

'Just keep talking to him in nice, calm tones,' Honey said to Penny, not changing her tone. 'Relax him with your words. Reassure him everything will turn out fine and that you love him. Can you do that?'

Penny held Honey's gaze for a moment before nodding.

'Great. Here. Take his hand. Just hold it. Stroke it lightly. Let him feel your touch. Let him feel your love.'

Penny did as she was told and a moment later Honey stood and stretched out her muscles then looked down at Edward. She was surprised to find him watching her with that same quizzical expression she'd seen several times during the week.

'Did you just…hypnotise the patient?' His tone was filled with incredulity.

'No.' She smiled at him. 'I used the pressure point at the base of the wrist to help him relax. Pressure there, combined with a soothing and calm tone, can work wonders on someone who's been traumatised.'

Edward shook his head in happy bemusement. 'You are amazing, Honeysuckle. At every turn, you're intriguing me further.'

'Good.' Her shining green eyes were bright and alive with life. 'That's just the way I like it.'

CHAPTER SEVEN

THANKFULLY, the first-aid team from Thredbo village came up with a stretcher and by the time the ambulance had arrived from Jindabyne, they'd managed to get Leonard safely back to the first-aid post, ready for his transfer to Cooma hospital.

'We can take it from here,' Sheldon, the paramedic, told Edward as the two men shook hands. 'Get back to enjoying your day away from the demands of patients.' Sheldon clapped Edward on the back before closing the rear doors of the ambulance and walking around to the driver's side. His partner, Raj, was safely ensconced in the back, monitoring Leonard's condition.

Penny's husband, Howard, and their other two children were going to follow in their car.

'Howard seems a lot calmer now,' Honey commented to Edward after both Howard and Penny had thanked them for their assistance.

'Perhaps he's starting to realise things could have been a lot worse.'

'Or perhaps he's thinking about whatever it was you said to him.' Honey looked up at the man beside her. 'I saw you having a quiet word with the blustering Howard while the paramedics were re-splinting Leonard's leg.'

Edward seemed self-conscious for a moment and

shrugged one shoulder. 'Life is too short to be blustering your way through it.'

'Is that what you told him?'

Edward's answer was to give another shrug as though he didn't like being in the spotlight, and Honey couldn't help but think he looked so cute when he did that. 'I may not have used those exact words, but—yeah, something like that.'

Honey leaned up and pressed a kiss to his cheek. 'You're a good man, Edward Goldmark.'

It wasn't the first time someone had said something like that to him and ordinarily it was the type of compliment that made him nod politely and move on to the next topic, but with Honey, the way she looked so intently into his eyes, the way his cheek still zinged with the sweet touch from her lips, the way she made him feel as though he was the only man who mattered in the world, caused his chest to swell with pleasure. The fact that Honey thought nice things about him mattered and while he knew he should probably be more concerned about that, he allowed himself to accept her heartfelt words.

'What's next on the agenda?' Edward needed to move things forward otherwise he'd probably spend all day dwelling on the way Honey made him feel and that would be of little use to anyone. He appreciated her bringing him out today and it hadn't been until he'd been on top of Mt Kosciuszko, yelling at the top of this lungs, that he'd started to realise just how tightly he'd been holding on to his life. Life was too short. Those were the words he'd said to Howard, to try and get through to the man just how lucky he was to have a wife and three children.

He glanced at the beautiful woman beside him, still struck by her generosity of spirit, how she was a giver, wanting others to feel the freedom of life she'd discovered. Yet at times he'd seen glimpses of a woman who wasn't completely happy. She wanted permanence, to find a home where she belonged, but even while she was searching for her own place in this world, she didn't lock others out. She nurtured, cared, gave her time and experience to others at the drop of a hat and never asked for anything in return.

Medicine was a vocation to her, something vitally important that she *must* do in order to be true to herself. She didn't look upon it as a ladder-climbing career and, given her qualifications, she could well be head of a hospital department by now. She was quite a woman.

'Well, I had thought we might have a nice warm drink at the restaurant at the top of the chairlift but as we're now down the bottom—' Her words were cut off as Edward picked up her backpack and took her hand in his, heading back to the chairlift.

'Then that's what we're going to do.' Once more they rode the chairlift to the top, noticing some mountain-bike riders heading down the steep slopes. Another daredevil was sitting in the seat in front of them, holding his push-bike as the chairlift continued to rise, taking them back to the top of the mountain.

'They're crazy.' Honey laughed as she watched them speed down the almost vertical track.

'Crazy but well padded and very safety conscious. Peter and Bartholomew used to do this when they were younger.'

'But never you,' Honey stated.

'No.'

'Did you want to?'

Edward thought about it. 'Maybe. I recall being more jealous at the fact they actually had the time to do it. I was either away at medical school or, whenever I was home for Christmas, there was always studying to be done.'

'Did you never grasp the concept of all work and no play can make Edward a very stressed-out man?' There was humour in her tone but also a large amount of caring concern. She cared about him. He wasn't exactly sure why the thought should warm him so much but it did. 'And after medical school, you had a different life to live,' she continued.

'Yeah.'

'So I guess daredevil mountain biking was then out of the question.' She raised her eyebrows and sat up straight as though an idea had just occurred to her. 'You should definitely add it to your bucket-list, though.'

'I need a bucket-list now?'

'Well, if you don't want to have one, I'll put it on my list and we can do it together.' Excitement danced in her eyes, the thrill of adventure in her voice, and Edward could only smile, captivated by her inner beauty.

When they reached the top, they stepped from the chair-lift and headed into the restaurant, glad of the warmth and homely atmosphere. They removed their wet-weather ponchos in the downstairs anteroom before heading upstairs.

'Oh, I'm so glad you came back up,' the restaurant's hostess greeted them as they entered. 'How did the young boy make out?'

'He'll be fine,' Edward said, and introduced Honey to Bernadette. 'We went to the same high school,' he told Honey.

'That's right.' Bernadette shook hands warmly with Honey. 'I was in the same year as the twins but even though Edward was a few years ahead, we all caught the same bus together every day.' She spread her arms wide, indicating a table for two. 'Now, both of you sit down and I'll bring you some drinks. Some nice hot cocoa to warm you up.'

And before either Edward or Honey could protest, Bernadette had disappeared behind the kitchen door.

'It's lovely up here,' Honey remarked, walking to the window to look out at the scenery. The clouds were moving again, rolling over the hills, the rain heading back in their direction. She breathed in, then caught a whiff of her Aran jumper. 'Oof, that's bad,' she remarked, and as Bernadette had lit a fire in the slow combustion heater, she removed the jumper and draped it over a chair. 'The jumpers keep you very warm but they don't smell the best when wet.' She rubbed her hands together and held them up to the fire.

'I think you smell gorgeous,' Edward remarked as he came to stand behind her, breathing in the cinnamony-earthy scent he was rapidly becoming addicted to. Honey felt warmth flood over her and it had nothing to do with the burning logs and everything to do with the heat radiating from Edward's close body. 'What *is* the name of your perfume?'

'I don't wear any.' Her tone was soft and she closed her eyes for a moment, wanting to absorb the exciting tingles that flooded down her spine and spread throughout her body as his breath fanned close to her ear.

'Impossible. You always smell incredible.'

'I do?' Honey was surprised at his compliment. It wasn't something she'd expected him to come right out and say but it appeared Edward was really starting to loosen up and she wasn't about to look a gift horse in the mouth.

'Distractingly so,' he admitted quietly, the heat from his nearness causing her cheeks to flush.

She shrugged and opened her eyes, turning to glance up at him, her shoulder brushing against his chest. She gasped at the connection. Pure masculine heat flowed from him through her, making her body tingle from the tips of her hair right down to her toes. Didn't Edward have any idea just how much he could affect her? That she was highly susceptible to his charms?

She'd been looking for *her* place in the world for some time now but she'd been looking at towns and people and houses. She hadn't been looking for a man. 'How do you know when you're in love?' she'd once asked her grandmother. Jessica had looked over to where Hubert had been reassembling the manifold of an old classic car, grease accidentally smeared on his face here and there. Her eyes had twinkled and she'd sighed peacefully. 'You just know, dear.'

Honey glanced at Edward once more, her heart doing flips of happiness at being so near him, her stress and tension ebbing away simply because he was there. 'Er… well…I use honeysuckle soap.'

'Honeysuckle soap?' he asked, trying to keep himself under control. She was close, she was almost leaning into him and, with the memory of their previous kisses still fresh in his mind, it was difficult to control the urge to simply bend his head and capture her glorious mouth once more.

'Well, quite a few honeysuckle things. It's like a little joke between me and my brother,' she continued, surprised her mind could even form words given the way her body was jumping for joy at this direct attention from Edward.

'And?' he encouraged, watching the way her lips formed words when she spoke, her soft tone soothing him. Deep down inside, he felt at war within himself, wanting to draw her close but knowing he needed to push her away. His life was too emotionally scattered at the moment, especially after standing at the top of the world and yelling his stress away…but he couldn't help wanting to know more about the woman beside him. 'You can't just leave it there. You have to explain further.'

'It's nothing major, Edward. Just a bit of fun.' When he raised his eyebrows in question she rolled her eyes, loving the way neither of them wanted to move. Instead they seemed intent on prolonging the conversation simply so they had an excuse not to shift. 'OK, then. My brother has always given me anything honeysuckle scented—all natural products, nothing artificial. Soap, shampoo or conditioner, or scented oil or hand cream—whatever he can find, whenever he can find it. He even once bought me honeysuckle-scented furniture polish—which does nothing for the complexion,' she joked. 'And I have quite a few candles as well. Woody recently told me that he'd found honeysuckle-scented lip balm in Tarparnii. Lip balm.' She shook her head as though this astounded her. 'So you see, it's just silly but I do love the scent.'

'It suits you.' He nodded with approval, his tone soft, deep, intimate. There was nothing artificial about the woman before him. She was definitely *au naturale* and he appreciated every part of her. 'The scent. The name. You *are* Honeysuckle.' Their gazes met and held and she licked her lips, unable to believe how aware she was of the mounting tension between them.

'Thank you, Eddie.' She was surprised at the huskiness of her voice but didn't bother to clear her throat. She was more than willing for him to realise she was as affected by him as he appeared to be by her. 'What a sweet thing to say.'

'I'm a sweet guy,' he murmured, his face completely straight, and Honey couldn't help the smile that touched her lips. It only made her look more irresistible. Edward's heart seemed to be pounding against his chest, the blood pumping faster around his body, his need for this woman mounting each time he was near her.

He swallowed and her gaze dipped to his neck, following the action of his Adam's apple. She licked her lips as though she wanted nothing more than to press tantalising butterfly kisses to his skin, gradually working her way up towards his mouth. He clenched his jaw. He wanted that, too.

'Uh...' She lifted her gaze back to his.

'Hmm?' His eyes were hooded and Honey could clearly read the desire evident in the brown depths. Her heart was beating so fast and her breathing had become so shallow, she thought she might hyperventilate simply from being near Edward. She swallowed. 'Uh...I think we should...' She forced herself to close her eyes, severing the connection.

Honey knew Edward needed to move slowly. He might be fine to admit the attraction here, on top of the world, so to speak, but it would be a different story once they arrived back in Oodnaminaby. When she wasn't looking at him, wasn't trying to control the need to wrap her arms about his neck and kiss him senseless, she could produce some semblance of logical thought. 'We should...uh...probably sit down and change the subject.'

'I can't even think what it is we're supposed to be talking about,' he confessed, which, when Honey opened her eyes to look at him, only made her instincts harder to fight.

'Anything,' she advised. 'Although I am having trouble thinking of a topic.'

'I'm not.' He raised his eyebrows in a suggestive manner before his gaze dipped to her lips. 'I want to kiss you again, Honey. I want to hold you in my arms without the wind and rain blustering around us. I want to feel your body pressed against mine. I want to run my hands through your hair, to press tiny kisses to your soft skin and to press my lips to yours in a way that makes my blood boil over.'

The primordial need in his tone was echoed in his eyes and it caused her to tremble as she never had before. It wasn't that she was scared of him, quite the opposite, in fact. She couldn't believe how powerful his words were, how they made her feel as though she was the most special woman in the world.

'Edward.' She rested her hands over his heart as she shifted to turn closer to him. Automatically, one arm came about her, drawing her close so he could fulfil his desires and *really* kiss her.

'Honey, you're so unexpected. You've burst into my life like a splash of colour over a dark canvas and you've made me question myself, made me focus my thoughts, made me release my tension by yelling into the wind.' He brushed some loose strands of hair back from her face, his fingers caressing her neck. Honey tipped her head to the side, granting him access, and slowly he bent to press a few tantalising, fluttering kisses to her skin.

'Divine,' he murmured. He lifted his head and stared into her face, placing his fingers beneath her chin and rubbing his thumb over her plump lips. Honey gasped at the touch, her eyes wide in wonderment at the way he was making her feel.

'Edward.' His name was a caress from her lips and while he wanted nothing more than to feel and taste the sweet flavours of her mouth, he also wanted to take his time, to memorise every contour of her face, every crease in her neck, every inch of her body. He couldn't fight the way he was drawn to her any more. He could see by the way she was responding ardently to his touch that she was as committed to these feelings as he was. He wasn't alone. Honey understood him and the realisation filled him with a powerful sense of peace.

He bent his head and kissed the other side of her neck, oh, so gently applying pressure as he tasted her skin, delighted with the way she seemed to melt further into his hold. She wanted him as much as he wanted her and that knowledge shot straight to his heart.

His heart?

Edward straightened, dropping his hand back to his side, and gazed down into her face. Her eyelids were closed, her body open towards him, displaying complete trust. When she opened her eyes, they had a dazed, dreamy look. Edward swallowed over the knowledge that he shouldn't be leading her on.

Yelling at the wind was one thing but he'd done that with Honey's direction. He needed to seek and find his own direction, to discover who he was. It wasn't fair to Honey for him to be wanting her so desperately like this.

'Edward?' When she'd said his name moments before there had been a sense of awe, as though she hadn't been able to believe he was really holding her, really touching her, really desperate to kiss her. Now he could hear the question in her tone, could see the slight confusion beneath her lashes, could feel her concern starting to rise. How had she been able to feel something had changed? She was a woman who seemed to be so in tune with him that she understood, sometimes even before he did, what was going on. Now was no different.

'What's wrong?' she whispered, licking her lips, her gaze still flicking between his eyes and his mouth.

'I want you.' The words were out before he could stop them, confusion creasing his brow.

Her smile was small. 'I know.' She leaned forward and rested her head on his chest, her hands tucked beneath her chin. He wrapped both arms about her but didn't draw her any closer. It was as though he so desperately wanted to hold her but knew he shouldn't.

Drawing in a deep breath, filling her lungs with the scent of him, Honey eased back. Edward instantly loosened his hold on her. She quickly reached out and grasped the back of the chair where her jumper was slowly drying, her legs still not strong enough to support her. The kisses he'd pressed to her neck had wound her so tight, she was still coming back to earth.

'We need to take things slowly,' she remarked as she sat down at the table.

Edward stood where he was for a second and then raked his hand through his hair. It wasn't that taking things slowly was the problem, as far as he could see, it was the fact that his feelings for Honey seemed to be increasing with every passing moment he spent with her.

Thankfully, Bernadette came over to them, carrying a tray of not only drinks but delicious-smelling food as well. 'Here you go,' she said. 'I had the chef whip you both up some banana and caramel pancakes. They're just new on the menu but on a blustery day like today they're just what the doctor ordered.' Bernadette giggled at her own joke and then left them alone, refusing to accept any payment for the food or drinks, telling them that all doctors involved in medical rescues deserved a free meal.

Edward picked up his fork and forced himself to eat

something, more to appease Bernadette, lest she think he didn't like the food, rather than because he was hungry. He searched for a topic of conversation and it appeared Honey was doing the same thing.

'So…on top of Kosciuszko, you said you were almost engaged?' She cut up her pancakes as she spoke.

'That's right.'

'Do you mind if I pry and ask what happened?'

Edward slowly drew in a breath before exhaling. 'Amelia and I met at medical school. I was a few years ahead of her and to earn extra money I started tutoring. She needed help.' He took a sip of his hot chocolate. It was strange telling Honey about his past, not because it made him feel uncomfortable but simply because it didn't. Shouldn't he feel odd telling a woman he'd just kissed about his past relationship?

Honey thought about what he'd said up on the mountain and nodded, the pieces falling into place. 'You both wanted the same things out of life, began to plan your life together and then when your parents passed away, she didn't want the instant family.'

'In a nutshell.' He ate a mouthful of pancakes, watching her closely. 'How about you?' he asked after swallowing. 'What happened to you? Why haven't you met the right man?'

'I was in a disastrous relationship about five years ago and since then I've been more concerned with finding the place where I belong. You see, Kennedy is now head of surgery at Brisbane General hospital. We met when I was doing a six-month locum in A and E. We dated. Things became serious. We started looking at properties, houses, schools for our future children, and it looked as though I was finally going to find that elusive home I'd always been looking for.'

'And then?'

'And then things started to change and I mean *change*. At that stage, my hair was a ginger colour with green tips on the ends. Well, now that we were serious, it had to go. He arranged a hair appointment with his mother's hairdresser to 'put my hair back the right way', I believe were his exact words. Kennedy wasn't happy with the way I dressed, so he went and chose my clothes for me. I came home from work late one night and found bags of beautiful designer clothes in my apartment but none of them were my style. None of them were *me*.'

'Sounds as though he was trying to change you, to make you conform to his idea of the perfect surgeon's wife.'

'Exactly.' Honey shook her head as she remembered, the pain surprisingly not as bad as it had once been. 'He also reserved two places for our two future children at the most prestigious boarding school in Sydney, without ever consulting me. I would *never* send my children to boarding school.' Honey stabbed the table forcefully with her finger. 'To send a child away? Never. I've lived the life of a lonely child and I won't allow it for *my* children. I want to give my children a legacy they can be proud of, just as your parents did for you and your brothers. Besides, I don't want to have only two children, I want a whole gaggle of them, and when I pointed this out to Kennedy, he said I was being foolish.'

Honey took a breath and forced herself to calm down, to shake off the annoyance she felt about Kennedy. 'I thought I'd found my home, the place where I belonged, but it turned out I'd found a prison instead. It made me wonder if I'd ever find the place where I really could spend the rest of my life.'

'So you left.'

'So I left,' she agreed with a nod. 'That was about five years ago now.'

'When you were *really* six years old,' he pointed out with a sad smile, wanting to cheer her up a little bit.

'Just a child,' she sighed.

'Did you return to stay with your grandparents or just move jobs?'

Honey nodded. 'I did actually go back to their place in Sydney and spent some time with them. I don't know, sometimes when things don't work out the way you planned, you need to head back to a comfort zone. It helps to regroup, to focus your mind, to put priorities in order.'

'And what about your parents? Have you ever been back to see them?'

Honey nodded. 'I have. Three years after I left, I returned for Woody's eighteenth birthday. He really wanted me there so I went. It was a disaster. My parents were ashamed I was studying medicine, telling me I'd been brainwashed by society, by my grandparents.'

Edward raised his eyebrows in surprise. 'They weren't happy?'

'No. They wanted me to become a vet, to treat the homeless animals, to run a shelter for them. I told you I was always very good with animals, with caring, with nursing poor little birds, especially oil-soaked penguins, back to health. We had a big row and almost ended up ruining Woody's birthday.'

'How did Woody take it?'

Honey smiled at the mention of her brother. 'He forgave

me. He said it was worth a try, getting the family together, but it had been a mistake.'

'So you've stayed in touch with your brother?'

'Always. I left my parents, not my brother. I practically raised Woody. There was no way I was breaking off contact with him. He was almost fifteen when I left so I sent him a cellphone and we were able to keep in touch. My parents don't approve of such devices but Woody always had a way of getting around them, of making them see his point of view, and so they let him keep it. We would talk every week—we still do—but rarely about our parents. I just…don't want to know. The hurt, the neglect, the feeling that everything else in the world was more important to them than their own children still runs deep.'

Edward nodded, understanding her hurt. 'Families aren't easy, Honey. Children aren't easy. I've had countless arguments with my siblings on a brotherly level and when I've been acting the parent. You saw how Hamilton and I were tearing into each other but, believe me, I'd do anything for him. He's my brother. I gave up everything I'd always wanted for him and Ben and I don't regret it. Not one bit, but I do wish I hadn't had to do it. Raising children is…hard. Sometimes I have no clue how my parents coped. Five boys! My poor mother, and I remember that the twins and I used to get into all kinds of mischief.'

'You appreciate your mother more, though, right? What she and your father did for you? How they provided for you? They left you with a legacy, one you have held up high and polished until it shines, but doesn't that make you want to continue passing it on to the next generation? To hand down stories of dreams and hopes?'

'Not really.'

Edward's words stunned her for a second. 'Really? You don't want to have children of your own?'

Edward slowly shook his head. 'Not particularly.' He put his fork down. 'I've done my time. I'm not sure exactly what I'm planning to do once Hamilton leaves home but it isn't to settle down and have children of my own.'

Honey blinked once. Twice, wondering why this news seemed to pierce her heart. Was that the reason why he'd been trying to keep her at arm's length? She'd seen the way he'd struggled with his desire to touch her, to hold her, to kiss her, and she'd been wanting him closer all the while, not putting up any resistance of her own.

'But you're such a good father,' she blurted, unable to keep the shock from her tone. 'How can you not want—?' She stopped herself, putting a hand to her mouth. 'No,' she said a moment later. 'That's your decision. I know it can't have been at all easy for you, taking on the guardianship, giving up your own dreams. Taking the weight of the world on your shoulders. It can't have been easy.'

'Just as it wasn't easy for you either.' Edward pointed out. 'You said you practically raised your brother.'

'Yes, but I wasn't alone. My parents were occasionally around.'

'I think that was the thing I wished for the most. To just spend one more day with my parents, to ask them all the questions I never thought to ask them before they passed away.' He swallowed and slowly shook his head.

'They were taken so suddenly. One minute they were called out to help with an emergency and the next, Pete called with the news that...' He paused, his voice thick. Honey felt a lump start to build in her own throat. 'That they were both dead. Gone.' Edward closed his eyes as the memories and the grief started to rise to the surface.

'See?' He asked a moment later, his eyes snapping open. 'This is why I don't like spending too much time by myself, too much time looking inwards, because nothing I say or do will *ever* bring them back.' He swallowed a few times then cleared his throat. 'You have your parents. They're alive, Honey. Nothing, no misunderstanding, no quarrel, no differing view points are worth it. They're not perfect. My parents weren't perfect. No parent is perfect—as I've discovered the hard way—but your parents are alive, Honey, and that's a good thing.'

She nodded and wiped at the tears stinging behind her eyes. 'You're right, Edward, but I just don't know what to say. How to face them. What do I do? You said before it was as easy as picking up the phone and saying 'hi' but is it? What happens after that?'

He shrugged. 'I don't know and maybe I'm not the person to advise you. I haven't even been able to go back to Charlotte's Pass since the accident. Lorelai has always done any house calls out there. Peter and Bartholomew took Benedict and Hamilton to see the memorial erected there in honour of those who lost their lives that fateful day but…I can't do it.'

Honey stared. 'You've never been back?'

'No.'

She looked down at their cold food, a crazy idea formulating in her mind…a crazy idea that might just help him out. 'What if…?' she said, raising her eyes to meet his.

'No.' He cut her off.

'Hear me out. What if we go to Charlotte's Pass today? We can go together. I'll hold your hand. I'll help you in any way I can.'

Edward was about to say no again but a stirring deep inside stopped him. Breathing out slowly, he met Honey's gaze. 'What if…we *do* go to Charlotte's Pass today? And what if…you call your parents?'

'They don't have a—'

'Someone in that commune they live in has to have a phone. Your brother would surely have a way to contact them,' Edward replied and Honey nodded, her face almost as pale as the clouds outside. 'I'll help you, if you'll help me.' He held out his hand, palm open.

'Deal?'

Honey pondered for a moment, knowing she'd do anything to help him achieve peace of mind. It seemed Edward was more than willing to do the same for her. She lifted her hand and slid it into his warm one, unable to ignore the exploding heat that shot through her body at the touch.

'Deal.'

CHAPTER EIGHT

As THEY drove along the road to Charlotte's Pass, Edward still behind the wheel of Honey's car, she wasn't sure what to say. She could tell he was concentrating on the road but the closer they drew to the alpine village, the tighter he seemed to be gripping the steering-wheel.

'Just as well it's summer,' he murmured as he slowed the car and turned off Kosciuszko road, onto the only road which led to Charlotte's Pass. 'During winter, the only way to access this place is via the SkiTube at Perisher.'

Honey nodded as he slowed the car and parked it outside the main hotel. 'I'm glad we decided to come today.' She climbed from the car and came around to the driver's side. Without hesitation, she reached for his hand and was pleased he didn't shy away. 'How are you doing?' she asked, looking intently into his face. It was colder here than it had been at the restaurant but, oddly enough, she didn't feel the chill. She was so focused, so intent on making sure Edward was really OK with this that for some reason the cold didn't matter.

Inwardly, she was still a little stunned at his declaration about not having children, especially when she knew he'd make such a wonderful father. Hamilton was proof of that and she was sure Benedict was equally as wonderful as the rest of his brothers. If Edward really didn't want to traverse the path of becoming a parent, then she knew she should start to disentangle her emotions from him. However, now was most definitely not the time. If she could do this one thing for Edward, if she could help him, be there for him as he took this enormous step towards healing the pain buried deep within his heart, that would be enough. Or so she hoped. 'Eddie?'

'I'm fine.' He looked at her, seeing the encouragement in her eyes. 'It's the right time.'

'All right.' She didn't let go of his hand but turned to look at the town, which was lush and green. 'Where do we go?'

'The little ecumenical chapel.' Edward pointed up the street to where a large triangular-shaped roof could be seen. 'Up the winding path,' he stated. 'In winter, this whole place is a beautiful blanket of white,' he murmured as they headed up the path. When they reached the top, standing outside the chapel, he turned and looked at the village before him. 'I'd forgotten how beautiful this place is.' He turned and smiled at Honey. 'The memorial is inside the chapel. Peter and Bartholomew spoke to the families of the others who died in the avalanche and it was decided to have the memorial indoors so that it wasn't snowed over during the winter months.'

'Sounds lovely.' He was hesitating a bit and Honey gave his hand a reassuring squeeze. 'Would you like to go in alone? Or would you like me to—?'

'Come with me.' It was a statement, not an answer to her question. Honey immediately nodded and took a step towards the door. Edward quickly opened it and together they went in, side by side, hand in hand.

They stood in the entryway where there were two tables by the door with the parish newsletter and several bibles and hymnals. The walls, to their left and right, were covered in beautiful mosaic art. The one on the right showed sunbeams shining down on the village of Charlotte's Pass. The wall on the left also had a sun shining its beams down but on this wall were a lot of white doves, flying upwards towards the sun, seeming to represent a feeling of complete freedom.

Edward stared at the wall with the doves, his grip on Honey's hand tightening. 'Forty-five doves,' he whispered.

As her eyes started to adjust to the dimmer light, Honey could see a tall, slim man walking towards them, his black and white clerical collar showing at his neck beneath his thin wool jumper.

'Edward!' The chaplain reached out his hand and placed it on Edward's shoulder. 'It's wonderful you've come.'

Edward tore his gaze from the wall to look at the chaplain. He opened his mouth to speak but found he couldn't and Honey realised he was too choked up with emotion. She stepped forward and offered her free hand to the chaplain.

'Hello. I'm Honey. I'm the new locum working in Oodnaminaby.' The chaplain dropped his hand from Edward's shoulder and shook Honey's hand warmly. 'I have to say your chapel here is quite lovely. Very relaxing.'

'I'm glad.' The chaplain looked from Honey to Edward, then down at their joined hands, Edward was holding onto her so tightly she thought she might lose all blood flow fairly soon. She didn't mind. 'I'll give you some privacy.'

Once he'd left, Edward sniffed and took a few steps forward towards the wall with the doves. As they drew closer, Honey realised each dove had a first name painted on it and a lump lodged in her own throat. Her gaze quickly sought out the ones named Hannah and Cameron and a moment later Edward reached out his free hand and touched each of them with trembling fingers.

He sniffed again and she leaned into him, putting her arm about his waist, drawing him closer. A tear slid down his cheek and he nodded slowly before pulling her close. It was as though he needed the warmth of her live body, to reassure himself that life did go on.

'It's…uh…beautiful.' He wrapped both arms about her and rested his chin on her head. 'I know they're gone. I've known for a long time but…um…this…' He sniffed again and she could hear the choked emotion in his tone. 'This makes it…more real.' He held his breath for a moment before sucking air into his lungs. 'They're gone, Honey, and I loved them so much.'

Honey couldn't hold back her own tears any longer and allowed them to flow silently down her cheeks. When she sniffed, Edward leaned back and looked down into her face, seeing how touched she was by the death of people she'd never met.

'I'm proud of you,' she whispered.

'Thank you,' he said, and bent to brush his lips lightly over hers, his voice filled with emotional relief. 'Thank you.'

The end of Honey's second week at Oodnaminaby wasn't as exciting as the first but that didn't bother her. They'd received word from Cooma hospital that Leonard was progressing well after undergoing orthopaedic surgery to stabilise his right leg and arm, as well as receiving sutures to the gash on the back of his head. It was hoped he'd make a full recovery in time.

At the clinic, her patient lists had settled down now that everyone had come and met the new doctor in town.

Even when she was out and about in town or surrounding districts, doing house calls or just seeing the countryside, Honey was always greeted with a cheery smile and a wave. It also meant that Lorelai could stay at home full time and off her feet.

The baby's head was now completely engaged and even though Lorelai was only thirty-six weeks, it was clear she could deliver at any time. Honey had arranged a briefing with Edward to ensure she knew the protocols for transferring Lorelai to Tumut hospital, should that become necessary.

Since their trip to Mt Kosciuszko and then to Charlotte's Pass, Honey had found Edward to be a little embarrassed around her. There was no disputing the fact they had feelings for each other but after the emotional moments they'd shared in the small chapel, Edward had been keeping his distance.

Professionally, they discussed their patients and went about business as usual. Twice during the week he'd invited her to share dinner with himself and Hamilton and on each occasion he hadn't made any move to touch her. He was polite and charming and obviously as confused about his emotions as she was.

With Edward declaring he didn't want to have children, Honey had started to figure out what meant more to her. Was it finding a place to call home or finding a place to raise her children? She'd always thought they'd be the same place but now she wasn't so sure. It was true that she'd fallen in love with Ood, not only with the breathtaking scenery but also with the people of the community. It was definitely a place she could call home and it was definitely a great place to raise a family but with the way her feelings for Edward were refusing to be quashed, she wasn't sure she'd be able to stay on past her twelve-month contract. Confusion continued to reign and she found concentrating on work was the best thing she could do right now.

'I'm so used to being busy,' Lorelai said as the two women caught up for a soothing cup of herbal tea. 'I've always been at the surgery, doing house calls in the district or visiting patients in Tumut or Cooma hospitals. Now I'm home all the time, I keep startling John.' Lorelai sipped her tea as Honey massaged her feet, using the pressure points to relieve the tension in the pregnant woman's back. 'Do you know, he walked into the room the other day, talking on the phone, and almost jumped through the ceiling when he realised I was lying on the lounge with my feet up, reading a book.'

Honey was surprised to hear Lorelai's husband was so jumpy. 'I thought John worked for the mining company as a demolition expert,' she remarked. 'I wouldn't have thought that was the type of profession to lend itself to a jumpy worker.'

'You'd think that,' Lorelai agreed. 'He says he has to be so alert and focused at work that at home he tends to let all his control go.'

'Hmm.' Honey heard something else in Lorelai's tone, something she couldn't quite put her finger on. 'How did the two of you meet?'

'On the ski-slopes. John's always been an avid skier.' Lorelai smiled, reflecting back on the past. 'We started dating almost straight away and before the next ski season we were married and he'd moved in here with me.'

'You didn't buy the house together?'

'No. I bought the house outright when I came back to

Ood to practise medicine.' Lorelai frowned and sipped her tea. 'Thank goodness it's still in my name.'

Honey was surprised at her words. 'Is everything all right with you and John?'

Lorelai's eyes instantly teared up and Honey quickly took the cup away lest she spilled the hot liquid and passed her a tissue. 'I don't know what's going on, Honey. He's snappy at me all the time. He says I'm fat.'

'You're pregnant,' Honey remarked, kneeling by her friend and putting her arms around her, anger building towards Lorelai's husband. She'd only met him once and her first impression had not been at all positive. John had leered at Honey's body, his lips smirking as though he thought she was a fruitcake because of the way she dressed, and then with a blink of his eyes he'd dismissed her. It had made her wonder what had attracted Lorelai to him in the first place.

'He wasn't like that when we met,' Lorelai said between sobs, and for a second Honey thought she'd mused out loud. 'He was attentive and sweet and kind. He was happy to live here in Oodnaminaby, to get a job in the district and to ski all winter long. He'd often stay up at the lodge in Thredbo, helping his friends who worked there pack up and set up each day. Sometimes the roads were too slushy to drive on, or he'd lend his tyre chains to someone else, which meant he couldn't drive home...' Lorelai trailed off as though all the excuses sounded too convenient.

'He didn't want to have the baby,' she confessed to Honey in a tiny whisper. 'I haven't told anyone that. Not my dad, not Edward or any of the boys.' She hiccuped, her bottom lip wobbling. 'When I told him I was pregnant, he told me to get a termination and then went to the pub.'

'Oh, Lore.' Honey's hatred for the man intensified. 'I had no idea.'

'No one does…and I've been able to keep my own mind under control while I was working but now that I'm home all the time, I keep going over and over things, my mind churning, and…' A fresh bout of tears erupted. 'And then I can't stop crying,' she blubbed.

Honey held her friend, passed her tissues and allowed Lorelai to let go of all the angst, pain and devastation she'd obviously been holding onto for far too long.

'Thank you,' Lorelai said, after blowing her nose again. 'I think I needed to get that out.'

'Another cup of tea?' Honey asked, but Lorelai yawned.

'No, thanks. I think I'll have a snooze.'

'Here on the couch? Or do you want to lie down in your bed?'

'Here's fine.'

'OK. Let's get you comfortable and I'll give your back a rub.' Honey shifted some cushions until Lorelai was comfortable and settled, then began a low back massage.

'Thanks for listening,' Lorelai remarked.

'That's what friends are for.'

As Honey continued to massage, her thoughts naturally drifted to Edward. Every day when she saw him at the clinic, her heart would leap and her body would warm with memories of his arms about her, his breath mingling with hers, his mouth pressing those soft, sweet butterfly kisses to her skin, heating her body until she thought she might explode. She thought of the way he'd held her when they'd been in that small chapel in Charlotte's Pass, about the way he'd kissed her and said thank you. Her heart started to ache for him, for the pain he must have felt seeing that beautiful memorial to his parents and the other people who had lost their lives in the avalanche.

After they'd left the chapel, she'd accepted the car keys and driven them safely back to Ood, letting Edward know how courageous he'd been and how much she admired him. As she continued to rub Lorelai's back gently, the pregnant woman dozing, Honey realised her feelings for Edward were intensifying with each passing day.

On Sunday evening, Honey had decided on an early night and was dressed in her tie-dyed pyjama bottoms and a matching snug singlet top. She'd made the garments a few years ago when she'd been working in Queensland and the weather had been particularly hot and humid. It wasn't particularly hot now but the garments gave her a sense of comfort, a sense of being herself.

When the phone rang, Honey rushed to pick it up, hoping, longing for it to be Edward. 'I've cooked too much food for dinner,' he would say, in that deep hypnotic voice of his. 'Why don't you come and join us?' At least, that's how it played out in her fantasy world.

'Hello? Honey speaking,' she said.

'Yo, sis.' Woody's deep voice came down the line.

'Yo, bro,' she replied in her usual way, but couldn't keep the slight hint of disappointment out of her voice. She leaned over to the kitchen window and twitched back the lace curtain, looking out to where she could just see the back of the main house, hoping for a glimpse of Edward, but she was out of luck.

'Expecting someone else to call?' Woody asked.

'What?' Honey returned her attention to her brother. 'Sorry. No. Uh…how's things? Recovering from your last trip to Tarparnii? How's Nilly and the girls?'

Woody laughed. 'They're fine. What about you? How are things going? Still being asked out to dinner every night? We didn't get much of a chance to talk last week you were such hot property.'

Honey sighed and curled up on a chair, closing her eyes. 'Things have settled down a bit.' Except for her heartbeat every time she looked at Edward. She shook her head, trying to clear her thoughts and concentrate on her conversation with her brother. 'The town is nice, the people are...' She paused. '*Very* welcoming.'

'Aha. I knew it. You've met a man.'

'What? How can you possibly tell that from—?'

'I know you, sis.' Woody's chuckle came down the phone line and she knew it was futile to try and kid him. 'Looks as though I'm going to have to come to town for a visit and check him out.'

Her eyes snapped open. 'Don't you dare.'

'In fact, that's not a bad idea. I was thinking of coming and catching up with you in person for a change. I'll be heading to see Mum and Dad next week and Oodnaminaby isn't too far from where they're situated at the moment so I can just pop on down, meet this bloke who's caught your eye, ask him if his intentions are honourable and slide on outta town, back to my own life.'

'I always love to see you, Woody, you know that.' Honey paused, remembering the deal she'd struck with Edward, the one where he would face his past if she faced hers. She swallowed and cleared her throat, knowing she had to follow through on that promise. The thought of letting Edward down was something she couldn't do. 'Uh...you said Mum and Dad were close by?'

'Yeah. They're in Victoria at the moment, at La Trobe Valley. About a day's drive from where you are.'

'Oh. That *is* close.' Closer than they'd been to each other in a very long time. She swallowed over the dryness in her throat but forced herself to go on. She'd promised Edward. 'Do you have a contact for them? A phone number of someone in their commune or—'

'They have a phone, Hon.'

She frowned. 'A cellphone?'

'Yeah. That way they can stay in touch with me whenever I'm in Tarparnii.'

'Oh. I never thought they'd ever—'

'A lot has changed, Hon. *They've* changed. So have you. It'd make me happy to have my family back together again. Have you got a pen? I'll give you the number.'

Honey took down the number and chatted with her brother for a few more minutes before a beep sounded, indicating she had another call coming through. 'Sorry, Woody. I have to go. I'll talk to you soon and…uh…thanks, bro. Love you oodles.' Honey disconnected the call and then pressed the button to connect her new call. 'Honey speaking,' she said.

'Honey?' It was Lorelai and she sounded incredibly upset.

'Lore? What's wrong? Are you feeling all right? Any contractions?'

'Everything's wrong,' Lorelai answered, bursting into tears over the phone. 'John's having an affair,' she mumbled between sobs. 'He just came right out and told me.'

'I'm on my way.' Honey wasn't a hundred per cent surprised at this news and quickly found a pair of flip-flops, sliding her feet into them, her cellphone still held to her ear. 'Keep talking to me, Lorelai. Tell me everything.'

She collected a torch and then headed outside, a brisk March wind instantly cooling her skin. She should have picked up a cardigan but it didn't matter. Lorelai was all that mattered. Her friend continued to sob and talk down the line with Honey only managing to understand about every third word, but it was when Lorelai groaned in pain, a deep guttural sound, that Honey stopped walking. She was in the driveway at the front of Edward's house.

'What was that?' she asked, and heard Lorelai almost panting. 'Was that a push?' When Lorelai gasped for breath and made another grunting sound, Honey raced up the front steps of Edward's house and rang the doorbell, trying desperately to curb her impatience to ring twice when he didn't answer immediately.

'Hold on. I'm just getting Eddie,' she told Lorelai as the front door opened. There he stood. The man she was hard pressed to stop thinking about, dressed once more in a pair of old denims and nothing else. His hair was damp from his shower and she wondered whether his delay in opening the door was because he'd just finished.

She breathed in, opening her mouth to tell him about Lorelai, but his fresh, spicy scent curled its way around her, teasing her, enticing her. She closed her mouth and swallowed as her gaze roved over the incredible contours of his chest.

'Honey?' Lorelai's upset voice came down the phone, which Honey still held to her ear. Honey blinked and quickly looked away from the sexy man before her. How was she supposed to fight the way he made her feel when he dressed like that and only created even more fantasies for her to think about?

'Honey?' Edward opened the screen door, his gaze roving over her body just as hers had over his. He sucked in a breath, wishing she'd had the sense to put more on before ringing his doorbell, especially at this time of night, when his thoughts had already been on her.

The tie-dyed hippy look suited her, especially when her long, silky hair was flowing loosely around her shoulders. The pants she wore were baggy enough but the top… He swallowed over the lump that came to his throat at the way the tight-fitting top highlighted her figure. She looked so incredibly sexy and he clenched his jaw, knowing he needed to fight the mounting attraction that existed between them.

'You could have used the back d—' It was then he realised she was talking to someone on the phone and that there was a crinkle furrowing her otherwise perfect brow. 'Honey? What's wrong?'

She lifted her gaze to meet his, trying desperately hard to ignore his manly chest in the process. 'It's Lorelai. She's in labour.'

Panic momentarily flitted across his face before he clenched his jaw and nodded. 'Right. Let me get my bag.' He disappeared for fifteen seconds and came back with his medical bag in hand. 'I've had it packed ready for a delivery as I had a hunch Lore wasn't going to make it to the hospital in time to have the baby,' he said as they walked, Honey still talking to their friend on the phone. She was thankful, though, that Edward had donned a shirt, covering up the skin her fingers were still itching to touch.

When they arrived at Lorelai's home a little later, they were met by a pacing, sobbing woman. She disconnected the phone and threw it down onto the lounge cushions before wiping furiously at the tears which were blurring her vision.

'I'm so glad you're both here,' she said between her tears. 'At least someone still loves me.'

'Oh, Lorelai.' Honey put her arms around her friend, providing much-needed reassurance. 'Let's get you sorted out,' she said as they walked further into the house. 'Have you had many contractions or just the really big one on the phone?'

'A few twinges. It's all been much the same for the past few days,' Lorelai answered, the usually calm and controlled woman completely flustered. 'I just thought they were more intense Braxton-Hicks contractions.'

'You've been under a lot of pressure, Lorelai,' Honey soothed. 'However, both Eddie and I are here and we're going to take excellent care of you.'

Edward put his hands on Lorelai's shoulders to stop her from pacing. 'You're in a right state, Lore. Let's get you to the bedroom where you can lie down and Honey can examine you.'

'No!' Lorelai spun away from him and resumed her pacing. 'No way. I'm not going into *that* bedroom ever again.'

'Why?' Edward looked from one woman to the other, his brow creased in total confusion.

'You didn't tell him!' Lorelai looked at Honey.

'I was talking to you on the phone the entire way here,' Honey remarked, keeping her voice nice and calm, cool and soothing. The fact that Lorelai was too caught up in the emotion of her husband's infidelities was starting to affect the baby. 'Sit down, Lorelai. I need to take your blood pressure,' she murmured as she opened Edward's emergency bag and pulled out the portable sphygmomanometer.

Edward ushered her to one of the comfortable armchairs. They were all quiet while Honey took the blood-pressure reading. 'Just as I'd suspected. Rising. We need to calm you down, sweetie.' Now that Lorelai was sitting,

Honey quickly removed the woman's slip-on shoes and applied pressure to the base of her big toe.

'*He* didn't do this,' Lorelai murmured after a moment, rubbing a hand over her swollen abdomen, her tension starting to flow away under Honey's care.

'Who?' Edward asked.

'John. I told him exactly where to press and told him it would relieve the pressure and pain I was getting but he didn't do it. He didn't care about me, or about our baby.'

'What did he say?' Honey asked, trying to keep herself calm yet internally she was completely riled up against the insensitive jerk Lorelai had married.

'What did who say?' Edward asked, completely perplexed as he plugged in the portable foetal heart monitor he'd extracted from his bag.

'John's having an affair.' Lorelai blurted the words out.

'*What?*' Edward went from complete and utter astonishment to a deep, angry scowl in a matter of seconds. 'Where is he?'

'He's gone. I confronted him tonight and he didn't deny it. Told me outright he'd been having an affair for the last eight months. *Eight months!* Then he said he was glad I knew. That he was relieved he no longer had to lie to me or to sneak around or to pretend to be interested in me and the baby.' Lorelai slumped further into the comfy chair, her expression filled with hurt and disbelief.

'He said I was always working and that I was more interested in my patients than in him.' Lorelai looked at Edward. 'Is that true? Am I?'

'No, Lore. This isn't your fault. His infidelities are not *your* fault. They're his. He's weak-willed and spineless. You're a kind, caring woman who is now in labour.' He glanced at Honey, as though seeking confirmation, and received a nod as the answer. 'Let's focus on bringing this baby into the world. That's what's important right now.' He clenched his jaw. He and his brothers would see to John later. No one hurt *his* surrogate sister and simply walked away without facing the consequences.

'Eddie's right. Listen to this.' Honey placed the microphone of the foetal heart monitor onto Lorelai's abdomen. The three adults were silent, the only sound filling the air was one of a fast but healthy heartbeat. 'Perfect,' Honey remarked after reading the display from the machine. 'Now, where do you want to have the baby?'

'At Tumut hospital,' Lorelai said, but Honey shook her head.

'Sorry, love. You pushed once while I was on the phone to you. That means we're not going anywhere, otherwise we risk you delivering in an ambulance. Better to keep you here, nice and comfortable. If you don't want to go and lie down on your bed, then what would you like? What's going to feel the most comfortable for you? Beanbag? Floor? Squatting?'

'Beanbag,' Lorelai remarked after a moment, then her lower lip quivered again as fresh tears sprang to her eyes. 'I can't believe he's gone. He was supposed to be here with me, watching our baby being born, but he told me tonight he doesn't want me and he doesn't want the b-b-baby.' Tears bubbled over but a moment later Lorelai was racked with another contraction.

Edward met Honey's gaze over Lorelai's head. His expression said they needed to get Lorelai settled and to focus on preparing for this birth. Honey nodded in agreement, not a single spoken word passing between them.

They worked together to get Lorelai into position, Edward going to the linen cupboard to gather some clean

sheets and towels and to prepare an area to receive the
baby once it was born.

'You *have* done this before?' he quickly confirmed as
Lorelai rested between contractions, which had now escalated to a firm five minutes apart. Concern and worry
peppered Edward's brow and Honey rubbed her hand up
and down his arm, wanting to reassure him, especially as
Lorelai was the closest thing he had to a sister.

'Yes, Eddie, I have. In fact, I've delivered twenty-eight
babies. This one will be number twenty-nine and only
two of those were in a hospital. All the others were home
births. Lorelai is almost fully dilated and at this stage the
delivery looks as though it's going to be textbook. You've
packed the medical bag with everything I need, the Tumut
paramedics are on standby, so we're good to go.' She
nodded for emphasis, then turned and looked at their
friend, sliding her hand down to his arm to squeeze his
fingers. 'Lorelai and the baby will be just fine.'

'Medically speaking or emotionally speaking?' Edward
asked softly, so Lorelai couldn't hear them. Honey could
hear the anger and disgust at John in his tone.

'She has good support. *That* makes an enormous difference.' Lorelai's breathing started to increase. 'Ahh...next
contraction on the way. That's our cue,' she remarked, and
they both shifted back into position.

Over the next four hours Honey and Edward supported
Lorelai, who was doing all the hard work. She listened to
Honey's instructions about when to push and when not to
push. Edward acted as support for Lorelai, sponging her
down and keeping her cool and as comfortable as possible,
as well as ensuring Honey had everything she required.

At twenty-eight minutes past two in the morning, Honey
finished delivering the beautiful baby girl. Edward did the

honours and cut the cord, before accepting the baby from Honey to wrap up and perform an Apgar test.

Lorelai had collapsed back onto the beanbag, not having the energy to care about any thing. Honey delivered the placenta and checked it carefully, pleased with the result. Meanwhile, little healthy cries filled the air as the baby made herself known.

'Sounds as though she doesn't like being poked and prodded.' Honey laughed, watching as Edward expertly wrapped the baby and held her like a loving uncle. She swallowed over the sudden lump in her throat at the sight he made. Man with babe. So gorgeous. So precious. So... right.

'What's the verdict?' Honey asked as she placed the placenta into a disposable container so it could be more thoroughly analysed at a later date. She continued to tidy things up and pulled off the gloves and apron she'd used to protect her clothes.

'One minute Apgar was a seven. Five minutes is a nine. She is strong and healthy and incredibly gorgeous. Lore? Do you want to hold her?'

A very weary Lorelai opened her arms, her eyes still closed, but the moment Edward handed her the baby Lorelai opened her eyes and looked at her daughter. Edward stood next to Honey and both of them watched as in that one instant Lorelai fell in love with her baby girl.

Tears filled Honey's eyes and she slipped her arms around Edward's waist, pleased when he didn't push her away but instead drew her closer, resting his arm on her shoulders.

'What are you going to call her?' Edward asked, his voice thick with emotion.

Lorelai smiled but shook her head. 'I don't know. The

names John and I chose no longer seem appropriate. Any suggestions?' she asked, unable to tear her gaze away from her darling cherub.

Honey laughed. 'Don't ask me. My name's so overly hyphenated it's not funny.'

'I think your name is the prettiest name I've ever heard,' Edward remarked softly. 'Honeysuckle Lilly-Pilly Huntington-Smythe.' He looked down at her and exhaled slowly. 'It suits you.'

Honey's throat went dry at the expression she saw in his eyes. It was of complete surrender as though in that one moment in time nothing else in the world mattered except for the two of them. Somehow Edward had the ability to make her feel more special, more precious, more feminine than anyone else she'd ever met. There it was again, the meeting of their two hearts, intertwining, drawing them together.

'Can you two stop making eyes at each other for a few minutes and help me to choose an equally lovely name for my baby girl?'

Lorelai's words startled Edward and he immediately shifted back, a little self-conscious at being caught. Honey knelt down beside her friend. 'Let me look at this cherub,' she said, and brushed the back of her finger over the baby's cheek. 'Oh, she *is* beautiful, Lorelai. So perfectly made.'

'She is. She's *my* baby girl. Mine and only mine.' Her voice choked on the last word but she shook her head, pushing the negative emotions aside. 'Happy thoughts. This is a happy moment. Honey, what's your mother's name?'

'Star.'

Edward looked at her. 'Seriously?'

'Yep. What about your mother's name, Eddie? That's

a pretty name,' Honey pointed out. 'I love that seat in the garden, the one dedicated to your parents.'

Edward nodded. 'Hannah.' He and Lorelai spoke at the same time.

'I always admired your mother so much, Edward. She was always there for me.' Lorelai looked down at her baby girl. 'Hannah.'

'Hannah means graceful and pure,' Honey remarked. 'What was your mother's name, Lore?'

'Emily.'

'That means honest and caring.'

'How do you know these things?' Edward shook his head in bemusement. 'You're like a walking name-meaning encyclopedia.'

'I've always found names interesting. Edward, for instance, means guard or rich guard, and you are certainly that. Guarding your family, keeping those who mean the most to you safe.' Honey smiled at him. 'It suits you.'

Lorelai sighed with happiness. 'That's it, then. She's definitely going to be Hannah Emily. That's my girl.' Lorelai kissed Hannah's forehead and the baby snuggled into her mother as though completely exhausted from being born.

'It's a perfect name,' Honey said.

'A perfect name for a perfectly made little girl,' Edward agreed. They were all quiet, absorbed in the tranquillity of the moment, before Lorelai turned sharply to look at her friends, her gaze narrowing on Honey.

'Sorry, but did I hear you call him *Eddie*?'

Honey smiled and nodded at her friend. 'I see your logical thought processes are kicking back into gear, and speaking of getting back into gear, let's get this place cleaned up so you and the lovely Hannah can get comfortable.'

Soon Lorelai was reclining on the couch, her baby still wrapped and in her arms. 'Isn't she going to want a feed? Shouldn't she be hungry? All the books say they're usually hungry when they're born.'

Honey shook her head. 'Sometimes they are and it appears Hannah isn't. Books tend to generalise too much. Don't you worry. Hannah will let you know when she's hungry and I'll be here to help you out.'

'You're a lactation specialist as well?' This question came from Edward, who was on the phone to Tumut hospital, informing them of the uneventful birth of Hannah Emily. 'Is there anything you can't do, Honey?'

'No,' she said with a smile. 'But again I've had a lot of practice with home births. There's no stress, no tension here, Lorelai. You can do whatever you need to do and relax whilst doing it. We can get a bath ready for Hannah and you can freshen up and have a shower. If you're hungry or thirsty, I can fix you something. There's absolutely no pressure.'

Lorelai took in a deep breath, letting it out slowly, and dropped a kiss to her daughter's sleeping head. 'No pressure,' she sighed, and looked at her friend. 'What I really want to know is…' she glanced over at Edward and then back at Honey '…what's going on with you two?'

'I don't know, Lore.' Honey looked over to where Edward was talking on the phone, her heart hammering against her chest with delight.

'But you were hugging him.'

Honey's smile was instant. 'We'd just witnessed the miracle of birth and, well…at that moment it felt right to hug him.'

'I think there's more going on between the two of you than either of you is admitting.'

'What makes you say that?'

'You keep calling him Eddie. *No one* but his mother ever called him Eddie and even then it was more a term of endearment than a common occurrence.'

'He hasn't asked me to stop.'

'That alone speaks volumes,' Lorelai pointed out.

'Besides, I think it suits him.' She thought of the way he'd stood on top of the mountain and yelled ridiculous things into the wind, a smile touching her lips. He was a fine man, an honourable man and an incredibly sexy one at that. Thinking of him opening the door tonight, wearing only jeans, made her mouth go dry.

'I also heard that the two of you went to Charlotte's Pass last weekend.'

Honey was surprised. 'How did you know?'

Lorelai shook her head. 'Honey, Honey, Honey. This part of the country is small and word tends to get around. I don't know how you managed to get him there but I am so glad you did. So are his brothers, but it does stand to reason that only a very special woman, one he lets call him Eddie, would have been able to persuade him to go. You obviously mean a lot to him.'

Honey glanced again at Edward, and when he looked across the room and caught her staring at him, she didn't look away. Instead she smiled and a moment later he returned that smile then gave his attention to whoever he was talking to on the phone.

Hannah started to murmur and squeak and wriggle. 'Looks as though she might be getting ready for a bath.' Honey rubbed her finger over Hannah's little cheek. 'It's exhausting work, being born. Isn't it, missy?'

Honey went and prepared the baby bath, pleased Lorelai was so well set up. Edward came over and watched as Lorelai expertly held her daughter, bathing her so carefully, so gently, so lovingly. Hannah relaxed, quite content, her eyes still closed tight as she allowed herself to float in the warm water.

'It looks as though Miss Hannah likes her bath,' Edward remarked, smiling down at the baby. He'd been watching the way Honey controlled the entire situation where Lorelai was concerned. The whole birth and the aftermath had flowed like a well-orchestrated ballet and he knew it was all Honey's doing. Given what Lorelai had discovered tonight, the fact that her husband's infidelity and the way he rejected her and walked out had caused her to go into labour, the whole situation could have been fraught with out-of-control emotions. Instead, Honey had kept Lorelai focused, had spoken calmly to her, reassured her every step of the way, making sure Lorelai and Hannah moved at their own pace.

Seeing her so in command, not flustered, not concerned, had only raised his opinion of her even more. She was an amazingly skilled woman and he knew how fortunate they were to have her at the Oodnaminaby practice.

He closed his eyes for a second as memories washed over him. Holding her in his arms, up on the mountain, their plastic ponchos blowing in the wind. Being close to her and brushing his lips across her long, smooth neck when they'd been in the restaurant. Feeling the reassurance from the little squeeze she'd given his hand when they'd been in the chapel. Having her close as he'd opened his past and grieved for his parents. All in all, Honeysuckle was becoming incredibly difficult to resist.

'Here, Uncle Edward.' At Honey's sweet voice, he

opened his eyes and looked directly into hers as she handed him a towel. 'Get ready to receive the baby and hold your new niece.'

Edward took the towel from her, their hands touching for an instant, awareness flaring between them. 'Wait.' He held her hand through the towel. 'You don't have your contacts in,' he murmured.

'No. Didn't have time to put them in so don't go asking me to read things that are far away.'

He looked deeply at her. 'Wow. Your eyes are…the colour of the sea on a stormy day. Vibrant blue and deep green, mixed together with a hint of grey.' He swallowed. 'Mesmerising.'

'Oh, Eddie, you do pick the strangest times to say and do the sweetest things.' Honey moved out of the way as Lorelai finished bathing Hannah and lifted her out, Edward more than happy to accept the newest addition to Oodnaminaby. He cradled her sweetly in his arms and brushed a kiss on her forehead.

'I'll go find her some clothes to wear,' Lorelai said, as she walked slowly up the corridor towards the nursery, leaving Honey alone with Edward, watching him hold the beautiful baby lovingly in his arms.

'You're good at that,' Honey remarked, her heart tightening at the sight of man and babe together.

'Holding babies? I've had plenty of practice. I was fifteen by the time Hamilton was born and as such was expected to pitch in wherever necessary.'

Honey stepped close and brushed her fingers over Hannah's forehead and cheeks. 'I know you said you didn't want children but look at you. You're a natural. You'd make such a wonderful father,' she said softly.

'That may be so but a family of my own isn't on my agenda at this point.'

Honey nodded and leaned forward to touch little Hannah's hand. She felt as though Edward had just put her in her place and that place was at arm's length from where he stood.

In less than twelve months she'd probably be getting ready to move from Oodnaminaby to… She sighed and clenched her teeth, unable to finish the thought. She didn't want to go from Ood. Of that much she was certain but could she stay in town, living near Edward, seeing him every day, when her feelings for him seemed to be sky-rocketing with each passing moment?

CHAPTER NINE

Two nights after the birth Honey was just sitting down to a bowl of soup and a piece of toast when there was knock at the coach-house door. Rising, she quickly went to open it and found Hamilton standing there, in his sports gear, dirt smudged on his face.

'Hi,' he said.

'Hi,' she returned brightly. 'Something wrong?'

'Uh…not really.' Hamilton looked past her and pointed to the food on the table. 'You've already eaten?'

'Just about to.'

'Well…uh…' Hamilton shifted from foot to foot.

Honey fixed him with a glare. 'What's wrong?'

'Come for dinner.'

'Did Edward send you over to ask?'

'No, but come anyway.'

'Hamilton.' There was a warning tone in her voice.

'OK, look. I might have done something a little crazy at school today and he's going to find out about it and I thought if you were there for dinner, then you'd be able to keep him all calm and relaxed like you usually do. He's different around you, Honey. He's…like a normal human being. You know…happy!'

Honey couldn't help but laugh. 'How's he going to find out about this thing that happened at school?'

'I have a note to give him.'

'Were you in the wrong? Did you do the wrong thing?'

Hamilton pondered this for a moment. 'Possibly.'

'Ahh.' Honey reached for her long cardigan, which was by the door, and slipped her feet into a pair of leather sandals. 'Then, before you give him the note, explain your side of the story, tell him what happened and whatever the punishment—do not dispute it. You keep saying you want Edward to treat you like a grown-up—that means you start taking the consequences for your actions. If you s*how* him you *are* an adult, he'll treat you like one.'

'Promise?'

'Promise.' She flicked off the lights and headed over with him to the house. 'Surprise,' she said when they both walked into the kitchen. Edward was just taking a dish from the oven. 'Hamilton invited me over for dinner. I hope you don't mind.'

Edward looked from his brother to the woman he couldn't stop thinking about. 'Uh…no.'

'Great. Knew it would be all right,' the teenager said. 'OK. I'm off to have a shower.'

'A quick one,' Edward called as Hamilton raced from the room. Honey was a little startled to find herself alone with Edward. Did Hamilton have another agenda as well? One that included giving the two of them a little push? 'How was clinic today?' he asked as he stirred whatever was in the crockery pot. 'I didn't get to catch up with you before I left.'

'It was good. No surprises. You?'

'Same.'

She walked closer and leaned over the bench, breathing in the delicious aroma of whatever he was making. 'Smells good.'

'So do you,' he murmured, unable to control his words.

He put down the tea-towel he was holding and reached for her hand, drawing her closer. 'I'm glad Hamilton asked you over because I was going to but I didn't want to bother you. I haven't been able to get you off my mind and...' He pressed his mouth to hers, effectively ending whatever it was he'd been saying.

Honey wasn't about to quibble and lifted her head, eager for the touch of his mouth against hers, eager to match his impatient hunger, eager to show him just how much she loved him.

'Good heavens, Honey.' He broke off a moment later, his breathing heavy as his arms came about her waist, needing her even closer. 'I can't stop thinking about you.'

'I know the feeling.'

'I keep wanting to contrive reasons for seeing you, for spending time with you, for being near.'

She smiled against his mouth. 'There's no need to contrive, Edward. I'm open to your suggestions and, in fact, I was actually going to pop over after dinner to ask for your help.'

'Really?' He kissed her cheeks, first one, then the other. 'What do you need help with? Kissing? Because I'm all ready to practise that with you.' To show her he meant what he said, he brought his mouth to hers again, capturing her lips with his, drawing forth a response that left her light-headed and very weak at the knees.

'What is this thing between us?' he murmured.

Love?

The word was on the tip of her tongue but she simply didn't have the courage to voice it. What if she said it and he pushed her away? She wasn't sure she was strong enough to deal with that. He kissed her again before eventually drawing back and putting a bit of distance between them.

'You're too distracting. Go and sit at the table or stand on the other side of the room because otherwise we risk the dinner being burnt or, worse, Hamilton catching us kissing in the kitchen.'

'Uh…I think he already knows.' Honey collected another place setting from the drawer and walked to the table.

'What?'

'He has some bad news to break to you and he wanted me here for moral support. He said I relaxed you, that you were happier when I was around. He's not a kid any more, Eddie.'

'So I'm beginning to realise.' He turned back to the dinner, putting the crockery pot back into the oven. 'So?' he asked a moment later, turning to look at her from the other side of the room. 'What did you need my help with?'

'I uh…spoke to my brother the other night. The night Lore went into labour, actually, so it's been a little busy since then but…uh…he…Woody gave me my parents' phone number.' She shrugged. 'Apparently, they have a cellphone now.'

Edward nodded. 'You're ready to call them?'

'No.' She laughed without humour and shook her head. 'I'm far too scared to call them. That's why I need your help. What am I supposed to say?'

'Hi. How are you? What have you been up to for the past decade? Would you like to come to town for a visit?'

'Visit?'

Edward wiped his hands on the tea-towel, then tossed it aside, closing the distance between them. He placed his hands on her shoulders and looked into her eyes. 'You're a strong woman, Honey. You're supportive, you're kind, you're caring. You can do this. You can reach out to them.

You can bridge this vast chasm that divides the three of you.'

Honey nodded, unable to believe how calm he made her feel. With Edward by her side she had the feeling she could accomplish anything. If he believed in her, she could believe in herself.

'I can put dinner on hold and we can call them right now, if you like.'

'Now?'

He nodded and returned to the oven, turning down the temperature before crossing to the phone on the wall. He took it from its cradle and carried it to her. 'Do you have the number?'

She tapped the side of her head. 'I've read it over and over so many times since Woody gave it to me that I've memorised it.'

'Go ahead. Make that call.' He steered her to the table and sat down beside her. Honey simply stared at the phone, paralysed with fear.

'What if they hang up when they hear my voice?' she asked.

Edward shook his head. 'Not going to happen.' He took the phone from her slim fingers. 'What's the number?'

Honey took a deep breath and looked at Edward. She thought about the way he'd looked at her when they'd been standing in that chapel and she remembered how brave he'd been and how proud she'd felt. Now it was her turn. Edward had lost his parents and would never see them again. She had the opportunity and the time to right past wrongs.

'You can do it,' he said, and leaned over to give her an encouraging kiss. Honey swallowed and cleared her throat before closing her eyes and breathing out slowly. Edward believed in her. That was enough.

Opening her eyes, she pressed the connect button. As the ringing tone sounded in her ear, she bit her lip, desperate to control her breathing. A moment later the call connected.

'Hello?' It was her mother's voice and at the sound Honey became paralysed with fear. 'Hello?'

'Go on,' Edward whispered and nodded, a smile on his gorgeous mouth.

Honey swallowed again. 'Mum?'

Her mother breathed in a sharp breath. 'Honeysuckle?' she whispered. 'Is that really you?'

'Yes, it is. Mum…' Emotion choked her throat.

'Oh, Honeysuckle,' her mother interjected, her tone instantly filled with deep apologetic emotion. 'We're so sorry,' her mother sobbed. 'For everything.'

At the sound of her mother's tears Honey felt a few slide down her own cheeks and soon those few turned into a few more. By the time her father came on the line, Honey was crying. Thankfully, Edward hugged her close, pulling a handkerchief from his pocket and dabbing at her tears. 'I'm proud of you,' he whispered.

'Thank you,' she mouthed, then smiled.

On Friday morning, Woody surprised Honey by arriving in town unannounced. Edward's first indication of the event was when he heard Honey's squeal of delight. He'd just come out of the shower and was wearing a pair of denim jeans with a white towel around his shoulders, rubbing at his hair. He'd rushed to the front window, his heart pounding beneath his chest, fearful something bad had happened to the woman who seemed to constantly be on his mind. As he watched, he saw Honey literally launch herself into her brother's arms.

The resemblance between the siblings was clear, even though Woody was a good foot and a half taller than his big sister. Edward's heart rate started to settle to its normal rhythm, pounding out a beat just for Honey. She was dressed in another pair of colourful pyjama bottoms and a tight-fitting singlet top, a long open cardigan hanging down to her knees as though she'd just thrown it on at the last minute.

Woody whipped her up and whizzed her around as though she were about five years old, Honey giggling with delight. The sound washed over him and he closed his eyes, wanting to savour the moment. There was no denying the strong feelings he had for her. Not any more. She was rarely far from his thoughts and he found himself almost desperate to contrive reasons to be in her presence. When he was there, when he was close to her, breathing in her hypnotic scent, trying not to stare into her beautiful eyes, he found it difficult to restrain himself from touching her, from taking her hand and hauling her into his arms. He wanted her body pressed as close to his as physically possible. Even thinking about it now made his heart ache for her.

She was *in* him. He had no idea how it had happened but his heart had connected with hers and he had no idea what to do about it. When he'd been with Amelia, he'd always been completely in control of his emotions. Not so with Honey. Even as he watched her now, his head and heart seemed to be warring with each other. One telling him she was the only woman for him, the other saying they had too many differences to overcome.

Honey wanted children, was almost desperate to have

'a whole gaggle' of them. Edward frowned as he started to wonder *why* Honey was so vehement in her need. What was it that had made this simple desire to reproduce such a necessity within her life? He recalled the way she'd stabbed her finger at the table, saying that no child of hers would be made to feel lonely and unwanted.

Perhaps her need stemmed from wanting to show her parents how they should have raised her and Woody? To let them see that children didn't necessarily want freedom, or to be left to their own devices, they wanted to be *valued* by their parents. She was trying to right past wrongs, wrongs that had been done to her.

Both of them had had responsibilities thrust upon them and both of them had assumed control. In that way they were the same but where Honey was desperate for children, Edward knew the thought of reproducing still scared him. His parents had had five children—and then his mother and father had died. They hadn't meant to. He'd always known it had been an accident but what if...what if he *did* have children and then something bad happened to him? Some freak accident that took his life and left his children—?

'Eddie?'

Edward was startled from his reverie to see Honey waving at him from the driveway, her other arm around her brother's waist. It was then he realised he was still standing at the window, watching them but not really seeing them as his thoughts had drifted off.

'Come and meet my brother,' she called, beckoning for him to come down. Knowing it was futile to attempt to argue with Honey, he did as she bid, mindful to pull on a T-shirt before heading downstairs.

Edward invited them inside, all of them walking into

the kitchen where Edward instantly put on the coffee machine. 'Cuppa?'

'Uh…have you got any herbal tea? I've been living on coffee for the past few hours to keep me awake.'

'I have some at the coach house,' Honey said instantly, and headed for the door.

'It's OK, Honey,' Edward said quickly, and produced a box of the same type of herbal tea she had at the clinic. 'I bought some.'

Honey's eyes widened. 'You drink herbal tea now?'

Edward shrugged. 'Well, no. Not necessarily but *you* do and you're here for dinner on a regular basis and so I thought that—' He broke off as Honey put her arms around him, hugging him close.

'You're wonderful,' she told him. 'Thank you.'

Edward looked down into her face, once again struck by the mesmerising colour of her eyes. He liked it when she wore her different coloured contacts but he much preferred her natural colour. He placed his free hand in the small of her back, delighted she had appreciated his gesture of buying the tea. 'You're most welcome,' he murmured, his gaze dipping to encompass her mouth before flicking back to meet her gaze.

'Herbal tea it is, then,' Woody remarked, rubbing his hands together. Honey and Edward looked at him as though they'd forgotten he was in the room. Woody winked at his sister as she released Edward from her arms and crossed back to his side.

'So, Woody.' Edward turned his attention back to filling the kettle and switching it on. 'Honey mentioned you've worked in Tarparnii?'

'That's right. I'm due to go back in another fortnight so figured it was the perfect time to come and see my sister and check out the area she swears she's fallen in love with. I have to admit,' he said, draping his arm around Honey's shoulders, 'it is quite beautiful around here.'

'I told you so,' she said with a wide smile.

'Yeah, you did.' Woody let go of Honey and picked up the duffle bag he'd brought in with him, before holding Edward's gaze. 'My sister only picks the best.'

Edward froze for a moment, unsure whether Woody was referring to the town of Oodnaminaby or to him. Honey had said she was very close to her brother but how much had she told him? Had she told Woody about the kisses they'd shared? The long talks they'd enjoyed? Edward swallowed, trying to read Woody's expression, but all he saw was open joviality.

'So, sis, why don't you show me the coach house and I can dump my stuff while we wait for the kettle to boil?' Woody suggested.

'You're going to stay in the coach house with Honey? Where will you sleep?' Edward looked at the tall man's stature. 'You won't fit on the couch.'

Woody chuckled. 'In Tarparnii we sleep on the floor,' he stated. 'I'll be fine.'

Edward looked at Honey for a moment before shaking his head. 'No, it's ridiculous for Woody to sleep on the floor when I have plenty of spare rooms here. You're more than welcome to stay in the house. Hamilton will be glad of the extra company,' he stated as the teenager came down the stairs and into the room, still half-asleep.

'Hey, man.' Hamilton blearily shook hands with Woody.

'OK,' Woody accepted. 'If it's no trouble, that would be great.' He looked at Honey who nodded and smiled, delighted that her brother and the man who had become so vitally important to her life were getting along well.

That evening they shared dinner with the rest of Edward's extended family. BJ brought Lorelai and baby Hannah over, whilst Peter, Annabelle and their children came to town for the night. Hamilton was in his element having so many people around and Edward and Honey quickly cobbled together enough food to feed everyone.

'Woody seems to fit right in,' Edward remarked as the two of them carried plates to the kitchen, Edward starting to stack the dishwasher.

'He's a very easygoing man. He always has been. Even when things don't work out as he plans, he seems to somehow pick himself up and soldier on. Woody recently suffered a great personal tragedy.' There was sadness behind Honey's eyes and Edward instantly found himself drawing her into his arms. She was about to say more but Edward quickly dipped his head and brushed his lips across hers.

'I'm sure he learned his excellent coping skills from his big sister. Where you felt abandoned by your parents, he didn't experience that sensation because he always had you to fill the void they left. We're the same like that, Honey. We've both worked hard to spare our younger siblings from feeling the same painful and lonely sensations we had to experience.'

'We're amazing,' she whispered as his mouth touched hers again.

'Oh, really?' Lorelai said as she walked into the room, Honey and Edward taking their time easing apart. 'You two have progressed to this stage already?'

Honey shrugged. 'Whatever "this stage" means, I guess we have.' She smiled as Edward winked at her. It was as though both of them knew their hearts had connected but neither were sure how to move forward from there.

Honey relieved Lorelai of the plates she was holding. Edward watched the two women as they chatted and laughed, moving around his kitchen, both of them feeling equally at home. Honey seemed to fit neatly into his life. Before they'd met he hadn't realised anything was missing but now, when he thought of his life without her, there seemed to be a large gaping hole filled with pain and loneliness.

Honey had experienced the same pain and loneliness as a child and there was no way he wanted either of them to feel that way ever again. Yet to discuss a future with her felt strange. Where children were concerned, they were at opposites. Slowly, though, an idea started to form in his mind. It was a plan that might help Honey to reconcile with her parents, to get her whole family back. Perhaps it would help her realise that her almost obsessive need to have children stemmed from the lack of control she'd had during her growing years. There was no way he could ever bring his own parents back but thanks to Honey he'd been able to finally make peace with their passing.

The least he could do was to support her while she took the next steps towards finding true happiness—and it was happiness he wanted to share.

CHAPTER TEN

'WHERE are we going?'

Honey was standing beside her car, an overnight bag in her hand, the crispness of the April morning making itself known. Edward took the bag from her hand and stowed it in the boot.

'Have you got the keys?' he asked as Woody walked out the back door of the house, sipping a cup of coffee. Her brother had been there for a week, fitting right in with the entire town and community. He'd been invited out for dinner almost every night and Honey was pleased he was being made to feel so welcome. He was more than happy to hang around for a few more days, delighted to be filling in for her and Edward at the clinic for the next two days. Edward had planned it all and she'd often caught the two most important men in her life chatting quietly, stopping as soon as she walked into the room.

'Almost ready to go?' Woody asked, taking a sip from his mug.

'Just about.'

'Where are we going?' Honey asked for the umpteenth time, spreading her arms wide.

'I've told you,' Edward replied as he opened the driver's side door for her. 'You and I are heading out of town for the night. Woody will hold down the fort at the clinic and can always call on Lorelai if he needs support. You were right, Honey. I don't take enough time out for myself, so now I'm going to rectify that matter.'

'But I'm going with you. That's not being alone, Edward.'

He stepped forward, sliding one arm about her waist and drawing her close for a quick, soft, body-melting kiss. 'I'm not going anywhere without you,' he whispered against her lips. 'Now, in you hop.' He stepped back. 'We're taking your car and you're driving.'

'But...where?'

Edward winked at her. 'That's for me to know and for you to find out!'

'Having fun?' he asked, looking over at her from the driver's seat, the two of them happy to share the driving. They'd been on the road now for just over six hours, having stopped here and there to admire the beautiful scenery they were driving through. Edward had been thoughtful in packing food and drink for them, allowing Honey more time to stop and browse through some of the craft and antique shops they'd passed along the way.

'Having great fun. I can't believe the bargains I've managed to get.'

'I can't imagine how these stores can claim they sell antiques. More like unwanted odds and sods no one else wants.'

'Except me.'

Edward glanced at the odd mix of packages wrapped in newspaper in the back seat and smiled. 'Except you,' he agreed.

'You have to admit, those sterling-silver sugar tongs I found were an absolute steal.'

He laughed. 'A steal for whom?' He reached over and took her hand in his, bringing it to his lips. 'You're unique, Honeysuckle. I like that about you.'

'Good.' Honey swallowed and smiled at him. 'I like it that you like that about me.'

'Even though you know where I've tricked you into coming today?' He set her hand back onto her lap and slowed the car down as they hit the outskirts of Rosedale.

'You didn't trick me, Eddie, and it didn't take me long to figure things out. You and Woody conspiring together was a pretty strong give-away.'

'You don't mind, then? Seeing your parents, I mean?'

Honey breathed out slowly. 'I'm nervous, I'm scared, I'm…nervous and scared. Oh, wait, did I already say that? See how nervous and scared I am?' She tried to laugh but it came off more as a sigh. 'It's time. It was time for me to call them and it's time for me to see them.'

'And I'll be there, beside you, the whole way,' he remarked. He slowed the car even more and flicked on the indicator to turn, driving them towards the location Woody had provided. It was the site of La Trobe Valley coal-powered electricity-generating plant. A group of protesters were starting to pack up their equipment as the sun was setting.

Edward parked the car and came around to Honey's side, opening the door and holding out his hand to her. She stood and he instantly pulled her close. 'Are you all right?' he asked. 'You're looking a bit pale.'

Honey breathed out slowly. 'It's good. I'm fine. Just stay close.'

He kissed her. 'I wouldn't be anywhere else except by your side.' It was as he said the words that he realised just how much he meant them, not only for now but for ever.

The thought didn't scare him as much as he had thought it might.

They turned and headed towards the protesters. Honey stopped for a moment and shook her head. 'They're not here.'

'What?' Edward looked around.

'That's their Kombi,' she said, pointing at the circa 1960s van that had most certainly seen better days. 'But I don't see them.'

'Who are you looking for?' one of the other protesters asked, having overheard them.

'Uh…Star and Red Moon-Pie?' she asked the thin woman who was dressed in a similar tie-dyed outfit to one Edward had once seen Honey wear.

'Oh, they're in the local lock-up,' the woman responded calmly. 'Things became a little heated earlier on and the police came out and, well, if you know Red, you'll know that when the police come, it's like a red flag to a bull.'

Honey nodded. 'I know him far too well,' she responded, shaking her head. 'Thanks,' she said, and turned around, taking Edward with her as they headed back to her car. 'Typical Dad.'

'Does that upset you?' Edward asked as he slipped back behind the wheel.

Honey thought for a moment. 'Actually, no. I'm not annoyed either, just…mildly amused that in all this time my dad hasn't changed. His values and beliefs are obviously still as strong as they've always been and you know what? That's a good thing.'

'Sounds like you.'

'Really?' Honey had never thought she was like either of her parents before.

'You have firm beliefs and values, Honey, and you live

them every day. You're an amazing doctor and it's clear you care for all your patients. You're smart, as has been proved by the numerous degrees you hold, and you're incredibly giving.' He turned in his seat, reaching out to cup her face in his hands. 'So very giving,' he murmured, and leaned over to kiss her.

Honey allowed herself to be swept away by his words, by his touch and by the glorious feel of his mouth on hers. She gave all of herself to him for in that one moment she knew for certain that she loved him. She had no idea what was going to happen in the future, whether or not he'd change his mind about wanting children, but right at this moment she didn't care if they never had children so long as she could stay with him for ever.

He broke off the kiss, leaning his forehead against hers as their breathing slowly started to return to normal. 'Shall we go to the police station and find out what's going on?'

Honey smiled and nodded. 'You sure know how to show a girl a good time, Dr Goldmark.'

So Honey's first sight of her parents, after eight years, was as they were brought out from the back room at the small police station. She gripped Edward's hand and was rewarded with a slight squeeze. 'I'm here,' he whispered near her ear, and when her parents stood before her, Honey found the anger she'd carried towards them simply drain out of her.

Edward was there. He was with her. Holding onto her. Keeping her grounded, keeping her safe from harm. With him by her side, she realised suddenly that she didn't need to worry about anything. The past was gone and she could do nothing to change it. The future was unwritten and anything could happen.

'Honeysuckle!' It was her father who spoke. 'That's my

girl. Coming to pick up her oldies. The last time you did this was…' Red stopped and scratched his almost balding head. He looked older, so much older than Honey had realised. Her doctor's brain immediately looked for signs of sickness but found none. He'd just grown older. Her mother, at almost sixty years of age, looked incredible. Her long silvery hair, which had once been a honey blonde like her daughter's, was pulled back into a ponytail and her blue-green eyes shone with happiness.

'Woody's eighteenth birthday,' Honey remarked. 'I came home for his celebration to find both of you had managed to get yourself arrested.'

'Woody understood, Honeysuckle,' her mother began, edging slowly forward.

'He may have but I didn't.' Where Honey had always thought there would be anger when she finally told her parents how she truly felt, there was only sadness. 'Even as an adult, I didn't understand how you could leave your own children to go and attend protest rallies instead of spending time with us. You've always been fighting hard to win everyone else's battles. Why didn't you fight to win mine? Why didn't you break down the walls I was putting up when I was younger?' Tears started to prick at her eyes. 'Why weren't you there for *me* when I needed you?' Tears ran down her face and she sniffed.

'Oh, Honeysuckle,' her mother said, and within another moment she had covered the distance between them, putting her arms around her daughter, both women crying tears of healing. 'We're sorry, Honeysuckle. So sorry. We had no idea until years later how much pressure we put on you.'

'You were always so competent, so strong and so determined to do things your way, there was no persuading you otherwise,' her father added, coming over to place a hand on his daughter's back. 'Stubborn and pig-headed. Just like your old man. Nurturing and powerful, just like your beautiful mother,' Red continued.

Honey sniffed and laughed at her father's words, wiping at the tears with her free hand, her other still firmly holding onto Edward. Star backed away and pulled a handkerchief from her pocket, dabbing at her eyes and blowing her nose. Red slipped his arm about his wife's shoulders and Honey took a good long look at her parents. After forty years together, they appeared still very much in love, very much in tune with each other. She looked at Edward. Her rock, her grounding force who had stood firm throughout this ordeal, showing her just how much he supported her. Honey knew she'd do anything for him, follow him to the ends of the earth, give up on her dream of children if he asked her.

Was this how her mother had felt when she'd met Red? Was this why she'd left home, defied her parents' wishes, headed off to live her life her way? Wasn't that exactly what Honey had done all those years ago when she'd walked out of the commune? Wasn't that what she was doing now, standing here with Edward by her side? Living her life her way?

'Now,' Red said, after blowing his own nose, 'aren't you going to introduce your ol' dad to this young whippersnapper who seems to have glued his hand to yours?'

Honey laughed and turned to introduce Edward, who suggested they all go out for dinner. Where Honey's parents had previously refused to eat in any restaurant given the food often had additives, they welcomed the opportunity to visit the local tavern.

'Food has certainly come a long way in the past decade,'

Star remarked as they looked at menus. 'Most places cater to different diets,' she continued, as though able to read her daughter's thoughts. Afterwards, they all piled into Honey's tiny car and drove back to her parents' van.

Her parents booked into the local caravan park, inviting Honey and Edward to stay with them.

'I hadn't planned on camping,' Edward remarked after they'd pitched the tent beside the van. Honey had used the foot-pump to blow up a large air mattress and unrolled the old sleeping bags her parents had provided them with.

'It's going to be wonderful,' she said with a giggle as she lay down. 'I haven't slept in a tent in well over a decade.' She stretched out her hand to him and after he'd taken off his shoes he lay down beside her.

Honey gazed into his eyes and sighed. 'Thank you, Eddie.'

'It was my pleasure.' He stroked her face, his fingers soft and gentle on her perfect skin. 'You are...exquisite,' he murmured, and a fraction of a second later she felt his mouth on hers.

Sighing into the kiss, she slid one arm around his neck, wanting to keep his head right where it was, desperate to memorise every minute emotion he evoked within her. She didn't hold back this time and put everything into the kiss. She had absolute faith that one day she and Edward would be together but until that day came she was determined to let him know just how important he was to her.

After a brief moment he deepened the kiss, slipping his tongue between her lips, amazed at how perfect she felt, how seamlessly they meshed as though they'd been made for each other. As he continued to plunder and probe the depths of her luscious mouth, Edward was pleased when she matched his hunger and need. This woman, this wild, vivacious woman made him feel as though he were the most fortunate man on the face of the earth. There was no way he would ever knowingly hurt her, his need to honour and protect her paramount.

No other woman had ever made him feel the way Honey could and that in itself was enormous for him. As much as he wanted to stay right where he was, as much as he wanted the emotions she evoked in him to take their natural course, they both knew now was not the right time. There were still a few things they had to address, namely if they *were* to get married, how were they going to solve the issue of children?

When they pulled apart, rapidly drawing breath, Honey leaned her head against his chest, secretly delighted at the fierce pounding of his heart. They lay there for a while, his arms around her as she snuggled into his chest, both seemingly content.

A few hours later, Edward woke to find he had little to no feeling in his arm and on trying to sit up rapidly remembered he was lying in a tent with Honey in his arms. They'd fallen asleep.

Carefully, he slid his arm from beneath her neck and quickly unzipped the sleeping bags, pulling them over her. When he returned to her side, she was still sound asleep but snuggled into him again.

'Mmm, Eddie,' she murmured, then slipped back into slumberland.

She was dreaming about him? A slow smile spread over Edward's face as he put an arm around her, the other one beneath his head. He closed his eyes, amazed to find that right at this moment he was incredibly content.

* * *

It was a little before four o'clock the following afternoon when they pulled Honey's car into Edward's driveway.

'That was a good trip,' she said as they headed into the house. 'And my parents have promised to come and visit on their way back to Queensland.'

Edward nodded. 'It's great. They're more than welcome to stay here.'

'That's so sweet of you,' she said, leaning up to kiss him. He opened the back door for her and they went inside. He dropped their bags just inside the door and pulled her quickly into his arms.

'The only problem with driving is that I can't hold you or kiss you properly,' he remarked, and was just about to lower his head when both of them heard the distinct sound of a baby murmuring happily.

They frowned at each other and then looked through the kitchen into the lounge room, where the sound had come from. Quickly, they followed the noise, Edward's eyebrows shooting upwards when he found his youngest brother sitting in a comfortable chair, Hannah in his arms, giving the baby a bottle.

'Hamilton?' Edward was stunned.

'Shh. Not so loud, bro. She's almost on her way to beddy-bye land.'

Honey and Edward came quietly into the room. 'Where's Lore? Woody? Where is everyone?' Edward asked softly.

'Emergency. The details are on the table over there.' He indicated a piece of paper on the coffee table. 'Woody said for you two to come as soon as you got home if I hadn't heard from him, and I haven't heard from him.'

Honey picked up the piece of paper and read what was written in her brother's usually illegible scrawl.

'OK, but where's Lorelai?' Edward persisted. 'Why are you looking after Hannah?'

'Lorelai had an appointment at the solicitors in Tumut and was pretty worked up about it so BJ offered to drive her and Woody said he'd stay with Hannah but when the emergency call came through, Woody wasn't sure what to do so I volunteered for Hannah duty.' Hamilton spoke softly but with an adult confidence Edward had never heard before.

Hamilton took the bottle out of Hannah's mouth when she'd finished, the little baby snuggling contentedly into him. 'Go. I'll be fine here.'

'Ham. You don't know how to—'

'I know how to do a lot of things, bro. Besides, I consider Hannah my niece, my family. And if there's one thing we Goldmarks know how to do, it's to take care of our family. You taught me that, bro. Now go!' Hamilton smiled. 'Ha. Go, bro. Man, I'm funny.'

Honey had her phone out and was trying to ring Woody. 'I can't get through but he's written down that the accident is on the road between here and Tumut.'

Edward nodded and pulled Honey's car keys from his pocket. 'Let me get my medical bag.'

Within a matter of minutes they were back on the road, heading towards Tumut. Given the cellphone reception was a bit hit and miss in these parts of the mountains, Honey tried Lorelai's and BJ's phones as well as Woody's but to no avail. Ten minutes later she was finally able to get hold of her brother.

'Woody! Thank goodness. What's going on?' she asked.

'Hang on. I'm going to put you on loudspeaker so Eddie can hear what you're saying, too.'

'Oh, Honey, I'm glad to hear your voice. Are you on your way?'

'We're about fifteen kilometres out of Tumut.'

'Then you can't be too far away. Listen, a car has crashed through the safety barrier and gone off the road. One man is trapped and a woman was thrown clear. They're about to take the woman to Tumut for possible airlift to Canberra. Lorelai is here with BJ, running the rescue side of things.' He paused. 'Edward, the man is John, Lorelai's husband. It's *his* car that went through the barrier.'

'John?' Edward repeated, astonished.

'Yes.'

'What about Lore?' Edward's tone was filled with concern and Honey noticed his face had turned ashen as his quick mind processed everything.

'She's OK. She's not hurt but she was first on the scene and called it through to me. Fire and rescue crews are here. Listen. I have to go. Get here soon and drive safe.' With that, Woody ended the call. The tension within the small car was almost palpable as both doctors mentally worked through the different scenarios they might be faced with when they arrived.

It was another five minutes before they saw the road block, traffic on the road already starting to back up. Edward slowed the car and drove on the wrong side of the road, getting as close to the accident as possible.

'Park it here,' Honey said, and Edward pulled the car up next to a fire truck, the police officer responsible for controlling the traffic having recognised Edward and waved them through the barricade. They were both out the car as soon as possible, Edward collecting his medical bag as they headed towards the crash site.

BJ, Lorelai's father, being a State Emergency Services

captain and an expert at this type of retrieval, was taking charge of the situation. He saw them and inclined his head towards the embankment. Edward nodded back, understanding the silent communication. BJ wanted them down at the crash site.

They moved to where the car had broken through the road barrier. It hadn't gone far but had rolled at least once, coming to rest on the driver's side, which was now completely mangled. Fire-retardant foam had been sprayed around the car, dousing any possible spark that might cause an explosion.

As they carefully picked their way along the ground, heading towards the crash site, the rescue crews peeled away part of the passenger roof, having cut through the door and roof-post, to allow easier access to John.

Lorelai was standing beside the car, her clothes and upper arms splattered with dirt, grime and dried blood, her face dirty here and there where she'd absentmindedly wiped herself. The look of complete anguish, complete desolation on her face almost broke Edward's heart.

'Lore?' Edward walked to her side, quickly putting his bag down as Lorelai turned instantly at his voice. He drew her into his arms and held his surrogate sister close.

'Oh, Edward.' Tears instantly flooded over the barriers she'd worked hard to erect. 'Edward, it's John.' She sobbed into his shoulder. He held her for a moment, wanting to reassure and help her in any way he could, but after seeing the wreckage he wasn't sure there was much he could say.

He saw Woody come up beside him. 'Come on, Lorelai. Let me take you home,' Woody offered, putting his hand on her shoulders as she eased back from Edward's comforting arms.

'Good idea. Go on up with Woody,' he offered softly. 'Let him take you home. Honey and I will look after John.'

Lorelai sniffed and nodded, swiping at her tears with her dirty hands. 'OK.' Swallowing, she turned and allowed Woody to help her up the embankment. Edward picked up his bag and turned, expecting to find Honey standing beside him, but she'd disappeared.

'Honey?' he called.

'Hey, Edward.' A fire-rescue crew member appeared from the other side of the car, walking towards him. 'Good timing.'

'Where's Honey?'

'She's taken over from Woody. She's in the car.'

'What?' He looked at the mangled car, then back to the fireman as though he was insane. Edward carefully moved closer, desperate to see Honey, desperate to know she really was all right, that she was safe. His head started to hurt and his heart hammered wildly against his chest at the thought that anything should happen to the woman he loved.

Loved?

He'd thought that before and now, in this one moment that seemed to stand still for ever, he realised it was true. He loved Honey—and nothing else mattered.

'She's fine,' the guy continued. 'Safety first. She's in no danger.'

'No danger? She's is a car that could slip down into the lake. She might get trapped. She might drown.'

'BJ has taken care of that. The car is tethered securely at the top so there's no way it'll move unless BJ wants it to.'

Edward quickly headed around to the car, being careful not to slip on the foam. 'Honey?' he called again.

'In here. We just need to secure the ropes and then, once he's in a harness, we can cut him out,' Honey called from the inside of the vehicle. 'Oh, and I'm going to need another IV bag pretty soon.'

Edward instantly shifted his attention to the car and, more importantly, to the woman who'd stubbornly crawled inside. He peered down into it, watching for a second as Honey shimmied slowly forward, a pair of pliers in her hand.

'Honeysuckle Lilly-Pilly Goldmark, what in the name of all that's sanity are you doing in that vehicle?'

His answer was one of her sweet laughs. She hadn't missed the change of last name and wondered if Edward had even realised he'd said it. 'Oh, shush, and see if that next bag of plasma's arrived from up top yet. I did radio BJ and ask for one.'

Edward checked, seeing one of the paramedics heading down with an IV bag in his hands. 'It's on its way. What's the status?'

'John's hand is wound around the phone charger cord. I need to free it to try and get the blood flowing through his limb again.'

'How is he?'

Honey sighed and when she spoke he could hear the dejection in her tone. 'Not good, Eddie. His pulse is weak, he hasn't regained consciousness and his legs are...' She stopped. 'Where's Lorelai?'

'Gone. Woody took her home.'

'Thank goodness.'

'What were you saying about his legs?'

'They're badly crushed, Eddie.' Honey freed John's hand and quickly tried to straighten it, searching for a pulse. 'Radial pulse is still not there,' she told him, before shifting carefully around to press her fingers to John's carotid pulse.

'John? John?' She called. 'Can you hear me?'

No response.

'Report?' Edward asked.

'Carotid pulse is weakening. Pass me the penlight torch,' she instructed, and held out her hand. When he passed it to her, his fingers gently brushed hers and she felt a renewal of energy. She accepted the torch and quickly shifted so she could check John's pupils. 'No, no, no.' She checked again.

'What? What is it?'

Honey sighed and closed her eyes for a moment. 'No pulse. Pupils fixed and dilated.'

There was silence and then she felt Edward's hand reach out and touch her arm. When she turned, it was to discover he was leaning in through the side of the car.

'Call it,' he said softly.

Honey reached around and found the walkie-talkie. 'BJ?' she said, and a moment later Lorelai's father's voice crackled back.

'Honey?'

'Time of death…' she checked her watch '…sixteen fifty-seven.'

Another moment of silence. 'Copy that,' BJ replied.

Edward's heart ached and he wanted nothing more than to hold her close. To let her know that she'd done all she could, that it wasn't her fault, that life went on, that he would *never* leave her, and that whatever the future brought, they would face it together.

'Let me help you,' Edward said, and with slow, careful movements Honey made her way out of the car. Once she was out, he instantly pulled her close, holding her tight.

'Poor Lorelai,' she murmured into his neck, her arms firmly around him.

'We'll get her through. Together.' He pressed his lips to hers, reassuring himself that the woman he truly loved was really all right. 'Honey, we have so much to discuss but…first things first.' He pointed to where BJ and the rescue crews were heading down towards them.

'You two go on home. Check on Lorelai and my grand-daughter,' BJ told them. 'I'll finish up here.' He clapped Edward on the shoulder. 'Thanks for telling Lore to go home. She's stubborn is my girl but she's always listened to you. You're a good man, Edward. Your parents would have been incredibly proud of you, just as I am, son.'

'He's right, you know,' Honey said an hour later, fresh from her shower, as she walked into the garden Edward's mother had loved and tended for years. Edward stood there, in the middle, just looking as the sun bounced off the different-coloured flowers and leaves. When they'd arrived back in Oodnaminaby, they'd checked in on Lorelai and Hannah, pleased when Woody had informed them that both were sleeping. Woody had offered to stay at Lorelai's for the night to monitor her. Relieved from being on Hannah duty, Hamilton had headed off to sport practice.

'Who's right?' Edward asked, pondering her question.

'BJ.' Honey slid her arms around Edward's waist, delighted when he held her close. 'Your parents would have been so proud of the man you are. The way you love and care about everyone, the way you have a calm authority that puts people at ease and gets the job done.'

'I'm just sorry they never got to meet you. My mother would have loved you.'

'Really? Most people find me a little…too flamboyant for their liking.'

'My mother loved things of beauty.'

Honey nodded. 'This garden is testimony to that.'

Edward looked down at her. '*You're* a woman of beauty, my Honeysuckle.' He breathed in deeply. 'I love your special scent, that sweet yet earthy spice that surrounds you.' He bent and kissed her left cheek. 'I love your laugh.' He kissed her right cheek. 'I love your sparkling, expressive eyes.' He kissed her eyelids closed, Honey gasping with sensual delight, her lips parting as her heart rate increased.

'I love your teasing, your verve for life, your essence.' He pressed kisses along her forehead. 'I love your smile and your plump, addictive mouth.' He brushed his lips across hers.

Honey wasn't sure she could deal with the wild pounding of her heart against her ribs, the blood thrumming through her ears with each word he spoke, with each caress he bestowed upon her as though she was the most precious person in the world.

'I love you, my Honeysuckle Lilly-Pilly.' And this time, when he claimed her lips, he deepened the kiss, letting her feel just how true his words were. A while later he pulled back and spread butterfly kisses over her face, before burrowing into her long, glorious neck, which had so often tantalised him. Now he was free to kiss her skin whenever he wanted, free to touch her, to gather her close and declare to the world that *this* was the woman for him.

Honey settled herself in his arms and sighed. 'Look at the sun. Almost down. Still radiant and breath-taking.'

He caressed her loose hair, delighted with the different colours sifting through his fingers as though making their own enchanting sunset. 'Yes.' He looked down into her face, his eyes alive with happiness. 'Just like you— chasing away my greys and bringing colour into my life.

Breath-taking.' He gasped as she leaned up and nipped his lower lip with her teeth. 'Literally breath-taking,' he said with a laugh, and kissed her again.

'Honey, you make me happy. I want to travel with you, I want to share new experiences with you, I want to be with you for the rest of my life. I don't care where I am or what we're doing, so long as we're doing it together.'

'And children?' Honey swallowed. 'Do you want to have children?' She held her breath, knowing this was a big question for Edward to answer. A moment later, when he didn't immediately jump in, she continued, 'I've been thinking about why you might not want to have any and, honestly, Edward, I don't think it's because you've "done your time", so to speak. I think it's because you're worried that if we have children and something happens to us, our children would be left alone—just as you were.'

'Accidents happen.' He nodded then shrugged. 'Having children means pressure and responsibility. What if something *does* happen, Honey? Then our children will be subjected to all the painful emotions I've lived with for the past eight years.'

'Then we'll do whatever we can to make it easier for them. We'll put counter-measures in place, just as your parents did.' When he frowned at her she smiled and leaned up to kiss his forehead. 'On my first day here you told me you'd had help in raising your younger brothers. Not only did you have Peter and Bart to lean on but you had BJ and Lorelai and the majority of the people in this community. Your parents provided you with the best back-up plan. They cared about you and your brothers and I'll bet they're looking down from heaven right now, incredibly proud of you.' She nodded. 'We don't have to have children straight away, Eddie. I still want to have one or two—'

'Not a whole gaggle?'

Honey smiled and shook her head. 'Seeing my parents again, talking with them, opening up has been good for me, which is probably the reason why you took me to see them. You realised, didn't you, that through my vehemence in wanting children, I was hoping to right the wrongs done to me?' She shrugged one shoulder. 'That's not a good reason to have children. We should have children because it's what we both want, deep down in our hearts. And I know, for a fact, that we will make excellent parents given we've practically raised our siblings and they've turned out pretty fantastic.'

'You don't want to have kids straight away?' he checked again.

'No. I want to have some time with just you and me. Together. Figuring out who we are as a couple. Besides, I'm young enough to wait a while. I am only seven and a quarter, you know.'

Edward's smile was bright as he leaned forward and kissed her glorious mouth.

'I love you, Edward Austin Goldmark,' she murmured against his mouth. 'I've always been looking for the place I belonged and I had hoped that Oodnaminaby might be that place…but I was wrong.'

'You were?'

'*You* are the place where I belong.'

'Home is where the heart is,' he recited, and she nodded.

'So long as we're together.'

'Together.'

'Home is where the heart is and my heart belongs to you.'

Edward nodded, then spun her from his arms but still

held onto her hand. 'Come with me. I have a present for you.'

'Really? A present?'

'I saw it on the table by the front door when we arrived back this afternoon but with the accident and all, I temporarily forgot.' She allowed him to lead her into his home, the walls feeling as though they were singing with delight. The house would once more be a home, home to two people who loved each other with all their hearts.

'Go and sit down. I'll be there in a moment.'

'Ooh.' Honey clapped her hands together, delighted excitement filling her. She did as she was told and a moment later he came into the room, stopping by the armchair she sat in, going down on bended knee in front of her. Honey's eyes grew as wide as saucers. 'Edward?'

'Honeysuckle,' he began, and took her hands in his, a long, thin rectangular box by his side. 'I saw these advertised in a medical journal and I knew I had to get one for you. It's right and I hope it shows you just how much I not only love you but appreciate you. You're a unique woman and therefore you require a unique gift.'

He picked up the box and placed it in her hands. 'Honey, I love you. I want you with me always and I hope you'll accept this as a token of my undying love.'

'Is that a proposal?' she asked.

'It is.'

'Of marriage?'

'Yes.'

'Good. Just wanted to make sure,' she said with a nervous laugh. She couldn't believe how badly her hands were trembling but it was curiosity that moved her forward. She removed the ribbon, then the paper. Finally, she lifted the lid on the box, pushed back the white tissue paper and gasped, covering her mouth with both her hands as she looked at what he'd bought her.

'Oh, Eddie.' Her eyes filled with tears. 'Really?' She looked at him and he nodded.

'Really.'

Honey looked back down at her gift, unable to believe the thin rectangular plaque that read, Dr Honeysuckle Goldmark General Practitioner and then had a list of her degrees underneath.

'You bought me a plaque of my very own. I've always wanted one.'

'I know. I remember you telling me. I've already contacted my solicitor to draw up the papers to make you an official partner in the Oodnaminaby Family Medical Practice. You belong in this town. It's your home…your home with me.'

Honey ran her fingers lovingly over the lettering before leaning forward to cup his face in her hands and kiss his gorgeous mouth. 'Honeysuckle Goldmark. I love it. This is the most *perfect* gift you could ever have given me. A place to belong. A place to call home. A place in your heart.'

'Is that you accepting my proposal?' he asked with a twinkle in his eyes.

'Yes, it is.'

'Good. Just wanted to make sure.'

With that, Edward stood and lifted the plaque from her lap before pulling her up and into his arms, kissing the woman of his dreams with all the love in his heart.

* * * * *

HEART SURGEON, HERO...HUSBAND?

BY
SUSAN CARLISLE

First published in Great Britain 2012
by Mills & Boon, an imprint of Harlequin (UK) Limited.
Harlequin (UK) Limited, Eton House, 18-24 Paradise Road,
Richmond, Surrey TW9 1SR

© Susan Carlisle 2012

ISBN: 978 0 263 89146 1

Harlequin (UK) policy is to use papers that are natural, renewable and recyclable products and made from wood grown in sustainable forests. The logging and manufacturing process conform to the legal environmental regulations of the country of origin.

Printed and bound in Spain
by Blackprint CPI, Barcelona

Dear Reader

I fell in love with Scott and Hannah long before they fell in love with each other. Their story has been with me for years, and I'm proud to share it with you. Scott and Hannah are two intelligent, well-educated and independent people, who think they need no one but soon learn that love is a bond they can't break.

Writing Scott and Hannah's story has been an emotional journey for me. In many ways their story was an easy one to tell, while in others a difficult one. I know personally what it's like to have a child waiting for a new heart. My youngest son received the life-giving gift of a heart transplant when he was one year old. He is now twenty-two and doing well.

I would be remiss in following my convictions if I didn't take this opportunity to encourage you to think about organ donation. Transplants do save lives.

I hope you enjoy reading about Scott and Hannah. I'd be honoured to hear from you. You can find me at: www.susancarlisle.us

Warmest regards

Susan

Susan Carlisle's love affair with books began when she made a bad grade in maths in the sixth grade. Not allowed to watch TV until she brought the grade up, she filled her time with books and became a voracious romance reader. She has 'keepers' on the shelf to prove it. Because she loved the genre so much, she decided to try her hand at creating her own romantic worlds. She still loves a good happily-ever-after story.

When not writing, Susan doubles as a high school substitute teacher—she has been doing this for sixteen years. She lives in Georgia, with her husband of twenty-eight years, and has four grown children. She loves castles, travelling, cross-stitching, hats, James Bond and hearing from her readers.

This is Susan's first book
for Mills & Boon® Medical™Romance

* * *

In Raina's memory

Special Thanks

To my Tuesday night critique group for steering me in the right direction each week, especially Lisa and Claudia.

To my editor, Flo Nicoll, for seeing something in my writing that showed promise and encouraging me until that something showed through. I appreciate you.

To Darcy for saying you should write this.
You were right.

To Sia for sharing your writing knowledge.
I'm better for it.

To Carol for reading, re-reading, and taking care of me.
Couldn't have done it without you.

To my mom, my husband and my kids
for being so supportive. I love you all.

CHAPTER ONE

"A HEART TRANSPLANT? My baby's only two years old."
Hannah Quinn stared at Dr. Scott McIntyre, the cardiothoracic surgeon who sat across the conference room table
from her. His familiar Mediterranean-Sea eyes were sympathetic, but his face remained somber.

The shock of seeing Scott again was only surpassed by
the pain of his words. Her son was dying.

When had she slipped down the rabbit hole to this hor-
ror at Children's General Hospital? As if that weren't tor-
ment enough, she now faced a mother's worst nightmare,
and the news was being delivered by Atlanta, Georgia's
supposedly best cardiothoracic surgeon, a man who had
hurt her badly years before.

In the movies this would have been called a twist of
fate, horrible irony. But this wasn't some screenplay, this
was her life. Her child, who always had a smile, her little
boy, who giggled when she kissed him behind his ear, was
in serious danger.

"He was doing fine. I was taking him for a scheduled
check-up. Next thing I know his pediatrician has ordered
an ambulance to bring us here." Hannah covered her
mouth, damming the primal screams that threatened to
escape. Moisture pooled in her eyes, blurring her vision
of Scott...now Jake's doctor. "You have to be wrong."

He glanced at Andrea, the heart-transplant co-ordinator, sitting beside him, before he reached across the table as if to take Hannah's hand.

"Don't." She straightened. He withdrew.

That night eight years ago had started with a simple brush of his hand. She couldn't go there, wouldn't go there again, or she'd fall apart. She had to hold it together until her world righted itself. And it would, it had to. "I knew that a valve replacement might be in his future sooner than I had hoped, but a heart transplant? Your diagnosis can't be correct."

Scott ran a hand through his wavy hair. The soft, silky locks had gone from light to golden blond with age. His fingers threaded through his hair again, a mannerism Hannah remembered from when they'd been friends, good friends. They'd shared warm banter when he'd come to work on the step-down floor. The banter between them had developed into a friendship she'd valued, and had thought he had too.

Leaning forward, he brought her attention back to why they were sitting in this tiny, barren room, acting as if they'd never known each other intimately.

"I'm sorry, Hannah," he murmured with compassion. His voice strengthened with the words, "But the diagnosis *is* correct. The condition is called cardiomyopathy."

"Isn't that when the heart has become enlarged?" Hannah asked.

"Yes, it is. In Jake's case, he must have contracted a virus that went undetected. It settled on the valve he has had from birth—the one that wasn't working correctly. His heart is inflamed and is no longer pumping efficiently."

"He's had nothing more than a little runny nose. I assure you that if it had been more, I would've taken him to see a doctor."

"I'm not questioning your care for your son. The virus may have looked like something as simple as a cold, but it attacked his heart, damaging it. Sometimes it takes weeks to manifest itself and sometimes, like in Jake's case, only days or hours. There is no way to know how or when it will happen. But you would know that, being a nurse."

"Most of my work experience has been on an adult orthopedic floor and, anyway, I'm not nursing at present."

His head canted questioningly, but he said, "Still, you should understand the only thing we can do for your son—"

"His name is Jake." The words came out frosted. She wouldn't allow Jake to become a hospital number, just another patient in a bed.

Scott's gaze met hers. "Jake needs a new heart." His voice softened. "He needs to be listed right away."

Could she melt into the floor? Disappear? Maybe run so fast reality couldn't catch her?

"There has to be another way. Isn't there medication you can give him? I want a second opinion."

The skin around Scott lips tightened. He shook his head slightly, forestalling any further argument. "Hannah, you're welcome to get a second opinion. But we can't waste any time. Jake will die without the transplant. He might only have a few more weeks. The first thing we'll do is see that he is put on the United Network for Organ Sharing list."

She wiped away the dampness on her cheek. The framed pictures of the smiling children lining the walls of the tiny room mocked her. Her child should be one of them. Instead, he lay in a bed in the cardiac ICU, fighting for his life.

"I've examined Jake. He's stable for now. We're giving him anti-clotting drugs to prevent blood clots, which are common with cardiomyopathy, and watching for any arrhythmia."

Her eyes widened. "Blood clots! Arrhythmia!" She leaned toward him, hands gripping the edge of the table. "I want Jake listed now."

"Before we can do that, you'll need to have a psychological exam."

Her dazed look met his. "You have to be kidding. Jake is dying and you want me to have a psychological test? There's nothing wrong with me. It's your job to get Jake a heart, not see if my head's on straight."

Scott shifted in his chair, one of his long green scrubs-covered legs bumping against the table support. Despite being terrified by what he was telling her, Hannah couldn't help but compare the man in front of her with the one she had once known. A tall man years ago, his shoulders had broadened since she'd last seen him. Cute, in an all-American way then, now he was handsome as a man with power. Maturity and responsibility had added fine lines to his face, which she bet only made him more appealing to the nurses.

Scott still possessed the air of confidence that had made him the shining star of his medical class and the desire of the female personnel in the hospital. She, fortunately, had managed to remain immune to his playboy-to-the-core charm for a while, but not long enough.

"You need to calm down. Take a couple of deep breaths."

"Don't patronize me, Scott."

"Look, the visit to the psychologist is protocol. You'll be asked questions to make sure you understand what's involved with a transplant. The care afterwards is as important as the transplant itself. We need to know you can handle it."

She pushed back in her chair and crossed her arms over

her chest. "I assure you I can take care of my son, both as a mother *and* as a nurse."

Propping his elbows on the table, Scott clasped his hands and used his index fingers to punctuate his words. "Hannah, I don't doubt it and I understand your frustration, but there are procedures."

At least he sounded as if he cared how she felt, unlike how he had acted years ago. Known for his excellent bedside manner then, in more ways than one, she'd never dreamed she'd ever be on the receiving end of his professional conduct.

"I have no interest in your procedures. I'm only interested in Jake getting well."

"If you really want that, you're going to have to work with me to see that it happens." His words had a razor-sharp edge, leaving her no room to argue.

"Okay then, I'm ready to do the interview." Hannah looked him directly in the eyes. "How much is all of this going to cost?"

He returned the same unwavering look. "Let's not worry about that. Keeping Jake healthy enough for the surgery is my primary concern."

Scott addressed Andrea. "Can you see that everything is set up for Han—uh...Mrs. Quinn's psychological?"

"I'll take care of it," Andrea responded.

Pushing the metal chair back, Scott stood. "I'll speak to you again soon. I'm sorry this is happening to your son." He hesitated as if he wanted to say something further but thought better of it.

Wishing this situation would just go away, she gave Scott a tight smile.

"Andrea also has some forms that need to be filled out, so I'll leave you with her."

With that, Scott made a swift exit. She shouldn't be surprised he'd showed no more emotion. He'd done much the same thing the next morning after she'd made the mistake of succumbing to his charms. Their friendship had died, and so had her faith in him. Hannah let her brain shut down, and answered Andrea's questions by rote. When Andrea had finished, Hannah asked, "How good a surgeon is Scott, I mean Dr. McIntyre?"

"He's the best," Andrea stated, her voice full of assurance.

Was she just another woman who had fallen under Scott's spell and could sing nothing but his praises? "I can't let Jake die."

"Mrs. Quinn." Andrea placed her hand on Hannah's arm. "Dr. McIntyre is a brilliant surgeon. He'll take excellent care of your son. You can trust him."

Andrea guided Hannah to the waiting room and to an area away from the other parents. Hannah sank onto a blue vinyl sofa and put her head in her hands, letting pent-up tears flow. She understood what she'd been told, but she wasn't entirely convinced. Hannah couldn't afford to be blindly accepting where her son's care was concerned. He was all she had.

Hannah studied the blue square pattern of the carpet. She had no idea that Andrea had sat down beside her until she laid a comforting hand on Hannah's shoulder.

Andrea said, "You'll get through this. Why don't you go back and see Jake? Visiting hours will be over soon."

Entering the cardiac unit, Hannah checked in with the clerk at the large circular desk situated in the middle of an enormous open room. Of the twenty or so beds around the wall, only one interested her, the third one on the left, where her little boy lay so still.

Her precious child looked small and pale stretched out

on the white sheet of the big bed. Wires ran from him to the surrounding machines. She'd seen this before, during nursing training, but this time it was *her* child lying there.

It's just you and me, honey. Don't leave me. Jake's usually sparkling blue eyes were clouded with fear as they pleaded for reassurance. Hannah took his tiny hand in hers, careful not to touch any of the IV lines. Her chest tightened. She placed a kiss on his forehead before stroking his dark baby curls while making a soft cooing sound that settled him.

"Mrs. Quinn?" A young woman stepped to the foot of the bed. I'll be Jake's nurse for today. You may come back to visit any time during the day but you need to call first and get permission."

What if something happens while I'm not here? Could I live with myself if it did? Would I want to? Her hands shook, and her stomach jumped. Wrapping her arms around her waist, she squeezed. "Can I stay with him tonight?"

She sensed instead of saw Scott step beside her.

"I'm afraid not." His words would've been harsh except they were said in such a low, gentle tone that they came out sounding compassionate, regretful.

"I don't see why not. I'm a nurse."

"But as Jake's mother you need to take care of yourself. Rest. Leave a number with the nurse and she'll call if you're needed." He gave Jake's nurse an appreciative smile.

The fresh-out-of-nursing-school girl blinked twice before she said in a syrupy tone, "I'll put it on his chart, Dr. McIntyre."

"I don't see—" Hannah began.

"Those are the rules. You have to be out of here by seven and can't come back in until eight in the morning," Scott said in a flat, authoritative tone.

"I guess I don't have a choice, then."

"No, you don't." Scott's words came out even and to the point.

Enunciating the numbers to her cellphone with care, Hannah watched to make sure each one was written correctly. The way the nurse was acting around Scott, she might make a mistake.

As Hannah gave the last digit Scott approached his patient's bed. "Hello, Jake. I'm Dr. McIntyre. You can call me Dr. Mac."

Jake didn't look at Scott's face, but focused instead on his chest, reaching his hand out.

Hannah moved around the bed to stand opposite Scott to see what Jake was so engrossed in.

"Oh, I see you found my friend." Scott smiled down at Jake. "His name is Bear. He rides around with me. Would you like to hold him?"

Jake's eyes lost their look of fear as they remained riveted on the tiny animal. His fingers wiggled in an effort to reach the toy.

Unclipping the toy from his stethoscope, Scott offered it to Jake.

Scott's charm obviously extended to his young patients. Jake didn't always take to new people but Scott had managed to make her son grin despite the ugliness of the place. Hannah sighed. Scott looked up and gave her a reassuring smile. She didn't like the stream of warmth that flowed through her cold body. Still, a kind, familiar face in her life was reassuring right now, even if it was Scott's.

"My bear hasn't been well. Could he stay with you?" Jake gave Scott a weak nod before Scott handed Jake the bear. "I need to listen to your heart now. I'm going to put this little thing on you and the other end in my ears, okay?"

Small creases of concentration formed between Scott's

eyes as he moved the instrument across Jake's outwardly perfect chest. She'd always admired Scott's strong, capable hands. The same ones that were caring for her child had skimmed across her body with equal skill and confidence. She shivered. Those memories should've been long buried, covered over with bitter disappointment.

She'd been around enough doctors to recognize one secure in his abilities. Scott seemed to have stepped into the role of pediatric surgeon with no effort. He certainly knew what to do to keep Jake from being scared, at least she'd give him that much. Maybe she could put her hope in him professionally, if not emotionally. She wanted to trust him. Desperately wanted to.

Jake's eyelids drooped but he continued to clutch the toy.

Scott removed the earpieces, looping the stethoscope around his neck.

"Scott, thanks for giving Jake the bear. He looked so afraid before. I still can't believe he needs a heart transplant," she said in little more than a whisper that held all the agony she felt. "He doesn't look that sick."

She prayed his next words would contradict the truth she saw on his face.

"I realize that by looking at him it's hard to believe, but it is the truth."

Hannah's knees shook. With swift agility, Scott circled the bed, his fingers wrapping her waist, steadying her.

She jerked away. The warmth of his touch radiated through her.

As if conscious of the nurse nearby, he dropped his hand to his side.

"I'm fine." For a second she'd wanted to lean against him, to take the support he offered.

Hannah peered at him. Had hurt filled his eyes before

they'd turned businesslike again? The unexpected look had come and gone with the flicker of his lids. Had she really seen it? Could she trust herself to interpret his looks correctly?

"You need to understand a heart transplant isn't a fix. It's exchanging one set of problems for another. Jake will always be on meds and have to come to the hospital for regular check-ups."

"I understand that. I'll take care of him."

Scott placed a reassuring hand on her shoulder.

"Don't touch me."

He dropped his hand. "Hannah, I know this is rough. But we were friends at one time. Please let me help."

"Look, Scott, the only help I need from you is to get Jake a heart."

"Hannah, we're going to get Jake through this."

"I hope so. My son's life depends on you." She couldn't afford for him to be wrong, the stakes were much too high.

"Hannah, with a heart transplant Jake can live."

Like before? Would he still squeal when she blew on his belly? Would he giggle when she blew bubbles and they burst above his head? Her sweet, loving child was dying in front of her eyes.

Scott was saying all the right things, but could she believe him? "It's not your kid, so you really don't have any idea how hard this is, do you?"

The muscle in his jaw jumped, before he said, "No, I guess I don't. But I do know I'm a skilled surgeon and this is an excellent hospital with outstanding staff. We can help Jake and we will."

"I'm counting on that."

In his office, using the time between surgeries, Scott waded through the stack of papers cluttering his desk. He leaned back in his chair. Hannah's face with those expressive green eyes slipped into his mind for the hundredth—or was it the thousandth?—time in the last few hours. She'd looked just as shocked to see him as he'd been to see her. It had required all his concentration to stay focused on what they had been discussing.

He couldn't have been more astonished to find a red-eyed Hannah looking at him expectantly as he'd entered the conference room. Andrea normally arrived ahead of him but she'd had to answer a page. He'd stepped into the room, and back through time.

Hannah's hushed whisper of his name had made him want to hug her. But she'd made it clear she'd never allow him. Guilt washed over him. Of course she didn't want his comfort. He'd hurt her, and for that he was sorry, but he'd believed it was for the best.

He'd wanted her desperately that night eight years ago, and she'd come to him so sweet and willingly, trust filling her eyes. If he could have stopped, he would have, but, heaven help him, he hadn't been able to. He'd handled things poorly the next morning. She had been too young, in her second year of nursing school. He had been an intern with a career plan that wouldn't allow him to be distracted. He'd refused to lead her on, have her make plans around him. He hadn't been ready to commit then, and he wouldn't commit now.

Andrea had entered before he'd let his emotions get out of control. Regret had washed over him, for not only what he had to tell Hannah but for what life would be like with a sick child and for their lost friendship.

Based on her reaction today, he'd killed whatever had been between them. She'd not been cool to him, she'd been dead-of-winter-in-Alaska cold toward him. Compared to the way she used to treat everyone when they'd worked together, almost hostile.

Not the type of woman that made men do a double-take, Hannah still had an innate appeal about her. He'd known it back then and, even while telling her the devastating news of her son, that connection between them was still there.

Speaking to any parent about their deathly ill child was difficult. Sending a child home with smiling parents after a life-giving transplant made it all worthwhile. Scott's intention was to put such a smile of happiness on Hannah's face.

Scott shook his head as if to dislodge Hannah from his mind. He let his chair drop forward, and picked up an envelope off the stack of mail on his desk. The familiar sunshine emblem of the Medical Hospital for Children in Dallas, Texas, stood out in the return spot. A surge of anticipation filled him as he opened it. Was this the news he'd been hoping for?

A quick tap came at the door and Andrea entered.

The statuesque, older nurse had worked with way too many young surgeons to be overly impressed by him when he'd arrived at Children's General. Still, she'd had pity on him and had taken him under her wing, helping him when he'd needed to navigate the ins and outs of hospital politics. They had become fast friends.

"Is that the news you've been looking for?" Andrea indicated the letter.

He'd been talking to the administrator at MHC for months about starting a heart-transplant program there. He opened the flap and pulled out the letter. "Not quite. They're still looking at other candidates. They'll let me know of their decision soon."

"You're still top man on their list, aren't you?" Andrea asked.

"Yeah, but they want to review a few more of my cases." He'd geared his entire career toward this opportunity. To set up his own program, train a team, and make the program in Dallas the best in the country.

"Don't worry, boss. I'm sure they're impressed with your skills."

With years of experience as an OR nurse, Andrea didn't look like she had a soft touch, but she had a talent for making parents feel comfortable. That was a gift he valued. Appreciative of the skills she brought to her job, Scott intended to persuade her to become a part of his new team in Dallas if he was offered the position.

"Thanks for the vote of confidence."

"I've got the latest blood work on the Quinn kid. You wanted it ASAP."

Scott took the lab sheet and studied it. "We shouldn't have a problem listing him right away."

"None that I can think of." With a purse of her lips and a glint of questioning in her eye, Andrea said, "I know I came into the meeting late, but I've never known you to call a parent by their first name. So I'm assuming you two know each other."

"Yes, we met while I was in med school, just before I left for my surgical training." Meeting her look, he refused to give any more information.

Andrea raised her brows. "Oh. Interesting spot you're in, Doc. She didn't sound particularly happy to see you again. History coming back to bite you?"

Few others would've gotten away with such an insubordinate question.

At his huff, she grinned and slipped back out the door.

Scott might have found some absurd humor in the situation if it wasn't such a serious one, and if he hadn't been so afraid that Andrea was right.

Hannah was the one nurse that had mattered, too much. The one that had gotten under his skin, making him wish for more. He'd pushed her away because she'd deserved better than he'd been able to give. He still couldn't believe Hannah had re-entered his life and, of all things, as the mother of one of his patients. Life took funny bends and turns and this had to be one of the most bizarre he'd ever experienced.

But it didn't matter what their relationship had been or was now. What mattered was that her son got his second chance at life.

Hannah made her way to the snack machine area on the bottom floor during the afternoon shift change. She was sitting in a booth, dunking her bag in the steaming water, when Scott walked up.

Her breath caught. He was still the most handsome man she'd ever known. His strong jaw line and generous mouth gave him a youthful appearance that contrasted sharply with the experienced surgeon he surely was. There was nothing old or distinguished about him, not even a gray hair to indicate his age.

He still wore the Kelly-green scrubs covered by a pristine white lab coat, which meant he'd been in surgery. She couldn't see the writing on the left side of his coat, but she knew what was printed above the pocket.

Embroidered in navy was "Scott T. McIntyre, MD" and under that was "Department of Thoracic Surgery." Reading those words over and over during their meeting had been her attempt to disconnect from the surreal turn her life had taken. She'd almost reached across the small table and traced the letters with a finger. He'd gotten what he'd wanted. She couldn't help but be proud for him.

Scott stepped to the coffee-dispensing machine and dug

into his pocket. Pulling his hand out, he looked at his open palm, muttered something under his breath and spilled the coins back into his pants.

"Here." She offered him some quarters in her outstretched hand.

Blinking in surprise, he turned. "Hey. I didn't see you sitting there."

"I know. You were miles away."

With a wry smile, he accepted the change. His fingertips tickled the soft skin of her palm as he took the money.

A zip of electricity ran up her arm. It was a familiar, pleasant feeling, one that her body remembered. But her mind said not to. She put her hand under the table, rubbing it against her jeans-clad leg in an effort to ease the sensation.

Scott purchased his coffee then glanced at her, as if unsure what to do next. She couldn't remember seeing him anything but confident. He appeared as off-kilter as she.

He hesitated. "Do you mind if I join you?"

"You know, Scott, I'm not really up to rehashing the past right now."

"I really think we should talk."

Hannah took a second to respond. Could she take any more emotional upheaval especially when she'd just started believing she could breathe again after their last meeting?

Her "Okay" came out sounding unwelcoming.

One of his long legs brushed her knee as he slid into the booth. That electric charge sparked again. She drew her legs deeper into the space beneath the table.

"I've just seen the psychologist. Is Jake listed?" Hannah asked into the tense silence hovering between them.

"I put him on a few minutes ago." Scott's tone implied it was no big deal, an everyday occurrence, which it might be for her. For her, it was a major event.

She breathed a sigh of relief.

Scott sipped his coffee, before setting the paper cup on the table. He looked at her. "I have to ask: where is Mr. Quinn?"

"That's not really your business, is it?"

"Yes, and no. If he's going to be coming into the hospital and making parental demands and disrupting Jake's care, yes, it is. For the other, I'm just curious."

"There's no worries where he's concerned." Her look bored into his. "He left us."

Scott's flinch was barely discernible. "When?"

"Just after Jake was born."

"You've no family?"

"None nearby. My sister is living in California now. I told her to hold off coming. I don't know how long we'll have to wait on a heart."

His sympathetic regard made her look away. "There's no one that can be here with you?"

"No. When you're a single parent with a small child, relatively new to town and you have to work, it leaves little time to make friends."

"I understand. Doctors' hours are much the same way."

"As I remember it, you didn't have any trouble making time for a social life." She softened the dig with a wry curl of her lips.

He chuckled. That low, rough sound vibrated around them and through her.

She took a sip of her tea.

Scott drained his cup before looking at her again. "Uh, Hannah, about us..."

"There *is* no us."

"You know what I mean. You have to admit this situation is unusual at best."

She placed her cup on the table. "Scott, the only thing

I'm interested in is Jake getting a new heart. Whatever we had or didn't have was over and done with years ago. You're Jake's heart surgeon. That's our only relationship." She probably sounded bitter, but she didn't have the energy to deal with her emotions where he was concerned. Particularly not today. She needed time to think, to sort through her feelings. Scott twisted his coffee cup around, making a tapping noise on the table.

"Hannah, I shouldn't have left like I did. I thought I was doing the best thing for you. I was wrong not to tell you I was leaving town."

She put up her hands. "Let's just concentrate on Jake. I don't have the energy to rehash the past."

He gave a resigned nod, but she didn't think the subject permanently closed.

"Then would you at least tell me why you're not nursing?"

"I took a leave of absence when Jake started getting sicker. I didn't think he needed to be in a day-care situation, and I couldn't find private care close enough to home to make it work."

"That's understandable. I thought you had quit altogether. I remember how much you enjoyed it. What a good nurse you were…are."

"Yeah, I still love it. I'll get back to it when Jake's better."

He'd made no attempt to be a part of her life in the last eight years, and now he was interested in her personal life? Picking up a napkin on the table, she wadded it into a ball.

Hoping to avoid further questions, she asked, "How about you? Where did you go…uh…for your surgery residency?" She'd almost said "after you left me alone in bed. Without saying a word."

He pulled his legs out from under the table, extended them across the floor, and crossed one ankle over the other.

"Texas, then to Boston for a while. I took a position here a couple of years ago."

"You always said you wanted to be a heart surgeon. You didn't change your mind."

"No. After hearing my first baby's irregular heartbeat during my cardio rotation I've been set on it. It took me years to qualify, but it was the right move." His gaze met hers. "But it meant making some tough decisions."

"So, is there a Mrs. McIntyre and any little McIntyres?"

Hannah held her breath, waiting for his answer. A part of her wished he'd found no one special, while another part wanted him to be happy.

"There's no Mrs. McIntyre or children."

Hannah released the breath she'd held. Why'd she feel such a sense of relief? "Why's that?"

"A surgeon's life doesn't lend itself to a peaceful private life. Somehow my patients always take precedence over anything or anyone else."

A dark shadow crossed his face that she didn't quite comprehend. Had he almost married? What had happened?

"As the mother of one of your patients I'm grateful you make them a priority. I believe that would be a part of being a great doctor. " She took a sip of tea. "So, are you still seeing a nurse on every floor and in every department?" The question had a sting to it that she couldn't help but add.

He chuckled. "You don't have a very high opinion of me, do you?"

Hannah chose to let that question remain unanswered. "Did you know that the joke in the nurses' station was that, when you had rotated to our floor, you'd asked for an

alphabetical listing of all the single nurses and were working your way through the list?"

"I did not."

"What? Know or ask for the list? Because you sure as
heck worked your way through the staff. I watched you.
With the last name of Watson, I had time to see you coming." Heavens, she'd gotten what she'd deserved. She'd
seen for herself what a player he had been.

"Yeah, and you refused to play along. That was one of
the many things I liked about you. You made me work to
get your attention."

"I wasn't interested in being another nurse you scratched
off your list."

Scott's hand covered his heart. "Ouch, that hurt."

She grinned. "That might have been too harsh."

He smiled, oozing Dr. McDreamy charm. "Same
Hannah. You never cut me any slack. But as it turns out,
believe it or not, being a surgeon doesn't leave me as much
free time as being a med student did. As for an answer, I
hope I've grown up some."

"I know I have. I understand things I didn't use to."
Like how it felt to be drawn to the bright fire that was his
charisma and get burnt. He was speaking as if they'd
shared nothing more than a casual meal all those years
ago, instead of a friendship that had ended with a night
filled with passion. She had repeated the same mistake
with Jake's dad.

"I'm sorry, Hannah, for everything." His beeper went
off, demanding his attention. "I have to see about this.
Thanks for the coffee." He picked up his cup, crushed it
and pitched it into the nearest trash can.

Scott moved down the hall as if he was a man in command, a man on a mission. He'd been intense and focused
as a medical student. That didn't seem to have changed,

but he also had the ability to laugh and smile effortlessly, which drew people to him.

Taking a deep breath, she slowly released it. She needed to think. Put things in some order in her mind.

Jake. Heart transplant. Waiting. Cost. Die. Scott. The words ping-ponged off the walls of her mind.

CHAPTER TWO

SCOTT peered over the unit desk toward Hannah, who sat at her son's bed. Her head had fallen to one side against the back cushion of the chair. Even with the burden of worry showing on her features, she caught and held his attention. Her chestnut-colored hair brushed the tops of her shoulders and hung forward, curtaining one cheek. If he'd been standing closer, he would've pushed it back.

Puffy eyes and stricken looks were so much a part of his profession that he had become impervious to them, but telling Hannah about Jake's heart condition had been the toughest thing he'd ever done. She was no longer the impressionable nursing student he'd once known. Hannah was now a mother warrior fighting for her child. He believed her strength and spirit would see her through.

She'd made it clear that their only association would be a professional one. He could be there for her as a friend, for old times' sake. The only sensible choice was to keep their relationship a professional one. Being involved with a parent on a personal level was a huge ethical no-no anyway. Lawyers didn't represent family members, and surgeons didn't treat loved ones, or, in his case, family.

Hannah shifted in the chair and shoved her tresses out of her face. She looked tired, worn and dejected. She stirred, causing her hair to fall further across her face. With effort,

Scott resisted the urge to go to her, take her in his arms and whisper that everything would be all right. She'd always brought out the protective side of him. She'd never believe it but he'd left her that morning all those years ago in order to protect her. Even then medicine had been his all-consuming focus. He'd gotten that trait from his father.

As a small-town doctor, his father had been on call day and night. Scott had watched him leave the supper table numerous times to see a sick child after eating only one forkful of food. More than once Scott had heard him return to the house in the early hours of the morning after seeing a patient. Their family had even returned early from a vacation because an elderly woman his father had been treating had taken a turn for the worse and was asking for him. Scott had never once heard his father complain. All Scott had ever wanted was to be like his father. He had thought he was the finest doctor he'd ever known.

Hannah woke with a start, blinking fast. Daylight had turned to darkness outside the window but the fluorescent lighting made it bright in the room. She straightened.

"Mommy."

She hopped up and went to Jake's bedside.

"Hi, sweetheart. We both had a little nap." She brushed his hair back from his forehead. "How you doing?" She kissed him.

The nurse pushed medicine into the port of the IV located at the side of Jake's tiny wrist. Giving the IV set-up a critical look, Hannah realized old habits did die hard. She still wished she could take a more active role in Jake's care. As long as he was in CICU she had to remain on the sideline.

"Would you like to hold him for a while?" the nurse

asked as she punched buttons on the IV pump and it responded with small beeps.

Moisture filled her eyes. "Could I, please?"

"Sure. You have a seat in the chair and I'll help you get him situated."

After a little maneuvering of IV lines and moving of machines, Hannah had Jake in her arms. It was pure heaven.

"Go home," Jake mumbled as he settled against her.

"I wish we could, but hopefully you won't be here long."

She looked over Jake's head at the nurse as he played with his toy bear.

The nurse spoke softly, "You know, Mrs. Quinn, I've seen some very sick kids come through here who are doing great after having a transplant."

The words reassured Hannah somewhat. At least she was getting to hold him. That more than satisfied her for the time being.

"If you don't mind, while he's sitting with you I'm going to step over to the next bed and help another nurse with her patient. Will you be okay?"

"Sure." Hannah's gaze shifted to Jake again. He looked like a small cherub. His lips were getting bluer, though. She had to admit Scott was right. Jake needed a heart. *Soon.*

She put her cheek against Jake's. "I love you."

"I luv 'oo."

Moisture filled her eyes. *Loving...was...hard.*

Her head jerked up at the sharp insistent beeps of the monitor that turned into an alarm. Staff rushed into Jake's cubicle. Scott came with them. "Hannah, let me have Jake." Scott took Jake from her and laid him on the bed, all the while issuing orders.

Hannah stepped to the bed. Her hands gripped the

rail. "What's wrong?" she whispered, fear coiling in her middle.

Scott looked at her as he listened to Jake's chest. "Hannah, you need to leave." His authoritarian tone told her he'd accept no argument. His attention immediately returned to Jake.

She was a nurse, Jake was her son. *She could help.*

But as much as she wanted to stay, Hannah knew he was right. She'd been involved in enough emergencies to know that the fewer people around the bed the better. If she wasn't allowed to assist then she would be in the way. Slowly, she stepped back.

Scott's gaze caught hers. "I'll be out to talk to you when Jake is stable."

Hannah walked toward the doors but took one final look over her shoulder as she left the unit. Jake's bed was no longer visible because of the number of people surrounding it.

Finding one of the small conference rooms off the hallway empty and dark, she stepped inside, not bothering with the light. Her eyes ached from the dry air and the bright lights. She dropped onto one of the chairs situated as far from the door as possible.

Unable to control her anguish any longer, Hannah's dam broke and her soft crying turned into sobs.

Now that Jake was resting comfortably, Scott needed to find Hannah. He paused in the hall.

What was that sound? There it was again. It was coming from the consultation room. He stepped closer to the entrance. Dark inside, no one should be in there. Was that someone crying?

He couldn't ignore it. In a hospital it wasn't unusual

to hear crying, but this sounded like someone in physical pain.

With tentative steps, he entered the room. "Hello?"

A muffled sob filled the space.

"Are you okay?"

"I'm fine. Please go away." The words were little more than a whisper coming from the corner, followed by a sniff.

Even when it was full of sorrow, he recognized her voice. *Hannah*. The stricken look on her face when he'd ordered her to leave still troubled him. He'd been surprised she hadn't put up more of a fight.

"Hannah?"

A whimper answered, then a muffled "Please leave" came from the corner. Moving into the room, he gave his eyes time to adjust to the dim light spilling in from the hallway. Scott had seen patients in pain, but her agony reached deep within him. Hearing Hannah sobbing knocked the breath out of him. It was killing him to stand behind professionally closed doors where she was concerned.

But if he did open that metaphorical door, would he be able to step through? Could he help her? Did he have the right to get involved so deeply in her life? What he did know with unshaking certainty was that he couldn't walk away. He couldn't make the same mistake twice. The consequences could be too great.

Coming toward her, Scott lowered his voice. "It's Scott. Hannah, honey, Jake is fine. He had a reaction to the new med. He's all right now."

Her head rose enough that he could see her eyes over the ridge of her arm. The rest of her face remained covered.

"Go. Away." The words were sharp and wrapped in pure misery. She turned her back to him and lowered her head again. "I don't need you."

Those words stung. Scott touched her and she flinched. He removed his hand. It wounded him that she wouldn't accept his help. Was she really that untrusting of him? "He's resting now, really."

Scott sank into the chair beside hers. He'd dealt with parents besieged by strong feelings. It was part of his job, but Hannah's pain reached deep to a spot he kept closed off. A place he shouldn't go with the parent of a patient, especially not with her. Somewhere he wasn't comfortable or confident in going.

Then again, his failure to recognize how distressed his mother had been when his parents had divorced had had disastrous results. He'd promised himself then to never let that happen again to someone he cared about. He wasn't leaving Hannah, no matter what she said or how she acted. Her obvious pain went too deep to dismiss.

Hannah made a slight shift in her seat toward him, then said in a hard voice, "I don't—want you here. Go away and leave me alone."

She was in so much pain she was contradicting herself. He could resist a lot, but Hannah's pain brought down the final wall. He had to do something, at least try.

A feeling of inadequacy washed over him. What could he say to make it better? Could he help her? Scott placed a hand on her shoulder, feeling the inflexible muscles. As if she were a troubled child, he began moving his hand in comforting circles along her back.

"Scott, stop." She twisted her shoulders back and forth, but he refused to let her have her way. He may not have the correct words or be able to change the situation but he could hold her, be there to comfort her.

"Hannah, I'm not leaving."

She stilled.

"Look, you're a fighter. And if Jake is anything like you, he is too."

He wrapped an arm around her shoulders and pulled her to him. She stiffened and pushed against his chest. "Let me help you get through this." His grip tightened and he tucked her head under his chin. Holding her as close as the chairs would allow, he said in a tender voice, "Let me be your friend. You need someone."

She remained rigid, but he refused to ease his hold. Taking several halting breaths, she gave up the battle and relaxed against him.

Hannah's distress was difficult to witness. He didn't flinch when he opened a child's chest or when making life-and-death decisions but he couldn't stand seeing Hannah in so much pain. He wanted to make it go away, make it his own.

"Why won't you leave me alone?" she murmured against his chest.

"You need to be held, and I'm going to do that. Cry all you want. I'll be right here when you're ready to talk."

Having her in his arms went beyond wonderful, even with her crying and heartbroken. It felt right. He'd not only stepped over the invisible don't-get-personally-involved line, he'd jumped. But he'd see to it remained one friend comforting another. He wouldn't, couldn't, let it become personal.

Holding her firmly against him, he made calm reassuring noises that made little sense. With his voice low, he spoke to her as if she were a hurt animal. After a few minutes she quieted. Pure satisfaction coursed through him like brandy on a cold night.

He placed a fleeting kiss to her forehead, which smelt like fresh apples. She still used the same shampoo. With his cheek resting against her hair, he took a deep breath, letting her scent fill him.

Neither spoke. Her breathing gradually became even and regular. The sensation of her body pressed against his made his thoughts travel back to what could have been. Was he taking advantage of her vulnerability? Yeah, but he still couldn't resist resting his lips against her skin again.

Scott comprehended for the first time in his life what it meant to want to carry someone else's burden. He longed to take Hannah's hurt away. Fix her problems. Yet he could never be her knight. His duty to others would always be pulling him off the horse.

With a sigh of resignation, she completely relaxed against his chest. She had to be drained in both body and mind.

Having Hannah in his arms brought back memories of that night. Even then he couldn't help but touch her, hold her. Now she needed to be held, desperately, and he was afraid that he needed the contact just as much. Everything about Hannah pushed his common sense away.

Heavens. She was being held by Scott.

"Better?" he asked.

In a quick movement Hannah straightened and shifted back into her chair. She should've never let him touch her. Mercy, it had felt wonderful. She was so tired of being alone, carrying the load for Jake's care. At least with Scott she had a partner until the transplant was done.

Under Scott's scrutiny, she refused to meet his gaze. "I've never fallen apart like that before," she muttered.

"Are you positive you're okay?" He sounded as unsure as she felt.

"I'm better now," she said, though her words lacked confidence. "You can go."

"Have you eaten today?"

Why wouldn't he leave her alone? She closed her eyes, then lifted them, looking through her lashes. "If I answer you, will you leave?" She didn't want to have a reason to start caring for him again.

Scott said nothing but gave her a hard look.

"Okay, I had a bowl of cereal this morning. I was going to eat during shift change…" she sighed "…but I just wasn't hungry. Satisfied?" Where was the ever ever-present sound of his pager going off when she needed it?

He shook his head. "You're one of the most intelligent women I know so I expected better from you. What did I tell you about taking care of yourself?"

"I heard you."

"But you don't plan to follow orders." Cynicism wrapped his words.

She straightened her shoulders. "I don't have to follow your orders. You're Jake's doctor, not mine." At his chuckle, she realized he'd baited her on purpose to make her show some kind of animation.

"That might be, but if you'd followed my orders…" He cocked his head to the side in question.

"It must feel good to be a know-it-all."

"It does have its advantages. Let's go get a bite to eat."

"Us?"

"Yeah, us. I eat too. I certainly can't trust you to see to feeding yourself. Anyway, I like to share a meal with someone when I can. I eat too many dinners alone."

"That's hard to believe. You can't find a nurse to eat with?" She'd never known him to have trouble getting dinner dates. Had he really changed that much?

"I did. You."

She huffed. "You know what I mean."

"I do, but I'm pretending I don't. Come on. Keep me company."

"I don't really want to go, but you're not going to give up until I agree, are you?"

He grinned and shook his head.

She'd consider it payment for him giving her a shoulder to cry on. And she was just too tired, too scared and too emotionally drained to fight him off. Besides, having one meal with Scott wouldn't change anything between them.

After a long moment she nodded her agreement. "But I'm going to check on Jake first."

"I never thought any different." He took her elbow and helped her stand. The pad of his thumb skimmed across the bare skin of her forearm. She shivered and stepped away.

Tugging at the hem of her pink T-shirt, she said, "I'm fine now."

He remained close as they moved toward the door. Her head seemed to be on straight again, but having Scott so near was making her nerves fire in double time.

What was happening? She'd given up acting like a schoolgirl long ago. Given up on him. She hadn't needed anyone in a long time, but she'd fallen apart in Scott's arms. Hannah shook her head to remove lingering feelings of being cherished while in Scott's embrace. Years ago he'd acted as if he cared, and she'd been crushed. She wouldn't let it happen again.

Jake was sitting up in the bed, playing with the toy that Scott had given him, when they walked into his cubicle.

"Mommy." He reached his hand over the rail of his bed.

She took his little hand in hers and placed a quick kiss on the top of it. "Hi, sweetie."

"Hello, Jake," Scott said, as he move around to the other side of the bed from Hannah. "While you're talking to your mom, I'm going to give you a little check. It won't hurt, I promise."

Scott slipped two fingers around Jake's wrist, feeling for his pulse before he stepped to the end of the bed. Pulling the blanket back, Scott placed the tips of two fingers on the top of Jake's foot to check his *dorsalis pedis* pulse.

At Scott's finger skimmed Jake's skin, her little boy jerked his foot away.

Scott looked up at Jake and smiled. "Do you like to be tickled?"

Jake nodded.

Cupping Jake's heel, Scott ran a finger down the bottom of Jake's foot. Her son laughed. Scott's low rumble of mirth joined Jake's.

Hannah couldn't help but smile. Her heart lightened. For the first time all day she believed Jake might get well.

Her laugh drew both males' attention as if they'd forgotten she was even there.

The overhead lights dimmed.

"It's time for your mom and me to let you sleep," Scott said to Jake as he pulled the blanket back over the tiny foot.

Hannah squeezed Jake's hand and kissed him on the forehead. "I love you, honey."

Scott nodded to a nurse standing behind her, who she'd not noticed until then. The nurse inserted a needle into Jake's IV port and emptied the syringe's contents.

"That should help him sleep," Scott said as he came to stand beside Hannah. "He'll have a comfortable night, so don't worry."

"Yeah, that's easier said than done." Hannah watched Jake's eyelids droop. When she felt his hand go limp, she placed it on the bed. Pulling the blue hospital blanket up, she tucked Jake in.

The urge to scoop Jake up and take him home to his own bed had never been stronger.

"Come, Hannah," Scott said in a sympathetic voice. "It's time to see about yourself. You need to eat."

As they waited for the elevator to go down to the cafeteria, Scott kept glancing at her. He'd been wonderful with Jake, but he was making her nervous now. Did Scott think she was going to fall into his bed again just because he'd made her son giggle?

She curled her hands together and intertwined her fingers again.

As close as they'd been at one time, they were little more than strangers now. She'd changed, was a mother now, and had been a wife. Maybe Scott had changed too. Relief flowed through her as the elevator doors slid open. Hannah stepped in and stood in a corner. She was glad that Scott chose to stand on the opposite side.

The jerk of the elevator as they dropped to the bottom floor made her grab the rail on the wall.

Scott moved nearer. "Are you okay?"

"Yes."

His gaze met hers then moved to her lips and lingered.

Her mouth went hot-summer dry. Her head spun. Had someone turned off the air-conditioning?

The elevator stopped and the doors slid open. Scott's eyes lifted. A smoldering look filled them. Hannah blinked. Gathering her wits, she slipped by him. As she exited, his warm breath ruffled her hair against her cheek.

He followed. "Let's go to the cafeteria instead of the snack machines. Wednesday is fried chicken day, the best thing they make."

Scott spoke as if the intense moment in the elevator had never occurred. Had having her back in his life affected him at all? Perhaps it hadn't.

"I think I'll just have a BLT and a cup of hot tea," Hannah said.

"I'm going for the chicken. Find us a table. Tell Lucy at the register that I'll pay for yours when I come through."

"I won't let you do that," she said as she stepped toward the grill line. "This isn't a date."

He held up his hand and grinned. "Okay, okay."

His boyish smile made her feel like she was sitting in the sun on a spring day, pure bliss. Her heart fluttered. He still had that devastating effect on her.

Don't stare. *Think*.

Hannah forced herself to turn around and go to the sandwich line. The mundane business of selecting a sandwich and the physical distance from Scott helped to settle her nerves. She'd moved into the register line when Scott came up behind her. Bending down, he said, "I'm getting yours."

He was too close. She was too conscious of him. He paid before she could form a protest.

Outside the high arched windows a slow, steady rain began to fall. The water on the concrete walk shimmered in the glow from the security light. The weather reflected her life. Dark, with hints of brightness.

Moving toward the dining area, she selected a table in the center of the room, if only to put a physical object between them as a way to regain her equilibrium. Scott glanced at an available booth and shrugged. His mouth lifted into the beginning of a grin before he took the chair opposite hers.

Hannah concentrated on keeping the bacon between the pieces of toast while Scott ate his fried chicken. It amazed her that after the heated moments earlier they could still manage a comfortable silence between them.

They'd slipped back into that easy place they'd enjoyed when he'd been in medical school.

Cleaning his plate, Scott sat back with a sigh, giving her a quizzical look. "Feel better now you've had some food?"

Her heart skipped a beat. He'd caught her staring. "Yes, much. But I do insist on paying for my meal."

"I owed you for coffee. Anyway, can't two old friends eat together without fighting over the bill?"

"We're just acquaintances." She fiddled with her glass a second before pinning him with a look. "True friends don't leave without saying a word."

His lips formed a tight line before he said, "Hannah, I realize you're still angry with me and I don't blame you."

She opened her mouth to speak.

"No, please hear me out. I know you don't want to go into the past. I appreciate that. You're having a rough time and I'd like to help if you'll let me." He laid a hand over hers, blanketing it.

Her heart thumped faster. She didn't know how to force her body to be sensible where Scott was concerned.

It would be nice to have someone to lean on. It was tempting to accept his offer, for at least a little while, until she could right her world long enough to think straight. But could Scott be that person, with their past looming between them?

And he was Jake's doctor.

"I guess we can try." They'd been friends before, maybe they could be again. She was just too exhausted in spirit and mind to argue. "But you'll have to earn my friendship and that will be *all* there is between us. Friendship." She tugged her hand from beneath his.

The stiffness in his body eased and, with a gentle smile, he said, "I understand."

With one finger, Hannah circled the salt shaker sitting in the middle of the table. She rolled it from side to side. The base of the glass knocked against the wood.

Scott took the shaker, setting it aside. "I wish I could make the situation with Jake easier for you."

"I appreciate that." She gave him a weary smile. "I hate not being able to help care for him. I am his mother and a nurse."

Scott opened his mouth to speak, but she forestalled him.

"I know. Protocol. I understand it, but don't like it."

He laughed softly. "And I understand where you're coming from. I know that right now it seems like all you're doing is sitting around, watching and waiting, but once Jake goes to the floor I promise you there'll be plenty to do. Plenty to learn."

"I hope I don't sound too whiny. I've been Jake's sole parent for so long it's hard to relinquish control. I understand why I'm not allowed to do more but that doesn't mean my heart accepts it."

He nodded. "So, do you plan to return to the same position when Jake recovers, or do you want to work elsewhere? Maybe a satellite clinic?"

Hannah leaned back against the chair, pulling her lower lip between her teeth. "I hadn't thought about doing that. Working at a clinic isn't a bad idea. The hours are better, and it may be easier to arrange care for Jake if I did." She sat up again, crossing her arms and leaned on the table. "Have I satisfied all your questions?"

"No, but I'll save some for another time." Downing the rest of his drink, he asked, "Are you ready to go? I've an early morning and you've had a hard day. We both need to get to bed."

At her surprised look he realized what he'd said. "I'm sorry, that didn't come out right."

She laughed. "I knew what you meant. Scott, I'm not holding a grudge against you. I got over what happened between us a long time ago. That's water down the river."

His blue gaze bored into hers and he said softly, "I wish that wasn't true."

Hannah swallowed. Her words weren't completely honest but she didn't want him to know that. Truthfully, their night still hung between them, but now wasn't the time to get into it.

As they left their trays on the cleaning rack Hannah said, "Thank you for the meal. It hit the spot." She looked up at him. "Even with the questions."

"You're welcome. I'd like to make one more start toward earning your friendship by seeing that you get home safely. I'll get someone to take you home. You don't need to be driving, but I'm on call and can't leave."

"There's no need."

"You're worn out. You need to go home."

"I'm staying here."

Scott leaned forward. She could see the lines around his eyes, indicating he'd smiled a lot through the years. Probably at all the women he'd seduced. She'd do well to remember that.

"Hannah," he said earnestly, "you need to rest, which you won't do here. Wouldn't you like to sleep in your own bed? Pick up some clean clothes? Take a hot shower?"

He'd known what would get to her. A shower sounded heavenly.

After sighing deeply, she said, "I'll go. For tonight."

"I know you'd like to see Jake one more time before you leave. I'll call up and let Jake's nurse know you're coming. While you're gone I'll arrange your transportation and meet you in the lobby."

Hannah made her way through the maze of corridors back to CICU. At a set of automatic doors she spoke into the monitor on the wall and requested entrance into the unit. She'd never been more acutely aware of hospital rules. It was her son in there, and she had to ask permission to see him. As a nurse, she'd never realized how much control she'd had over a patient's life.

At Jake's bed, she whispered goodnight to her sleeping child and gave him a kiss.

Her baby…needed…a heart. If not…

She refused to let that thought catch hold.

Scott stood at one side of the lobby, talking on his phone, when Hannah approached a few minutes later. As if he sensed her arrival, he turned and looked at her. He ended the conversation and started forward.

Watching him saunter down the long corridor of the hospital used to be a favorite pastime of hers. She still found it absorbing.

As he approached, he smiled. "Your carriage is waiting."

Taking her elbow, he ushered her out the sliding glass doors at the front of the hospital. Waiting beside one of the hospital's vans was a security guard.

"Hannah, this is Oscar. He's going to be escorting you home."

The large, toothy man smiled. "Nice to meet you, Ms. Hannah. Climb in." Oscar opened the door nearest her then went around to the driver's side.

"I thought I was taking a taxi."

"Hush and appreciate the ride. Oscar believes he owes

me a favor, so this is my way of letting him think he's paying me back."

"I'm grateful for the ride, but I don't understand why you're going to so much trouble."

"Let's just say I need to do it for me more than you. This way everyone wins." Scott helped her into the van. "You get a safe ride home with someone I trust, and Oscar gets to feel good about what he's doing. I'll see you tomorrow. I'll keep an eye on Jake and let you know if you're needed. Trust me."

Trust him? She'd trusted him one time with her affection and her body. He'd disappointed her. Could she trust him with Jake's life?

Oscar returned to her house early the next morning to bring her back to the hospital. He informed her that Dr. Mac expected it. Hannah agreed to the service, not wanting to hurt the sweet man's feelings.

At the hospital, she killed time in the waiting area until she could visit Jake. Her heart skipped when she saw Scott. She stepped toward him, pushing panic away, and asked, "Has something happened to Jake?"

His hand cupped her shoulder. "He's fine. I've spent most of the night in the unit, so I've been close by. He was sleeping when I left. You can go back to see him just as soon as shift change is over."

Hannah released an audible breath.

Scott held out a box of donuts. "I was hoping to find you. I thought you might like these. The 'Hot' sign was on."

"Did you go out especially to get these?"

"Yeah, but the bakery is just a few miles away. I promised the nurses I'd bring them some today. And I remember how crazy you were about them."

Hannah took the box. "You are really going above and beyond the call of duty on this being-a-friend thing." She looked up at him. "I really can use one right now. Ah, and they're still warm. Thanks for remembering." She brought the box up to her nose and inhaled deeply.

"I remember everything about you." He smiled, as a pensive look came over his face.

Heat rushed to her cheeks and she avoided his gaze. She didn't want to be sucked in by his charisma again, but he was making it awfully difficult not to be. "I thought you could use a blast of sugar to keep you going today. I've got a couple of minutes before I have to be in surgery. How about sharing those..." he nodded his head toward the box of donuts "...and a cup of coffee with me?"

"Sure, the parents' lounge has a coffee machine and a table and chairs. How about we go there?"

"Sounds great." He grinned.

It was still early enough in the day that they had the lounge to themselves. Scott's bulk filled the small area, making her conscious of how large a man he was, his scent reminding her of being outdoors after a rainstorm.

He sat at the small table after her. Hannah placed the box of donuts in front of him, and grinned as he struggled to work his long legs under the table. He gave up and stretched them out in front of him.

Sharing an intimate breakfast with Scott was something she'd expected to do that morning after they'd made such passionate love. By a twist of fate, instead she was sharing a meal with him years later in a pitifully utilitarian room of a hospital with nothing more than tentative friendship between them. She forced the emerging hurt to one side.

She crossed to the automatic coffee machine and poured two cups of coffee.

"You don't have to pay?"

"No, this is here for the parents." She smiled. "Maybe they'd let you get a cup here the next time you're out of change and I'm not around."

A disquieted look came over his face for a second, and then he said, "That's a thought. I'm going to remember this place."

Placing their cups on the table along with some napkins, Hannah took a chair at the table. She really looked at Scott for the first time that morning. Absorbed his appearance. He looked incredible, even after a night with little sleep. He'd always been intriguing, larger than life, and that hadn't changed. If anything, he'd become more appealing.

Dressed in jeans that had seen better days and a yellow snug-fitting T-shirt with "Come Paddle with Me" printed in bright red letters across his chest, Scott looked nothing like the white-coated doctor she knew him to be. His hair was a crowd of unruly waves, with a lock falling over his forehead.

Did he still spend his days off kayaking and rafting? He'd loved the water and adventure when he'd been in school. After rounds, he had sometimes come by the nurses' station and told her a funny story about something that had happened on one of his trips down the river. She'd always looked forward to those stories, because he'd shared them with such flair, making her wish she could go with him some time.

"You're not dressed like you're going to work. More like you're going to the river."

Somehow the thought that he might not be around for the rest of the day bothered her. What if Jake needed him?

His soft laugh filled the room. "These are my spare clothes. I keep them in a locker for nights like last night. Nothing was wrong with Jake."

Relief filled her. He wasn't going anywhere.

"You must be getting plenty of time in down the river because you haven't changed much in the last eight years."

"Why, thank you for noticing." He dipped his head in acknowledgement. "I don't kayak as much as I'd like but that's where I usually spend my days off."

"I see your ego is still in good shape."

"It isn't as large as you might think," he said softly.

Had something happened that had damaged his confidence? "Was your night so difficult that you didn't go home?"

"Not bad, just constant."

From his causal demeanor, she would have never guessed he'd spent the night at the hospital.

"We got a new patient."

It made her chest tighten to think how the parents of the child must be feeling. Had it just been yesterday morning that she'd been in the same spot?

Scott opened the green and white box containing the donuts and pushed it toward her. "Ladies first."

Hannah picked out one sugary ring. She took a healthy bite and shoved the box toward him.

"You know what I've been doing for the last few years— how about you?" He picked out a chocolate-covered one.

Hannah didn't want to talk about the last few years. The future was what she was interested in, one where Jake was better and at home. She'd tell Scott the bare facts to satisfy him, and hope he'd leave the subject alone.

"Well, since we worked together I received my MBA in nursing, got married, got pregnant, got divorced and moved to Atlanta after getting a job at Fulton Medical. And here I am." She raised her hands in the air in a dramatic pose.

That sounded like a well-rehearsed litany of events, even to her ears.

"Have you tried to contact his father since Jake was listed? I'd want to know if my son needed a transplant."

"No." The word came out jagged and tart.

"Why?"

Yes, why? Why wouldn't he leave it alone? "He wouldn't be interested." She couldn't conceal her bitterness.

"Why not?"

Hannah took her time finishing the bite of donut she'd just taken before she said, "He left us." She paused. "I shouldn't have married him to begin with. I think I just fell in love with the idea of being married. For him, I think his mother thought I could settle him down. By the time I realized we had no business being married, I was pregnant. Turns out I didn't have to leave him. He packed his bags and was gone. I found out later he already had someone else by then."

Scott's harsh, crude words filled the space between them.

"I couldn't agree with you more. He wasn't too sure about having children to begin with and when Jake was born with a heart problem he couldn't get past the idea that his child wasn't perfect. His answer was to run." She made it sound like she was giving a statement to a newspaper reporter. Just the facts. "Anyway, I have Jake, and he's the best thing that has ever happened to me. He's my life. All I've got. I won't lose him too."

"We'll do our best to get Jake out of here soon."

"I sure hope so." She picked out another donut. Her eyes closed in delight as she took the first bite out of it.

"Like these, do ya?" The words were filled with Scott's mirth.

She opened her eyes and nodded as she licked the sticky sweetness from her upper lip, and began to flick away the grains of sugar that had fallen on her chest.

Scott's laughter stopped as his eyes followed her movements.

An uncharacteristic warmth settled over her. The fine hairs at the nape of her neck stood as straight as corn on her granddaddy's farm. She tried to concentrate on what she was doing. Seconds ticked by.

His gaze rose and locked with hers, held.

Scott's pupils had widened and darkened, giving him the intent look of a predator. Suddenly, the light button-down top she wore seemed heavy and hot against her skin.

Mercy, she was in over her head. He could still do it to her. She placed her donut on a napkin and stood. "Um, I think I need some cream for my coffee. Can I get you some?"

She needed to move away from him, get out of the room, but she had to pass Scott to do so. His intense look still clung to her.

"It hurts you don't remember I take my coffee black," he said in the indulgent voice of a man who knew she was trying to escape and why.

Hannah moved to step over his legs at the same time he drew them in. Her feet tangled with his. Falling, her head landed on his chest. The quaking of Scott's low rumble of amusement only added to her frustration, compounded by the molten heat she felt from being against him.

A zing of awareness zipped through her. It was happening again, just like it had all those years ago. Despite her embarrassment, Hannah longed to stay. She struggled not to show a response to the continued emotional assault, but she had to stop this now. If she didn't, it would end no differently than it had last time. With heartache—hers. Pushing against Scott's muscular thighs, she made an ineffectual effort to stand.

"Hannah, stop struggling and I'll help you up."

The words reverberated pleasantly beneath her ear. She stilled. He gripped her shoulders, pushing her away until she found her footing.

"Thanks," she murmured.

Scott stood, maintaining eye contact. "My pleasure. I rather like having you sprawled across me." As he closed the bottom button of his lab coat he said, "I'd better go check on a patient."

The nuance of his words and the heat of his touch lingered well after he'd disappeared down the hall.

CHAPTER THREE

WATCHING the clock, Hannah called to see if she could see Jake the second the minute hand clicked to eight. The clerk said she could come in, but she would have to stay at least thirty minutes because Scott was doing a procedure on a patient and couldn't be interrupted.

The automated doors swooshed opened when Hannah pushed the silver entry button on the wall. She went straight to Jake's cubicle. He was still asleep. Hannah placed a kiss on his forehead and the nurse told her that he'd had a good night.

She wanted to believe that a heart would be available soon. Scott had spoken with such confidence that one would be found. For her own sanity, she was desperate to trust him. Searching for something positive to cling to, Scott's optimism was all she had. Yet Hannah wasn't ready to believe him without question. If she lost Jake...

Dropping into the chair next to Jake's bed, she looked out into the unit. From her vantage point, she had a direct view of Scott.

He'd changed into scrubs. Holding a mask in his latex-covered hand, he said to the nurse beside him, "Has she been given meds?"

"The morphine and Pavulon are on board," the young nurse responded.

Donning the mask with the nurse's help, Scott gave calm orders in a crisp tone that generated an instant response.

Hannah was impressed by the way he managed the situation, but not surprised. Scott demanded attention out of respect, without being dogmatic. Being witness to how he remained cool in a literal life-and-death situation reassured her. The staff followed his lead.

These attributes were priceless in the operating room. No wonder she'd heard such glowing reports about his abilities. A surgeon had to have the respect of the people who worked with him.

Scott raised the edge of the dressing covering the child's open chest. "Patch."

The nurse at his right handed him the six-by-six white bandage. He placed it over the incision.

Despite her lingering cynicism, Hannah appreciated Scott's efficient but tender manipulations as he worked with the infant child. She'd always admired the way he'd had a gentle touch for his patients and had gone to great lengths to make them feel comfortable.

Scott had done the same with Jake and herself. He'd been nothing but caring and helpful towards them both.

Over his shoulder, Scott spoke to the clerk behind the desk. "Call OR. Tell them we're coming down in fifteen." He turned back to the nurse. "Thanks for the help."

The nurse nodded and smiled.

Scott stepped away from the bed, pulled off the mask and gloves, then removed his gown with minimal effort, before tossing them into a basket. The actions were automatic. Hannah found the ordinary spellbinding when Scott was involved. It was like watching a thoroughbred horse go through his paces. She couldn't help but be riveted.

Going to the row of sinks on the wall, he scrubbed before moving to another patient's bed, where he spoke to a nurse. When he was finished, he approached Hannah.

She stood and asked in a hushed voice, "Is the baby going to be all right?" As irrational as the thought pattern was, when another child wasn't doing well, Hannah felt like it might rub off on Jake. As if heart problems were contagious.

"Yes, she should be fine with time. How's Jake doing?"

"Sleeping peacefully, but I think he may be breathing heavier."

"Let me have a listen."

Hannah watched as he examined Jake.

When Scott had finished he turned to her. "He may be having a little more difficulty. I'll have the nurse keep a closer eye on him."

Scott flipped the stethoscope around his neck and took her by the elbow, leading her away from Jake's bed to a corner of the room where they couldn't be easily seen.

His look sobered, telling her he was debating whether or not to say something.

"What's wrong? You're scaring me."

"I wasn't sure if I should tell you, but I had a call about a possible heart for Jake a few minutes ago."

Hannah grabbed his arm and squeezed. "You did?" It was the first time she'd voluntarily touched him. Scott just wished it had been for another reason.

He wanted to reassure her, make her understand. "Yes, but it wasn't good enough. I had to turn it down."

Disappointment, disbelief, and fear all showed in her eyes before anger pushed them away. Her fingers tightened on his arm, biting into his skin. "What? You can't do that." She glanced around as if she were caged and looking for a way out.

Scott hated having to telling her. He'd anticipated this

reaction. Unable to wrap his arms around her, he took her hand. "It'll be fine." Softening his voice as if to calm a scared animal, he added, "I want the best heart we can get for Jake. The right one will come."

He believed that, but wanted her to accept it as truth. To have faith in him again.

She pulled her hand away, clasped her hands together and looked straight ahead. "I hope you're right."

The sharpness of her voice cut him.

"Hannah, I can't imagine how hard this must be." His fingers wrapped her forearm, unable to keep from touching her. "I'll take good care of Jake. I'll get him the right heart. Trust me."

"Dr. McIntyre," the clerk called.

Scott let his hand drop and stepped away from Hannah.

"Dr. Stevens would like to speak to you and the OR called to say they're ready," the clerk finished, giving them a speculative look.

Scott regretted the interruption. "Please tell Dr. Stevens I'll call him as soon as possible and let the OR know I'll be down in a few minutes." He shocked himself. He'd never said anything but, "I'll be right there."

Hannah needed him and neither of the other issues was an emergency.

"Hannah, please sit down." She eased into a chair, and he pulled a rolling stool up close.

He unclasped her hands, taking one and smoothing her fingers out across his palm. Lowering his voice, he said, "The perfect heart for Jake will come. You just have to believe that. He's stable for now. We have to wait on the right one."

"I know. I understand. I just don't like it."

He ran a finger along her jaw, making her look at him. "That's my Hannah, tough when you have to be. I hate to leave you but I have to go. I have a patient waiting in surgery."

"I know. I understand. That little baby needs you. I'll be fine."

Guilt gnawed at him for having to leave her when she needed him but he had no choice. When duty called he would always go.

Scott entered the large open area of the waiting room and stopped. The nurse had said the parents were here. He wished he could delegate this job to someone else, but that wasn't the way he worked, or would let himself work. Despite feeling inadequate, it was still his responsibility to talk to the mother and father of his little patient.

He'd let his mother down when she'd needed him, and he wouldn't do the same with the parents of any of his patients. Sometimes he wondered if his struggle to speak to the family was his penance for failing his mother so miserably. Was it his way of atoning for past mistakes, to involve himself so totally with his patients?

The surgery on the girl had been more difficult than anticipated but the medical whys and wherefores wouldn't mean anything to the girl's parents. They were only interested in him fixing the problem and making sure their daughter went home with them. It wasn't, unfortunately, that simple.

He understood their fears, sympathized with them, sometimes to his own emotional detriment. Caring so profoundly made him a sought-after surgeon but it left nothing to give to others. He'd heard that complaint on more than one occasion from a woman.

Scott searched the area again. He scanned past a person, and came back. *Hannah.* He'd not seen her since earlier that morning.

His gaze met hers. She sat up ridgcd in her chair. *She thinks I've come to give her bad news.*

Summing his most reassuring smile, he watched as the tension drained from her like a rubber band being released. Her chest rose as she took a deep breath and let it out slowly. She met him halfway across the room.

"Jake's fine. I just checked on him. He was even sitting up and playing with his bear."

"Thank goodness." Hannah gave him a weak smile. "From the look on your face, something is wrong. Are you okay?"

"I should be asking you that."

"I'm all right. Just don't be turning down too many hearts."

"I won't, I promise."

"So what's putting that frown on your face?" Her hand made contact with his forearm for a second.

The simple gesture calmed him, giving him confidence. Telling him it was all right to care. "How did you know?"

"I've always been able to tell when you were upset."

"Yeah, you were good at that. You were the one nurse who was willing to go with me when I talked to parents."

"Thankfully, that didn't happen too often."

Scott glanced around the room and found the couple he'd been looking for in the far corner. "I've got to speak to those parents."

As he turned to leave, Hannah touched his arm again. "You're better at talking to parents than you think. The truth is always hard to take, but they'll want to know it and will appreciate you giving them honesty."

"Thanks." Hannah's words were gratifying, making what was coming seem less daunting. She made him believe he was up to the task.

He'd always cared too much for his own good about his patients, unable to keep a professional distance like other physicians. It became more of an issue after his mother's overdose. The next morning in the hospital she'd made some ugly accusations about him. When she'd shouted that he'd abandoned her for his own patients, just like his father had, and she didn't need Scott any more either, he'd felt like he'd been slapped.

He'd seen that she received the care and services she needed and became absorbed in his work. Their relationship still wasn't what it should be. He wished for more but it was difficult to put the unpleasant words she'd thrown behind him completely. If he had a question about his ability to manage a high-pressure career and a solid relationship, after that morning he'd known beyond a shadow of a doubt he couldn't. Even his own mom wanted little to do with him after he had disappointed her.

But he refused to disappoint his little patients' families. Squaring his shoulders, Scott made an effort to look less like a man bearing bad news and walked toward the girl's parents. Hannah watched Scott approach the couple. They stood, but he waved them down before he sat. He raked his hand through his hair, leaving a wavy lock hanging across his forehead, adding to his vulnerable look.

Elbows on knees, Scott leaned forward, occasionally raising a hand to punctuate a point. He maintained eye contact with the mother and spoke in a low tone. One filled with compassion, she was sure. She'd heard the caring there when he'd told her Jake needed a heart.

He appeared confident, but she knew better. In the past, they'd talked a number of times about how difficult it was for him to speak with parents. She'd tried to reassure him, telling him that feeling so deeply for the patients and their families was part of who he was and what made him a good doctor.

The mother's shoulders jerked up and down and Scott

reached out and touched her. She turned to her husband, and he took her in his arms.

Hannah's sympathy went out to the three. Scott looked like he was the one that needed a friend. She was tempted to go over and take Scott's hand, be his moral support.

She'd had a taste of his bedside manner when he'd held her. Based on what she'd learned about him during their reacquaintance, he wouldn't be a doctor who didn't tell it like it was, even if he had bad news. He'd always felt more deeply than he let on. They'd talked about different patients' problems in the past. Hannah had been able to tell by the tone of Scott's voice when he'd taken a patient's issues more to heart than he should have. Not being able to heal every person had worried him more than it had the other interns.

Scott was a soft touch with a hard outer covering, and was careful not to let that gooier side show. If he appeared weak, then the patient would feed off that. Their will to get better would be diminished and Scott wouldn't allow that. She'd often wondered if he was so cavalier in his personal life because he was trying to compensate for how deeply he cared for his patients.

He might have been, maybe still was—despite his implied remarks in the negative—a playboy but he'd always had a kind heart. She wasn't sure why he had treated her the way he had. Had she done something wrong to make him leave that morning? Only looking back on it, that really hadn't been like him.

Scott rose and spoke to the mother again. The woman nodded. Scott didn't even look in Hannah's direction as he left. He hurt for the parents, and that about Scott hadn't changed.

He'd comforted her yesterday. Today she wanted to run after him, reassure him. Maybe she'd been too hard on him? He'd been a great friend before and he seemed to be trying hard to be one again.

Who did Scott go to when he needed to talk through his problems?

Maybe she could at least make an effort to meet him halfway. She could use a friend right now, a shoulder to lean on. Could he also use one?

Hannah remained in the waiting room a while longer before going to visit Jake. It was quiet in CICU but she noticed two nurses and one of the interns standing beside the bed of a patient. It must be the child Scott was concerned about.

The parents had to be terrified.

She found her usual chair and settled in. Already she'd slipped into a hospital routine. The hours of waiting dragged by and the sky darkened as the sun set. The only thrill in the day was when she got to hold Jake for a short while. She craved the closeness of having him in her arms. Even now she missed his little body nestling next to hers.

Jake's nurse pulled Hannah out of her staring stupor with the statement, "I need to change Jake's IV. It's not flushing as it should."

Light-headed when she stood up, Hannah shook it off and moved to the bedside opposite the nurse. Hannah watched as the nurse removed the old IV port and began inserting a needle into a vein near Jake's wrist. Bright red blood dripped from the port onto the bed before the nurse could cap it off.

Hannah's stomach rolled like a wave hitting the shore. She'd witnessed IV ports being placed hundreds of times, done them herself more often than she could count, yet this was her son's blood.

Come on, Hannah. Keep it together.

She gripped the bedrail.

This is nuts. I'm an experienced nurse.

Closing her eyes, her head spun. Her body swayed. Opening her eyes wide, she focused on a spot on the white wall and took a gulp of air. Her grip on the rail became painful. The whirling worsened.

Her world went black.

Was that a hand pushing her hair off her forehead? There it was again. Opening her eyes a slit, Hannah could only make out a tiled ceiling. There was also a hard bed beneath her. Where was she? How had she gotten here?

Fainted. She'd fainted. She couldn't believe it.

A scraping noise of metal chair legs being moved across the floor caught her attention. Turning her head towards the sound, she saw a pair of khaki-covered legs.

Her gaze lifted past sprawled legs, to the hem of a white pressed cotton lab coat with an unfastened bottom button. Her eyes followed the row of secured buttons to the open neck of a light blue shirt that looked familiar, over a square chin covered in enough evening shadow to be TV sexy, to full lips where a faint smile rested below a Roman nose and arresting eyes. They peered at her with a mixture of frank concern, humor, and maybe...longing.

Scott.

Could she be more embarrassed? Putting her hands over her face, she said between her fingers in a strangled voice, "Oh, no."

"Are you all right?"

"I'm fine. Just mortified." She groaned. "I've never fainted before in my life."

His soft chuckle would've made her knees go weak again if she'd been standing. He propped an elbow on a knee and put his chin in his hand, bringing his face closer. His eyes twinkled. "It's okay. Don't worry about it. We see it in the unit pretty often."

She shook her head in denial. "But I'm a nurse. It shouldn't be a problem for me!"

After a tap at the door, an aide entered with a soft drink can in one hand and a glass of ice in the other. Scott took both, setting them on a table.

"Is there anything else I can get or do?" She glanced at Hannah with concern.

"Thanks, Susie. No, I think Mrs. Quinn's going to be fine."

The aide left, closing the door behind her.

Hannah moved to sit up. Scott put a hand on her shoulder in gentle deterrence. The heat of his hand seeped through her cotton top like the sun on a hot day. That comforting warmth was becoming addictive.

"You need to stay put a few more minutes. We don't want you to fall and hurt yourself."

Resigned, Hannah settled back. "Where am I?"

"In the on-call attending's sleep room." Scott stretched back in the chair, extended his legs and folded his arms across his chest. He acted as if he was in no hurry to leave.

"How'd I get here?" Hannah murmured.

He gave her a cheeky grin. "I carried you."

"You did?" She hid her face. She hated the thought of facing the people in CICU after that show.

"Yeah. I was coming through the doors when I saw your knees buckle. I managed to catch you before you hit the floor."

"Th-thanks," she stammered.

"I wish I could say I've always been as aware of people's needs, but I can't. I was just lucky to be in the right place at the right time."

"Whatever it was, I appreciate it. How's Jake?"

"He's just fine. Fared much better than you. He's a tough kid."

"I guess you think I'm a complete basket case after yesterday's show and now this today."

"Truthfully, I'm impressed with how well you're holding it together. I know of others with much less stress that haven't coped nearly as well as you."

The compliment brought a glow of pleasure. Had he been thinking about an old girlfriend, friend or family member?

"Let's see if you can sit up now." He reached out and helped by supporting her back as she righted herself, though Hannah wasn't sure the physical contact wasn't putting her further off center.

"I'm fine. You don't have to baby me, even if I seem like one." She moved away from his hand.

She didn't want to contemplate her strong reaction to Scott's touch. Heaven help her, having Scott's attention was getting to her. Maybe this thing she had about him was her mind's way of helping her remain sane. Giving her something to dwell on besides Jake.

Scott stood, pushing his chair out of the way. Pouring the soft drink into the cup, he offered it to her.

Hannah looked flushed, but beneath it a healthy color had returned. Was the pink from embarrassment or because he remained so close? Maybe both?

Setting the cup on the table, she tried to stand. She plopped back on the low bed.

The next time he slid his hand around her waist as she stood. "Let's try that again, a little slower." He left her no opportunity to move away from him. "Better? Head bothering you?"

Scott sucked in a breath as the gentle heat of her body pressed against him. The yearning to lean into her grew. Under his scrutiny, Hannah looked away but, using a finger under her chin, Scott brought her focus back to him. Her moss-colored eyes had darkened, and she blinked.

Heaven help him, he wanted to kiss her. Unable to stand the tug of need any longer, he leaned towards her.

Hannah's eyes widened as his mouth lowered to hers.

Fearing she might push him away, he placed his lips lightly at the corner of her mouth, tasting, testing, and asking for her acceptance.

A hot flare of desire flashed through him. History was repeating itself, and he was incapable of stopping it.

Scott wanted Hannah as much as he had that night so many years ago. His hands shook with the depth of it. She was a soft yet demanding siren, drawing him. Her vulnerable appearance masked an iron strength he admired. He'd fought his desire once but he couldn't do it twice. His emotions drove him, his mind was no longer in control. He had to savor her once more.

Her lips parted, and he gave thanks for the opportunity. He took the invitation offered and pulled her tight against him, bringing his lips down to completely capture hers.

Seconds ticked by before her hands ran along his arms, stopping at his biceps, squeezing them slightly as if to steady herself.

She tasted of tea, lemon, and well-remembered Hannah. He felt a quake of emotion ripple through her as her fingers flexed on his arms. No longer able to hold himself in check, his desire flowed over its banks. Without constraints the kiss escalated into a crushing assault.

Hannah shivered, and Scott groaned low in his throat. This was going to get out of hand if he didn't put a stop to it. He didn't need to ruin the cautious friendship they were building again.

Hannah clung to him. Having her in his arms was a heady feeling.

He had to put a stop to the fever threatening to become wildfire out of control. Easing his mouth from hers, he tenderly brushed his lips across hers as he murmured, "What are you doing to me?"

He knew he'd missed their friendship but he'd not realized how much he'd missed touching her, having her in his arms. "I've thought a lot about kissing you since this morning," he muttered. "You make eating a donut look incredibly sexy." He glanced at the hard, narrow bed behind her. *The* question flickered in his gaze.

Hannah squirmed and he eased his hold. He watched the rapid throb of her pulse on her delicate neck.

If he asked the question out loud, would she?

Long, sizzling seconds hung between them. Scott closed his eyes then opened them again. Remorse washed over him. He'd promised friendship, she'd made her expectations clear. She was the mother of one of his patients. What he was suggesting was wrong on many levels.

Scott stepped back, releasing her. "I'm sorry. I shouldn't have done that. You had my word we'd remain just friends. I think we're both experiencing emotional overload." The words came out flat and measured. "Please, forgive me."

She smiled shakily. "You're forgiven. I think it's the least I can do for someone who brings me hot donuts."

Hannah was on her way through CICU to visit Jake for the last time that evening. She'd relived the kiss between her and Scott numerous times. She understood he was just being human, that maybe he'd needed someone after the day he'd had. As a way to let off steam. But somehow his apology for kissing her felt worse than being left in bed alone.

She couldn't be mad at him. He'd been so wonderful with Jake and had cared for her when she'd needed a shoulder to cry on. That tenderhearted person she'd known before had still been in him when he'd spoken to those parents.

As she reached Jake's cubicle a deep baritone growl filled the air. The sound was followed immediately by a roll of giggles she recognized. *What was going on?*

She stopped short at the sight of Scott sitting in a rocker with Jake in his lap. Scott held a book so Jake could see the pictures. Neither of them noticed her as she stood in the doorway.

"And the pig goes…"

"Oink, oink, oink," Jake said with a big smile. "You do."

"And the bear goes grrrr…" Scott drew the sound out.

Hannah had never expected to find Scott taking the time to read to any of his patients. She enjoyed listening to his rough voice as he read to Jake. The sight and sounds of the two of them having a good time together soothed nerves that had been piano-wire-taut.

"And the horse goes?"

"Me do, me do. Heehaw, heehaw."

Scott's deep chuckle made her feel mushy inside. He was enjoying himself as much as Jake was. Her heart softened. She ran a finger under her eye. Once again Scott had managed to push the unpleasantness of what was happening to Jake away for just a few minutes. Her son was a kid, instead of just a patient.

"More. Me do," Jake said as he helped Scott turn the page.

"Okay, how does the chicken go?" Scott said as he smiled down at Jake.

"Cluck, cluck, cluck."

"Yes, that's right. Cluck, cluck, cluck. Smart boy."

Jake clapped his hands.

Scott looked up. Hannah couldn't help but grin at his disconcerted look. He shrugged his shoulders and grinned.

She smiled back, hoping to convey her appreciation. "Hi, guys. You two sound like you've been having fun."

"Mommy." Jake lifted his arms toward her.

"Hi, sweetheart." She stepped over to take him from Scott, being careful not to get tangled up in the IV lines. She pulled the little boy close for a hug. Jake was warm from being held by Scott.

"So, have you been having a good time with Dr. Mac?" she asked against his cheek before kissing him.

Jake nodded up and down. "He funny."

She looked at Scott and grinned. "He is, is he?"

Jake bobbed his head with enthusiasm.

"I was here when the Child Life lady came by with the books and the next thing I know I'm making animals noises."

She nibbled at her boy's neck. "Jake loves to have someone read to him."

Jake yawned.

"I think you might have had too much fun," Hannah said as she moved to Jake's bed and laid him down. His eyes were already closing as she kissed him on the cheek. He had such a small energy reserve. Despite the earlier lift to her spirits they were suddenly dampened by the reminder of why he was here.

Scott came to stand beside her. "He's a wonderful kid. You've done a great job with him, Hannah."

"Thanks. I think he's pretty outstanding too." She pulled the blanket up around Jake.

She looked away from him a few seconds later when she thought she'd heard Scott say Jake's mother was pretty amazing also, but he was gone.

* * *

Scott didn't want to tell her, but he had to. Hated what he had to say. Hated to see the little boy who had such a cute personality so sick.

Some patients he connected with better than others but Jake had captured his heart. Scott wanted to say it was because he was Hannah's son but that wasn't all there was to it. Jake's willingness to be held by him, to giggle when he was around, made Scott feel taller and stronger for some reason. It made his heart swell to see the boy grin up at him.

Hannah should be waiting on him in one of the consultation rooms down the hall. He'd had the clerk call her soon after she'd left the unit, asking her to wait for him. She had to be scared to death, wondering what was wrong. He lengthened his strides.

She was pacing the room when he opened the door.

"What's wrong? Can I see Jake?"

"He's okay but—"

"But what?" Fear sharpened her voice.

"I've given orders for Jake to be put on the respirator." He stepped closer to her. "Things are under control. He just needs a little help breathing."

She took a couple of halting breaths, and let out a soft moan.

"Hannah, honey, this is just a precaution. Jake's all right." His chest clenched at seeing her upset. He'd give anything to take the burden away.

She looked up. Even in the dim light he could see the moisture glistening in her big, sad eyes.

"W-w-will he be okay?"

Hannah was struggling bravely to keep her composure. Scott took her in his arms, pulling her securely against him. A tremor went through her, and a sob escaped. He couldn't really know her fear. He wasn't Jake's father. But he could comfort her, let her know she wasn't alone. When he placed a kiss on her temple, she made a soft, incoherent sound.

"We've got everything under control," Scott whispered as he took a handful of silky hair and moved it out of her face. "The fellow is a good man. He'll take care of Jake tonight." He tipped her chin up, drawing her focus. "This is nothing more than a precaution. Jake's breathing became labored and we don't want him to wear himself out before surgery. Hannah—" his tone gained her complete attention again "—a heart will come."

"I don't know how much more of this he can take. Or I can take," she murmured.

Scott skimmed a tear from her cheek with the pad of his thumb. "You're strong. You'll get through this. Trust me, we're doing all that can be done."

She leaned into him as if she was drawing strength from him.

Scott liked having her next to him for any reason. He tightened his embrace, needing the contact almost as much as she did. He lowered his voice to soothe and comfort. "We have everything under control." He sure hoped he was telling her the truth. All that could be done was being done, but sometimes things went wrong. He ran a hand across her shoulders and down her back. "You can—*we* can—get through this together."

He desperately needed her to feed off his confidence. To believe in what he said, in him. He wanted to be her haven, someone she turned to. Hannah nuzzled her cheek against his chest. Dampness touched his skin. "I hope you're right." She shuddered against him, as if she was accepting that with him was where she should be.

Holding her close, he continued to whisper nonsense. Despite all his skill as a surgeon, there were times he still felt helpless. He wished he could prevent what Jake was going through, but that was out of his power. Hannah needed support, and he would see that she got it.

He wasn't going to make the same mistake twice with someone he cared about. He'd misread how emotionally depressed his mother had been, and he refused to take the chance of doing the same with Hannah. The first time there had been major repercussions to his inaction. He would not repeat it. He couldn't promise that he'd be there for her for ever, but the least he could do was to be here for her now.

This time he would make time. At this moment he had no doubt he was needed, and he refused not to act on it. Regret was something he wasn't prepared to live with. But there was a major difference between the two women. His mother had demanded his attention and Hannah was pushing him away.

He breathed a sigh of relief when she moved. She turned her back to him, took a deep breath and squared her shoulders. "I'm okay now." He couldn't help but admire her. She was already gathering courage, preparing to fight her fears bravely again.

"Hannah," he said softly, "I know you're going to hate this suggestion, but I think you need to stay at my place tonight."

She spun to face him. "What? I can't do that!" The words had a ring of panic to them.

"Calm down. Hear me out. It's late and you're upset. Tired."

"I don't plan to go home. I bought a bag with me this morning. I'm staying at the hospital."

"No, you're not. You need a good night's rest. You'll stay at the hospital a lot after Jake's transplant. Anyway, my place isn't far away. You can be here in no time if you're needed. You can use my extra room."

A yawn escaped her, confirming visibly how drained she was. She covered her mouth. "I'm staying here."

"I don't think so." The words were said in a firm, blunt tone. His voice softened with the next ones. "Be reasonable Hannah. If you stay at my place you can visit a few minutes before shift change tomorrow morning."

"That's blackmail."

"Yes, it is. Now, come on."

CHAPTER FOUR

Scott's condo was in a nice upscale area, but nothing over the top. Done out in beiges, tan and a touch of black, it had a masculine appearance, with the only hint of a woman's touch being two bright orange pillows on the sofa. What girlfriend had been responsible for those?

Outdoors magazines were strewn across the dark wood coffee table and the black leather sofa, and a shirt hung over a chair next to the door. The room had all the markings of bachelor living, of a person who didn't have time to waste on the small stuff in life.

She liked the place. It suited Scott.

"How about something to drink before we call it a night?" he asked as he threw his jacket on a chair and dropped her small overnight bag on the floor.

"A glass of iced tea would be nice, if you have it."

"Sure."

Scott led her to a kitchen lined with windows. It would be a perfect place to enjoy a leisurely breakfast but he probably never had time to do so. He pulled a pitcher of tea from the refrigerator and opened a cabinet. He was taking out two glasses when his cellphone rang.

"Hey, hold on a sec," he said into the phone, and then told Hannah, "I need to get this. Help yourself. I'll be right back."

"The hospital?"

"No, honey. It's one of my kayaking buddies. I'll be right back."

She had to stop overreacting every time Scott's phone rang. Relieved but with her nerves still unsteady, she began filling a glass with ice from the fridge door. As she placed the glass on the counter, it toppled and began rolling over the edge, leaving ice in its wake. She bent and fumbled with the glass, taken aback when an arm brushed her breast. A quiver like that of a bow with the arrow just released went through her. Scott clasped the glass before it shattered on the floor. Reaching around her, he put the glass back on the counter.

His body heat blanketed her from head to foot. Her body came to full attention.

She strengthened and looked at him. Their gazes met and held.

Scott's hands came to rest on her waist. Why she didn't argue, she couldn't fathom. Maybe because her mind was fuzzy, so completely filled with him. Or because she didn't want to.

He nudged her backwards, until her bottom pressed against the cabinet. Caging her in with an arm on each side, he trapped her between the hard surface of the cabinet and the equally firm plane of his body.

She should be pushing him away, but it felt good to be sharing someone's warmth. Being in Scott's arms calmed her nerves, pushed the worry away for a while.

His hands cupped her face. The slight tremor to his fingers made her understand the effort he applied to control his need. The pad of his thumbs caressed her cheeks. In a low and raspy voice he said, "I know I promised...but I can't quit thinking about this—you." He gathered her into a firm embrace before his mouth claimed hers.

Hannah made a soft sound of acceptance, and wrapped her arms around his waist. Her eyelids fluttered closed as her fingers kneaded his back. She leaned into the warm, sweet taste of his lips. The memory of how he'd made her feel years ago and the sensation of his lips on hers earlier mingled together and made this kiss even sweeter.

The pressure of his mouth intensified, taking on a sense of urgency. Excitement filled her at the thought she made Scott spin out of control. He held her so tightly it was almost painful. The demand of his lips against hers was hard and unrelenting as he thrust his tongue into her mouth. A flurry and churn like that of a rocket going off swelled within her. Caught in the spinning sensations, she met his powerful demands with those of her own, and hung on for the marvelous ride. A pleasure-filled way to escape.

After the initial combustion of their lips meeting, Scott eased the kiss into a tender caress. Soothing, sinful and sensual all at once but Hannah missed the throbbing pressure and heat. She wanted more. To replace the debilitating fear and heartache, even if only for a few minutes.

Bringing her hands to his head and spreading her fingers to run through his hair, she guided his mouth closer, opening her own. Scott took and countered with a challenge of his own. He shifted closer, making the evidence of his longing clear.

A steady hum of pleasure built upon itself until it became an unrelenting, pulsating yearning. Unaware of anything else in her world, Hannah's only reality became what Scott's lips were doing to her.

She made small purring sounds.

Scott lifted her to sit on the counter. There was a clank as the glasses tumbled along the counter behind her.

He lifted his mouth. Resting his forehead against hers

for a moment, he took a deep breath and let it out. He looked as regretful as she that they'd been interrupted.

Scott's gaze met hers. His eyes had turned a dark, velvety blue. "I think I'll pass on the iced tea and go for you." Still in a Scott-induced haze, Hannah fought hard to comprehend what he'd said. He'd twisted her thoughts around like a tornado going.

Hannah shook her head and looked away. Heaven help her, she was no more immune to his charm and desire than she had been as a young nurse. She had to clear her mind. "I think I'd better get down."

His mouth dipped towards hers. She stopped the motion with a hand on his shoulder. He didn't immediately back away but soon helped her down. She wobbled as she moved, then swayed. Scott released a low chuckle. Putting out a hand, he steadied her and with the other hand he swiped the ice cubes into the sink.

"As much as my ego would appreciate believing you're weak in the knees from my kisses only, I'm afraid some of it's because you're worn out. Come on. I'll show you where you can sleep." He kept a hand on her elbow as they moved down the hallway.

He stopped, opened a door wide and turned on the light. "I'll go get your bag. That door over there is the bathroom. Make yourself at home. You should find everything you need in there." His arm brushed her as he pointed. "My mother usually keeps extra here for when she visits."

Hannah's breath caught. She balled her fingers to keep from reaching out and touching him. If she couldn't control her growing attraction, she'd embarrass them both. They needed to be comfortable around each other, for Jake's sake.

Just friends. That's what they were. If she repeated

it enough maybe she would believe it. Despite the red-hot kiss.

Before she could do something she'd regret, he'd turned and headed toward the living room. She wanted to call him back. Beg him to kiss her again. Instead, she watched as his loose-hipped strides took him away.

Hannah sucked in a breath. *This has to stop.*

Scott looked confident and relaxed, while her insides quivered. She must've developed brain rot to have agreed to come to his place. He was too much. Heck, he made her feel too much.

Hannah stepped into the bedroom. It had the basics—bed, end table, and dresser. The navy spread and curtains were the out-of-a-package kind that could be found in any large household chain store. The room had the look of a functional but otherwise forgotten space.

Scott returned and handed her the bag.

"If you'll toss the clothes you have on into the hall, I'll throw them in the wash."

"Scott, I've needed a friend and you've gone out of your way to be a good one. I appreciate it."

He nodded. "You're welcome."

The husky thickness of his voice beckoned her. She wanted to step into his arms. Feel safe. The heat of their earlier kiss hovered, waiting to flare up again, like a spark starving for fuel.

He made no move to leave. "Hannah?"

As if he willed it, her gaze lifted to meet his.

"I'm sorry I treated you so badly back then, that you had such a lousy marriage, and that this is happening to Jake."

Hannah nodded, unable to say anything as he closed the door quietly behind him.

Going to the bed, she lay on it and covered her eyes

with an arm. Her thoughts bounced around like ping-pong balls inside a lottery machine. She was caught up in the vortex called life. Jake needed a heart and Scott's mind-numbing kisses were becoming additive. The emotional pressure of having a child waiting on a heart transplant and this, this...

She couldn't even put a name to it. A crush? An attraction? Sexual desire? Why did these emotions have to be swelling all at the same time? It would be hard enough one after another. Her feelings were all tangled. Scott and Jake. Jake and Scott.

Scott cracked the door open, allowing a dim shaft of light into Hannah's room. Had he heard her call out?

"No, no, no," she cried as she tossed, kicking at the covers.

She was having a nightmare. He hurried to her. Sitting on the edge of the bed, he gathered her into his arms. She trembled. The musky, warm smell of sleep surrounded her.

The T-shirt she wore left an exposed expanse of slim thighs. Scott stared, feeling the first stirring of arousal. He couldn't have stopped looking for the world. His eyes remained riveted to where the edge of the T-shirt barely covered her panties. He summoned the presence of mind to say in an even tone, "Hannah, wake up. You're having a nightmare."

She opened her eyes but he could see she wasn't completely focused on him. "Scared."

"I know, honey. But I'm here now."

"Stay," came out in a pleading whisper.

His heart jerked to a stop before it found its pace again. "Hold me."

Her quiet, pleading words tore at Scott's heart. He could help this time and he wouldn't let her down. He was being a friend. But they couldn't remain friends if she continued to snuggle up against him like he was her savior. It was difficult to keep her at arm's length physically as well as emotionally. His wasn't that strong. Taking a deep breath, he vowed to comfort her—nothing more.

Scott scooped her into his arms and placed her in the middle of the bed before crawling under the covers and snuggling her to him, her back against his chest. He'd never spooned with a woman before. Never stayed long enough to form a bond. Women had asked him to stay but he had always refused. His affairs had been more about physical release. Because he'd guarded his emotions so closely and refused to open up, all his relationships had slowly dissolved over time.

Hannah had already broken through one of the barriers he'd erected to distance women. He'd never experienced this kind of confusion before where a woman was concerned.

It felt good to have Hannah cloistered under the sheets alongside him as if he were fighting off her fiery dragons. She wriggled closer, then sighed deeply. Seconds later her breathing became soft and regular. He couldn't give in to his growing desire, refused to make promises he couldn't ever keep.

What would be next? Would she expect more from him? Would he be disappointed if she didn't? He wouldn't like it if she was the one pushing him away.

He'd seen the damage a job like his did to a relationship. Others managed, but it wasn't in his genes to handle it. The chance he might fail Hannah and Jake was one he wouldn't allow himself. He couldn't have two people depending on him emotionally, just medically. He refused to let the demands of his career ruin their lives, because he couldn't reset his priorities.

Still…wouldn't it be heaven to have Hannah to come home to after a long night of emergency surgery?

Pain and pleasure warred within him. There would be no more sleep for him tonight.

Hannah woke with a start. She needed to check on Jake!

Snugly tucked against warmth, she wished she didn't have to move, but she had to find her phone. Riding quickly behind that thought was the realization that Scott's arms surrounded her. The solidness of his chest resting against her cheek was a sweet contrast to the gentle hand stroking her arm. Hannah felt a tender, dewy touch at her hairline. He'd kissed her.

She'd fallen asleep in Scott's arms! Even asked him to stay with her. In her bed. There were no social guidelines for what to do when you've begged a man to join you in bed. She had to maintain her self-respect, but checking on Jake took priority.

"Hannah?" Scott asked. The warmth of his voice swept across her cheek.

"I need to call the hospital."

The mattress shifted as he rolled away and back again. He handed her the cell phone she'd left on the bedside table. "I've already checked on Jake, but I know you want to hear for yourself."

Hannah punched the speed-dial number for the hospital. The phone rang.

Her heart beat in double time. Scott's arms no longer encompassed her, but he remained close enough that she could still feel his heat. She almost broke into hysterical laugher. How many mothers of transplant patients slept with the surgeon?

The nurse assured Hannah Jake was doing fine.

Had the nurse noticed how fast and shallow she was breathing?

Hannah disconnected the call, keeping her back to him.

"Are you all right?" Scott asked. "Jake is fine?" She could tell he'd moved out of touching distance.

"Yeah."

"Look at me," he said, sternly enough that she complied.

She tugged on the sheet as she sat up. Scott stood before her in a pair of red plaid boxer shorts. Her gaze moved past his bare chest, which she ached to run her hands across, and lifted until it met his eyes.

"You needed someone to lean on last night. You've nothing to be embarrassed about. So don't act as if you do."

She said nothing, her gaze locked with his. She licked her suddenly parched lips.

"Hannah…" Scott stepped toward her, passion flaring in his eyes. He halted beside the bed and looked down at her. The question hung in the air.

Time stood still between them.

She'd been forced by circumstances to trust Scott with her son's care, but had he changed enough that she could trust him where her heart was concerned? Could she take that chance again?

When she said nothing he took a deep resigned breath and said, "Why don't you get dressed? We still have time to get to the hospital before shift change. We can check on Jake together."

CHAPTER FIVE

SCOTT stepped into the bedroom, carrying Hannah's freshly laundered clothes as he'd promised. The hairdryer was buzzing in the bathroom so she was still in there. He laid the clothes on the bed. What would her reaction be if she stepped out and found him there?

Those precious, heartbeat-suspending seconds when he'd stepped toward the bed slipped into his thoughts. A tingle of anticipation still lingered. He'd wanted to return to her warmth, had all but begged to. Had she had to force herself to say no? From the look in her eyes, he thought she might have. What had kept her from saying yes? Did she still not trust him? If he had been in her shoes, he probably wouldn't either.

Was she still embarrassed about last night? To have her begging him to join her, to hold her had been so out of character for her. He was glad he'd been the one here when she'd needed someone. She was no weak ninny who pleaded for comfort often. If she was out of control enough to ask him to stay then she was really hurting. This morning she had to be working to regain her pride.

He'd tried to put her at ease in the kitchen, which was next to impossible since he was humming with need like a taut wire in the wind. He'd held her because she'd needed it, despite it being unbearably difficult for him to stop there. She'd needed companionship and caring, not a lusty male. He'd been the gentleman last night that he should have been years ago. At least he'd made sure he'd still been there when she'd woken up this time.

His eyes lingered on the bed a second before he walked out the bedroom door.

Five minutes later Hannah entered his living room. Dressed in jeans and a red T-shirt with a sweater draped around her shoulders, she looked like a fresh-faced sorority girl out for an afternoon of shopping. She carried her bag in her hand. He'd not seen her look lovelier.

With a gruff "Let's go," he took the bag from her and opened the front door. She gave him a quizzical look but said nothing. If he just didn't touch her again he could make it without turning around and pulling her back into the bedroom.

As they approached his car, Hannah said, "I see you got that BMW you were always talking about. You've definitely moved up in the world."

"Just a little."

She gave a little huff of disbelief. "From that worn-out car you used to drive to this beauty is more than a little."

Warm pleasure at her appreciation filled him, and he smiled. "I bought it after I finished my surgical training. The old car had given its all, so I had to let go."

"That happens with people too."

Scott studied her a moment. Was she thinking about how badly he'd treated her after she'd given him her virginity?

He didn't want to believe that. Guilt had become something that he lived with every day, but he wanted to believe that Hannah really had forgiven him.

Opening the passenger door, he let her scoot in before closing it, then put the bag in the backseat. He climbed in behind the wheel. Hannah had already buckled up and was running her hands across the leather seat.

He smiled. At least she liked his car.

The sky was just turning pink on the eastern horizon as Scott drove to the hospital. He and Hannah spoke little on the way. Scott let her out at the front door, saying he would meet her outside the unit.

"Okay. Uh...thanks for your—uh—help...last night."

"No problem." Scott waited for her to close the door before he drove away. He hated having to leave her there. Didn't like the feeling they were sneaking around. After all, nothing was going on.

Yeah, right. He had to be fooling himself. If she'd said the word they would be in bed together right now.

Scott watched as Hannah came down the corridor from where he stood waiting for her. "I've cleared it for you to stay for just a few minutes."

They walked together to Jake's bed. A machine making a puffing sound with a long tube leading to Jake's mouth was the new fixture beside his bed.

"I hate this machine."

"I know, but you also understand it is necessity."

Jake's small chest rose with a huff of the pump. His eyes were opened but were glassed over from the drugs Scott had ordered to keep him calm. His small fingers flexed as he strained against the Velcro strips that secured his hands to the bed, preventing him from trying to pull out the tube. He struggled to speak and looked frustrated when he couldn't.

Hannah put her index finger in his palm. She trailed the back of her finger down his pale cheek. "Shh...honey, Mommy's right here. I love you." She repeated the words almost as a chant.

Jake fell asleep as they stood watching him. Seconds ticked by. Hannah glanced over her shoulder at Scott.

"You really are a wonderful mother. Jake's a lucky little guy to have you," Scott said softly.

"I'm just doing what any mother would do."

Scott knew better than that. "No, you're not. You're here, letting him know you love him, no matter what, and that's the important thing. You're always thinking of him and not just yourself."

"Doesn't every mother?"

"No." The word came out harsher than he'd intended. "Some mothers reject their children because they aren't what they want them to be." His mother certainly had.

She gave him a thoughtful look, then said, "I can't imagine ever doing that to someone I love."

"I don't imagine you could." Hannah loved too freely and unconditionally for it to be any other way.

"I don't feel like a very good mother right now. I can't do anything to help Jake."

"You will soon. A new heart will come." Scott picked up the chart on the end of the bed and looked at it. "He's just getting a little help. We don't want him to wear himself out. He's on half a liter of oxygen and five breaths."

"You do know Jake's more than what you read on that darned chart."

"Yes, I'm aware of that." A tone of sadness entered his voice. "I hate to see him this way too."

"I'm sorry. I shouldn't have said that. I know none of this is your fault. It's just nerves talking." She looked at Jake.

"I won't hold it against you."

She gave Scott a wry smile, and he tried to return a reassuring one.

Her smile grew and reached her eyes. "Thanks, I appreciate that. No more falling apart for me. I'm going to be a big girl."

"I think you're doing just great." He raised his eyebrows in a wolfish manner. "I don't mind helping out at all."

Hannah looked away, but he didn't miss her pink cheeks. "Hey, there's a hospital event being held downtown tonight to raise money for a new cardiac MRI. I have to attend. I was wondering if you might like to go with me?" Scott tried to insert a casual friendly tone to cover his eagerness to spend an evening with her.

"I don't think that would be a good idea."

He wasn't going to give up easily. "I'd have more fun if I were with someone, especially if that person was you." What he didn't say was that he only wanted to go with her. "You can't stay with Jake at night anyway. Come, please. Food and dancing. No pressure, you've my word." He put his hand up as if he were taking a pledge in court.

"I don't have anything to wear."

Scott's mouth lifted at the corners. "Searching for an excuse, are you? All you need's a nice dress. These events are usually fun and it'll take your mind off Jake for a couple of hours."

She shook her head. "I don't—"

"Look, we'll go late. At nine. After you have to leave CICU. It's not good for your health to be sitting and stewing twenty-four seven. Look what happened yesterday. I'm alone. You're alone. So why can't we do something together? For old times' sake?"

"I don't know…"

"A heart won't come any faster because you're sitting here day and night. I'll be paged if anything happens."

"Scott, you and I shouldn't be going out. I don't need any more emotional upheaval in my life." She laid her hands on the rail of Jake's bed.

His heart flip-flopped. "So I cause you emotional up-heaval?" He lowered his voice. "Come on, Hannah. Just because you're taking a break from here doesn't mean you care any less about Jake."

She wrinkled her nose and pursed her lips. He grinned. That dig had hit home.

"I think our relationship should only have to do with Jake and the present."

Scott said nothing for a few of seconds, letting the space and time between them grow. "But it's not, is it? I don't normally have mothers of patients to my home. This thing between us is too powerful to ignore."

Hannah blinked, and blinked again. She was aware of the *thing* he was talking about.

He stepped closer. "You don't want me to have to go alone, now, do you?" He purposely sounded like a little boy pleading for his first puppy. "You've got some pretty intense days ahead. Why not have one night of fun while Jake's in good hands? It might help keep you sane." Scott shifted from one foot to the other. Was she going to turn him down? He'd never been more anxious to hear a yes to a date invitation.

"Okay, but only this one time."

He grinned in triumph, tempted to give the air a high five. "Gee, that's not the most enthusiastic response I've ever received but I'll take it. I'll have Oscar take you home. He'll be waiting out front. I'll see you at eight?"

"I thought you said nine."

"I did, but you don't need to be here after shift change anyway."

"It's nine or not at all. I want to stay until Jake goes to sleep."

"Okay, I'll accept that if you will make an effort to at least try to enjoy yourself this evening."

"All I can promise is that I'll do my best."

She gave him a slight smile. Genuinely relieved to hear a positive answer, he decided to leave well enough alone. He wasn't used to feeling insecure when asking someone out on a date.

The clerk and tech gave him a curious look as he left. Had they noticed his special interest in Hannah?

The single desk lamp provided the only illumination in Scott's windowless office. Resting his elbows on the desk, he covered his face with his hands. What was happening to him?

He'd promised Hannah they would keep it simple and easy. He shouldn't push for more. They had no future. He'd known all those years ago that she was the type of woman who would want to settle down and have a family. She would expect and deserved someone that could be there full time. Not someone with divided loyalties.

What would happen when he could no longer step away? She and Jake were slipping under his defenses. That didn't matter. He still had to let them go.

Heck, he'd not only fallen for the mother but her kid. Jake had managed to wrap him around his finger as well. Scott felt like a car being pushed by another one. No matter how hard he applied the brakes, he was still moving forward. He was in deep with no hope of getting out gracefully. Was it possible for him to have a solid relationship and still be the kind of doctor he wanted to be?

Hopefully if he got the position in Dallas, that would solve the problem.

He didn't want Hannah to be hurt again. When she'd made that comment about being let go he wasn't sure she'd been referring to years ago. Her ex had hurt her too. No wonder she was so cautious.

Scott understood why Hannah had been angry and dis-
trustful of him initially, but she acted as if she was coming around. He'd been honored she'd trusted him enough
to ask for help during the night.

It would've been fabulous to be inside Hannah's warm,
welcoming body. Instead, he'd been left with a hunger that
might drive him mad. A cold shower had been his reward
for being a gentleman.

He'd not stayed around long enough the last time they'd
been in bed together to enjoy the ruffled morning look that
was so cute on Hannah. Now he wished more than ever
he'd crawled back into her bed the morning after they'd
made love.

Kissed and bedded the mother of a patient. It wouldn't
have been a quick consoling trip down memory lane. He
hardened at the memory of the vulnerability and longing
that had been in her eyes. Once he'd started kissing that
generous pink mouth, he wouldn't have stopped until they
had both been satisfied. He'd have missed rounds for sure.
And he never missed rounds.

Despite the gnawing longing, he refused to take advantage of her need for simple human contact. She was alone,
in a stressful and fearful situation. She'd only been in his
home because of her son. He wanted Hannah to desire *him*,
not just let him into her bed because she needed someone.

Tapping on the open door drew his attention. Andrea
entered. "Daydreaming, boss?" she asked with a grin.

If the truth be known she was more his boss than the
other way around. As his right-hand woman, she kept him
on track.

"Just thinking. Did you let UNOS know that Jake Quinn
had been placed on the respirator?"

"I called just a few minutes ago."

"Good. I was…wondering if you would do me a favor."

"What's that?"

"Would you sit with Mrs. Quinn while the transplant is taking place? She has no one and I think she should have someone with her while Jake's in surgery. I need to know she is taken care of."

The protective part of him had been more pronounced since Hannah had re-entered his life. When he'd seen those sad, sorrow-filled eyes he'd wanted to take all her cares away.

"Sure, boss. I'll be glad to. This one's getting to you, isn't it?"

"Yeah, this transplant needs to go smoothly."

The one way he could achieve that goal was to make sure that Jake got better, and soon. He had no control over the allocation system, or the number of children on the waiting list, but he had control over the type of care Jake received. Confident in his abilities as a surgeon, he'd been right when he'd told Hannah not to worry. The odds were in Jake's favor.

"I wasn't referring to the patient."

Scott didn't respond. Andrea gave him a knowing smile and left him alone with his thoughts. He needed to face facts—his greatest fear wasn't for Jake, but for his own heart when he had to give Hannah up. And he would give her up because he did care so much for her.

Scott groaned. He couldn't go around half-aroused all day. He leaned back in the chair and raked his fingers through his hair. The sexual tension between Hannah and himself was like no other he'd ever known. What he didn't understand was how she'd managed to flip his ordered and planned world upside down in a matter of days.

The doorbell dinged again.

"I'm coming," Hannah yelled, managing to make it

into the living room just after the third ring. Swinging her front door wide, Hannah stood stunned by the sight of Scott, dressed in a navy suit.

Gorgeous. Breathtakingly handsome. All healthy male.

Scott looked like the cover guy on a magazine. The color of the suit deepened the blue of his eyes. The ones twinkling at her now.

His broad shoulders filled the entrance. She swallowed a "Wow," trying not to embarrass herself. A crisp white button-down shirt and a silk tie in striped shades of blues finished his impeccable appearance. He'd shaved that evening. She caught a hint of his earthy aftershave. She liked it.

What would he do if she ran her palm across the plane of his cheek? She shoved her hands into the pockets of her robe.

Scott's hair had been trimmed, but the thick waves were mussed. She grinned. He'd been running his fingers through it. He did that when he was anxious. Had he thought she wouldn't let him in?

He represented sophistication right down to the bouquet of yellow roses in his hand. Her favorite color. Right now Scott appealed to her more than a chocolate sundae on a hot Saturday afternoon. She could almost taste him.

"That good, huh?" A grin lined his full lips and broadened to a smile.

Hannah bit the inside of her cheek to keep "Yum" from seeping through her lips. "Good-looking suit."

"Just the suit?"

She waved her hand at him as if dismissing the question. "Stop fishing for compliments."

Scott's smile and laughter were a lethal combination, hard to resist. He was pulling her under his spell again, making her revisit all those feelings she'd long hidden, making her think, *What if?* Making her remember why they had been such good friends at one time. Why she'd enjoyed his company so much. Hannah hoped he had no idea of the magnitude of her mental and physical reaction to him.

She didn't want to feel anything for him. She'd already been there and done that, and had the broken heart to show for it.

"Come in. I'm not quite ready. I still need to put my dress on." She sounded more out of breath than she should've been.

"I don't know, that furry thing you have on looks interesting," Scott drawled as he entered. "I particularly like those silver shoes with it." He nudged the door closed with a foot and offered her the flowers.

Hannah took them, inhaling their sweet smell. She smiled. "They're wonderful." She sighed with delight. "Thank you. I love them. Let me get a vase. I'll only be another sec. Have a seat."

When had she become such a chatterer?

"We've plenty of time," he said, chuckling.

He knows he rattles me. I've got to be on guard or I'll be overwhelmed.

In the kitchen, Hannah pulled a chair toward the counter below the cabinet where she stored vases. She removed her shoes. With her robe gathered in her hand, she stepped on the chair, opened the cabinet and reached in for a container.

"Hey, let me help with that." Scott stood beside her. Effortlessly, he grabbed the largest crystal container from the shelf, then closed the cabinet door. The vase clinked as he placed it on the counter.

Scott's gaze dropped to the long expanse of her exposed

leg, then lifted to meet hers. Appreciation, heat, and humor warred to dominate, making his eyes darken.

Hannah released her bathrobe, letting it drop to cover her thighs.

Humor won, leaving a twinkle in his eye. "Let me help you down." His hands circled her waist, lifting her. Her hands automatically braced on his shoulders and she could feel muscles bunching beneath the fabric of his suit jacket. She longed to explore their breadth, but resisted the urge.

Their gazes locked, held as she slid at a snail's pace toward the floor. Her toes were inches from touching when he pulled her against his solid frame.

Acutely conscious of her body's reaction to his nearness, Hannah made no effort to be released. Her core heated, glowed, grew brighter and flowed outwards, like a river of lava. Would she burst into flame? Her fingertips kneaded his muscles, asking for something she wouldn't put into words. Scott's quick, heavy breaths mingled with her expectant ones.

The air crackled around them.

For one beautiful, suspended moment Hannah thought he'd kiss her. Hoped he would. Instead, his hands tightened at her waist as he eased her away, letting her feet rest on the floor. Scott stepped back, his hands falling to his sides. Disappointment washed over her. Hannah missed the pleasure of his touch and the promise of his kiss. She shook her head, clearing the cotton-candy fog.

"I'll take care of the flowers. You go get dressed." His words had a rough edge to them, as if he were in pain.

Hurrying across the living room, she closed the bedroom door and let out a soft sigh. Her heart thumped in double time. Darn the man. He didn't seem rattled at all. Would it be considered irony if a heart doctor caused a heart attack?

Keeping her hands off Scott would prove difficult. She'd never responded to another man the same way as she did to him. *That* thrill had been there before, and had returned with a vengeance. She stood stock still. The truth of that reality would mean heartbreak but she was older and wiser now. She'd handle it. Her vow just to remain friends was like a stick that had been thrown into a fast-running river. Long gone.

Hannah slipped her dress over her head. It was the nicest thing she'd ever owned. She'd bought it as a splurge. Had fate known she'd meet Scott again and need it? With a fluttering heart, she took a deep breath. The effort did nothing to calm her anxiousness.

At the mirror, she checked her hair. She'd pulled it into a loose French twist. Tendrils fell to frame her face. Ignoring them, she added a princess strand of pearls to her neck and single pearl studs to her ears.

Taking another fortifying breath, holding it for seconds before letting it go, she stepped out to meet the man that flustered her and sent her heart racing.

While he waited, Scott wandered the living room, trying to get his libido under control. It was becoming almost impossible to maintain the "just friends" concept between them. Sweat nearly popped out on his brow from the effort he made not to touch Hannah whenever she came near. Taking a deep breath, he tried to focus on something beside the woman dressing a few feet away.

Her condo was small, but adequate for a mother and young child. Floral artwork hung on the walls, adding a bright hominess to the rooms. The furnishings spoke of comfort first, looks second. There was a bit of a backyard where toys of all shapes and colors were strewn. A sandbox was tucked away in the corner. Knowing how Hannah needed space, it was no surprise she'd found a home that would give Jake a place to play.

Framed pictures of Jake and Jake with Hannah rested on tables throughout the room. Scott picked up one where Jake was giving Hannah a kiss on the cheek. Jake looked full of life and Hannah's face held an almost angelic appearance as she smiled with pleasure. It was heartwarming to see such love between a mother and child.

He remembered seeing pictures of his parents with him and his brothers as small children, but as they'd grown it always seemed his father had been too busy to make time for the family portrait appointment. It wasn't only those his father had missed. The picture taken after Scott's winning run in baseball didn't have his dad in it either.

Scott had tried to understand. He'd known what his father did was important, even admired him. Still, it had hurt when his father hadn't been there for the state baseball play-offs. At first, Scott had thought that if he went into medicine then he would have a connection to his father, but had soon realized that he loved everything about the profession. That, after all, he was his father's son.

He studied the picture of Hannah and Jake again. *What would it be like to be encircled in that glow of emotion?*

He didn't have any business having those kinds of thoughts. He shouldn't be thinking of Hannah in regard to a future. It couldn't include him. He had hurt Hannah before but this time whatever happened between them would also affect Jake. He wouldn't do that to them.

Scott carefully returned the picture to its spot.

Hannah came into the living area. "I'm ready." Her words tumbled out as she reached for the tiny beaded clutch lying in one of the chairs. With a self-conscious flourish, she faced him.

Scott didn't miss the smallest detail as his eyes took in

the amazing vision before him. Hannah must be what angels in heaven look like. Air left his lungs as if he'd been sucker-punched, while his heart rate kicked up ten notches. All his good intentions had fled.

Supported by thin straps at the shoulders, her dress left an expanse of her smooth skin bare. From there the palest of pink fabric fit like a glove across her high breasts, and along her slender waist, to create a cloud of folds that swirled down around her hips and ended an inch above her knees.

He'd never had a lovelier date.

The same rose tint of her dress rested on her cheeks. She was nervous, self-conscious. A feeling of satisfaction filled him to know that it mattered to her what he thought. He grinned. She refused to meet his gaze. The small jingle of the linked chain of her purse made the lone noise in the room as she wrapped it around her fingers, undid it, and rewrapped it in rapid succession.

His whistle was low and appreciative. "You look amazing."

"Thank you, kind sir. You don't look half bad yourself." Her eyes had a shy look, but her words indicated her confidence was returning. "Shall we go?" She stepped toward the door.

From her head to the tips of her delicate feet, she was perfection. Except for...

He stooped and picked up her thin strapped shoes. They dangled on the ends of two of his fingers. "I believe you might need these." She'd forgotten them when she'd left the kitchen. With a question in her eyes, she looked at him, then down at her feet. He watched with satisfaction as she blushed crimson, making her even more becoming. *She's absolutely captivating.*

Scott liked the strong, demanding Hannah and the give-as-good-as-you-get one, but this sensually unsure Hannah was the best yet. It would be extremely difficult to keep his promise of no pressure when his body was already making demands to have her.

"I guess I do need those." She took the shoes, making an obvious effort not to touch his hand.

Sitting in an armchair, she adjusted the straps around her feet, treating him to a fine expanse of her shapely legs. She caught his appraising stare and pushed her skirt down, effectively closing the curtain on his view. Finding her tiny bag, she stood. "I think I'm ready now."

"I'll have the best-looking woman there on my arm. My colleagues are going to be jealous."

She smiled. The first unwavering one he could remember her having that evening.

"I do believe you're flirting with me, Doctor."

Scott grinned wickedly. "You might be right." He held the door for her. She slipped past him, and Scott had his first view of the back of her dress. From each of her shoulders, the folds of chiffon dropped to scoop below her waist, leaving her back bare.

The rise in his body temperature was instant, probably high enough to break a glass thermometer. He feared he would combust on the spot.

Breathe man, breathe. His mouth went dry. With effort he remembered to put one foot in front of the other as they went down the walk. All he could think about was placing a kiss on the ridge of one of those golden shoulders while his hand glided along every silky inch of her back.

"That dress is incredible."

"It's not too much for this event, is it?" The insecurity in her voice reminded him of a girl on her first date.

"No, it's perfect, absolutely perfect," he said with almost too much enthusiasm. Taking her hand, he pulled it through the crook of his arm and gave her a broad smile. "And so are you."

She returned the smile with a bright one of her own.

Unaware of her sex appeal, Hannah exuded it with no effort or consciousness. Did she realize his libido was running wild because of her? His body sang in response. His reactions were displaying themselves like a flashing billboard, but she didn't seem to notice. If he didn't focus on keeping the evening light, he could scare her off.

Guiding her to his car, he opened the door and helped her in. The least a mere mortal could do for this celestial being.

Hannah settled into the supple leather seat as Scott maneuvered the low sports car through the late-evening traffic. A tangy smell encircled her. She inhaled, appreciating Scott's own special essence. He smelled like a combination of sun and rain, with a hint of pine. She resisted the yen to lean closer.

"Hey, I'm sorry I gave you a hard time about coming tonight," she said. "It does sounds like a good time, but I'm not sure I'll be much fun. I seem to be unhappy at the hospital and miserable when I'm away. Until Jake gets a heart I'm not sure I'll be satisfied anywhere."

Scott reached for her hand and briefly squeezed it. "Why don't you try not to think about that for a few hours and attempt to enjoy yourself?" He flashed a smile.

One of her favorites. But each of his smiles was jockeying for a spot as favorite. This smile wrapped around her like a blanket on a cold winter day, making her believe that all could be well. A fluttery feeling developed in her stomach. Afraid she might be learning to love more than his smiles, she didn't dare let herself go down that path. "I'll try."

"These events are always laid back and fun. There'll be games, a silent auction, dancing with a good band. We should have no problem finding something distracting to do."

In no time Scott had pulled up in front of a building with massive glass windows. Inside a huge ballroom a band played a fast rock and roll number. Enormous records and pictures of movie stars blown up bigger than life decorated the area. An old '53 Chevy with girls in poodle skirts and guys with slicked-back hair greeted them.

"The fifties. My favorite decade." Hannah smiled, giving Scott's arm a slight press in her enthusiasm. The band struck up the first notes of another song. She swayed to "Earth Angel." With a sheepish grin on her lips, she looked at him from under lowered lashes. "What?"

"I was thinking how appropriate that song is. I've my own earth angel."

Tongue-tied, Hannah could only stare at him.

Scott suppressed a smile…barely. He said close to her ear, "Knowing you, you need to eat before we play."

His lips brushed the shell of her ear, making her body quiver. Her breath caught. Did he have any idea what he did to her? Her stomach did loop-di-loops. She was hungry for more than food.

Scott took her hand. "Let's go and see what's on the buffet."

They wove their way through the crowd towards a group of tables set up on the far side of the room. Her hand fit comfortably into his as if it belonged there. Scott held her hand tight enough to be possessive but not so tight she couldn't have removed it if she'd wished. Her heart missed a beat when he gave it a gentle squeeze, as if he knew what she was thinking.

* * *

With their meal completed, Scott took Hannah's hand again as they headed toward an area set up for games. His body needed some type of physical contact with hers, otherwise it felt like a piece of him was missing. He spoke to a couple of his colleagues as he and Hannah walked across the large room. He introduced her only as an old friend, leaving out that she was the mother of one of his patients.

In the game area, they waited their turn after he'd talked Hannah into playing a round of table tennis. He watched her remove the silver shoes, finding the artless action very sexy. Keeping things light was turning into work.

"Did I mention I've been the Watson family reunion champion three years running?" She grinned at him across the expanse of the green table.

"You failed to share that information."

"Don't let that intimidate you."

"I'll try not to." He served his best fast ball.

"Not bad." She nodded with approval. "All those hours in the interns' hideout in the basement of the hospital must've paid off."

"Just serve, Quinn, and know I'll be giving no mercy."

Hannah grinned, obviously pleased with her efforts to rattle him. At least he'd succeeded in helping her forget her problems for a few minutes.

After a couple of spirited games Scott had a newfound respect for Hannah. She didn't beat him but managed to hold her own.

"You don't feel the need to let my male ego go undamaged by letting me win?" It wasn't a trait he'd normally found in the women he'd been out with.

"No. Why should I? My motto is 'Let the best man or woman win.' Your ego is the last thing I need to feed."

He pulled his lips back in mock pain. "You always did

tell me like it is. That's one of the things I always liked about you."

Scott took the final game, barely. Coming around the table, she gave him a quick hug of congratulations. Their laughter merged.

The tinkling sound that he loved placed him hopelessly and completely under her spell. He wanted to hold onto this moment for ever. His days were spent with such serious matters. It was nice to laugh and have fun for a change. Her sharp wit and love of life was infectious.

"That'll show you not to mess with me. That was fun," she said after most of her mirth had dissipated. "I needed to do that. You always could make me laugh. Even when I was having a tough day on the floor," she said. "That's a gift, you know."

"My pleasure." And it was. He always liked her laugh. It reminded him of a breeze moving through wind chimes on a hot summer day. He had an idea she'd not laughed much in the last few years, certainly not in the last few days.

It was nice to see her smiling, letting go a little. She needed to. Her emotions had to be swinging one way and then the other. She needed a release.

"What?" she asked, sounding a little ill at ease.

"I was just contemplating what an interesting woman you are."

"How's that?"

"Well, you play table tennis like a demon, love donuts, you're evidently a self-sufficient single mother, you appreciate nice cars and you like the oldies."

Scott noticed the worry lines on her face had decreased. For that he was grateful. She had looks that went beyond attractive. Hers was still a wholesome beauty, the kind of loveliness that came from the inside. The type that had drawn him to her in the first place, making him want to get to know her, and later to consider the impossible.

Turning her shoulder in a saucy manner toward him, she said, "What more could a man want?"

"I can imagine."

She immediately flushed red, making her even more desirable.

"Don't be using that charm on me, Doctor. It won't work. I've seen it in action too many times. That's just a figure of speech."

He chuckled. "Yes, Hannah, I know what you meant." It was nice to see that some of the spunk that had attracted him when they'd first met hadn't disappeared. His plan was working. He'd been right to insist she accompany him. She needed fun in her life. If he could, he would have it be that way for her always.

"I'm thirsty." Her eyes shined as she smiled.

"Then let's get you something to drink." He hoped none of his colleagues saw the sappy grin on his face. He could imagine the unmerciful fun they would make of him. The grapevine would no doubt run with that information. "Don't forget your shoes."

Hannah found them under the playing table and slipped them on.

"I think it adds something to your dress when you're barefooted." Hannah's nervous laughter sent heat to a part of his body that didn't need any encouragement. "Come on, hotshot, I think there's a soda stand over this way." He pointed to a red and white awning.

As they made their way across the room, Hannah exclaimed, "I thought you meant a place to get a cola! This is a real soda parlor."

They found a small empty table. A young man, dressed

in a yellow striped shirt, took their order. She wanted a chocolate shake. He ordered vanilla.

"I'm really enjoying myself." Hannah's eyes sparkled. "There must be thousands of nurses wishing you'd invited them."

"I think it is more like a hundred." He gave what he hoped was his best wolfish grin.

She laughed. "At least."

The young man returned with their shakes. Hannah stuck her straw into hers. Her cheeks drew together as she sucked. A look of pure joy touched her features as she drew up the rich liquid. He grinned. Releasing the straw, she ran her tongue with slow deliberation across the curve of her top lip. Closing her eyes, she made a sound of unadulterated pleasure.

Had all the air been sucked out of the place? Scott couldn't breathe. Captured by the sight, he wished he'd been the one to put that look of delight on her face.

Hannah's smiled broadened. "I'll race you to the bottom. On your mark, get set, go."

He shoved his straw into his glass. The thick liquid moved up their straws at a slow pace. Watching her over the top of the glass, Scott raised a brow, taunting her. Smirking around the straw, he continued to suck hard.

"You won't beat me." Determination filled her eyes as her lips drew on the straw again.

Scott put his hand under the table and caressed her knee. Hannah's eyes widened in surprise, then narrowed. He beamed. She shoved his hand away and moved her knee to where he couldn't touch her with ease. With a negative movement of her head and a gleam in her eye, she continued sucking with gusto.

He broke contact with his straw and let out a laugh that came from his belly. It was loud enough that others sitting around them stared. The last noisy slurp of nothing being left in her glass could be heard by the time his mirth had died into a chuckle.

"I won." Hannah clasped her hands over her head in a victory sign. "And you tried to cheat!"

Scott laughed again, feeling no guilt. "Yeah. In the end you got the better of me. I could tell that, no matter what I did, you planned to win this contest."

"You're right." Hannah grinned. "We should've set a prize."

"How about this?" Not allowing her time to answer or caring if he was seen, Scott slipped a hand behind her neck and pulled her to him.

Her lips were cool under his. In a slow, methodical motion his tongue slid over her lips, not wanting to miss any of the sugary flavor. Hannah brought her hand to his shoulder and made a low sound of acceptance. Her mouth heated under his. Long, perfect seconds went by before he lifted his mouth.

CHAPTER SIX

SCOTT's hooded eyes and the sensual curve of his lips made Hannah's blood speed through her veins. A blur of shapes and colors whirled around them. Scott was the only person who remained in focus.

Her gaze locked with his blue one. The air snapped round them. He leaned toward her. Her lips parted.

A man moving between the tables jostled Scott's chair. Pulling back, Scott sat straighter. The moment evaporated. He'd been thinking about kissing her again. She would've let him.

"I think, no, I know, kissing you could get out of hand and I promised no pressure."

As far as Hannah was concerned, he could forget that pledge. She wanted him and she wanted to feel wanted. Even if it was just for a little while.

"There's a silent auction going on. I read a trip down the Colorado River through the Grand Canyon was being offered. I'd like to bid on it. After we check that out, maybe we could dance, if you'd like," he said, standing.

Scott sounded a little formal all of a sudden. The abrupt shift in his attitude made her feel a little lost. He'd been so warm minutes before. Had that kiss affected him as much as it had her?

Lifting a finger, Hannah touched her bottom lip. She

should be grateful for the interruption. It gave her time to get her emotions corralled.

As they strolled side by side toward the auction area, she noticed the number of admiring looks that came Scott's way from other women. Hannah glowed with feminine one-upmanship, knowing he was with her.

The area where the auction was set up was quieter. A few other couples strolled around the tables. Scott located the Canyon trip and wrote his bid on the sheet. Hannah coughed to cover her gasp of shock when she saw his bid amount.

He must've known what she thought because he said, "It's for a good cause."

"Yours or the hospital's?" she asked with a grin.

"Both."

Hannah realized he could afford it. A reminder of how different their worlds were.

They continued down the line of tables filled with auction items. An exquisite blue floral teaset caught Hannah's eye. Picking up the cup, she checked the bottom to find it had been made by a quality British company. She ran the tip of her index finger along the scalloped rim of the fragile cup. Returning it to the matching saucer, she lifted the pair to admire what a beautiful pair they made.

"It's beautiful." She spoke more to herself than Scott. The magnificent set was one she'd enjoy owning and using.

"Would you like to bid on it?" Scott asked from behind her.

She'd been so engrossed in admiring the set she'd not seen Scott put down an autographed baseball and join her.

"No. No. I was just looking." Even the starting bid was way beyond what she could afford.

"I'd be glad to bid for you." Scott studied the auction sheet.

"No. I don't even have a good place to put it," she assured him. "And I've a small child. Nothing like this would survive long in my home."

"You're probably right. How about a dance now or would you rather play some more games? I could let you win this time."

"Funny. It's not a real win unless you earn it." She looked at him. "But let's go and see if you're as good on the dance floor as you are at table tennis."

He draped her arm through his. She'd noticed he'd made a point all night not to touch her back. During the last few days she had especially liked him placing his hand at the small of her back, like an old-world gentleman. Why wouldn't he touch her back now?

The music became louder as they approached the tile-covered dance floor.

"I wonder if my *must-attend* cotillion lessons when I was thirteen will stand up to this." His lips curve into a boyish smile.

"You'll be better than me. My skills come from dancing in the living room with my father. Most of the time on his feet."

"As a kid I use to watch my dad swirl and twirl my mom around the house. Mother always wanted my father to take her dancing. She loved to dance. Still does."

"That's a nice memory."

He didn't say anything for a second, as if he'd never thought of it like that before. "You know, it is. Come on, let's give it a shot. What do you say?"

"Lead on, Mr. Astaire." She beamed up at him.

Scott placed his hand low, but not too low, on her back. Hannah's breath jerked to a stop for a second. Heat radiated out from where his hand moved over her skin. Maybe it'd been a good idea for him not to touch her. It'd been a long time since she'd allowed an adult male's interest.

He maneuvered them across the floor to where other couples were preparing to dance. A fast tune began. It took a few steps for Hannah to adjust to Scott's closeness and the rhythm of the music. She settled into his lead. He was an excellent dancer. With his lithe and athletic body, he moved across the floor with natural grace. Scott twisted her in his arms, spun her one way then another and even dipped her following one number.

"How about a cold drink?" he asked after a set of songs. She nodded her agreement and he took her hand, leading her off the dance floor.

"Please. This is the most exercise I've had in days," she said, breathless from exertion and being in his arms. "I should've known when you suggested dancing you would be good at it."

Scott found a cart selling sodas, and then they located a spot out of the way where they could sit.

"Thanks," she said when he handed her the drink. "I thought you said you didn't dance well."

"No, what I said was it'd been some time." He smiled down at her. "I'm rusty at it. I don't have much spare time to go dancing."

"You're still a great partner. Mr. Astaire wouldn't be disappointed in you."

"Thank you, ma'am." He gave her a regal nod. "As are you." He took a swallow of his drink. "I was wondering why I never took you dancing."

"I wouldn't go out with you, remember? I saw you for the womanizer you were." She grinned at him. "Anyway, if we'd gone out it would've ruined a friendship. I wanted more than a date. What happen between us proved I was right."

"I see your point. I'm sorry. I handled things badly." His words seemed to include more than not taking her on a date.

"You can stop apologizing. I've grown up. Moved on. I have Jake to be concerned about. Men that come into my life affect him too. It's not just me getting hurt any more, it's Jake too."

"You're a strong woman."

"I don't know about that. I'm simply a mother doing the best she can for her child. He has no one else but me." She took a swig of her drink, and put her cup down.

He nodded in understanding. Slipping his hand in his pocket, he pulled out his cell phone and handed it to her. "Here, why don't you call and check on him? The hospital is number one on speed dial."

"I'm not surprised." His eyes clouded over for a second. Had she said something wrong?

"I would be paged if there was a problem, but I know you wouldn't be happy unless you heard he was fine from the nurse."

"You know me so well."

"Not as well as I would like to." His voice took on a suggestive note. Time held still between them then he said, "You go find someplace quiet enough to check on Jake, and I'll go and have a look at how the silent auction is going. I'll meet you back here by Elvis."

"I won't be long," she said over her shoulder as she walked away.

Ten minutes later they were both standing beside the life-size Elvis cutout.

"How's Jake?" Scott asked as she joined him.

"Resting. And I know you want to say I told you so but please don't."

"You're a great mom. I see a lot of mothers who

shouldn't have the job. It's nice to see a parent who has a connection to their child. Sadly, it doesn't always happen."

"Thank you. Sometimes I think I'm fumbling around in the dark."

"You're more in the daylight than you know." A slow song began and the lights dimmed above the dance floor. "Would you like to see some of my best moves?" he asked, his voice going low. He led her into the center of the already overflowing floor.

"I can't imagine them being any better than what I've already experienced."

Gathering her into his arms, Scott placed a hand on her back. She couldn't help but tense at the stimulating contact, but soon relaxed enough to lean into him. One of her hands found his and the other slid along his arm to rest at his shoulder. When another couple bumped them, Scott flexed his arm at her waist bringing her closer.

The solidness of his body met hers from head to toe. Hannah had a sense of being protected from the ugliness of the world. His hand dipped low on her waist before it moved inch by tantalizing inch up the length of her spine to her neck. A hot trail of consciousness flowed through her as his fingers paused at each dip in her vertebrae then worked his way down again. She simmered in the heat his touch created in her. His hand came to rest in the bow of her back.

His lips touched the sensitive spot behind her ear, sending a jolt of awareness rocketing through her.

"Scott..."

"Shh, let me enjoy having you in my arms."

Hannah's hand gripped his upper arm. Every fiber of her being strained toward him, hyper-responsive to each nuance of Scott's touch. His chest rose and fell against hers. When his heartbeat increased, she felt it. Skimming her hand over his shoulder, she curled her fingers into the waves of hair at the nape of his neck. Stepping closer, she breathed deeply, taking him in. A soft sound of pure pleasure escaped.

Scott groaned, pulling her tighter. His thigh slipped between her legs as they swayed slowly to the music. Scott no longer led to the beat of the music, but to his personal one.

His fingertips followed the edge of her dress along her back until his hand came to rest in the folds. He slowly slipped his fingers under the material to settle near the curve of her breast.

A tingle ran through her. Her nipples strained upward, pebble hard. Her step faltered. Scott compensated with a flawless move, holding her snug against his length, his desire hard against her belly.

His pager vibrated between them, bursting the blissful, sensual balloon they'd been floating in.

He expelled a scalding word and eased his hold.

Her body throbbed with need left unmet.

Scott unclipped the phone from his waistband, glanced at the screen, then muttered a blunt curse under his breath.

Hannah put more space between them. "Is it about Jake? Is something wrong?" she asked, fear filling her voice.

"I don't know yet, honey. Let me answer this." His voice was husky with disappointment. He led her off the dance floor and into a quieter area.

"This is McIntyre," he said sharply into his phone. "Yes. Can you see to it? Yes. That sounds good." His manner had turned all business.

She put a hand on his arm, and caught his gaze. "Jake?" She whispered the plea.

Scott put his hand over the receiver and mouthed, "He's fine, honey," before continuing his conversation.

Hannah took a deep breath and released it, listening to the low rumble of Scott's voice. If the call had come an hour later they would've been making love. She would've been a willing partner. Very willing. The tornado of sensations still swirled through her. Scott had set her on fire. She'd never before experienced the all-consuming need he elicited from her.

Now he stood discussing a patient. His mood had shifted lightning quick. She'd been forgotten. He'd morphed into doctor mode. But with something as simple as catching her hand, she'd be lost again.

Her feelings overpowered all logical thought, shocking her. Maintain control, that's what she needed to do. Think first. Not to expect more than Scott could give. None of that mattered. Scott had already left his mark.

Hannah watched as his jaw tightened and he looked off into the distance. His questions came out short and succinct.

As if he suddenly remembered she was there, Scott reached for her hand and pulled her close, wrapping an arm around her waist. Already her plan had a huge hole in it. She couldn't control Scott. The heat from his body surrounded her.

"I'll be there within the hour." He flipped his cell phone closed, and turned her so she could look at him.

"Something has come up that will require our attention. He curved his lip into a confident smile. "We think we've found a heart for Jake."

"Oh, thank God."

He squeezed her shoulders. "Now, remember we're in the beginning stage, and it'll take hours before we know for sure, but the heart looks promising."

"Please let this be the one," she whispered.

"I'm going straight to the hospital to review the information about the possible donor and check on Jake. Timing is everything now."

"I'll go with you."

"No," he said firmly, "you don't need to be sitting and fretting at the hospital. I'll drop you at my place. That way you'll be close. It could be hours before I know more. I'll call you."

She refused to let him dictate whether or not she should be there for her child. "I'm going with you. Jake's my son and I want to be with him as much as I can. Anyway, I have a change of clothes at the hospital and a sleep room in my name. It makes more sense."

He nodded his agreement but didn't appear happy about the arrangements.

In a hurry, Scott left her where the hallway divided, one hallway going to CICU and the other to the waiting room. She missed the security he represented the second he was out of sight.

With Scott gone, Hannah stood in the middle of the corridor, suddenly unsure what to do next. She couldn't move. This was it, what she'd prayed for. Only she'd never have dreamed she'd be involved emotionally with the doctor who would be saving Jake's life. She'd stopped thinking straight the minute Scott had arrived earlier that evening. With the possibility of a heart for Jake, the situation had become more desperate.

Change. That's what she needed to do. She rode the elevator to the upper floor and found the small sleep room she'd been assigned that afternoon. She'd made arrangements for it so she wouldn't be tempted to stay at Scott's. The room held a single bed and end table. It wasn't much, but it was close to Jake. Withdrawing her bag from the locker where she'd stored it earlier, she dropped it on the bed and began to change.

A flood of heat washed over her as she removed her dress. She overflowed with longing. If it hadn't been for the tremors of Scott's pager she'd no doubt be in his bed right now. Her heart rate quickened. A flood of hunger washed over her as if Scott was near.

She couldn't deny she'd been as willing a participant as he. No way could she place all the blame on him.

Pulling a pair of comfortable jeans out of the bag, she slipped them on, added a favorite T-shirt and tennis shoes, grabbed a sweatshirt, and hurried out to check on Jake.

"Mrs. Quinn wants to come back. Is that okay?" the clerk asked the midnight shift nurse.

Scott, standing by the desk, looked up from the chart he'd been reviewing. He'd asked her to wait. It figured she wouldn't listen. Hannah had certainly never been intimidated by him. The nurse looked at him and he nodded his consent.

The clerk had hardly replaced the phone receiver before Hannah entered the unit. She glanced at him but continued straight to Jake's bed.

Scott appreciated the view of Hannah's shapely backside as she stretched and leaned over the rail of the bed to place a kiss on her sleeping son's head. He needed to get his thoughts off the mom and on the son.

To give her some time alone with Jake, Scott waited before he approached. "Hannah." The word came out sharper than he'd intended. Lowering his voice to a more mellow level, Scott said, "I told you to wait until I came to get you."

Hannah glared at him. "I couldn't wait." She turned

back to Jake. "I had to see him." Her voice caught. She was in protective mode.

"You're right." Scott understood her feelings because he felt that same need to protect her. He admired her strength. There was no begging and pleading or demands on her part. She just did what had to be done because she loved her child.

The desire to wrap her in his arms pulled at him, but he would have an audience. The best he could offer, though inadequate, was the reassurance of knowing what she could expect in the next few hours. He moved to the other side of the bed in order to put some space between them. Hannah had a way of making him do things he'd not planned to whenever she was within touching distance.

She looked at him in expectation with a gleam of moisture in her eyes. Her hand clasped one of Jake's.

"Let me explain what's happening and going to happen. Right now, we're waiting on the family of the possible donor to agree to donation. Most of the time the recipient family never knows this far in advance about a possible donor."

"You get to know sooner if you're out dancing with the surgeon," Hannah said, averting her eyes.

His lips became a thin line. The acute sting of the remark registered.

Hannah brought her eyes back to his. "I'm sorry. That was uncalled for."

Glancing to see if anyone watched, Scott reached across the bed and captured one of her hands. His thumb brushed over her knuckles before he released it. "I understand, but don't regret what almost happened between us. I certainly don't."

She gave him a wry smile.

"As I was saying, the family will have to agree, which

will probably take place in the morning. Afterwards there'll be more tests, and it may not be until tomorrow…" he looked at his watch "…or I mean this afternoon, before things will really start moving along. The thoracic fellow will go after the heart. I plan to stay here with Jake. He won't go into surgery until after the fellow has left. We'll be in constant contact until the fellow walks into the OR with Jake's new heart."

"Will I know what's happening?"

"Yes. Andrea will be coming into the OR and I'll be sending messages out to you."

"So nothing may happen until tomorrow evening?"

He nodded. "That's why I insisted you didn't need to be here."

"I couldn't stay away."

"I realize that now. It's just part of who you are. If I hadn't had my mind on other matters I might've been thinking more clearly."

Even in the dim light he could see her blush. She knew exactly what he'd been referring to.

"So why don't you go up and try to get some rest? I'll call you when there's something new to tell. I'm even going to bunk in the attending's room for a few hours so I'll be ready for surgery."

"You don't have to stay right here?"

"No, they'll call me with any questions. We're good at transplants here, Hannah. My staff knows their jobs and they do them well."

"Dr. Mac, Lifeline is on the phone," the clerk called, holding the phone out.

Hannah spun around to look at the nurse.

Scott circled the bed, stopped beside her and said, "Wait for me outside the unit. This call shouldn't take long. I'll walk you to the elevator." He made a few steps and stopped, turning back to her. "Please wait," he pleaded softly. "Jake is hopefully going to have his new heart soon."

Hannah kissed her sleeping child, wishing she could hug him close, and left the unit. She lingered outside the CICU doors. "Still thinking of me?" Scott quipped as he came out, a slight grin on his lips.

He was obviously trying to add some levity to this anxious and unsure time. "Mighty confident of yourself, aren't you?" Her smile grew, despite her effort to control it.

His grin disappeared and his look turned solemn. "Not where you're concerned."

Scott's intense gaze bored into hers for a long moment before he took her arm and directed her down the corridor. They walked in silence, with uneasiness hanging between them. At the elevator Hannah pushed the "up" button.

"I want to kiss you." Scott's words were a husky demand.

Hannah's body tingled. Her pulse pounded. Her fingers itched to touch him. "I...I...don't think that's a good idea. I think we both should focus on Jake."

Scott stepped away, his jaw tight. "Jake will be getting my very best care. In no way will I let what I feel for you affect my performance as a doctor."

"I didn't mean to imply—"

"Hannah, I know you're beating yourself up over what was happening between us on the dance floor. I wish you wouldn't. I know all the negatives to this relationship. You still don't completely trust me and I understand. I can't make you any promises, but I also know there's something special between us."

She remained silent. There was something amazing between them. She felt it too. But she needed to be sure about her next move. She'd misread him before, had completely missed the mark with her husband, and she couldn't af-

ford to do it again. Scott had convinced her to trust him
with Jake's heart but she still didn't know about hers.

"Try to get some sleep. I'll call you as soon as I know
something more concrete."

Scott turned, going back toward the unit. She'd wanted
him as much as he'd wanted her. Scott wanted her sexu-
ally, but she was looking for someone to share her future.
He hadn't been willing to do that during medical school.
Could he feel differently now? If she invested her heart,
she had to know he wanted the same things in life she did.
She owed it to Jake, and to herself.

The trouble was, she was weak around Scott, and so
very alone.

In the hospital the next morning, Hannah's cell phone
hadn't completed a full note before she snatched it up.
Her heart jumped when she heard Scott's voice.

"Hannah, we think this is the heart for Jake." His tone
sounded professional, somber. "But it'll be hours before
we'll go to collect it. Jake's resting and everything looks
good on the donor end."

"Thank goodness." She closed her eyes and said a silent prayer.

"I'm sorry I can't tell you more. I'll see you later. I've
gotta go."

His abrupt end to the conversation startled her. She
wasn't sure she appreciated the return of his all-business
manner. She'd come to enjoy, anticipate, the warmer ver-
sion. It had become part of her comfort zone.

Despite her jumbled emotions, the chain of events leading to Jake getting a new heart registered. On a human *and*
parental level she knew another family had lost their child
in order for hers to live. Her chest constricted. As wonderful as Jake getting another chance to live was for her,

at the other end of the spectrum was the donor family's devastation. Moisture blurred her vision. The thought of what those parents must be feeling was almost impossible to endure. Their two families would be forever linked.

Clutching a pillow, she caught herself wishing for the security of Scott's arms. He'd really been wonderful and supportive, not only with her but with Jake. She had to admit she'd felt a twinge of jealousy when Scott had managed to get Jake to laugh. She hadn't been able to do that. Wiping tears away, she took a fortifying breath. There were things to do, calls to make.

Phoning her sister in California, Hannah told her about the available heart. Despite the distance, Hannah felt better just talking to her. Jake was getting a new heart. She could scarcely comprehend it.

Scott managed to get a few hours of sleep at the hospital between calls from Lifeline and thoughts of Hannah creeping into his dreams. The long hours leading up to a transplant were often tedious. Reviewing the donor's history, checking the heart size to see if it would fit into the chest cavity and assessing blood work were a few of the many details he'd organized that morning.

A heart transplant took careful and well-timed actions. An amazing life-and-death dance. It never ceased to fill him with awe that he had a part in something so phenomenal.

Dancing. For ever after, dancing would be synonymous with Hannah. He loved holding her, wanted her in his arms again. Soon. It had hurt when she had refused to kiss him at the elevator, but she'd made the right call. They needed to take things slower.

They were on two different paths. Her life was hearth and home, and he couldn't commit to that. He wasn't capable of giving Jake and Hannah what they needed or deserved. It would be another failed relationship to add to his list.

The life he'd chosen made it impossible for him to be doctor and family man. He couldn't foresee doing both well. He already carried the heavy weight of guilt from letting his work get in the way when his mother had needed him. Hurting Hannah or Jake was something he wasn't prepared to accept. Some people could manage different parts of their life effectively, but he couldn't. The McIntyre family history bore that out.

He was just too much like his father. His patients had always come first, and Scott felt the same way about the children he cared for. That the idea he and Hannah could have more even crossed his mind came as a surprise.

It would be late evening or early morning before the major part of his day would be complete. Now wasn't the time to consider what-ifs.

Scott looked up to see Hannah coming through the CICU doors. He met her beside Jake's bed.

Jake's eyelids opened a moment and then slid closed again.

"I've ordered something to make him sleep. Jake needs to be well rested before going into surgery," Scott said. "Did you get any sleep?"

He stood close enough to catch a whiff of the fresh apple smell of her hair when she turned to him. Scott ached to pull her into a dark corner and kiss her until her cool demeanor fell away. Until the hot passion he knew she held in check boiled over.

"Some," Hannah said, before taking Jake's hand. "Is there any news?" she asked, her attention totally focused on her son.

"Yes. The family has agreed to donate. Now Lifeline

has to see that all the organs being donated are placed before the retrievals."

"All the organs?"

"Yeah. The family can agree to give other organs."

"Other children will share the same donor as Jake?"

"They could. Depending on what organs the family agrees to donate. I think we'll be going after the heart around six this evening." Scott forced his voice to remain flat, showing none of the concern he felt about the upcoming surgery. He'd grown attached to the little boy. This would be one surgery where he couldn't leave his feelings at the door.

"Where's the heart coming from?"

"I can't say, but not too far away. A heart has to be transplanted within four hours so that doesn't let it travel a long distance."

Hannah nodded, and he watched her thick hair bounce around her shoulders. His fingers flexed and curled in an effort to keep him from succumbing to his longing to touch it.

They stood by Jake's bed, doing nothing more than watching her sleeping boy. Scott practiced equal care and concern for all his patients, but this particular little patient had become a personal case despite his efforts not to let it happen. He wanted to save Jake's life. He must.

"It won't be long now," he said with all the confidence he possessed.

"Mrs. Quinn?" Andrea placed a light touch on Hannah's arm long hours later.

Hannah blinked. "What?"

"It's time to get Jake ready to go down. You need to say goodbye to him." Compassion filled her voice. It held something encouraging in it, maybe a note of excitement.

"He's going now?" Jake needed the transplant, but it was difficult to let him go. At least now he was alive. He might not live though surgery. The known was better than the unknown. The terror of losing Jake filled Hannah's body like a sharp wind on a bitter winter morning.

"No. He'll actually go down in about an hour. It takes a while to prep him," Andrea said.

Hannah tensed. A film of wetness blurred her view. She needed to absorb him, afraid this would be her last memory. Studying every detail of Jake's precious face, she wanted to remember him happy and smiling, laughing with Scott…

Stop. She inhaled, letting the breath out in measured puffs. Jake had to live.

Sedated and on a respirator, her precious son had no idea what was happening. Jake lay pale against the white sheets of the bed, the only color in his face being the dark circles under his eyes. She wanted to drop to her knees and cry, howl at how unfair it all was.

"I love you, honey. Be strong. See you soon." Kissing his cheek, she released his tiny hand and cringed when it fell limply on the bed. She refused to use the word *goodbye*.

Jake would be fine. She'd accept nothing less. She believed Scott would allow nothing less.

"Mrs. Quinn," Andrea said in a low, gentle voice. "They're expecting him in the OR. Why don't you go on down to the surgery waiting room? Do you know where it is?"

"Yes." The word came out as a croak.

"Good. I'll be down to join you in a little while."

Hannah balanced on her toes, leaned over the rail and placed a kiss on Jake's forehead. A tear dropped onto his face. Hannah wiped it away. "I love you, sweetie."

Andrea put a hand on her shoulder. The comfort was appreciated. "I'll tell Scott where you are. He'll want to talk to you before going into the OR." Hannah wiped her cheek with the back of her hand as she made the long, lonely walk to the waiting room.

Her chest tightened. Would she be able to draw another complete breath until Jake came out of surgery?

Be positive. Straighten up. Jake will be fine.

Taking a seat in the far corner of the waiting room, Hannah settled in for the night. A few minutes later Andrea entered and took a seat close by.

"You'll see a big difference in Jake right away," Andrea said.

Hannah appreciated Andrea trying to make conversation while at the same time she just wanted to be left alone. "That's what the nurses tell me."

Scott came through the door dressed in blue scrubs with his ever-present white lab coat. Hannah stood, meeting him in the center of the room. If he'd opened his arms, she wouldn't have thrown herself into them, but he didn't.

Instead he said, "Let's sit. We need to talk." He placed his hands lightly at her waist, turning her. Hannah wanted to lean into his strength, but found her chair again as directed. Scott sat in the one beside her, which put Hannah between him and Andrea.

He took her hand. Desperate for his offered comfort, she didn't pull away. Looking into her eyes, he promised, "I'll take good care of Jake."

"I know you will," Hannah whispered, making her trust evident.

"Jake's getting settled in surgery. He's had his first dose of Prograf, which is the anti-rejection medicine. The team going after the heart has been gone almost an hour. I'll be in touch with them at regular intervals until they return. As close as I can to the heart's arrival, I'll open Jake's chest."

Hannah winced. He shifted closer, giving her hand a squeeze.

"You need to understand this is an iffy process right up until the new heart gets to the OR. Something could happen to the heart, the time could go too long, or we might find out at the last minute that the heart isn't good enough. There's a chance we may not be able to do it tonight."

She looked at him, saying nothing, praying, *Oh, God, please let it be tonight.*

Scott tightened his hold on her hand. "Surgery will probably take around four to six hours. Don't expect to see me any time soon. I'll be out when Jake's ready to go up to the unit."

He glanced at Andrea. Standing, he pulled Hannah into his arms. Hers went around his waist, absorbing his warmth, strength and assurance. His confidence and support was like balm to her nerves.

Scott ran his hand over her back, making no move to leave. He brushed his lips across her temple, then released her.

Hannah gripped his upper arms. Tears, swimming in her eyes, blurred his handsome face. She silently begged him to tell her that everything would be okay.

Scott's hand cupped her cheek and he looked directly into her eyes for an extended moment before he said, "Next time you see me, Jake will have his new heart."

CHAPTER SEVEN

SCOTT stood at the surgery wash basin, running a small white brush beneath his fingernails. The antibacterial soap formed froth.

He'd performed numerous heart transplants. Being well trained, he knew what to expect. Yet he hadn't been this nervous since his first surgery.

It added pressure to an already hyper-sensitive situation. Why hadn't he at least waited until Jake was out of the hospital to get to know Hannah better?

He'd tried to resist her, but it seemed like he was always there when she needed help. Touching her had become addictive. He didn't understand this unfamiliar emotion. She'd slid his world sideways.

His heart had soared when Hannah had said she trusted him. Looking in the mirror above the basin, he saw the amazed look on his face. He loved Hannah.

Scott stood shock still. Muttering an inappropriate word for a children's hospital, Scott's foot slipped off the water control, stopping the flow over his hands. How had he let this happen?

What was he going to do? He couldn't act on that emotion. He refused to. Loving someone meant making them happy, and he could never make Hannah happy.

Pain squeezed his heart. He'd never be really happy

without her. She'd become his world. But he would never tell her so.

The surgery nurse next to him cleared her throat, drawing his attention. She handed him a sterile towel.

There was no time or energy to waste dwelling on the revelation. His needed to focus on Jake getting his new heart.

Another nurse helped him into gloves before he shouldered through the door of OR Four. The coolness of the room surrounded him. He'd soon be grateful for the lower temperature. It not only kept the heat from the operating lights reasonable, but helped slow the patient's blood flow. Right now he was glad to have the cold bring his mind back to the job at hand. He knew this routine. Understood this world. He had control here.

Jake lay on the operating table with his hands held securely and under sterile drapes. Scott didn't make a habit of viewing a patient, but he couldn't help but look at Jake. The boy's soft laugh as he himself had made animal noises came to his mind. He touched one of Jake's hands briefly. Like a punch in the stomach, the realization came that he'd fallen for this little guy as well.

This surgery *must* go well.

The anesthesiologist sedating Jake sat at his head. "Mac, are you okay?"

Scott nodded. He had to get in the zone and let his training take over from his emotions. Jake's life was in his hands. "Is everyone ready?" he asked. The smell of sterilizing solution wafted through the brightly lit OR.

The phone on the wall rang.

"Heart's on its way. It looks good. It should be here in two hours. They'll call back when they're in the air," the nurse announced.

Flipping down the small but intense light stationed between surgical magnifying glasses, Scott stated, "Let's get the chest open and this young man on bypass. Scalpel."

He made an incision down the center of the chest, opening it. The heart looked exactly as he'd told Hannah it would. Large and flabby.

"Needs a new one," one of the assisting fellows remarked from across the table.

"Let's see that he gets it." Scott glanced at the clock.

The shrill ring of the phone drew his attention. The team was in the air. Forty minutes away. No time to waste.

"Let's get him on bypass," Scott stated.

Minutes later the swishing and bumping of the heart-lung machine became a constant sound in the room.

The phone rang again.

"The helicopter's on the roof. The heart's on its way down," the nurse said.

"We're ready." Scott concentrated on his patient.

Minutes later the door swung open and a two-man team entered with the new heart. One man carried a small white cooler. On top, printed in red, were the words "Live Organ."

Looking at the heart with care, Scott said, "Looks good. Time?"

"Two hours, eighteen minutes."

Great. He had leeway. He'd have time to get the heart into its new home and some to spare.

"Scalpel." With skilled precision, Scott removed Jake's damaged heart and replaced it with the donated one. "Nice fit. Sutures."

The new heart looked wonderful. Strong. Healthy. The tests indicated the match was a good one but, still, you never really knew for sure until the heart was in place if the body would accept it. The match needed to be good enough Jake wouldn't have any major problems with rejection but there were never any guarantees. Despite medical advances, heart transplants were still medical miracles.

"Coming off bypass."

The rhythmic sound of the heart-lung machine ceased as the transplant team stood around Jake, holding a unified breath.

"Releasing the clamps," the fellow said.

Blood flowed through the new heart.

It quivered.

It shifted.

With a jerk, it began to beat.

Scott always felt a sense of awe when he watched a transplanted heart begin beating on its own. It took a few seconds before the heart moved into a steady pace of thump...bump...thump...

Surgery couldn't have gone more textbook perfect. Scott felt like a weight had been lifted off his shoulders.

"Andrea, you can let Hannah...uh...Mrs. Quinn know that the heart is in and looks great. Jake is stable."

Hannah saw the smile on Andrea's face as she came through the waiting-room door. She could tell the woman had good news and Andrea's words confirmed her confidence in Scott.

"Thank God," she cried in relief, as joy bubbled up and escaped.

She hugged Andrea. "What happens now?"

"Scott will watch closely for bleeding and then close." Her tone was reserved, but she wore a smile.

"How long will that take?"

"If all goes well, about an hour." Her look turned more serious. "We still have some hurdles to get over. Jake's not out of the woods yet."

Hannah sank into a chair, her knees going weak. *Jake has a new heart.*

With an impatient clasping and unclasping of hands, Hannah stared at the waiting-room door, then glanced at the clock on the wall. An hour had passed. Where was Scott? Was something wrong? Why didn't he come?

As soon as Scott entered the waiting room, Hannah jumped up. He grinned at her. *Jake was doing well.* In her happiness, Hannah wrapped her arms around Scott's neck. He felt solid and secure, safe. Scott pulled Hannah close, lifting her off her feet.

"Oh, Scott..." she whispered into his neck. "Thank you, thank you, thank you." He lowered her, letting her feet touch the floor. Taking her hand, he led her to a chair, indicating she should sit. He sat in the chair next to hers.

"How's Jake?"

"He's doing as well as can be expected." Scott gave her hand a reassuring squeeze. "I wanted to explain what'll happen next."

Andrea rose. "I'll let you two talk."

"Thanks," Scott said. "For everything."

"No problem, Mac. I'll be back in a few minutes to walk up to the unit with Hannah."

Scott gave Andrea an appreciative smile. "I owe you one."

She smiled. "Glad to be of help." Andrea went out the door.

Hannah's attention returned to Scott. "What was that about?"

"I asked her to sit with you during surgery. I didn't want you to be alone."

She gave him a grateful smile. "I'm glad you did. It was a long night and would've been even longer sitting here by myself." She scooted closer. "Now, tell me about Jake."

After taking both her hands in his, Scott said, "Jake did well through the surgery. The new heart looks great." He absently played with her fingers as he spoke. "The heart even started on its own, which is always a good sign. He's in CICU now. You can see him after he's settled. The plan is for him to be in the unit for three days, then be moved to the cardiac step-down unit."

Hannah sighed. "I can't wait." Some of her fear and worry fell away. "I'll get to hold him again. Take care of him."

Scott stood, and pulled her up beside him.

Slipping her arms around his waist, Hannah lifted her gaze to his. "I can't thank you enough," she said pouring all the gratitude she felt into the words.

He looked deep into her eyes and returned her hug. "You're welcome. You have to remember, Jake isn't out of the woods yet. He has to come off the respirator and be moved to the step-down unit before he's well enough to go home. There's rejection to be concerned about and med adjustments to be made."

Hannah refused to let her happiness be dampened. "I understand, but getting the heart was a giant step. He'll make it through the rest. I just know he'll be all right."

"That's what we're working towards." Scott followed the line of her cheek with the tip of his index finger. "I love your spirit."

At the insistent buzzing of Scott's pager Hannah moved away but remained in his arms. She was close enough to read 911 Quinn on the pager screen.

At Scott's look of alarm, her stomach dropped, and rolled. She clutched his arm. "Something's happen to Jake."

Scott pushed her away and set her in a chair. "I have to go."

Andrea returned as he rushed out the door. "Take care of Hannah," he called over his shoulder.

Scott ran along the hallway, took the stairs two steps at a time, ran down another corridor and shoved through the unit doors.

Oh, God. This can't be happening. Not to Jake.

His bed was already surrounded by staff working at a fast but efficient speed.

Frantic, Scott made his way into the thick of things. His heart had almost stopped when he'd read the page. What was going on?

He felt small beads of moisture popped out across his forehead as he pulled on plastic gloves.

"Report," he snapped.

"BP 80 over 20. Unresponsive," a female voice stated.

Keep your cool. Think, man, think.

"Push meds."

He jerked off his stethoscope from around his neck, placed it on Jake's chest, and listened.

The beats sounded strong but slow.

"Epi—"

"BP rising," someone called from behind him.

"Eighty over fifty. Ninety-three over sixty-five and rising."

Rolling his shoulders, Scott released the tension knotted there, hard as a baseball. He turned to Jake's nurse. "Give another dose of Prograf. Check level in one hour. Blood gases every fifteen minutes till the hour and then every thirty minutes if stable. BP?"

"Low but steady."

"Okay, we're going to let him rest. Let his body adjust to the new heart. Stop any possibility of rejection. Watch him carefully. Page me if I'm needed."

Scott's hands shook. He'd almost lost control. Now he had to tell Hannah that Jake still wasn't out of danger.

Andrea placed a hand on his arm and said in a low voice, "Hannah's in the hallway. She's almost hysterical."

Scott took a deep breath and let it out slowly. He must get his rattled nerves under control before he saw Hannah. He pushed through the unit doors.

Hannah leaned against the wall, her face drained of color. She looked like she'd slide down the wall any second. When he opened his arms she stepped into them. A tremble went through her as she clung to him. He tightened his embrace.

"Scott, what's happening?"

He ran a hand down her hair, smoothing it, allowing himself time to form the words he resisted saying.

"Jake is in rejection."

"Oh, my God, no."

Her tears dampened his shirt where her face was pressed to his chest.

"We've seen this before. But it'll be touch and go for a while. We may even have to relist him if the rejection can't be controlled. He'll have to be watched closely through the rest of the night. All we can do now is to wait and see if Jake's body will accept the heart."

Hannah pulled away and looked up at him. Terror, desolation and weariness filled her eyes. "Can I see him?"

"Yes, but only briefly."

Hannah noticed Scott's usual reassurance and confidence was missing. He wasn't telling her everything would be all right. A sick feeling hit her again. Scott was worried.

It was difficult to believe Jake had gotten his new heart and now it might kill him. She wanted to curl into a ball and hide, but she wouldn't. She had to remain strong, see Jake over this hurdle.

With effort Hannah prepared for what Jake would look like. She'd been warned he'd be swollen from being on the heart-lung machine. Tubes, a lot more than before, would be inserted into his body. It hurt to think of her small boy having to endure pain.

After washing her hands, she shakingly pulled on a gown and gloves. One of the nurses helped her with a mask. She found Jake behind glass doors, which were closed to form an isolation room.

The steady whoosh and puff of the respirator was ever-present. He was surrounded by beeping pumps and three of the staff. Hannah tuned all of it out. Taking slow, steady steps, she approached the bed. The light touch of Scott's hand at her back steadied her. He was her rock in the face of this ugly reality. She was thankful to have him there.

Jake wasn't as puffy as she'd feared. That was one positive. "He looks so pink," Hannah whispered. She hadn't seen such a healthy color on Jake's cheeks in a long time. The difference was remarkable. The dusky blue around his lips had disappeared. He looked beautiful. If only his body would embrace this heart.

The incision site made her flinch. Taking his small limp hand in her gloved one, she'd make do with meager contact until she could hold him.

Hannah looked at Scott and whispered, "This heart has to work." She refused to believe otherwise.

Scott's hand flexed against her back.

To Jake she whispered, "I love you, honey." She watched for any indication he'd heard her. "Hang in there."

"Tomorrow we'll know more," Scott said from behind her. "We'll let him rest, give him a chance to adjust to the heart. If he improves we can start weaning him off the respirator. But the next twelve to twenty-four hours are crucial. You'll want to stay close."

Hannah slumped against him as tears ran down her cheeks.

Apparently Scott no longer cared what the staff thought or what the grapevine would say in the morning. His arm supported her as they walked out of the CICU.

Hannah had asked Scott a couple of times during the wee hours of the morning if she could come into the unit. He allowed it once but the next time he had to say no. Jake's blood pressure had plummeted again. Scott feared they were losing him, but Jake came through the episode and started doing much better. It looked like the adjustment period was over.

He'd wanted to sit with Hannah and give her some much-needed support but Jake required his attention. He couldn't remember a time when he'd felt so torn. Scott managed to go to the waiting area and check on Hannah around six in the morning. The lights were still off, and he found her staring into space in the dark room. The TV was in snow mode.

He flipped the switch, doing away with the electric storm, and gathered her to him. She laid her head on his chest and a soft sigh slipped through her lips. They said nothing for a long time. He struggled with having to leave her all alone when it was time to return to the unit.

At midmorning Scott returned to the waiting room to find Hannah asleep sitting up. His heart went out to her. It was pouring with rain outside, and despite the weak light Scott could see the exhaustion on her face. The weariness had to be both emotional and physical. A person could only take so much, and she'd had more than her share.

Scott hated to wake her but she needed to be in a bed. Outside the hospital rest area. He gave her a gentle shake.

Hannah's head jerked up. "What?" A wild look filled her eyes. She rose quickly. "Is Jake okay?"

"He's fine, honey. Doing much better, actually. I thought you'd like to go back for a visit."

She blinked once, twice. Her hair was mussed and she looked adorable. He wanted to gather her into his arms, take her home and tuck her into his bed.

Unable to act on the impulse, he settled for taking her hand and walking beside her down the hall. "Jake needs to rest and stay quiet the rest of the day. If he's still improving by this evening, we'll start weaning him from the respirator."

After gowning up to visit, Scott followed Hannah to Jake's bed. "I've ordered he remain sedated to prevent pain and to let him rest. That'll put him in the best shape for when the respirator is removed. I've left orders for the meds to be decreased later this evening allowing him to wake up a little."

"Is he out of the woods?"

"I believe so, but I'll know more when I see him this evening."

"Thank God." Hannah leaned over, picked up Jake's unresponsive hand and brought it to her cheek.

Scott's chest constricted to see the love Hannah expressed. What did it feel like to be on the receiving end of that kind of devotion? His heart ached with longing for something that could never be. He needed to leave before he said something that might end up hurting her. "I need to check on another patient. I'll be a minute."

He went to the nursing station and glanced at his notes, not really seeing them. Inhaling deeply, he let the breath out slowly. His hands trembled slightly. Hannah and Jake made him wish he was a different kind of person.

The nurse seated beside him gave him a curious look. He managed a smile, hoping it looked more normal than his rattled nerves indicated. Taking another deep breath, he returned to Hannah. "It's time to go. You can come back later."

Her green eyes fixed on his. "May I kiss him?"

Scott couldn't say no. "Sure. Just be careful."

On her toes as far as she could stretch, Hannah leaned over the rail. The bed had been adjusted to a higher than normal position. She couldn't quite reach Jake's head.

Without hesitation, Scott circled her waist with his hands and lifted her. Hannah's lips touched Jake's forehead. Holding her a second longer, he lowered her. She glanced back at him, her eyes full of gratitude. His chest swelled.

A hand still at her waist, he said, "Let's go. You need to rest too. You're almost dead on your feet." He lowered his voice. "You're coming home with me."

She gave him a defiant look and said in a low whisper, "No, I'm staying here."

He grinned. She hadn't disappointed him. Even worn out, she could put up a fight. "No, you're not, and that's the way it's going to be." His tone left no doubt he meant it. "Think about it. If anything were to happen to Jake I'm the first person who'd be called, which means you'd know right away." With complete confidence he knew his statement would put a stop to any argument she might make.

They made their way to the parking deck in silence. As the elevator doors closed, he slipped an arm around her waist and gathered her close, tucking her against him. She accepted his support. He liked having Hannah next to him. She fit.

As they exited the elevator and walked to the car, Hannah made no effort to leave his embrace. He helped her into his car, and she rested her head against the seat. Exhaling a sigh of exhaustion, she closed her eyes and immediately fell asleep. Scott adjusted her head so it rested on his shoulder.

Scott and Hannah stood in his living room, watching each other. Indecision hung in the air as if they were two magnets pulled together while at the same time being pushed apart. His gaze lingered on Hannah's brown hair then traveled over the curve of her cheek, paused at her breasts before following the length of her jeans-covered legs.

He wanted her in his bed, but she'd get no rest there. It wouldn't be fair to her. A physical relationship would imply there could be something more between them. That wasn't going to happen. He would leave her. He had to.

His eyes returned to hers. Those expressive green orbs had gone wide. The tell-tale rapid pulse in her neck caught his attention. Hannah recognized his desire. He had to send her to her bed before he tumbled her into his. "Get some sleep, Hannah."

She said nothing, turned and walked down the hall.

Scott decided he needed a shower. An ice-cold one.

Needing rest after a long night, he'd installed the one thing that could keep him awake right next door to his bedroom. What had he been thinking?

On the way to his room, Scott hesitated at her closed door. He brought his fist up to knock, but dropped his hand to his side. It would be disastrous if she opened the door. He would lose control. His body ached to have her. All the tension, emotion and adrenalin of the last twenty-four hours would find release. With a force of will he hadn't known he possessed, Scott moved on down the hall. The firm click of the door closing behind him echoed in his too-empty bedroom.

Scott was stepping out of the bathroom a few minutes later when the door to his room opened. Hannah stood partially in the entrance, as if she wasn't sure she'd be welcome. She wore the same T-shirt she'd had on the other night. One sleek leg came into view. He wanted more.

His heartbeat rose, along with another part of his anatomy. He was grateful for the boxers he'd pulled on.

She didn't move. He waited. The next step had to be hers.

"I…uh…I don't want to be by myself." She made a movement towards him.

"Hannah, I can't just hold you."

"I know." The words were said so softly he almost didn't hear them. "I want to forget all the ugliness. To start living life again. To feel. I want you to make the loneliness go away for a little while." Scott enveloped her in a hug. Hannah wrapped her arms around his trim waist and pulled his warmth and strength closer. She wanted to burrow into him, to push the loneliness away. A ripple of awareness went through her, and she released a soft moan of pleasure. It felt wonderful, even right, to be in Scott's bedroom.

His look intensified. Drawing her snugly against the breadth of his chest, his lips came down on hers in a crushing kiss. Those same lips had brought her pleasure on many levels, smiling at her, reassuring her, making her laugh. A ripple of excitement raced through her body. She'd found her protective harbor.

Scott eased his hold, but his body remained tense, as if he was restraining his desire with effort. His kisses became a succession of gentle nibbles against her mouth. She leaned into him, asking for more, demanding it. Her hands slid up his arms to circle his neck, offering herself to him completely.

The sound of a man released from his pain surfaced from deep within Scott. He became the aggressor again. Giving her a couple of long caressing kisses, he then probed her mouth with a gentle flick of his tongue. She opened to him, surrendering. His tongue explored her mouth, conquering.

He lifted her, his hands cupping her behind. She tightened her arms about his neck.

A sound trickled out of her, a cross between a mewl and a hum.

She trusted him. Scott would take care of her.

Scott groaned in delight at the discovery Hannah wasn't wearing panties. He feared his need might pour over the dam wall of his control. Hannah had surprises. Sweet surprises.

His finger traced the place where a band of lace should've been circling her thigh, before his hand traveled over the curve of her hip. Hannah pulled away and searched his face for a suspended moment before bringing her mouth to his again. Her kiss became damp, dense and daring as she caressed his lips with her own, as her tongue searched and found his.

She fed his raging need. He surrendered with a growl of unadulterated male desire.

Hannah giggled. She had to know exactly what kind of effect she was having on him.

His mouth feasted upon hers. Their tongues dueled. The hot, forceful motion of her tongue tasting and exploring his mouth tantalized him, testing his control. His manhood stood ridged between them. He would have Hannah, and there was no going back.

"Hannah…" Scott drawled in a strangled voice when

she dragged her mouth from his. "You're so hot." He reached for her again, pulling her along the evidence of what she did to him. In a raspy whisper he said, "You do the sweetest things to me."

"You're kind of wonderful yourself." Her look was shy, sending a completely different message from the suggestive shift she made against him.

Her bashfulness ebbed and flowed. It was one of many facets of her personality Scott found intriguing. A lioness when fighting for her son, yet in a heated moment of passion she could still act and look like a lady. Someone he wanted to care for, protect. Scott found the combination of strength and timidity intriguing.

He studied her earnestly.

"What's wrong? Am I hurting you?" she asked, stirring as if she'd leave his arms.

He held her in place with a firm clasp of his hands under her amazing behind. Oh, yeah, she was hurting him, but in a good way. "Stay. I like you here. I want to look at you."

Hannah lowered her eyes then brought her gaze back to meet his.

"I want you in my bed." His words were little more than a husky sigh.

Her cool lips touched the fevered skin of his chest in acceptance, before moving her attention to his lips.

With her secure in his arms, Scott walked her backwards to the bed. Her lips remained tightly pressed against his as she followed his lead. Half seated, half lying, he brought her down with him. She shifted, gaining a more intimate position against him, pushing his ache higher. Searching her eyes, Scott found trust and openness and wanting there.

He needed to have her crave him as much as he did her. Something he'd never experienced before.

Scott found he was experiencing numerous firsts where she was concerned.

Hannah broke the heated kiss and smiled down at Scott. His lips curved into one of the sexy grins she loved so much. "Hannah..." The word drifted across her cheek like a sea breeze. Blood zipped through her veins. With a tender slip of his hand along her neck he guided her mouth down to meet his. She saw the reverence in his eyes before her lids lowered. The pure, perfect pleasure of his mouth against hers again made her heart soar.

His index finger crawled cross her thigh to the edge of her shirt, and slipped under. His hand gained her complete attention as it slid further up over her hip and across her back to settle at the curve of her breast. His fingertips danced away, leaving behind a straining ache to be touched.

She shuddered. The hunger throbbed low in her belly as primal as a native drum. Her hips lifted towards him, then pulled away and lifted again, before he brought her on top of him. The hard length of his desire pulsated against her belly. Their tongues touched, darted away, and came together to meet again.

Hannah's fingers wandered across his chest. Warm and solid, her hand hovered over the fine mat of hair there. Scott shifted beneath her as she continued her exploration. His heartbeat thumped steady and strong under her palm. Ignoring his murmur of protest, she lifted her mouth from his and placed a kiss above his heart.

His chest stilled, his breathing faltered.

With a rumble of pure manly pleasure coming from deep within him, Scott flipped her. He pushed the shirt she wore up and off, exposing her breasts.

He placed a tender, reverent kiss on the soft curve of one of the exposed mounds before his mouth moved to hover over the tip of the other breast. Hannah inhaled and her nipple brushed his partially open mouth.

With the tip of his tongue, Scott flicked the nipple straining to reach him. A shiver moved through her. Her eyes widened. Was the hunger she felt reflected in them?

"Please," Hannah begged, as she pushed at his boxers.

Scott stood, letting his underwear fall to the floor. He reached into his bedside-table drawer, found what he needed and sheathed himself. He rejoined her, taking her mouth in a long and lingering kiss. Moving between her legs, he entered her slowly. Reverently.

Hannah welcomed him into her heat, basking in it. Wrapping her legs around him, she pulled him to her. She joined him in the special dance of life as they found a rhythm that was theirs alone.

She tensed, gripped his shoulders and voiced her pleasure before a rumble of satisfaction began deep in his throat and built like thunder rolling into the night to boom as he joined her in paradise.

A feeling of power swept over Hannah as she lay cradled in Scott's arms. She'd made the always-in-control doctor lose it. The knowledge fueled her desire.

She'd never been the aggressor in lovemaking but with Scott it had been different. It amazed her. The freedom he allowed her to be herself endeared him to her even more. The curtain surrounding her heart and concealing her feelings fluttered open after years of stillness.

She was in love. Mountain high, valley low and river wide, in love.

Scott pushed her hair away from her forehead and kissed her.

"That was wonderful," Hannah said against his chest.

"The kiss or...?"

"Fishing for a compliment?"

"No, actions speak louder than words."

Hannah nipped his skin with her teeth.

"Watch it. That might lead to retaliation."

She giggled. "I wouldn't mind."

His hand skimmed over her hip. "I wouldn't either."

Neither said anything for a few minutes.

Was this the time and the place to ask? She had to know. She'd wondered for years. If she asked it might ruin everything but if she didn't she might never know. She needed to understand why.

Hannah brushed her hand back and forth over the mat of hair on his chest. "Scott, can I ask you something?"

"Sure." The word came out slowly, as if he was drifting off to sleep.

"Why?" With her cheek resting against his warm skin, she felt the catch in his breathing.

"Why what?" His voice no longer sounded drowsy.

"Why wouldn't you talk to me after that night?"

He stilled. His hand no longer caressed her side. "Because it couldn't go anywhere," he said quietly. "I would've only hurt you more. It should never have happened."

Hannah twisted around so she could look at him. "You think I didn't know that? I'd watched you with all the other nurses. But I did think our friendship deserved more credit than you gave it."

He didn't say anything for a long moment. "You're right. You were a stronger person than I gave you credit for being."

"Self-esteem get in the way, did it?" The question had a bitterness to it she'd not intended.

"I'll admit I was a little more than confident about my success with women, as you know."

She smiled. "A little?"

"Well, if it's any consolation I'm not as confident as I used to be." He shifted, moving away from her slightly. "As for the way I acted, for the first time in my life I found something I wanted as badly as I wanted to be a surgeon— you. I had no idea you were a virgin. I couldn't believe you chose to give that gift to me. I knew you were the type of woman who needed a forever kind of guy. I wasn't prepared to be the guy. The truth is you scared me."

She swallowed hard. There was nothing to lose by asking, "And now? Do I scare you?"

"No, now I'm scared *for* you."

"Why?" she asked softly, fear prickling her heart. Something told her she wouldn't like his answer.

"Do you remember me telling you my father is a doctor?"

She nodded.

"He's a wonderful guy, and a great doctor who loves people. He still makes house calls. But my father has a problem. He can't say no. It made my mother miserable and in turn it made him miserable. When I decided to go to medical school my mother cried. Not with joy but in disappointment. She said I'd be just like my dad. Married to my job."

Hannah wanted to yell that Scott was different. He already proved it in so many ways. Their relationship had nothing to do with his parents' marriage. Scott needed to give them a chance. There must be another reason he wouldn't let her get close.

"That's not all there is to it, is it? Because all kinds of people have high-pressure careers and solid relationships."

"No, that isn't all. My parents divorced during my surgical fellowship. If anything, Mother got worse. She became more demanding, more in need of attention, but now it was from me and my brothers. Mother called us all the time, wanting this or that. During one period the calls numbered as many as ten or fifteen a day. My brothers have families so I tried to run interference and asked Mom to come and visit me for a few weeks. While she was staying with me she had an emotional breakdown and took an overdose of pills."

"Oh, Scott. I'm so sorry." She squeezed his hand. "Is she all right?" she asked quietly.

"She's fine now. Doing well. For the first time in a long time I really think she is starting to be happy."

He continued, as if he needed to talk.

"I had no idea she'd become so depressed. I should've known but I was so involved in my work I couldn't see it." He looked down at their clasped hands. "She called me, and I didn't go, didn't even answer her call. She'd gotten to where she was calling me almost hourly, day in, day out. Sometimes I answered, other times I didn't. I didn't want to encourage her.

"That day was no different. It had been a crazy day, with one patient going into cardiac arrest, two more being admitted. My voice mail was full of messages begging me to come home, but I still had afternoon rounds to make.

"I arrived home to find her passed out on her bed in her best dress with a pill bottle in her hand."

"And you've been blaming yourself ever since."

"Yeah." The word was said so softly she almost didn't hear it.

She cupped his face. "It wasn't your fault."

"It's easy to say, but I don't think I'll ever really believe it. The overdose was bad enough but Mom said she wanted nothing more to do with me."

"That can't be true!"

"Well, it was at the time. Now we do have some semblance of a relationship but we're just going through the motions. Both of us are dancing around the elephant in the room when we see each other."

"Have you sat down and really had a heart to heart with your mom?"

"No, I just want to forget and move on."

"I don't think you ever will until you two kick the elephant out the door."

He squeezed her to him. "You might be right." He hesitated. "It also hit home that horrible day that I was no different from my father. I knew then I had no business having a wife and family. I'm incapable of setting boundaries for myself. I'm too wrapped up in my work. My job will always come first."

Hannah wrapped her arms around him and gave him a hug. She said nothing for a long moment. She couldn't let him know how she felt. He was already starting to run. She was done being the goodbye girl. Maybe with more time she could convince him he was wrong about himself, that his mother had been speaking out of her own pain. For now she had to tell him what he needed to hear. "I don't expect any more than your friendship."

The tension in Scott's body eased.

CHAPTER EIGHT

No LIGHT beamed through the bedroom window when Hannah woke up.

Jake. How's Jake?

She reached for her cell phone on the bedside table. The space beside her was still warm. Scott hadn't been gone long.

Battery dead.

Flinging the spread off, she looked for a phone. Finding none, she pulled on the first thing she saw. It was one of Scott's T-shirts. Her bare feet made a padding noise as she went to the door and pulled it open. A gurgle came from down the hall. Coffee-pot. Kitchen. There'd be a phone there. Her throat tightened as she hurried toward the sound. Panic welled. She had to check on Jake.

She stopped short at the sight of Scott at the kitchen table. He held a newspaper, a cup of coffee within his reach.

He glanced at her. "Evening," he drawled.

"I've got to call the hospital." She frantically searched the kitchen for a phone.

"Settle down. Jake's fine. I checked in. They're already starting to wean him from the respirator."

The calmness in his voice annoyed her, but her heart slowed its pace. "Really?"

"Yes. Really." He gave her a lazy smile.

Relief washed over her.

"I'm his doctor, remember?" Scott grabbed her arm and pulled her into his lap. His lips found hers. They'd slept and loved the afternoon away without Scott's beeper sounding an alarm. Even after the time they'd shared in bed, Hannah still hungered for him. He'd left her in bed again but based on his actions earlier in the day and again later in the afternoon she knew he wouldn't go far. Scott had been a wonderfully attentive lover.

She couldn't resist returning his kiss but she had to put a stop to this before she went past the point of no return. The truth was, though, that had already happened.

She pushed away and stood, moving out of his reach. "Uh, about last night, I mean today, I—"

"You needed someone and I was there. Being a friend. How about a cup of coffee or tea before we go to the hospital? Would you like something to eat now or wait until we get back?"

Scott certainly wasn't placing any importance on what had occurred between them. His calm demeanor almost made her smack him. Those had been the most amazing moments of her life and Scott was treating them as if they had been no big deal. If he could act cool about their love-making then so could she.

Resting back in his chair, with a slight grin on his lips, he acted as if it was a normal everyday occurrence to have her in his home. Despite the lack of sleep during the night and today, he appeared well rested. He'd already dressed. His royal blue polo shirt and khaki pants made him look like he was ready for a round of golf.

Heavens, she was wearing one of his thin white shirts. Her eyes dropped to what she wore. His shirt barely reached the top of her thighs. Heat rushed up her neck and settled in her cheeks. She crossed her arms over her breasts. Scott had seen much more, touched every inch of her, but she wasn't used to parading around half-dressed in front of a man.

"Why didn't you say something?" she squeaked. "I'm going to get dressed."

He raised an eyebrow and made a low chuckle. "Are you kidding? I was enjoying the sight of you in my T-shirt, in my kitchen."

She whirled to leave.

Scott pushed back his chair, stood and caught her arm. "I'll get you something to cover up with. Fix yourself a cup of tea. Settle for a minute." He left.

Going to the pot, Hannah found a teabag and poured water into a cup. After the stress of the last couple of days, and especially yesterday, on many levels, she needed to soothe her nerves. She was still standing by the counter when Scott returned.

He handed her a robe. Scrambling into it, she found it fell below her knees, giving her some sense of security. She pulled the belt tight. The tangy smell of Scott permeated the robe.

"Better?" he asked.

"Much, thanks."

Scott returned to his seat and picked up his coffee mug, still grinning. It was clear he was enjoying her discomfort.

Pushing against the leg of a chair, he scooted it out. "Come and sit next to me."

Hannah approached the chair with trepidation. The whole scene smacked too much of marital bliss. It made her wish for things Scott had said could never be.

She sank into the chair. "Why're we taking our time getting to the hospital? Don't you need to check on Jake? I need to see him."

"You didn't get much uninterrupted rest. I was giving you as much time as possible to sleep. Instead of doing that, you came storming through the door." His lips turned up at the corners.

Hannah flushed all over. Yes, he had kept her busy as if he'd held himself in check for all the years they'd been apart. "Please don't make fun of me. My first thought was of Jake. He's all I've got."

Scott's face sobered and the skin along his jaw tightened. He acted as if he was going to say something, before his face eased and he returned to his easygoing manner. "When you finish your tea, we'll go."

"I need to get a quick shower."

His eyes turned dark and his voice dipped low. "Would you like some company?"

Heat coiled within her. For a second Hannah was tempted to say yes. "No, I think I can manage by myself." She hurried out of the room, fearing she might change her mind.

Scott groaned.

How much could a healthy male take? Waking with Hannah's warm body nestled close and having her come into his kitchen with the scent of him lingering on her was one of the most erotic things he'd ever experienced. He longed for it all. Hannah, the job, a family. Could he have that ideal life?

She'd said Jake was all she had. He'd wanted to argue the point. Tell her she had him too. But could he honestly make that promise? Pulling out his cell phone, Scott checked on Jake and another patient in the hope Hannah would be dressed by the time he'd finished. He needed to get his mind on something else. If he didn't find a way to keep busy, he might do something stupid, like stepping into the shower with her. Or telling Hannah he loved her.

Would she welcome him with open arms?

Scott groaned. There were other problems. Jake's recovery concerned him more than he'd let on to Hannah. There was always a chance Jake could have difficulty getting off the respirator because he had been on it before going into surgery. Scott hoped and prayed removal went smoothly for everyone's sake.

"Ready?" Hannah had entered the living room without him noticing. A quizzical look crossed her face. "You're deep in thought."

There was a fresh, wholesome smell to her. Perfect. She wore a simple light green shirt and a short blue denim skirt that showed off her incredible legs. Scott resisted the urge to pull her to him and kiss her past all reason. If he did that, they'd never make it to the hospital any time soon.

She stepped closer. "Everything okay with Jake?"

Her question brought him back to reality. He had to leave. He'd never run away from a woman before, but he felt the need to put some space between himself and Hannah. "How about we see for ourselves?"

Scott pulled into the hospital parking lot a few minutes after seven. Hannah had to wait until after shift change before she could see Jake. Scott regretted he couldn't let her come back with him, but shift change was the one time of day the nurses' word was law.

When most of the patients' reports had been given, Scott asked Jake's nurse to call the waiting room and tell Hannah she could come through.

His lips curved upward as he watched Hannah hurry to Jake's bed. Her smile made him feel like the greatest man on earth. A superhero. His skill as a surgeon had helped to put a joyful look on her face. With that knowledge came immense satisfaction.

Scott moved to stand beside her. "Jake's making great progress so far. We'll be going down five breaths at a time over the next few hours and then try to remove the tube first thing in the morning.

"Nurse, I want a blood gas drawn every fifteen minutes. Cut back on the dopamine and Captopril." He made a notation on Jake's chart.

"He looks better than he did yesterday. Even his incision area doesn't look as awful." Hannah ran a caressing finger along Jake's arm.

Hannah showed her caring through touch. Scott especially enjoyed it when he was on the receiving end of emotion. The stroke of her hand had a way of making him feel as if he was the best man in the world for her. It was already killing him to think about having to let her go.

"During the night we will work toward removing the respirator. The longer we wait the harder it is to remove. Because Jake was on the respirator before surgery it's even more important he comes off it soon," Scott said. "You'll be surprised at how fast things will improve afterwards. We'll continue to keeping a close watch on him."

"Jake certainly doesn't need any additional problems."

"I don't want him to have any more problems either. He's a special little guy. I'm doing everything I know to see it doesn't happen. I think he's past the worst." Scott gave her shoulder a quick squeeze. Something as simple as giving Hannah a reassuring touch sent heat hissing through him.

She continued to look at her amazing little miracle.

"Do you think you could eat now?" Scott asked.

"Yeah. I'm starving, but I hate to leave him."

"His nurse knows we're but a phone call away. Hunger's a good sign your nerves are settling down."

His certainly weren't. A different kind of hunger gnawed at him.

After picking up a drive-through meal, they returned to Scott's place. With their dinner completed, Scott gave Hannah one of his piercing looks that said in no uncertain terms he wanted her. He scooped her up and carried her to his bed. This time their lovemaking was slow and sweet. Afterwards Hannah curled into him and settled into a peaceful, deep sleep, enhanced by dreams of what could be.

The next morning Scott left her with a swift, but fervent kiss before they parted in the stairway. With Jake improving and a kiss from Scott on her lips, Hannah's heart felt lighter than it had in years.

She'd barely been in CICU a few minutes when Jake's nurse asked her to leave. It was time for the respiratory therapist to remove the respirator.

Hannah sat, paced and sat again. Would Jake be able to come off? Would he stay off? What if he had to be put back on?

Stop.

She had to quit thinking. Thinking led to an all-consuming fear. Despite her efforts not to look at the clock, she watched each slow minute pass. With any luck this would be the last time she'd have to endure this type of wait.

The desk phone rang. Hannah stared at the pink-coated volunteer who answered it. She looked at Hannah. "The nurse says you can come back now."

The tube was gone from Jake's mouth. He lay at a slight angle, propped on pillows with an oxygen canula under his nose. A weak smile came to his lips as Hannah approached. Her heart swelled. It felt like years since she'd seen his lips curl upwards.

"Hello, honey." She beamed to the point that her cheeks ached. The bed had been lowered and she leaned across Jake, placing her cheek against his.

The nurse still had his hands secured. Hannah put her index finger in his palm and he wrapped his fingers around hers. His breathing remained labored, but not enough for her to be too concerned. He was breathing on his own. That was what mattered. Catching the corner of her shirt, she wiped the moisture away from her eyes. "I love you."

"M-o-m-m-y." He mouthed the word but she heard no sound.

"Do you have anything to put on his lips? They're so dry and cracked," Hannah asked.

The nurse handed her lip balm. Hannah applied it, welcoming the opportunity to have even such a small part in his care.

Jake's eyes focused on Hannah for a second before his eyelids drooped. The sparkle of his childhood had yet to return but it would soon. She said a prayer of thanks for Scott's surgical skills and for the family who had given her child life again. The knowledge of what the family of the donor was suffering troubled Hannah, but she was grateful for the gift of Jake's life. She would make sure their gift was honored by taking excellent care of Jake.

The nurse allowed Hannah to remain at his bedside most of the day. The time passed in a blur of activity, which was a relief from the mind-numbing worry and boredom of the past few days. Hannah hadn't seen Scott since earlier that morning, but knew he had to be in surgery. She missed him. He'd come to see them when he could, she had no doubt.

By the middle of the afternoon only one nurse was required for Jake's care. The central line had been removed, along with the catheter. The machines monitoring vitals, two chest tubes and a pacemaker were all that remained.

Scott finally made it by to see them in the early evening. The nurse smiled knowingly at Hannah and Scott then left them alone.

"Doesn't he look wonderful?" Hannah asked, unable to contain her happiness.

"He does." Scott's smile reached his eyes. "He's doing great. If tomorrow goes as well as today, he'll be going to the floor."

"Wonderful. I can stay with him all the time then."

"I'll miss having you next to me when that happens, but it's nice to see you happy." Scott's look turned solemn. "I wanted us to have dinner tonight, but I've got emergency surgery. Please don't stay too late. I don't like you being in the parking deck by yourself." His finger traced the line of her jaw. "Go to my house. Get some rest," he whispered, and slipped her keys.

Her heart contracted. She felt cherished, as if she had someone to stand beside her. It was wonderful to no longer be alone. Not having experienced those feelings for a long time, she wrapped the sensation around her and basked in its warmth. "I won't. I'll go after I see Jake, I promise."

Scott nodded, his gaze never leaving hers.

Hannah glanced around, then lowered her voice. "I appreciate you taking care of both my son and me. You've been a great friend. I'm glad you were here when we needed you." She gave him a bright smile.

"My pleasure."

In response to his husky tone, a sizzle of delight zipped through her.

In the same sensual timbre, he said, "I wish I could kiss you…" he glanced around "…but…"

She reached for his hand, catching his little finger for a moment then releasing it. "I do too."

He looked into her eyes for an extended moment filled with wishing, regret, and a promise before he left. The warmth that had surrounded her went with him. Hannah understood why he hadn't kissed her but that didn't keep her from being disappointed.

Much later Scott slipped into bed beside her. She scooted next to him. The contentment she'd been missing had returned, engulfing her.

"Shh…go back to sleep," Scott said softly in her ear as his arms drew her back against him.

"Jake?"

"He's fine, honey. Sleeping when I left."

She glanced at the clock. One a.m.

"Are you okay?" The blood hummed through her veins, being so close to him. The roughness of his beard brushed across her cheek.

"Yeah, tired. Sorry to wake you."

"A doctor's life isn't always their own. Coming home at all hours is part of my life. I understand."

"A lot of women wouldn't see it that way."

"Well, I'm not just any woman. I know firsthand what you do is important." His arms tightened around her for a second then eased. Goose-bumps popped up along her arms.

He placed a quick kiss behind her ear. "Thank you."

The words were thick with emotion, as if she'd given him a precious gift.

"Okay, we're off." Hannah made a buzzing noise like an airplane as she circled the white plastic spoon in a flying motion toward Jake's mouth.

He giggled. Like a baby bird waiting for a worm, he

opened his mouth. Hannah dipped the spoon into his mouth. Scott stood at the door, watching mother and child totally absorbed in each other. His chest swelled with pride. This was his reward for the years of medical school and lost sleep of his intern years. If only he could keep Hannah as happy for the rest of her life. He shook his head. He had no business contemplating such things. They were never to be.

Scott winced at the memories of his family meals. There had been a few nice ones early in his life, but as his parents' marriage had disintegrated during his teenage years, few if any had been peaceful. It was hard to remember the warmth that he felt in this small hospital room at any meal.

Hannah might understand now what his job entailed, but after a while his dedication to his profession would grow stale, start to divide them. He didn't want what had happened between his parents to happen to him and Hannah. That would be a pain he couldn't bear.

He ached to be on the inside of the love he was witnessing, instead of standing on the outskirts. Could he manage having a family and a growing transplant program at the same time?

What if he set boundaries? Learned to say no? Accepted help? Could he make his professional life different than his father's?

No. He wouldn't take the chance. He loved Hannah and Jake enough to protect them from him.

Scott left without disturbing them.

By the end of the day most of the tubes and lines attached to Jake had been removed. The two large chest tubes used to drain fluid and the pacemaker wires were all that remained. They would be taken out after he went to the floor.

Hannah disliked Jake's hands having to remain tied.

She *ached* to hold him. She'd have to settle for small hugs
for a while longer. They weren't as satisfying as having
him sit in her lap, secure against her chest, but that would
come.

She'd thought Scott would've been by to see them before now. At least visit between surgeries.

Life would be busy during the next year. There would be
little time to devote to a relationship, even if Scott wanted
one—and he gave no indication of wanting that. She wasn't
fooling herself into believing he gave any thought to a future with her. She wished she could get Scott to see they
could be a family if he would open his mind to the possibility of a relationship. But it was more than she could
hope for.

This thing between them had simply been a convenient
interlude.

She had to stop driving herself crazy with what-ifs. One
question still wouldn't go away. How had she let Scott become such an important and necessary part of her life so
quickly?

"They're ready for Jake on the step-down unit," his
nurse said, interrupting Hannah's musings.

Jake was sitting up in the middle of his bed with a smile
on his face. His nurse had already loaded his belongs onto
the far end of the bed.

"Ready to go, sweetheart?" Hannah asked him.

"Go, brrmm, brrmm," he said, driving his pretend car.

It was hard to believe how quickly he was recovering.
Almost hourly he gathered more strength. His personality was returning too.

Hannah laughed. "Yes, brrmm, brrmm."

With Hannah's help, the nurse maneuvered the bed
down the hall and into the elevator. It felt so good to be
doing something active after so many hours of waiting

and worrying. They pushed Jake's bed into a wing of the hospital Hannah had never seen.

The charge nurse met them in the hall. "We're glad Jake's doing so well. We've been looking forward to meeting you."

Hannah didn't understand the comment. Why would the nurses be interested in her? Had the grapevine been talking about her and Scott?

The nurse settled Jake into his room and checked his IVs. Hannah watched as the telemetry to monitor Jake's heart rate in the nurses' station was attached. His nurse also hooked him up to a blood-pressure and a pulse-ox machine.

Hannah scrutinized everything. Being a nurse was an innate part of her. She may not be nursing at present but she'd not forgotten the safety precautions.

"You'll need to continue to wear a gown and gloves," his nurse said.

"Even when I sleep?"

"You can go without covering if you sleep on the other side of the room. And there can be no visitors outside immediate family."

"That won't be a problem. There's just me." Those words sounded sad to even Hannah's own ears.

When Jake slipped into a peaceful sleep, Hannah went down the hall to buy a canned drink. On her way back she passed a partially open door to a patient's room. The respiration and heart monitor were buzzing. No parent was staying with the child. She'd mentioned the patient to Jake's nurse earlier, saying how difficult it must be for the parents not to stay with their child. Hannah was grateful she wasn't in the same situation.

Searching the hallway, she saw no staff members headed her direction. She looked into the room. A child of about two years old was lying on his back unmoving and turning a dusky blue.

Hannah pushed the door open as a man from housekeeping came around the corner.

"Get some help. Stat!" She didn't wait to see if he did as ordered. She plopped her drink on the table on her way to the bedside. Reaching the child, she pushed the nurses' call button. No answer.

She placed her hand on the child's chest. There was no rise or fall. Quickly lowering the bed rail, Hannah rolled the boy on his side. She placed her cheek near his mouth. No breath.

The beeping of the monitor still pierced the air, but she tuned it out. This child would die if she didn't do something. Had he aspirated into his lungs? She checked the child's airway.

She had to start CPR.

Where were the nurses? Why wasn't someone coming?

The boy was turning bluer. She couldn't wait.

Covering the child's mouth with hers and holding his nose closed, she blew enough air into his lung to raise the child's chest, then began compressions to the sternum.

Minutes crawled by. Still no one came. She continued working.

Where was everyone? Couldn't they hear the monitor? People as far away as Africa should be able to hear it.

She was going to have to use the defibrillator. Hadn't the crash cart been outside the door? It was her sole chance to save this child.

The housekeeping man stuck his head in the door and said help was on the way. There'd been a code blue at the other end of the hall.

"There's a code blue here," Hannah snapped between compressions.

The man stared at her.

"Two, there is, three, a cart, four, outside, five, the door, six, get it, seven, now."

The housekeeper didn't return pushing the crash cart. Instead Scott appeared.

"Hannah, I'll handle this. You push the meds. They're in the cart." He handed her a keyring with a key held between two fingers. "We'll worry about the legalities later."

She found the meds. Double, triple checking the dosage on the code card against what was in her hand, she stepped to the other side of the bed. Pushing the needle into the portal of the IV, she said words of thanks that it had already been placed. She pressed the plunger down slowly.

"Step back," Scott commanded.

He placed the paddles of the defibrillator on the child's chest.

With the electric shock, the boy's chest rose then fell, then rose and fell again on its own.

"Get the oxygen mask on him. Two liters."

"Yes, sir." Hannah unwrapped the plastic tubing and turned on the oxygen at the head of the bed. Fitting the small plastic mask over the child's nose and mouth, she watched as Scott checked the boy's pulse. Scott pulled his stethoscope from around his neck and began listening to the boy's chest.

"We've got him back. Good work, Hannah."

A charge nurse rushed into the room, stopping short. "I just heard."

"He's stable. A CBS, panel, and gases need to be drawn. Let Dr. Carter know what happened. This is his patient. Also let the supervising nurse know I'd like to see her," Scott told the nurse in a stern voice.

He turned his attention to Hannah. "You did a fine bit of

nursing here. This boy wouldn't have lived without you."
He smiled across the bed at her as he reset the monitor and
continued to check the numbers. "You can have a spot on
my team any time."

She glowed under Scott's praise. He was right, they *had*
worked well together. "Thanks. It was pretty scary there
for a few minutes."

CHAPTER NINE

HANNAH glanced at her sleeping child when Scott opened the door enough to stick his head in. He'd been stopped by a staff member when they'd passed the nurses' station on their way back to Jake's room. Smiling, he backed out, returned with a mask in his hand then came inside and closed the door behind him.

The dark shadow along his jaw gave him a roguish look, a bad-boy appeal. She liked it. Her fingers itched to skim across his cheek while her heart raced at the sight of him. Hannah met Scott halfway across the room. A slow and sensual smile covered his lips. She had no doubt his thoughts were running similar to hers. They'd not really spent any time together in the last couple of days. She'd come to depend on him, accept him as part of her life. She'd missed him.

His smoldering eyes made her afraid she might flash-burn on the spot. Reaching for her, Scott took her hand and towed her toward the door. There they wouldn't immediately be seen by anyone entering the room or through the window to the hall. With his back against the wall and his feet spread apart, he pulled her close.

"I've missed you." His words rumbled as his lips skimmed over her cheek en route to her mouth as a finger pulled her mask down over her chin.

A tingle traveled along her spine. Hannah shivered as she molded her body to Scott's and brought her mouth to his. Scott took the invitation, grazing her lips, before he dipped to explore her more completely. The kiss pushed any thoughts away except for those hot and heavy with need that begged to be fulfilled. Scott's kiss communicated the same desperation.

A bolt of longing shot through Hannah. She gripped his waist. Molten heat pooled in the lower part of her body. With a sigh Hannah met his demands with those of her own. Her hands slid over the expanse of his chest to wrap around his neck. A fire blazed in her center. By the time Scott's lips had left hers, their breaths came in small gasps.

Hannah traced the nape of his neck with her fingertips. His hand scanned her ribs, down her hip until it cupped her behind. Shifting, he fit her more snugly to him. The light, caressing kisses Scott was placing down one side of her neck made her knees buckle. Pressed against him, she didn't have to guess at his desire. It was evident. Hannah shifted her hips forward. He held her securely, a moan originating deep in his throat.

The prickle of his whiskers sent a shudder along her spine. They brushed her sensitive skin as his mouth found the hollow of her neck and he murmured, "You sure taste good."

Heat simmered then boiled in her as it flowed to her center. She wanted to hold onto this feeling for ever.

Hannah surrendered her neck and pushed closer. Scott's hand aided her movement forward. A yearning built in her like a summer electrical storm. He retraced his path with tiny nips of his teeth. His low rumble of satisfaction brought her a wave of delight. Going up on her toes, she silently asked for more.

Scott's tongue followed the shell of her ear. A tingle shot

through her like water sizzling in oil. Her fingers dug into his back in an unspoken demand for more of everything.

"Mommy…" The soft call pierced the mist of sexual need. Hannah jerked away. Once again, Scott's hands had made her forget where she was. Scott groaned at the interruption.

"Bad timing?" Hannah giggled.

"You've no idea," Scott muttered. His body had some type of radar that zeroed in on Hannah's like a heat-seeking missile. The woman didn't have to be looking at him for his body to react.

"I think I might."

It was nice to know he wasn't the only one who forgot where they were when they were together. Hannah met his gaze and her hand cupped his cheek. Scott eased his hold but didn't let go of her. "I seem to lose control around you."

"Mommy…"

"Coming, honey."

What had he been thinking? Kissing his patient's mother in the little boy's room certainly showed poor professional conduct. That was just it, he didn't think around Hannah. He gazed down at her. Hannah's eyes were wide with expectation. Her sweet lips were plump and cherry colored. She had the look of a woman who'd been thoroughly kissed, and wanted more.

Oh, yeah. He'd like to do it again.

The need for her still throbbed within him.

He gave her a quick peck on the lips, then let her go. "I need to be a heart surgeon and check on my favorite patient." Pulling the mask out of his pocket, he fit it over his mouth before he approached Jake's bed.

"Hi, there, buddy," Scott said. "Remember me? I'm Dr.

Mac." Scott pulled down his mask and gave Jake one of his Hollywood smiles before replacing the covering.

Scott picked up the disposable stereoscope hanging on the rail of the bed and listened to Jake's chest. "I need to give your new heart a listen for a sec."

"Mommy," Jake whispered. Hannah turned to pick up her mask before she stepped beside Scott.

"I'm right here. Be real still for Dr. Mac."

Jake watched his movements with interest. He was a bright little boy anyone would be glad to call his son. It wasn't a thought he should be having.

"His heart has a strong, steady beat. But I do want to pace it for a couple of days." Scott glanced at Hannah and saw the look of panic wash over her face. "Nothing's wrong. If I pace the heart it'll fall into a solid rhythm. The pacemaker gives the heart a little help so it doesn't have to work too hard."

She nodded.

"I see you still have Bear," Scott said to Jake as he touched the toy clipped to the bed. "We'll get those chest tubes out today so you can get out of bed and play some." To Hannah he said, "I'll write the orders before I go back to surgery."

"You're going back to the OR? You look like you need some rest."

"That bad, huh?" Scott chuckled. He appreciated the concern in her voice. It felt good to have Hannah fuss over him.

"I didn't say you look bad."

His grin grew. "So I look good?"

"Oh." She swatted his arm. "You know what I mean."

"I do. But I like seeing you flustered." Hannah returned his smile. Scott looked back to find Jake watching them. "I've got to go. They'll be waiting for me in surgery. Hannah?"

Her eyes lifted.

"Have dinner with me?"

"I...don't know. I need to be here with Jake."

"What if we make it a late meal? Jake will be asleep. I'll order Chinese take-out and we can eat in the garden. We wouldn't be too far away."

She didn't answer right away.

Was Hannah trying to put some distance between them? He should be doing the same thing, instead of acting like the family man he could never be. But he couldn't back away yet. "Please. You don't have to stay any longer than you feel comfortable."

"Okay, but I want sweet and sour chicken, and fried rice."

He grinned. "You've got it. I'll see you around eight."

"Don't forget the fortune cookies."

He raised his thumb in the air and said goodbye to Jake before pulling the door closed behind him.

For Hannah the rest of the day was spent caring for Jake. The interruptions continued with doctors and nurses checking in. She and Jake did take a nap, but her peaceful sleep was sabotaged by thoughts of Scott. Where did she fit into his plans? Did she fit at all? Was this relationship going anywhere? She wanted him, but did he want her? Even with all the unknowns she still looked forward to seeing him again.

The thoracic surgery fellow came in to remove Jake's chest tubes. The nurse had warned Hannah it would be painful for Jake. The fellow asked Hannah if she wished to leave the room, but she declined the offer. She was a nurse. She'd be able to handle it. Besides, the fellow wasn't someone Jake knew. He'd be scared without her.

The fellow clipped the sutures holding the chest tubes in place then pulled them out with a steady motion. Jake's body tensed, tears streamed over his cheeks. His hands pulled against the restraints securing them.

Moisture welled in Hannah's eyes and fell. Never in her life had she wanted to scream "Stop!" louder or longer. Her hands gripped the metal rail until her knuckles turned white and her fingers blue. She knew this pain was necessary, but her mother's heart howled to have it done with.

"It'll be over soon, honey," Hannah said as calmly as she could in spite of the knot lodged in her throat.

As the fellow finished he told Hannah she could remove the restrains. Whimpering, Jake reached out to her. She lifted him into her arms, holding him tight as she cooed.

Exhausted, Jake soon quieted and fell asleep. Hannah settled into the wooden rocker, enjoying the feel of his small warm body against hers. Finally, she was able to hold her baby close.

When she finally put Jake down for the night he made a noise as if awakening. She patted his bottom until he settled again. Glancing at the clock, she saw she was running late and had to rush to change into tan slacks and a red cable sweater for her date with Scott.

The phone rang.

Her heart jumped. Was Scott calling to cancel?

The floor clerk was on the line, telling her Dr. McIntyre would be there soon. He was seeing a patient in CICU. Hannah's heart settled into a steady rhythm again, but her breathing remained faster than normal.

Twenty minutes later, Scott came to the door. "Sorry I'm late. I hate you always having to wait for me."

"I don't mind."

"You really don't, do you?"

"No. I know the importance of what you do. I'm just glad to see you."

Scott dressed in jeans and a striped button-down shirt reminded Hannah of how appealingly male he was. His shirt was tucked in, which emphasized his trim waist. His sleeves were rolled up over tan forearms. No man had ever looked better.

His smile reached his eyes. "It's nice to see you too. Our food's at the front desk. We'll pick it up on the way to the garden."

Hannah started in the direction of the elevator, but Scott took her hand and directed her into a stairway.

"Where're we going?"

"Down this way." He pinned her against the wall of the stairwell and his lips found hers. Long, lustful and luscious moments later he released her. "There's way too much interest in what I do around here. And I get a kick out of sneaking around, don't you?" He winked at her.

Hannah laughed and followed him down the stairs. Scott even made dinner at the hospital an adventure. She enjoyed seeing the kid come out in him. His job was a serious one. He needed a release from the life-and-death decisions that made up his world.

At the bottom of the stairs, Scott peeked out the door and gave her a quick peck on the lips before they stepped through it. "Wait here," he said in a conspiratorial tone, before walking across the lobby. Scott spoke to a woman behind the welcome desk. She smiled and handed him two big bags. "Thanks, Helen. I owe you one."

Scott charmed young and the old. He'd gone one better with her, he'd made her fall in love with him. Hard. Could she convince him to make her and Jake a part of his life?

Looking both ways, as if he were a spy, Scott returned to her and took her hand again. Hannah snickered at his antics. His lips lifted into a sexy grin. Her breath caught. He led her to the drink machines, where they made their selections.

The garden looked lovely in the dusk of the summer day. A few late-blooming flowers gave off sweet scents. The setting sun shone brightly on one side, while the other side of the garden remained encased in shadow. They followed a curved walk around to the most secluded area. At a stone bench, Scott stopped.

"Wait before you sit." He poked through one of the bags, pulling out a camping lantern and a green and yellow plaid blanket. Flipping the blanket a couple of times, he settled it across the bench.

Hannah watched in fascination as he lit the lantern and placed it on the ground in front of the bench. Bowing like a maître d', Scott offered her a place on the bench.

Picking up the other bag, he handed her a white box from it. "Sweet and sour chicken, ma'am."

"Thank you, sir."

He dug further and came out with another container.

"What did you get?" She leaned over to peer into the container as he opened it.

"Nosy, aren't you?" he teased.

"I am. What're you having?"

"Mongolian beef."

"Ooh, that stuff's hot."

"Yes, like me," he quipped, making his brows rise and fall.

Hannah laughed. Something she did a lot when Scott was around. There had been little laughter in the last few years in her and Jake's life. It was nice to have it back, even for a short while.

"Here's your fried rice."

Hannah took it. "This is nice, thank you. I'm glad to get out of the room for a while." She picked at her chicken with her chopsticks. "I haven't been out here before. I'll have to bring Jake. No, I can't. He can't be around people for a few months."

"I wish I could tell you it was okay, but we can't take any chances he might catch something."

"I know. I'll bring him when we come for a visit. By the way, why didn't you tell me taking chest tubes out was so horrible?" She screwed up her face at the memory.

"It's rough. That's why I didn't do it myself. I don't want Jake to have that memory of me."

"Why not?"

"I want us to be friends and removing chest tubes isn't a friendly thing to do."

Her chest contracted to think it mattered to Scott whether or not Jake liked him.

As they ate, Hannah enjoyed the deep roll of Scott's voice. They discussed the movies they'd seen. She learned they both enjoyed Westerns and wished more were being made. Another thing they had in common. When they'd finished, Scott started gathering their empty containers. He pulled a couple of small packages out of another bag, like a magician performing a trick.

"Want your fortune cookie now?"

"I'd love it."

Opening his, he laughed.

"What?" she asked, leaning over until her shoulder rested against his. "Let me see." She took the small slip of paper from him. "What's so funny?" She handed it back.

"Haven't you ever heard about adding 'in bed' to the end of the fortune? 'Your talents will prove to be especially useful this week...in bed.'"

A flush covered her face. She couldn't meet his eyes. "It does give it a new meaning."

"Yeah, it does." The humor in his voice had disappeared, leaving it deep and raspy. She glanced at Scott from hooded eyes. His sea-blue gaze captured hers.

Hannah saw his desire. Hot, rich, deep. It pulled at her. But that was all it was, she had to remind herself, sexual desire. She couldn't let it drag her under. He'd made no promises. She wanted, no, needed more than a meeting of their bodies. Especially from Scott.

Scott leaned toward her as if planning to kiss her, but when a mother with a child in a stroller came around the curve in the walk, he straightened. Saying nothing, Scott began gathering the rest of the remains of their meal. Hannah helped. When her hand brushed his, Scott captured it, turned it over and kissed the inside of her wrist. A tremor rolled through her. With everything packed away, he took her hand and they slowly walked back into the hospital.

Hannah didn't want the evening to end. Scott seemed to agree.

In the stairwell, before he opened the door to the floor, they shared a passionate meeting of lips that was much too short. With a final kiss to her cheek, Scott said, "I'll miss having you in my bed tonight."

Her stomach fluttered. "I'll miss being there, but you know I have to be here with Jake."

"I do and I'd expect nothing less from you. You're a wonderful mother."

"Thanks for understanding. I know what it is to be left and I'd never do it to Jake."

Darkness filled Scott's eyes.

"I didn't mean you."

A dry smile came to his lips. "I realize you could mean me."

Hannah cupped his cheek and smiled at him. "I could, but in this case I don't."

At Jake's room, Scott stopped long enough to review the med chart posted on the outside of the door. Dressed to enter, they stepped toward the sleeping child's bed.

Careful not to disturb Jake, Scott pulled off the sheet and checked the tube sites. "They look good."

"I'm proud of him. He's a trouper." Hannah tipped her head toward Scott. "Thanks for your part in saving his life."

"You're welcome. I'll let you both get some rest. See you tomorrow." He pulled her to him and gave her a tight hug because having a mask on didn't lend itself to kissing.

Hannah was returning to Jake's room after breakfast the next morning, and noticed the door stood ajar. Someone was talking to Jake. She recognized the rich voice. Jake giggled. Her pulse went into overdrive.

She gowned up and pushed the door open. Scott sat in the rocker with Jake in his lap. Scott had his mask pulled down to his chin, and Jake was busy feeding Scott cereal.

Hannah's heart stopped, and lurched again. It could be a Norman Rockwell picture. Jake let out a squeal of joy every time Scott lost a piece inside his mask. *Scott would make a wonderful father. If he would only believe that.*

He pulled at her heartstrings. Was he beginning to care for Jake less as a patient and more as a son? Would he ever consider being a parent of a heart patient when he worked with them all day? Dared she hope so?

Scott smiled up at her. "Hey. Jake woke up when I came in, and I didn't want to leave him here by himself."

"I went down to the cafeteria for breakfast. I thought he'd sleep until I got back."

"Would you like some of ours?" Scott asked.

She noticed Scott made no effort to hand Jake to her and Jake was content to stay where he was as well. Their coloring was close enough they could be family.

Jake offered the plastic bowl of cereal to her. Some fell to the floor. Both males laughed.

"Which ones are you guys giving me? The cereal off the floor or that in the bowl?"

Jake brought the bowl to his chest in a protective manner.

"The floor must be it," Scott said, with a grin. "Jake, I think we could be nicer to your mom."

Jake shook his head.

"I can see you're feeling much better this morning," Hannah told Jake. "Maybe too good. Dr. Mac might have done too fine a job on you." Hannah smiled at Scott.

Her heart swelled with the contentment of seeing her son so happy and comfortable with Scott. Hannah couldn't believe how quickly it had happened.

Jake and Scott had bonded. It would make it even harder when Scott stepped out of their lives. With all her heart she wanted this moment to last. But could it? Would Scott allow it? She didn't want Jake hurt by becoming too attached to Scott. That feeling she was very familiar with. Jake didn't need the loss of another man in his life.

"He's acting like a mischievous boy should," Scott said as he took another offered piece of cereal. Jake continued to stuff Scott's mouth with more than it could hold. He chewed and swallowed the mass before he rose with Jake in his arms. "Well, I've got to finish rounds."

Jake complained when he was handed over to her.

Reaching out, Scott tickled Jake's belly. He squealed.

"I'll be back to see you soon, bubby." Scott gave her a quick kiss on the lips.

Had she wanted to see a wistful look in Scott's eyes? Had it really been there?

Jake's day nurse entered soon after Scott left. She checked Jake's vitals and adjusted the settings on the monitors.

"Looks like Jake's doing great. He should be going home soon," the nurse said with stethoscope in hand as she prepared to listen to Jake's chest. "Dr. McIntyre's a great doctor. We're going to miss him when he leaves."

Bile rose in Hannah's throat. Her heart skipped a beat. She stopped rocking and sat up straight. "Leave? Where's he going?"

It was happening again. Scott was going to leave without saying anything to her again.

"The rumor is he's been offered a position as head of a transplant program in Dallas. He'd be starting the program from scratch, which is a big deal if you're a transplant surgeon," the nurse replied in an offhand manner.

Hannah's shoulders sank. Leaving? She couldn't believe Scott hadn't said anything to her. Why hadn't he?

She shouldn't have expected more, hoped for more. He'd made no promises. Hadn't he made it clear where he stood the afternoon they'd spent in bed? She hadn't wanted to accept it.

"When's he supposed to leave?" Hannah made an effort to make the question sound nonchalant, despite the tightness in her chest.

The nurse adjusted the blanket over Jake. "Soon, I think. It's pretty much a done deal, I understand."

Hannah not only wanted Scott around because she loved him but because he was Jake's doctor. It gave her a sense of security to know Scott was close by if Jake needed him.

"Dr. Mac is such a great doctor I can't imagine him not getting the job." The nurse looked at her. "Uh, are you all right, Ms. Quinn?"

Hannah nodded, her stomach rolling like a ship in a storm.

"I thought you knew," the nurse said in an unsure voice.

"No, I didn't know and I'm concerned for Jake. Who'll care of him if Dr. McIntyre is no longer here?"

"Oh, don't worry there. We've other great doctors." She patted Hannah's hand, gave her a bright smile and went out the door.

A tear rolled down Hannah's cheek as she slowly started rocking again. It was the same old scene of the same old play. Scott hadn't changed. He planned to leave without saying a word. Again.

She knew what she had to do. End it.

Scott had managed to get out of the OR earlier than he thought possible and had every intention of spending the extra time with Hannah and Jake.

He took a few minutes to stop by his office to check his mail. While there he received a call from Dallas. Despite the short notice, they wanted him to fly out to speak with the committee the next day. Thankfully, his patients, including Jake, were doing well enough that he could agree. He made some quick travel arrangements.

He'd put off telling Hannah about Dallas because it wouldn't have mattered by the time he thought he would be moving. She would've gone on with her life, making it a non-issue.

Scott couldn't believe how fast Hannah had become important to him. Jake too. A chance to be with someone like Hannah didn't come along more than once in a lifetime. Well, maybe twice. He knew what he was letting go of, but still he had to do it.

In another few days or so Jake might be going home. Scott's relationship with Hannah would change then anyway. With Jake recovering, she wouldn't need him any more.

Could he and Hannah maintain a long-distance relationship? Would seeing her occasionally fill his need for her? He didn't think so. It didn't matter he had to be a different person than he was for it to ever work.

Hannah didn't stand to greet him when he entered and closed the door to Jake's room behind him. She continued to hold Jake and rock.

Scott leaned down to kiss her, but she only offered her cheek. "How's Jake been doing today?"

"He's had a great day." She sounded pleased, but the words were stiff. She didn't look at him.

Was something bothering her? Jake's nurse had said nothing about there being a problem when he'd stopped at the nurses' station. "Hannah, is something wrong?"

Hannah looked up at him. "Why didn't you tell me you were planning to move to Dallas? Was it a secret? You didn't have to hide it from me. You've made it perfectly clear we have no ties on each other. I understood. But *friends* don't keep secrets."

The knot forming in his chest ached. There were ties between them, but he couldn't tell her that. Scott raised his brows. "How'd you come by that bit of info?"

"The hospital grapevine works for everyone." Her eye remained fixed on him. "So, are you leaving?"

"I've been interviewed by a hospital in Dallas. They want to start a transplant program. It's been my dream to head my own."

"When're you leaving?"

"I'm still in the discussion stage. But...I have to fly out first thing in the morning to meet with the committee."

"What about Jake?" Anxiousness crept into her voice.

His desire to help patients was already coming between them as he'd known it would. He didn't want her to live her life worried he wouldn't be there when she needed him. He was making the right decision, for both of them as well as Jake. "He's doing well. He'll soon be followed by Cardiology. My job is almost done." Scott tried to make the words sound matter-of-fact.

"I think, under the circumstances, it would be better for Jake if things remain professional between us. Jake doesn't need to get attached to you." She looked out the window as she spoke.

"Better for Jake?" His words came out softly.

She looked at him. "Okay, better for me. You're leaving, so what're we doing anyway? Having great sex? I want more, you don't or won't let yourself have more, so I think now is a good time to call it quits, before either one of us gets hurt."

Scott's chest felt like a band was being tightened around it. There was no longer an ache but a cavernous hurt. He had no one to blame but himself. "I told you—"

She shook her head, silencing him. "I know what you told me. The problem is you have issues that you need to resolve with yourself and your parents. I care for you more than you care for me. But I've been left behind or set aside for the last time. I have to think of Jake. He doesn't need to get attached to someone who won't be there for the long haul or want to see him make the first step. Jake deserves someone who will stick with him and fight for him, and I do too." The last few words had a bite to them.

Scott said nothing. He couldn't refute anything she'd said. He wished with all his heart he could.

"Stupid me," she murmured. "I'd hoped this time you'd feel differently." She gasped, swiping her hand across her cheek. "It's been fun while it lasted. Nice seeing you again."

Scott stood looking down at her for a long moment. He wanted to argue with her, but how could he? She was right. "One of the other surgeons will see about Jake while I'm gone. I'm sure he'll be discharged before I return. Goodbye, Hannah."

"Thanks for taking such good care of Jake and for helping me get through some stressful moments. I wish you the best in Dallas. Bye, Scott." The last few words had an iceberg chill of finality to them.

The pain of leaving Hannah was so searing and deep Scott found it difficult to breathe. For the first time in his life he was asking if he was doing the right thing.

CHAPTER TEN

HANNAH'S next few days were spent preparing to take Jake home. Hannah was grateful to be busy because it left less time to think about Scott. She pushed thoughts of him aside the best she could. At unexpected moments, like each time the door opened, Hannah's heart raced, thinking it might be Scott. It never was.

She missed him. Hurt with the want of him. As disappointed as she was that he didn't need her, it didn't make her love for him disappear, which only intensified the pain.

Jake had his first biopsy to determine if he was rejecting the new heart the morning after Scott left. Jake would continue to have biopsies regularly throughout his life. Hannah waited in Jake's room while the nurse took him to the cath lab for the procedure.

Wringing her hands until they were almost raw, Hannah watched the clock as an hour crawled by. Dr. John Reynolds, the cardiologist now following Jake's progress, came in to see her. The test had shown no rejection and Dr. Reynolds planned to release Jake from the hospital the next day.

The news was like the sun coming out after a long, cold winter. Elated with Jake's recovery, Hannah's first thought was to share the good news with Scott. It was too late for that. The day turned gloomy again. Her sense of loss seemed as vast as the ocean.

Hannah was packed and ready to leave before Dr. Reynolds made rounds the next morning.

Once back at home, fretting over missing Scott took a backseat to caring for Jake. She gave medicine four times a day, checked Jake's blood pressure, temperature and weight at regular intervals. Feeding Jake took extra time, coaxing him to eat enough to gain weight. His incisions required attention as well.

Jake napped a number of times during the day, giving Hannah an opportunity to take care of her everyday matters. Bills arrived daily, and there were phone calls to make and return. Holding Jake became the highlight of her day. Reminded of how much she'd almost lost, she was grateful for each precious moment.

The nights were different. They dragged. Thoughts of Scott wandered in and camped. She relived all the wonderful times they'd had together, and yearned for his breath-stealing kisses, his body next to hers, his lovemaking. Despite being exhausted, it took hours for sleep to find her.

As the days lapsed into weeks the loss of Scott became a dull pain Hannah learned to live with. Like splinters, barely touched memories would flood back with a sting when she saw a tall man wearing a white lab coat or heard shoes tapping across a tile floor. Thoughts of Scott never completely left her.

No one liked being left behind, but it was a part of life. When had she become so scared of living? Chances had to be taken if happiness was ever to be found. She wouldn't have missed her time with Scott for anything. The pain was worth those amazing hours she'd spent in his arms.

Other people, sometimes more wonderful people, would

enter to replace him. The secret was not to let fear close any door. She didn't want Jake to grow up with a mother fearful of life. She wanted to be a positive role model, strong, resilient, no matter what happened to her.

Hannah glanced at Jake as he swung in his swing and played with his bear. She wasn't the only one who'd been left behind, but her ex had given her a wonderful gift in Jake. Each positive report Jake received was a thrill. He'd grown since the transplant and was becoming more active. Still, the only time they left the condo was when Jake had an appointment at the hospital. She even had groceries delivered.

A thump of a toy falling on the floor and Jake's squeals made Hannah look up from balancing her checkbook. The toy Scott had given Jake had slipped from his hand. The little bear was Jake's constant companion.

Hannah smiled and leaned down to pick up the toy. Giving it to Jake, she kissed him on top of his head. "Time for meds, sweetie."

Hannah slipped into doing Jake's care as easily as putting on old shoes. Maybe Scott had been right. She should think about being a clinical nurse instead of working in a hospital. With a few extra courses, she could work with children. Perhaps working with transplant families would be a good place to consider. With leave pay still coming in for a while longer and her savings in fair shape, she had time to look into jobs when Jake had recovered enough to be left with a sitter.

Jake had been given a second chance at life and she planned to live her life to the fullest, for her sake as well as Jake's.

One afternoon the doorbell rang. Hannah answered it and found a delivery man there.

"Hannah Quinn?"

A huge box sat at her feet with the word "Fragile" written across the top.

"Yes, but I'm not expecting anything."

The man in the brown uniform smiled at her, and handed her an electronic device for her to sign. The return address indicated it was from one of the best gift shops in the area. There had to be some kind of mistake.

Hannah pulled the box indoors and cut through the packaging tape. Picking up one of the items in the container, she removed the plastic bubble wrap. Beneath it, she found a teacup from the set she'd admired at the fundraiser. Gently, she set it back with the rest of the set.

Reaching for the invoice under another item, she located a phone number. Calling the store, the manager explained she couldn't return the set because it had been donated to the hospital. Her name had been identified as the highest bidder.

Hanging up the phone, Hannah sat staring at the box. Scott must have bid on it when she'd gone to call about Jake.

She removed each piece with loving care until the completed set was arranged on the coffee table. Spying a white gift envelope pushed against the inside wall of the box, she pulled it out. Opening the card, she read: *"Don't even think about returning it. Enjoy. Scott."*

Hannah's hands shook and her eyes watered as she held the envelope to her chest.

Scott drummed his fingers on the desk as he waited to be connected with Dr. John Reynolds.

"Scott, how you doing?"

"I'm working more hours than should be humanly possible. What I was calling about—"

"You want to know how Jake Quinn is doing."

He was too transparent. John had to know Scott was checking on Hannah too. "Yeah."

"He's doing as expected, like I've told you every time you've called. His mom is taking excellent care of him."

"I appreciate the report." Scott smiled. Jake was doing great. Was Hannah? He couldn't ask. But if Jake was getting better, Hannah had to be happy. He'd have to find contentment in that knowledge.

"I'll be in Atlanta in a few days to clear up some business. I'll stop by."

"Sounds great. I'd like to hear firsthand how your program is shaping up," John replied, and Scott rang off.

Maybe he should make arrangements to see Jake while in Atlanta. After all, Jake had been his patient. Who was he kidding? He wanted to see Hannah. Needed to see her.

Scott shouldn't have had time to think of Hannah with the amount of work he'd done in the last two months but she crept into his thoughts continuously. During meals, he thought of their shared ones. At night, it took him hours before sleep found him. Even after he fell asleep, Hannah filled his dreams. He ached to touch her and ached to have her touch him.

His hunger for her hadn't died. If anything, it had intensified.

For the first time in his life he wanted more than to be a great heart surgeon. He wanted Hannah. And Jake. Wanted to be a husband, father, a family man. He would do whatever was necessary to convince Hannah to take a chance on him. Without Hannah and Jake, nothing mattered.

Hannah had gotten his attention about more than setting his priorities in regard to work. He needed to set things right between him and his mother. Hannah would expect that, want that for him.

With Hannah as his life partner he could find that balance between his professional and private life. She had already helped to do that. Hannah would keep him centered, support him, while at the same time reminding him of what was really important. They could make it work— together.

He wanted it all. Would fight for it, beg for it if he had to.

But would Hannah have him?

"We need to hurry honey or we'll be late," Hannah said when she hiked Jake further up on her hip as they went down the hall of the hospital. Jake, with a mask covering his mouth, looked like a miniature doctor as he bounced along in her arms.

"If Dr. Reynolds says you can go out in public, we'll stop and get some ice cream on the way home," she promised.

Absorbed in her conversation, Hannah didn't notice the man standing next to the door of the pre/post cath lab. She reached for the doorknob.

"Hannah."

Her breath caught. Had her name ever sounded sweeter? Her thoughts swirled, and her blood hummed. She looked up into the most beautiful blue eyes she'd ever seen.

"Hello," Scott said.

"Hi."

"Dr. Mac," Jake squealed and reached out to him.

"Hi, big guy." Scott opened his arms to take Jake. He jerked toward Scott in his eagerness to be held by him. Hannah let Jake go to him. "You look like you're doing well."

Hannah gave up trying to slow her heartbeat. "What're you doing here?"

"I'm visiting. I had a few loose ends to take care of in Atlanta."

"Oh." Hannah tingled from the tip of her fingers to the ends of her toes. Now was the time to sound intelligent. *Talk to him.* "By the way, congratulations. I heard you got the job you were after. That's great." She meant it. She was proud of him. He was an outstanding surgeon.

"Thank you." Scott studied her a moment. "It's good to see you." He captured her gaze. "You look wonderful."

Her heart fluttered, his words a soft caress.

Scott stepped forward, tentatively reaching out a hand to touch her but not doing so. Jake demanded his attention by pulling on Scott's tie.

Sharp disappointment filled her at the abandoned connection.

Jake put out his hand, showing Scott his toy.

"What've you got there?" Scott asked. "Is that Bear?"

Jake looked at the toy and smiled, pulling it closer to his side.

Hannah had tried for weeks to replace the little toy with another one, but Jake had refused. He had to have Bear with him when he came to the hospital or when he fell asleep. For Hannah, the toy had been another constant reminder of Scott.

"Does Bear go everywhere with you?" Scott asked.

Jake thrust the toy at Scott. He studied it. Looking up at Hannah, with a twinkle in his eye he said, "Bear has gotten a lot of wear."

"Jake won't let him out of his sight." She didn't meet Scott's gaze. Instead, she focused on his broad smile as he returned the animal to Jake.

"Um…I'm glad we ran into you," she said. "It's nice to—"

"You didn't run into me. I've been waiting on you."

A stream of warmth Hannah hadn't felt in months raced through her. She didn't trust herself to say anything, so she just waited.

"Could we meet somewhere and talk?"

"I guess so." She brushed Jake's curls back as he squirmed in her arms. "How long are you going to be in town?"

"Until tomorrow."

"Would you…uh…" she'd promised herself she'd take chances "…like to come to dinner tonight? I owe you one or two." If he said no, could her heart stand it?

A look of surprise crossed his face before the grin she loved so much found his lips. "I have some meetings this afternoon but I'll make it work. Thanks."

Delight filled her at the sparkle of pleasure in his incredible eyes. "Six okay?"

"I'll be there."

She returned his smile with a bright one of her own. Hannah reached out to take Jake again. "We have to go. They're expecting Jake for a biopsy."

When Jake whined about having to leave Scott he said, "I'll see you this evening buddy. We'll play then."

Her hand shook as she opened the door of the cath lab.

Hannah shifted the candle a little to the left, then moved a book back to its original spot on the end table. She'd blurted out her invitation to Scott without thinking it through. The delivery boy had had to make two trips from the grocery store before she'd had everything she needed for the meal. The boy's face had brightened at the large tip he'd received on the last trip.

After trying on a couple of outfits, Hannah settled on a pair of jeans and a peach-colored sweater. The one she'd been told looked particularly nice on her. Tonight she wanted to appear at her best.

Hannah wouldn't let her hopes get out of hand enough to expect things to be different between her and Scott. She wanted to pull off the evening without seeming pathetic or needy. If he wanted some kind of relationship more than friendship but less than marriage, would she take it?

With a final check in the mirror, she went to the kitchen to finish preparing their meal. She was preparing to put the shrimp with white sauce on the linguine when the doorbell rang. With a deliberate movement she laid the spoon down. She adjusted her sweater at her waist and walked to the door. The bell rang again. Jake squealed as she passed, and she stopped to pick him up. With more flourish than intended, she opened the door.

Scott stood on the front stoop, shifting his weight from one foot to the other as if he thought she might not let him in. He didn't look like a self-assured surgeon. Instead, he appeared uncomfortable. Surely he wasn't uneasy about seeing her again.

Had anyone ever looked more appealing? Dressed in a green knit shirt and tan slacks he filled out perfectly, Scott had never looked better, which was helped by the fact she'd missed him so desperately.

Her stomach quivered. Scott was there.

His smile reached his eyes before his gaze fell away. He ran his hand through his hair in that uneasy gesture she recognized. What could he possibly be nervous about?

Shifting Jake to the other hip and stepping back, she said, "Please come in."

As Scott entered, he cleared his throat and said in a raspy voice, "For you." He handed her a small gift bag.

He reached for Jake. "Why don't you let me take Jake while you finish supper?"

Hannah wasn't surprised when Jake gave no argument to switching rides. Jake had bonded with Scott. She left the room to the sound of her son's laughter as Scott sat Jake on his foot to play This Little Horsy. A feeling of rightness washed over her.

In the kitchen, she poured the noodle mixture into a bowl. She turned to the bag Scott had brought her and pulled the light blue tissue paper out. Inside she found a tin of tea leaves and a tea diffuser in the shape of a house. Warmth filled her. The gifts were perfect.

At the sound of footsteps behind her, she turned.

Scott, with Jake in his arms, stood in the doorway. Scott appeared less out of sorts as he stood there than he had at the front door. It was as if Jake had soothed his anxiousness. Scott looked like he belonged in her home. "I thought you could use them with your teaset."

"I love them." She beamed, hoping her smile showed all the delight she felt. "I should've said thank you for the teaset earlier. It's beautiful. You shouldn't have done this either." She dangled the diffuser from two fingers. "Did you pick it out yourself?"

He smiled. "No. The lady at the store helped me. I thought you'd appreciate them more than a bottle of wine."

"I do. They're wonderful."

Scott tickled Jake's belly, causing him to giggle. Looking down at him, he said, "Amazing, aren't they? How tough and resilient children are."

"Yes. Jake, come on. It's time to eat." She reached to take him but he clung to Scott.

Scott grinned. "Where does Jake sit?"

Hannah pointed to the highchair next to the table.

Their meal was pleasant, because she and Scott both

focused their attention on Jake. Hannah enjoyed having a man at her table but she had the feeling Scott was anxious about something. Was she reading too much into him being there? He'd said he wanted to talk. The anticipation kept her on edge and apparently he was too. The one time she relaxed and he did also was when she asked Scott about his new job and got caught up in his excitement.

"I've been working a lot of hours and hiring staff. I've also had to spend time writing procedures and going to meetings, which aren't my favorite things. But I think we'll have a great program that will help many children."

"You must be very busy." Probably far too busy to have thought of her.

"Yeah. It's been nice to get away for a few days."

The meal completed, Scott helped her clear away the dishes and clean the kitchen while Jake played with a pot and spoon. Scott watched TV while Hannah got Jake ready for bed.

As she rocked Jake to sleep, Hannah sensed Scott's presence. She glanced at the door and found Scott leaning against the frame with his arms across his chest. He had a solemn, contemplative look on his face. What was he thinking?

Happiness had filled her at having Scott there, but by the way he was acting it had been only to see how Jake was doing. Was he here to say goodbye for ever?

Hannah continued to move back and forth despite being hyper-conscious about Scott's presence. Jake shifted in her arms as if he was responding to her reaction to Scott. When Jake eyelids lowered, she kissed his sweet-smelling forehead and started to rise. Scott stepped over and took Jake, gently laid him in his bed.

Hannah joined Scott at Jake's bedside. "Thank you for this. For these precious moments I might not have had."

Scott offered his hand, and she placed hers in his. He smiled as he laced his fingers through hers and gave them a gentle squeeze. "Hannah, can we talk now?" His words were soft and earnest. Without releasing her hand, he led her to the living room. At the sofa, Scott said, "Let's sit."

To Hannah's disappointment, he took a chair opposite her. Balling her trembling hands in her lap, she mustered up her courage. Hadn't everything already been said between them? He'd given no indication he'd change his mind. Supper had been two friends sharing a meal.

"I was surprised to see you at the hospital today. I'm so glad your new job is going well. I know they're glad to have you. Jake's growing and happy. I'm so proud of him."

Scott chuckled and moved over beside her. "Are you almost done? Can I speak?"

He smiled at the glow his comment brought to her cheeks. His heart lurched. *She hasn't shut me out entirely.* Was she as unsure as him? Maybe he had a chance.

"I was just trying to see how—"

Apparently she wasn't going to be quiet until he did something to get her attention. His mouth came down to claim hers, tugging at her full bottom lip until she opened for him. Scott registered her hesitation then acceptance and the moment she returned his kiss with complete abandon. He'd come home. With Hannah was where he belonged. What they shared weeks earlier still smoldered between them, and found oxygen again.

Before the kiss went beyond his control, he had to talk to her. Know what she was feeling. If she would take a chance on him—again. Scott ran his hands up Hannah's arms, cupped her shoulders, and put her away from him. Their lips remained inches apart. She made a small sound of protest, which added fuel to his already raging desire.

"I want..." Her eyes shined with a longing begging to be filled.

He smiled. "What do you want, honey?"

"You." The word came out like a caress.

Scott watched with pleasure as her face went crimson. "I want you too, but we need to talk first." He gave her another quick kiss, resisting the urge to take it deeper, despite Hannah's efforts to draw him closer.

Looking as if she'd been in a dream and reality had returned, she scrambled away and put some space between them. Her eyes were wide, her cheeks flushed and lips full. She'd never looked more beautiful, more desirable. His body throbbed for her. Battling the hunger roaring in him, Scott had to let her go. He couldn't carry on a rational conversation with her sitting so close to him.

He took one of her hands in his. Absently, he moved the pad of his thumb over the back of her hand. "We need to talk."

Her green eyes searched his, weary. She looked unsure. He'd not meant to make her feel anxious.

"I've been a plan follower all my life. The plan was working well until you showed up again. My life was no longer as clear cut as it had once been. But you didn't demand anything. You were strong and supportive of me even when your own child was sick. You understand the work I do and why it drives me. It has been made clear on more than one occasion you're nothing like my mother.

"Even when I woke you in the middle of the night, coming home late, you welcomed me, comforted me. I hadn't known how much I'd missed that in my life until then. I've realized that I share many wonderful traits with my father but I don't have to be like him in all ways. He should have set priorities, learned to say no, taken on a partner when he saw that his marriage and family were suffering.

"When I went to Dallas I knew I'd miss you but I had no idea how much. I ached with it. I dream about how nice it would be to come home to you and Jake every night. The comfort you would offer after a long, tough day." He grinned. "Or days. You wouldn't make unreasonable demands I couldn't meet. You would just take me in your arms and hold me."

Her eyes glistened with tears, and she squeezed his hand.

"I thought getting the position in Dallas would make my life perfect. It's everything I've worked for, sacrificed for. Today and this evening when Jake came so trustingly to me I knew I wanted to be his father, to feel that love every day. I couldn't return to Dallas without telling you how I feel. No job is worth sacrificing you for. Without you and Jake it means nothing. The most important thing in life has been missing in mine, and I found it with you and Jake. I want to settle down. Have a wife and a family.

"I want you and Jake. For Jake to have brothers and sisters. I wanted *that* with you. I love you."

Her lips parted and her eyes remained fixed on his. A knot of fear formed in his chest. Why didn't she say something? Had he misread her kisses?

With a sudden tiny squeak Hannah threw herself at him, wrapping her arms around his neck. Scott pulled her tight, his lips meeting hers in a searing kiss.

Her mouth left his, to slide across his cheek to his ear. "I love you so much. It almost killed me when you left. Please don't ever do it again."

His lips found hers again, the contact a gentle stroke of promise. He broke the kiss and looked straight into her eyes. "I know you have good reasons for being afraid I'll leave, but if you'll take a chance on me, I promise never to leave you again." His tone held all the sincerity he felt.

The kiss that sealed the pledge was sweet and spicy. After long, perfect moments Scott released her and his hand came up to brush her cheek.

Hannah's lips touched his palm.

Closing his eyes and breathing deeply, Scott labored to control his passion. Hannah was too close for him to think straight. He shifted, putting her at arm's length, but kept his hands on her shoulders.

With his gaze fixed on hers, Scott said, "I know I won't be around a lot at first and I'm already looking to bring another surgeon on to help. With you, I know I can find that balance between work and family. Together we can do anything. Please give us a chance. Marry me and move to Dallas?"

She wrapped her arms around his neck. "Yes, yes, yes." Scott's heart beat faster. A thrill better even than the one he had each time he saved a child's life.

He drew Hannah against him. His lips found the softness of hers. Her fingers fanned through his hair as she tugged him closer. Hannah opened her mouth, offering him the honeyed taste within. With a murmur of satisfaction his tongue reached out and found hers.

When Hannah broke away Scott tried to pull her back, but she stayed him with hands to his chest. His fingers settled with a light touch at her hips.

She beamed up at him. "What took you so long, you big lug?"

Scott grinned. The feisty Hannah he loved so much had shown up. Tightening his grip, he brought her hips against his. "I fought it at first. But I knew I was a goner when I found myself calling the hospital a couple of times a week to check on Jake. I convince myself that I was only calling to check on Jake. When I realized that I wanted to ask more questions about you than him, I knew I was in trouble.

"Thanks to you, I've spoken to my mother and really cleared the air between us. She's even planning to visit soon. Things are better now between us than they have been in years. Surprisingly, she and Dad are even talking."

"I'm so glad." She leaned over and gave him a quick kiss.

His hands moved upwards until he could skim the undersides of her breasts. His reward was a smoky comehither look.

"I've been doing some thinking too," she said. "I believe you're right. I should consider working in a clinic situation. My appreciation for your skills has me thinking about how I can use my own."

"You know, I happen to need a good clinical nurse to work in the Dallas transplant program. Do you know anyone who might be interested?"

"I just might." With a grin on her face, she said, "I'd certainly have insight where others wouldn't." Her hands moved up over his biceps and across his shoulders. "Would *you* be my boss?" Her voice took on a Marilyn Monroe quality.

The combination of husky voice and twinkling eyes was intoxicating. Flirty Hannah sent a fire through Scott. He growled low in his chest. "You can count on it." He punctuated each word with small kisses.

Hannah guided his mouth down to hers.

Scott loved the way she couldn't seem to get enough of kissing him. As her lips traveled along his jaw, he said, "I've been living at the hospital the last few months. I've put off looking for a place to live in Dallas. Do you think you could help me find the right house? Maybe one with a big yard? A place for our kids to play?"

"I believe I can."

"In that case, I've something else I need your help with." At her expectant look, Scott chuckled. "But we'll need to find a bed."

"I know just where to find one." Hannah stood. Taking his hand, she tugged him down the hallway.

A feeling of pure satisfaction filled Scott. *I'm home.*

* * * * *

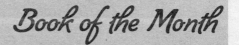

Medical mini-series

Sydney Harbour Hospital

Welcome to the world of Sydney Harbour Hospital

From saving lives to sizzling seduction,
these doctors are the very best!

Sydney Harbour Hospital: Lily's Scandal
by Marion Lennox
Sydney Harbour Hospital: Zoe's Baby
by Alison Roberts
On sale 3rd February

Sydney Harbour Hospital: Luca and the Bad Girl
by Amy Andrews
On sale 2nd March

Sydney Harbour Hospital: The Pride of Dr Tom Jordan
by Fiona Lowe
On sale 6th April

Sydney Harbour Hospital: The Socialite's Secret
by Melanie Milburne
On sale 4th May

Sydney Harbour Hospital: Shrinking Violet's Guide to Life
by Emily Forbes
On sale 1st June

Sydney Harbour Hospital: The Untamed Italian
by Fiona McArthur
On sale 6th July

Sydney Harbour Hospital: Fixing Ava's Marriage
by Carol Marinelli
On sale 3rd August

Find out more at
www.millsandboon.co.uk/medical

Visit us Online

0212/03/MB360